W9-BDP-266

DISCARD

Date: 9/7/16

FIC ALTEN
Alten, Steve,
Meg /

SPECIAL ANNIVERSARY EDITION

This is number 4440 *of 5000 copies*

SPECIAL ANNIVERSARY EDITION

MEG

SPECIAL ANNIVERSARY EDITION

STEVE ALTEN

MEG: SPECIAL ANNIVERSARY EDITION

ISBN: 978-1-68102-011-2

Published by Rebel Press, an imprint of Next Century Publishing Las Vegas, NV 81948

Printed in the United States of America

ACKNOWLEDGMENTS

It is with great pride and appreciation that I acknowledge those who contributed to this special edition of MEG and its prequel, MEG: ORIGINS.

First and foremost, many thanks to the great staff at Next Century Publishing/Rebel Press— CEO Ken Dunn, Mike Murphy, Rod Larrivee, Shannon Lutz, and D.J. Gothe. My heartfelt appreciation to my literary agent Danny Baror at Baror International and my manager, Melissa McComas at Tsunami Worldwide Media Productions.

As I write this, the MEG movie is in pre-production, thanks to the tireless efforts of my friend and producer, Belle Avery. Very special thanks to Wayne at Gravity Pictures, Ben at Reach Glory in Beijing and Mr. Liu at FFD in Tianjin.

Thanks as always to the tireless Barbara Becker for her dedication and hard work in the Adopt-An-Author program and to my webmaster Doug McEntyre at Millenium Technology Resources for his excellence in preparing my monthly newsletters and maintaining the Steve Alten website.

This collector's edition features the amazing artwork of Erik Hollander, who has been creating my cover art for years—many thanks, E. Thanks as well to Gavin North.

MEG was my debut novel back in the summer of 1997 and I owe much of the success that followed to literary agent Ken Atchity at AEI in Los Angeles for his guidance, faith, and hard work. And to those individuals who have contributed to the MEG franchise – Nick Nunziata, James Gelet, Ed Davidson, Tim Schulte, Tom Doherty, Bob Gleason, John Scognamiglio, Eric Raab, Whitney Ross, Scott Gere and Mike Donovan at Gere

Donovan Press, Trish Stevens at Ascot Media Group, and the staffs at Bantam/Doubleday, Kensington/Pinnacle, Tor/Forge, and Cedarfort Books … my gratitude.

Finally, to my wife and soul mate, Kim, our children, my parents, and especially to the MEGheads: Thank you for your correspondence and contributions. Your comments are always a welcome treat, your input means so much, and you remain this author's greatest asset.

Steve Alten, Ed.D.

To personally contact the author or learn more about his novels, go to www.SteveAlten.com

The MEG series is part of ADOPT-AN-AUTHOR,
A free nationwide program for Secondary School students and teachers.
For more information, go to www.AdoptAnAuthor.com

Dedicated to my father

LAWRENCE ALTEN

A kinder soul never lived ...

MEG

SPECIAL ANNIVERSARY EDITION

STEVE ALTEN

MEG: Origins

PROLOGUE

Aboard the H.M.S. Challenger
Philippine Sea
October 5, 1874

CAPTAIN GEORGE NARES stood defiantly on the heaving gun deck, his weight giving at the knees as the broiling Pacific tossed his command within the valleys of its fifteen foot swells. Each rolling crest of blue levitated the British warship's bow, each rise ended with the crash of copper keel meeting ocean. For the Scot, the spray of sea and the flap of canvas from the three mainsails defined the mantra of the past seven hundred-odd days; despite the danger, he much preferred the ocean's fury to the mission's incessant ports of call.

George Nares knew from day one that this command would be far different from his others. Once the flagship of the Royal Navy's Australia Station, the Pearl-class corvette had been stripped of all but two of her guns and her spars reduced. The

15

extra space had been converted to laboratories brimming with microscopes and chemical apparatus, water sampling bottles and specimen jars filled with alcohol—and not the kind her captain much preferred. In addition to the equipment and labs, the main deck had been altered to accommodate dredging platforms. These stations projected outward along either side of the ship like scaffolds, so that their occupants could work without fear of running afoul of the fore and main yards. The men who worked on these platforms were scientists, their crew skilled in troweling and dredging the bottom. To accomplish this feat required netting and containers rigged to great lengths of hemp, the coils of rope exceeding 140 miles, with an additional twelve and a half miles of piano wire reserved for sounding gear. Motorized winches released and gathered these lines—a chore that still took most of each work day to accomplish.

Science was the mission of the H.M.S. *Challenger*, a voyage of discovery for the two-hundred and forty-three men aboard—a mission that would take four years while trekking nearly 69,000 nautical miles.

Popular among his men, Nares led with an even temperament; what he lacked in physical stature he more than made up for with his cunning. Standing by the mainsail, he watched with a mixture of trepidation and amusement as a heavily bearded professor warily made his way aft along the swaying deck. "Professor Moseley. What is it to be then?"

"Sink lines, followed by more dredging. The crew's been rigging longer lines, the depths seem to have no end in this area of the archipelago."

The captain glanced to starboard. For weeks they had been following a course that took them past the Mariana Islands, each mountainous mass carpeted in green jungle. "I would have thought the depths around these islands far more shallow."

"As it turns out, these volcanic islands sit in the deepest

waters we have yet come upon. The sea bed is ancient, yielding a treasure-trove of fossils and manganese nodules. This morning's sink line exceeded thirty-five hundred fathoms and still there is no sign of bottom. We had to splice in another …"

The captain grabbed the teetering scientist and held fast as the bow lifted again, then crashed back into the Pacific. "How soon until a new length of cable can be made ready?"

"I'm told another twenty minutes."

"Very well. Helm, come hard to starboard. Mr. Lauterbach, lower the mainsails; prepare to engage steam engines."

"Aye, captain." The first officer rang his copper bell, the signal mobilizing two dozen crewmen as the *Challenger* leaned onto its starboard flank to shed the wind within the valley of a swell.

Captain Nares waited until the scientist disappeared safely down a hold, then returned his gaze to the Pacific, staring hard at the heaving waters.

Thirty-five hundred fathoms … more than six kilometers of ocean. How deep could these waters run? What strange life forms could they be concealing?

The depths surrounding this strange archipelago had certainly offered a bounty of clues, from cetacean vertebrae and whale ear bones to thousands of shark teeth, more than a hundred of these manganese-encrusted fragments as large as his hand. Moseley had identified these larger specimens as the genus, *Carcharodon*, those teeth exceeding four centimeters belonging to the species Megalodon, a true ancient sea monster.

The spectacular size of the creature's teeth led to nightly debates in the galley as to whether these sharks might still be alive. The dark lead-gray serrated triangles were fossilized to be sure; only a white specimen would bear proof of the Megalodon's continued existence. For his part Professor Moseley carefully inspected each haul, hoping to find one ivory treasure among the fragments—so far, to no avail.

"Some of these fossils are not that old, captain," the scientist had cooed the night before last, draining his third brandy. "This tells me the creatures might still be around, prowling the deeper fathoms."

"Exactly how big would these mega-sharks of yours be?"

"Some say thirteen meters, but these fragments tell me different. I've held an eighteen centimeter tooth in my hand; its owner had to measure twenty meters from snout to tail."

"Good God, man! That's more than half the length of the *Challenger*. A creature that size ... we'd need a bigger boat. Has any man ever spotted such a beast?"

"There have been rumors, whalers mostly. Lots of blood in the sea attracts all kinds of sharks."

"Attracts them? How so?"

"Unknown. Perhaps they can taste the blood. Sharks are not my specialty, but a devil like this Megalodon ... I'll confess, captain, each time we retrieve the nets I find myself watching the sea, secretly wishing our cast would lure one of these monsters up from the depths, if only so I could lay eyes on such a magnificent animal, surely nature's most feared creation of all time."

Staring at the foam-covered swells, Captain Nares shook his head, trying to imagine a shark that could consume four of his men in one bite, wondering if such a fish could still be alive, inhabiting the unexplored realm harbored by these ungodly depths.

1

CAPTAIN RICHARD DANIELSON stood defiantly on the main deck, his ears assaulted by the thirty knot winds swirling southeast across the broiling Pacific. Each gust disturbed the twenty-nine ton beast held aloft above the stern, each sway threatening to tear harness from machinery and cast the "white whale" from its perch.

For the American naval officer, the spray of sea and the incessant rolling steel beneath his feet were a constant reminder that his scheduled twelve day mission was now entering its third week. A commander who commanded best from behind a desk, Danielson was clearly out of his element. Three years ago he had

19

transferred to the U.S. naval base at Guam seeking a non-combat position where he could spend his days pushing papers until his retirement. Guam was exactly what the doctor ordered—a tropical island paradise brimming with pristine beaches, deep sea sport fishing, and world class golf courses. And the women—exotic islanders and Asian delights. True, the job was flavored with the occasional "readiness at sea" command, but these maritime exercises occupied no more than a few of his days every quarter.

Danielson knew he was in trouble the day the *Maxine D* arrived in port. More research ship than naval vessel, the boat was essentially a steel camel designed to transport its charge—a Deep Submergence Vehicle. Unlike his other maritime exercises, his orders were being sent directly from the Defense Department. The DSV's deployment site was prioritized as top-secret, its location—a six hour voyage from Guam in the Philippine Sea. The DoD had made it clear from the onset that while the Guam Naval Base commander was technically in charge of the tender, the eggheads on board would be running things.

The problem was that up until last week, barely anything had been running. First it was the A-frame's winch, then the primary generator, then the DSV's sonar relay. The seemingly endless breakdown of equipment had rendered Danielson a prisoner to a mission he knew little about, and the scientists on board only served to irritate him more. Compounding the repeated delays was the weather, which had grown uglier by the day. Danielson had puked-up his last solid meal ten days ago; even the most experienced sailor felt perpetually queasy and hung over.

Ironically, it was Mother Nature that decreed an end to the assignment. P.A.G.A.S.A., the Philippine Atmospheric, Geophysical and Astronomical Services Administration, was tracking a powerful category 2 typhoon, dubbed Marian. The name was apropos; the storm's predicted path would take it south from the Sea of Japan on a long sweeping arc that traced the Mariana Island chain before channeling it farther east away from land. Packing ninety-two-mile-an-hour winds, the typhoon's eye wall would be upon them in twenty-six hours.

Protocol should have sent the *Maxine D* on its way back to Guam, the southernmost island in the chain. At the urging of the scientists on-board, however, the Pentagon had insisted on one last dive on what would be their fourth venture into the Mariana Trench's *Challenger Deep.*

The Mariana Trench was the lowest point on Earth, a seven-mile-deep, 1,550 mile-long, forty mile-wide canyon formed by a volcanic subduction zone. Named after the British research vessel that had dredged its depths more than a century earlier, the *Challenger Deep* was its deepest section.

Why the navy would want to expend time and money to explore this hellhole was beyond Dick Danielson. At this point his only concern was getting the scheduled seventeen hour dive underway as soon as possible, allowing him as large a window as he could get to recapture the DSV, secure it to the deck, and race back to the naval harbor at Guam before Typhoon Marian turned the surface of the Pacific into a watery version of the Himalayas.

As the outer storm bands played havoc with the teetering *Sea Cliff* and the DSV's pit crew struggled to ready its launch, one man was screwing up Captain Danielson's plans.

* * *

The late afternoon sun was hot, the beach crowded. Jonas Taylor rose off the blanket onto his knees, his lower back sore from lying on his stomach. He stretched, then turned his gaze to the model gorgeous blonde stretched out in the beach chair next to him, her tan, oiled breasts two swollen grapefruits in the skimpy red bikini.

Jonas beckoned his wife to join him for a dip in the ocean.

Maggie waved him off.

Jonas jogged to the shoreline. The Pacific was calm, barely a ripple. He strode in up to his waist, joining a dozen other bathers.

Turning to his right, he saw an Asian boy standing next to him, the child no more than ten years old. Piercing almond eyes matched an expression of deep concern.

"Don't go."

Jonas stared at the boy. He scanned the crowd for a potential parent. Curious—the other bathers were now gone.

He turned back to the beach. Maggie was standing, ready to leave. She was no longer in her bikini. Instead she was wearing a topaz dress with stiletto heels. She walked away without so much as a glance.

Bud Harris was there with her. His best-friend was decked-out in a tuxedo, his slicked back dark hair in a ponytail. Jonas waved at his friend.

Bud waved back, then followed Maggie up the beach.

Jonas turned to the boy.

The boy was gone.

Jonas was alone.

His heart pounded, disrupting the silence. Every breath echoed in his ears.

A deep rumble built like distant thunder. The sky remained clear.

A mile out to sea the tidal wave appeared, levitating the horizon. It crested slowly, majestically—a mountain of curling dark water rising twenty stories high.

Jonas turned to flee, but his legs felt like lead.

He looked up. The sheer wall of water blotted out the sky. With a clap of thunder it fell …

"Ahhh!"

* * *

Jonas Taylor sat up in bed, his flesh and the tangled sheets drenched in so much sweat that for a moment the thirty-year-old naval commander wasn't sure if the tidal wave had been a nightmare or real.

The familiar gray cabin walls assured him it was a dream.

And then the room began to spin.

He closed his eyes, but the nausea said no and he reopened them. The suddenness of the vertigo returned him to a similar sensation experienced a decade earlier as he lay semiconscious on a grass football field, the junior tight end's head ringing and Beaver Stadium rolling sideways in his vision. Penn State's team physician had shouted his name over the crowd noise. "Don't move, J.T.! Focus your eyes on one spot until your vision clears!"

His first choice back then had been to focus on the football, still clutched in his hands; the choice now was the porthole, but with the ship swaying he held up his left hand and stared at his wedding ring.

As his pupils locked on, the vertigo passed.

An insistent knock demanded his attention.

"Shut up already and come in."

Michael Royston entered, the DSV pilot's East Tennessee State University tee-shirt soaked in sweat from a morning workout. "Sorry to wake you, boss. Heller wants you in sick bay for the pre-dive. Jonas, you okay? You look like hell."

"Been there. Three times in the last eight days. Don't have a fourth in me. Not today anyway."

Royston's eyes widened behind his glasses. As the mission's back-up hydronaut, the twenty-seven year old was accustomed to playing Robin to Jonas's Batman. Twice in the last year he had accompanied his mentor to the bottom of the Middle America Trench, but co-piloting a DSV at 20,000 feet and making a solo dive to 36,000 feet suddenly seemed worlds apart—the equivalent of asking a Single-A pitcher to strike out Mickey Mantle in game seven of the World Series.

"Jonas, you think I'm ready? I mean, hell yeah, I'm ready. I'm your back-up, right? If you need me to stand in, then sure, let's do it."

It was a bad play. Royston's cockiness was gone, replaced by trepidation. A healthy dose of fear was warranted before any deep sea dive; what concerned Jonas was that his young co-pilot was a better actor than this. Clearly he wanted to be bailed out.

"Let's see what Heller says. Tell him I'll be there in five."

* * *

From his porthole, Jonas could see the shadow of the DSV as it rocked back and forth within its harness, forcing its "pit crew" to hold on. Thirty feet long, with a twelve foot forward beam that tapered back to an eight foot propeller shaft, the *Sea Cliff* (DSV-4) and her sister ship, *Turtle* (DSV-3) had been the navy's workhorses since they were commissioned back in 1968. White with an orange-red dorsal hatch, the sub was designed around a six-foot-in-diameter, four-inch-thick titanium sphere that held its three-man crew. The exterior hull was neutrally buoyant fiberglass, supporting a propulsion unit, ballast and trim system, lights, cameras, steel weights, grappler arms, and a series of collection baskets.

What few people outside the Pentagon knew was that the *Sea Cliff* had recently received an extensive overhaul, the titanium pod and aluminum chassis upgraded to withstand 18,000 pounds per square inch of pressure. Life support capacity was doubled to thirty-two hours, descent weight increased by eight hundred pounds—features necessary when taking an elevator to a bottom floor whose basement exceeded Mount Everest's height. Of course, if something failed on Everest's summit, the pressure didn't implode your skull.

It took a cool customer to pilot a DSV; it took the best the navy had to offer to guide the upgraded *Sea Cliff* into the *Challenger Deep*, the deepest most unexplored realm on the planet. Only four men had ever ventured into these depths—both in 1960 aboard bathyscaphes. In both cases there was no piloting involved, the vessels simply went down and came back up. On one of these dives, the lone viewport had actually cracked, four inches of reinforced glass buckling under 16,000 pounds per square inch of pressure.

In the three decades that followed, no human had returned to dive the Mariana Trench.

Jonas Taylor had been preparing for the *Challenger Deep* for six months. His nerves were rock-steady, his attitude evolving from "cavalier cowboy" to a higher, zen-like state once he'd entered the DSV's titanium sphere—a claustrophobic life support chamber somehow deemed large enough to accommodate three passengers for upwards of twenty hours.

The top-secret mission was as straightforward as it was dangerous; Jonas would pilot the DSV six miles down, hovering just above a silty warm oasis of ocean created by the superheated mineralized water pumping from the abyss's hydrothermal vent fields. Once the sub was in position, the two scientists on-board would release a robotic drone which would enter the *Challenger Deep* and sink another five thousand feet to the bottom where it would gather samples of manganese nodules via a remotely-operated vacuum assembly.

Jonas had no idea what was so special about these pineapple-sized chunks of rock, nor did he care. As he told Danielson at their first meeting, "To me, the descent becomes routine the moment we pass beyond the light, right around twelve hundred feet. There's a lot going on in the universe outside that porthole—bioluminescent creatures, mating rituals, schools of jellyfish and things that glitter in the night—but until I get down to the basement, all I'm watching are my control panels. I don't want to know what's out there, I don't want to think about anything other than operating the DSV. Once I slip on my headphones and tune into some classic rock, I'm pretty much on auto-pilot for the next fifteen hours."

The first descent, eight days ago, had changed his tune.

Deep dives into the Hadal zone meant longer missions, the additional "on" time affecting the pilot's mental and physical attributes. Like an airline pilot or radar control operator, stress and fatigue quickly become a dangerous twosome, compromising the mind's ability to reason. Work-rest cycles of both submersible pilots and their surface support crews have to be strictly monitored, with back-up personnel on hand lest mental acuity be affected.

Diving the *Challenger Deep* was like nothing Jonas had ever experienced. The water pressure was tremendous, causing an unnerving rattle in the titanium sphere. Worse was the hydrothermal plume. Temperatures below this raging river were tropical, above the layer near-freezing, and the temperature differential created unpredictable water currents that threatened to flip the submersible into oblivion. It was like hovering above Niagara Falls while balancing on a tightrope.

Sixteen hours after the first dive had begun, the DSV surfaced. Jonas had been so exhausted that he had to be carried out of the sub.

Two more dives had followed in less than a week. Over fifty hours spent in a six-foot titanium sphere with two scientists, and now they wanted him to do it again.

Every man has a limit. Jonas knew he had surpassed his after the last dive when he could no longer tell if he was piloting the *Sea Cliff* or dreaming that he was piloting the *Sea Cliff*.

* * *

Dr. Frank Heller may have been a first generation medical man, but he was third generation navy, his grandfather having served in World War II aboard an aircraft carrier, his father and two uncles assigned to the battleship *USS Missouri* during the Korean war. Younger brother Dennis was an Assistant Chief Engineer aboard a Los Angeles Class attack sub, their older sister a former diving officer.

Heller knew that Chief Warrant Officer Carolyn Heller-Johnston would never have certified the pilot seated on his exam table as dive-ready. But then, his big sister didn't have to deal with a pencil-pusher like Dick Danielson or the other desk jockeys back at the Pentagon.

Taylor's last dive had yielded the type of manganese nodule the team of scientists had apparently been hoping for. Now they were demanding that Taylor make another descent before the brunt of Typhoon Marian arrived by noon tomorrow. Rough weather, a subterranean current, even a school of fish could cause their bounty to drift to another location, making it impossible for a returning mission to locate the same patch of volcanic rock.

Danielson essentially gave Heller little choice. As long as Jonas Taylor appeared reasonably coherent, he would be cleared for one more dive.

* * *

The forty-four-year-old physician with the graying crew cut removed the blood pressure cuff from Jonas Taylor's left bicep. "One-thirty-seven over eighty. Slightly elevated, nothing to write home about."

I'm normally one-ten over sixty."

"You're anticipating this morning's dive. Arms out to the side, eyes closed. Now touch your nose with your right index finger."

"Whoa!" The vertigo washed over him, causing Jonas to lose his balance. He reopened his eyes, struggling to stop the room from spinning.

"Vertigo?"

"No thanks, I have enough."

"It'll pass."

"As reassuring as that is, Frank, I'm pretty sure my brain is milk toast."

Captain Danielson entered. "How's our boy?"

"Grumpy. I'm prescribing Antivert for his vertigo and a shot of B-12 to alleviate the fatigue, otherwise he's good to go."

"Wait, what?"

"Excellent. Commander, I'm sure the good doctor will have you feeling ship-shape in no time."

"The good doctor must have fallen off the wagon. My brain's in a fog, my dexterity's off-kilter, and I'm working on three hours sleep."

"Navy SEALs do it all the time. Man up, Taylor. Get some caffeine in you, a few calisthenics. You'll be right as rain."

"Right as rain? I'm not driving Aunt Bea in the squad car to deliver apple pies to Mayberry's church picnic, Dick. This is the Mariana Trench. I need to think clearly down there. And don't get any ideas about Royston. He's nowhere near ready."

"The navy obviously disagrees or he wouldn't have been selected to be your back-up."

"Regulations demanded a back-up. The other two candidates in training quit. Royston was the only pilot available who had dived beyond 15,000 feet."

"Then, technically, he's qualified."

"Technically, Frank here is a doctor, but I wouldn't trust him to lance a boil on your ass, which in your case is probably the equivalent of brain surgery."

Danielson's face turned red. "Dr. Heller, have you certified Commander Taylor fit to dive?"

Frank avoided Jonas's eyes. "Yes, sir."

"Commander Taylor, I am ordering you to pilot the DSV at oh-nine-hundred hours. If you fail to do so you will be subject to a court martial and Mr. Royston shall take your place. Is that clear?"

Jonas stood. For a long moment he and Danielson stared at one another, then the DSV pilot unbuckled his pants and ceremoniously dropped his boxer shorts, exposing his bare buttocks. "You can plant your B-12 shot right there."

Forty minutes later, Jonas Taylor was in the DSV *Sea Cliff* going through his pre-dive checklist—his life about to change forever.

2

Guam Naval Base

LOCATED IN THE REGION of the western Pacific known as Micronesia, the Mariana Island chain is an arc-shaped archipelago consisting of fifteen volcanic mountains. The islands were birthed millions of years ago when lava was released along the Philippine Sea floor as a result of the western edge of the Pacific Plate subducting beneath the Mariana Plate. This region, the most volcanically active convergent plate boundary on Earth, forms the deepest point on the planet—the Mariana Trench. Water trapped in the fault line, heated by the subduction process, is the source of the hydrothermal activity that proliferates throughout this seven-mile-deep, 1,550-mile-long crevasse.

The largest and southernmost island in the Mariana chain is Guam. Home to the Chamorro, a seafaring people whose heritage dates back over four thousand years, Guam's identity underwent a drastic change when it became part of the United States following the Spanish-American War. Guam's location between Hawaii and the Asian mainland rendered the island a strategic location for a U.S. military base, and it is now home to five installations, including the main naval base on Orote Peninsula on the central west coast and Andersen Air Force Base on the northeastern tip.

* * *

Command Master Chief Steve Leiffer's gaze shifted from the dark gray skies to the black Cadillac SUV now approaching the main gate. Rear Admiral Kevin Quercio's unannounced visits were more social call than inspection, his V.I.P.s always political allies or elite members of the military industrial complex. At the end of the day (or days) everyone had a good time, entertaining themselves on a taxpayer-funded holiday.

With Danielson gone and a typhoon on the way, the last thing Leiffer needed to deal with was the renowned partying admiral and his inebriated guests.

Leiffer saluted Admiral Quercio as the imposing man climbed out of the SUV. "Admiral, welcome back to Guam."

"Chief, good to see you. You remember Senator Michaels?"

The Republican from Alaska nodded.

"And these two gentlemen … well, let's just call 'em Mr. Black and Mr. Blue to make life easier."

Leiffer recognized the two executive officers from Brown and Root and BP Oil. "Gentlemen. My apologies. Admiral, Captain Danielson is away on a mission, and we're busy preparing for Typhoon Marian. However, if you need me to arrange accommodations off the base—"

"Already handled, Leiffer, we'll be staying at the Radisson. But I promised our guests a helicopter tour of the island. Where's Mac?"

Leiffer's heart skipped a beat. "Sir, Commander Mackreides is securing his airships in their hangars. Perhaps I can arrange for

Commander Rosario to escort your party."

Admiral Quercio placed a hand on Leiffer's shoulder, leading him away from his guests. "Let's dispense with the horseshit, son. Go find Mac and tell him to meet us at the helipad in exactly ten minutes, or it's your ass and his."

* * *

Commander James "Mac" Mackreide's hawkish eyes moved from the pair of jacks in his right hand to the D-cupped breasts barely contained beneath the brunette's olive-green tee-shirt. "You're bluffing again, Rudd. I can always tell when you're bluffing because your nipples get hard."

Natalie Rudd blew him a kiss. "The bet's a hundred, Mac. Like your hookers say, are you in or out?"

"They're not hookers, Rudd, they're military escorts." Mac glanced down at the dental assistant's remaining chips. "Tell you what. I'll see your hundred and raise you two hundred."

"Asshole. You know I haven't got two hundred, I only have sixty."

Warrant Officer Vicky Baker rolled her eyes. "Here we go again. What's it going to be this time, Mac? Shots at Geronimo's or a drive down to Facpi Point?"

"Quiet, Baker, we're negotiating. Actually, Rudd, if you lose, I was thinking about a weekend's stay at Pago Bay. Just you, me, and the twins."

"Vic, lend me the buck-forty so I can call this gorilla's bluff."

"Let me see your cards."

Rudd passed her friend the hand.

"Call," said Vicky, adding her own chips to the pile.

"If you're so sure, Baker, why not raise me?"

"And give you a chance to raise the pot again and draw me into your childish games? Not a chance."

"Think about it, Baker. You, me, and Rudd, alone in a

bungalow."

"Sounds like fun, Mac, but what will you do?"

The enlisted men whistled cat calls.

"Okay, Rudd, I call. Show me your pair …and your cards, too."

The brunette turned over her hand. "Full house, tens over threes."

Mac ground his teeth, snapping the wooden match in his mouth. "Take it."

Rudd high-fived her friend. "Pleasure doing business with you, James."

"Aw, poor guy," Vicky pouted, "He looks like he's gonna have a Mac Attack."

Mac was about to reply when he saw a jeep skid to a halt in front of the open hanger doors, Steve Leiffer hustling inside.

"Well, if it isn't our second-in-command. What's wrong, number two? Danielson drown at sea trying to retrieve his golf balls?"

"This is serious, Mac. Rear Admiral Quercio just arrived, along with a GOP Senator and two civilian hard-ons. He wants you and your chopper ready to go in ten."

"No way, Stevie. First, my crew just finished tucking the birds in their nests. Second and more important, Quercio stiffed my girls the last two times out. I'm not taking him to the lagoon until he settles his tab."

"Mac, please—"

"Forget it. Get Baker and Rudd here to entertain them."

"Like that's ever gonna happen," Natalie said, cashing out her chips.

"Mac, he'll have both of our asses in the brig."

Vicky smirked, "Is that why they call him a Rear Admiral?"

Leiffer ignored the joke. "Mac, you owe me. I covered for you twice last month with Danielson."

"My girls have families they support, Stevie, they expect to get paid. No tickee no shirtee."

"Okay, I didn't want to bring this up, but if you don't handle this for me, I'll tell Danielson about Linda Kushnel."

Natalie Rudd's eyes widened. "The ER nurse with the tattoos? Man, Danielson fell head over heels for that chick. Remember her, Vicky?"

"How could I forget, he kept asking me for advice. That boy was whipped. He wined her, dined her; he even picked out a ring. Two days after he popped the question she put in for a transfer."

"All Mac's doing," Leiffer said.

"What did you do to her, Mac?"

"Nothing. In fact, I only met her once, at which time I simply offered her my professional opinion of her would-be fiancé."

"Professional opinion? You're a chopper pilot."

"True, but first and foremost I consider myself a life coach."

"Stevie, how did Sir Galahad here manage to get a woman he met once to listen? Did he get her drunk?"

Leiffer grinned. "Nothing like that. Kushnel received an order to report to the base counselor for her annual psychiatric evaluation."

"Base counselor? We don't have a base counselor."

"Who did the evaluation?"

"Dr. James Mackreides."

Mac winked. "We spent four hours together, plus the following weekend in Honolulu. Poor girl, she had a lot to get off her chest. I'd tell you about it, Rudd, but that would violate doctor-patient confidentiality."

* * *

The H-3 *Sea King* was a twin engine, all-weather

33

multi-purpose helicopter used by the navy to detect, classify, track and destroy enemy submarines. Phased out in the 1990s by the SH-60F *Sea Hawk*, the four 73-foot, six-ton airships relegated to Guam were maintained by the mechanics under the command of pilot James Mackreides.

The *Sea King* followed the southwest coastline of Guam, battered by thirty-five-mile-an-hour winds. Mac headed for the village of Merizo, located on the southern peninsula by Cocos Lagoon. Admiral Quercio rode up front, his guests strapped in back in the cargo area.

"Mac, those two lovely young ladies you introduced me to last time …what were their names?"

"Their Chamorro names are too difficult to pronounce. I just call them Ginger and Mary Ann."

"Nice. Once we get my guests settled, you'll arrange a rendezvous."

"Ginger's father lost his leg last year to diabetes, Mary Ann has a kid. They expect to be paid for their services."

"So pay them." The admiral squeezed Mac's shoulder. "I know you take a nice cut from every transaction, son. Consider my on-the-house excursions a necessary business expense."

Mac ground his teeth, then offered Admiral Quercio a Cheshire cat grin. "We've actually added something new for our V.I.P. customers. It's sort of our own version of the mile-high club. I've got two inflatable mattresses in back. I fly us out over the lagoon—the privacy makes the girls less inhibited—plus the sound of the rotors blocks out their screams."

"A flying bordello, huh? What about the wind?"

"Ginger and Mary Ann prefer a bumpy ride."

The admiral grinned. "Let's do it."

3

PROPELLED BY DUAL 653-horsepower engines, the 275-foot research vessel *Tallman* continued its erratic southwestern course. Privately owned by Agricola Industries, the ship and its crew were routinely leased out by the Canadian company to the oil industry for completing pre- and post-dredge surveys, pipeline inspections, and wreck imaging prior to salvage operations. While these jobs helped pay the bills, what the ship's owner preferred were the more challenging academically-oriented assignments—like the one they were now close to completing.

An international science expedition had brought the *Tallman* to its present location in the Philippine Sea, hiring Paul Agricola, the CEO's son, to gather data on NW Rota-1, a deep submarine volcano. Since its discovery three years ago, the erupting volcano had added another eighty feet to its already imposing cone, which now towered twelve stories off the bottom of the world's deepest trench.

Surveying the deepest sea floor in the world required a sophisticated sonar array. Fastened to the *Tallman*'s keel like a twelve foot remora was a gondola-shaped device that housed a Multi Beam Echo Sounder (MBES), its dual frequency deepwater sonar pings designed for mapping the abyss. The bigger challenge was penetrating the hydrothermal plume, which played havoc with the sonar signal six miles down. The solution was the *Sea Bat*, a winged, remotely-operated vehicle. Tethered to the MBES, the *Sea Bat* dropped below the plume like an underwater kite, using its on-board sonar to relay signals back to the mother ship, identifying every object within acoustic range.

For three months the *Tallman* had circled the area above the undersea volcano, gathering water samples while imaging a thriving ecosystem feeding off the heated bottom. Clouds of shrimp and crab would flee each eruption, then return to feast on the fast-growing bacteria, begetting a unique food chain that enticed massive schools of eighteen-foot albino cuttlefish and the occasional giant squid.

Having completed its mission, the crew of the *Tallman* was recalling the *Sea Bat* when a large object suddenly appeared in the sonar array's field of vision. There was no doubt the blip was a biologic. The question: what was it?

Sonar painted the picture of a very large animal, with a length exceeding fifty feet and a girth that would place its weight between fifteen and twenty-five tons. That ruled out even the most giant squid, and the sheer depth of the blip—32,332 feet—eliminated a sperm whale or any other mammal from the list.

The consensus among three of the four oceanographers on-board was that it was most likely a very large whale shark.

The youngest scientist on the team disagreed.

Paul Agricola was not a capitalist like his father, Peter, but, the thirty-two-year-old biologist rarely allowed an opportunity to slip through his fingers. Delaying the ship's departure, he ordered the captain to circle while he conducted a few experiments with the *Tallman*'s sonar, using the *Sea Bat* as bait.

Actively pinging the ROV's sonar at 24 kHz had no effect on the mysterious creature, however the lower 12 kHz sound waves sent the monster charging up from the depths—a behavior not observed among whale sharks. To Paul, the biologic was clearly a carnivore and not a krill feeder, and yet, as aggressive as it was, it refused to ascend beyond the hydrothermally-warmed bottom layer of the hadalpelagic zone.

"It's definitely not a whale shark, but it *is* a shark. Sensitivity to the array's bio-electric fields suggests a biologic possessing an ampullae of Lorenzini ...I think we're looking at a member of the genus *Carcharodon*."

"Based on what evidence?" challenged ichthyologist Eric Stamp.

"Size, for one. Its girth exceeds any whale shark sighting I can think of."

"Ah, yes, but an increase in size can be an adaptive response to the frigid waters of the abyss. Don't forget Bergmann's Rule: larger body size is consistent with colder water creatures—an adaptation that keeps proportionately less of a fish's body close to the outside environment, reducing its loss of internal heat. I'd say that makes it a bottom feeder, a trait not found among *Carcharodon*."

"It's a deep water feeder, professor, but not necessarily a bottom feeder, and neither bottom feeders nor whale sharks attack ROVs. Anyway, I suspect the shark could leave the warm layer if it desired."

"Okay, genius, tell us how you know that." Lucas Heitman

was the *Tallman's* captain and Paul's former fraternity brother, a New Jersey native who never missed an opportunity to deflate his friend's ego.

"It's simple deduction, based on the science of a shark's body mass, something you know nothing about. Take *Carcharodon carcharias*, the Great White shark. Nature endowed big sharks with an anatomy that can handle the cold—their lateral lines contain a web-like structure of veins and arteries. As the shark swims, its moving muscles generate heat in the venous blood, which warms the cooler arterial blood like an internal bellows. It's known as gigantothermy. Our shark must be similarly equipped, which means it can easily generate the heat needed to reach the surface waters, but it doesn't. Why? Because it's been conditioned to remain in its tropical habitat."

"Conditioned by what?"

"The last Ice Age. Stay with me on this, Lucas, I'll try to explain it so that even a fifth grader can understand it. We know glaciation from the last Ice Age affected the flow of warm water currents, shunting off food chains in the three temperate oceans. But these deep water trenches sit on volcanic hot spots. As we've seen from the Rota-1 volcano, warmth equals bacteria and bacteria anchors food chains. If these sharks inhabited surface waters that contained a Hadal Zone, they had a survival option to go deep into the hydrothermal layer beneath the plume. The rest of their kind couldn't handle the extreme cold and perished."

"The rest of their kind? Paul, you sound like you know what this creature is."

"I do. Based on its size, its ferocity, and the fact that it hunts alone, I'd say with ninety-seven percent certainty that we've been tracking *Carcharodon megalodon*."

"A Megalodon?" Professor Stamp scoffed.

The two visiting oceanographers seemed intrigued. "Megs hunted whales, Paul. From the tens of thousands of fossilized teeth we've found near land, it seems obvious the Megs preferred the shallows."

"Maybe man finds most Megalodon teeth in the shallows because that's where it's easier for us to find them. However, we also find Megalodon teeth in the depths. In fact, the *H.M.S. Challenger* found them in these same depths, in these very waters. No, gentlemen, this is definitely a Megalodon, and I intend to prove it."

Captain Heitman's skin tingled. "How, Paul? How are you going to prove it?"

Paul flashed his father's smile. "Lucas, old pal, you and I are going to coax it up."

4

Aboard the DSV-4: *Sea Cliff*

THE 58,000 POUND BEHEMOTH sank slowly away from its detached harnesses and out of the dive team's view, trailing streams of air bubbles. The fiberglass hull, fashioned over the four-inch-thick titanium crew sphere, was essentially a chassis, designed to secure the silver-zinc batteries that powered the electrical and life-support systems, as well as the two hydraulic units that drove its propeller. Mounted outside the hull were television and still cameras, external lights, short-range sonars, two 7-function hydraulically operated manipulator arms, a collection basket that could hold up to 450 pounds, and a "super-sucker" device used for collecting samples.

Ballast tanks, set in pairs forward and midship, prevented the submersible from plunging to the bottom like an anchor. Should the vehicle pitch in the currents, the pilot could employ the sub's Battelle trim system—sintered tungsten carbide balls in a hydraulic fluid, moved along stainless steel coils at either end of the sub.

Steel plates were fastened along the bottom of the craft. When it was time to ascend, the pilot simply jettisoned the six tons of ballast, the change in buoyancy launching the DSV to the surface.

Limited to an hour's forward velocity of 2.5 knots, restricted to controlled descents and ascents, the *Sea Cliff* was essentially a deep-diving mechanical turtle, its three passengers sealed within its watertight titanium shell.

* * *

Of the three teams of scientists assigned to the mission, Jonas enjoyed the company of Richard Prestis and Mike Shaffer the most. Unlike the other stuffed-shirt professors, these two middle-aged geologists had a boyish comic side to them, especially at chow time when Prestis would often attempt to steal his friend's food, causing Shaffer to retaliate with a "titty twister."

The interior of the titanium capsule was far too small for goofing around—the equivalent of placing three grown men inside an empty Jacuzzi encased by a five foot curved ceiling of equipment. The three 4.3 inch portholes did little to relieve the sensation of claustrophobia lurking a wandering thought away, forcing both scientists to balance their cognitive responsibilities with their intake of Valium.

Jonas had no such luxury, and could ill-afford a lapse in concentration, especially today.

In a sense, piloting a DSV was similar to the dangers of driving a truck solo cross country; fatigue was the result of the hypnotic effect of long journeys on monotonous interstate roads. Operating an eighteen wheeler at night was ten times more dangerous than during daylight hours. The mind wandered, impairing decision-making and slowing the driver's reaction time.

Of course, a truck driver could always pull over at a rest stop to stretch his legs, even grab a few hours of sleep. In the DSV it was always night, at least after the first thousand feet.

Three dives in eight days...

Fifty-one hours of piloting in just under 190 hours.

Gazing out the forward viewport above Mike Shaffer's shoulder, Jonas watched the blue void deepen to violet as the *Sea Cliff* slipped below eight hundred feet, sinking beyond the shallows of the mesopelagic region. 400 feet later, the depths officially extinguished the last gray curtain of sunlight, casting them into the mid-region's velvety darkness.

The journey had officially begun.

Approaching the first quarter mile ...one of twenty-four quarter miles that leads down to the warm layer. Five hours down, three to five hours collecting samples, then another four back to the surface, maybe less if I push it. The sea will be even rougher by tomorrow morning with that damn typhoon right on our ass. The highlight of the day will be watching Danielson bent over the rail.

Shifting his weight within the tight confines, careful not to kick the dozing Dr. Prestis, Jonas looked down at the viewport between his feet—a grapefruit-size window revealing only blackness.

As he watched, the dark void suddenly came alive with thousands of twinkling lights.

The *Sea Cliff* had transported them into another universe—a mid-water region known as the bathypelagic, home to the largest ecosystem on the planet. Encompassing upwards of ten million species, the life forms inhabiting this "twilight zone" had adapted to an eternity of living in darkness by evolving large, bulbous eyes that could pick up slivers of light ...and by creating their own light.

Bioluminescence in living organisms was generated through a chemical reaction, in this case a light-producing luciferin and its catalyst, called luciferase. Fueled by the release of Adenosine

Triphosphate (ATP), the luciferase caused the luciferin to oxidize, creating a bioluminescent light. Jonas was familiar with these light-emitting photophore organs, having dissected a Vampire Squid in the navy's lab.

The deeper they descended, the more curious the fish became. Hatchet fish bashed their fanged jowls against the thick glass in alternating swarms, attempting to reach the twinkling lights of the control panels. For several minutes an anglerfish escorted the starboard viewport, its illuminated rod fin casting an eerie yet enticing reflection back at the hitchhiker, who was unknowingly snapping at itself.

Finding himself becoming mesmerized, Jonas looked away, focusing his attention on his gauges. The sea temperature had dropped to a bone-chilling 51-degrees Fahrenheit, the water pressure increasing beyond 1,935 psi.

Closing his eyes so as not to cheat, he attempted to calculate their depth, a mental exercise designed to keep his mind sharp. *Water pressure increases at a rate of 14.7 pounds per square inch for every 33-feet of depth. Dividing 1,935 pounds per square inch by...*

The sudden sensation of vertigo nearly tossed him from his cushioned bench. Quickly reopening his eyes, he glanced around the sphere.

Richard Prestis was still snoozing on his left, curled under a blanket in a forced fetal position.

Michael Shaffer was staring at him on his right, the geologist's eyes as wide as the Hatchet fish's, his white-knuckled hand clutching a frayed paperback book. "Tell me you're okay."

"I'm okay. Right as rain."

"Good. Then maybe you ought to strap in...you know, your harness?" He pointed.

"Harness? Yeah. Good idea." Retrieving the two straps, he attempted to insert one end into the other, only his hands were trembling far too much to accomplish the task.

43

Shaffer waited patiently, while on the inside his pulse raced. The scientist glanced up at the depth gauge as its orange LED numbers flickered past 7,100 feet. *Barely a quarter of the way down and Taylor's already losing it. Better lighten the mood …ease his mind, at least what's left of it.*

"Hey, Jonas, did I ever tell you about the best toast of the night contest? It was won by a fine Irish lad, John O'Reilly, who hoisted his beer and said, 'Here's to spending the rest of me life …between the sumptuous legs of me big breasted wife!' When John returned home that night, drunk as a skunk, his wife demanded to know what the prize was for. 'Mary,' he said, 'I won the prize for the best toast of the night. Here's to spending the rest of me life, sitting in church beside me beautiful wife.'

"Well, the next day Mary ran into one of John's drinking buddies. Staring at her massive boobs, the man said, 'So Mary, did ye hear John won the prize the other night at the pub with a toast about you?' 'Aye, he told me,' Mary said, 'and I was a bit surprised myself. You know, he's only been there twice in the last four years. Once he fell asleep, and the last time I had to pull him by the ears just to make him come.' "

Jonas smiled. "It's a long ride. I hope you saved your 'A' material for the *Devil's Purgatory.*"

"Now there's something I've been meaning to ask you. Who came up with that name for this stretch of trench?"

"I'm told it originated from one of the scientists aboard the *H.M.S. Challenger.* According to his journal entry, it was in this area that they netted some of the biggest fossilized shark teeth of the entire voyage, including a few that dated back less than ten thousand years."

"How big were the teeth?"

"Six to seven inches, the edges all serrated. Like a steak knife."

"What kind of—"

"Megalodon. A prehistoric relative of the Great White shark. If you figure an inch of tooth equals ten feet of shark …well, you get the idea."

"That's a big-ass shark."

"Here's the real scary part: if the teeth were less than ten thousand years old, then that meant some of these sharks had survived the last Ice Age by going deep to inhabit the warm layer heated by the volcanic vents. Lots of heat along the bottom. The hot zone. As in hell."

"As in devil, I get it. But the term purgatory makes it sound as if the sharks had been stuck down there."

Jonas pointed to the temperature gauge, the ocean now registering an icy 42-degrees. "Seventy degree temperatures along the bottom, separated from sun and shallows by six miles of cold. If you lived in an oasis with plenty of food, would you risk crossing the desert to reach another oasis you had no clue even existed?"

Shaffer smiled. "Only if it was Vegas. I'm a bit of a shark myself. Card shark. Plus I love stalking the ladies. *Grrowl.*"

Aboard the *Tallman*
17 miles north-northeast of Guam

Lucas Heitman unfurled the bathymetric map across the fluorescent table top. "We're here, about fifteen miles northeast of Guam. Your monster's about a half mile ahead of us, cruising in 33,000 feet of water at a steady five knots. We're pinging at 16 kHz, which is low enough to maintain a reading but high enough not to piss it off—at this range."

"What if I want to tag him?"

"Tag him?"

"Him. Her. It. All I know is that it was sheer luck detecting this shark. I don't want to risk losing it because of some damn typhoon. Therefore we need to tag it."

"Okay, it's time for a reality check: these fifteen-foot seas from that damn typhoon? By tonight they'll become small mountains. If we don't head south soon we'll be caught in its eye, and that's the last thing we want, trust me. Next reality check: your monster won't abandon the warmth beneath the hydrothermal plume. That's a major problem, Paul. The plume is like a raging river of minerals. It will tear the transmitter dart's assembly from any launch platform you send down there, eliminating any possibility of tagging your shark."

"Okay, Lucas, so maybe it won't abandon the warm layer for good, but I bet we could lure it up for a quick shot. Rig the *Sea Bat-II* with the transmitter gun and the remains of the tuna we netted yesterday morning. We bring the Meg up with *Sea Bat-I*, then lure it in real close to *Sea Bat-II* and blam—right in the mouth!"

The intensity in Paul's eyes bordered on manic.

Lucas stared at his friend. "Shoot it in the mouth? Dude, what are we doing? We're messing with a shark that's the size of the *Tallman*'s beam. What happens if we lure it away from its habitat and it surfaces? What's to stop it from following the ROV straight up into the shallows?"

"Can you imagine those headlines? It'd be bigger than the *Alvin* discovering the *Titanic*."

"Paul, be serious."

"I am being serious. And if you had any idea how difficult it's been to convince my father to keep this little venture of ours going, then you'd be serious about this too. Decent paying jobs outside of inspecting oil pipelines are few and far between, and most of them are going to the more established boats. We need something big like this to put *Tallman* on the map."

"All I'm asking is that you think this through. You bring this monster up from the depths, pal, and you own it."

"Don't tease me."

"I'm talking about liabilities, Paul."

"First we tag it, then we figure out the next step. Fair enough?"

"Fine. You have until six tonight to play tag, then we're heading south."

"Make it eight."

"Paul, ever see the movie, *The Poseidon Adventure?*"

"Okay, okay, six o'clock. Just have both *Sea Bats* rigged and ready to launch within the hour."

5

Mariana Trench

THE MARIANA TRENCH was birthed along the subduction zone where the massive Pacific Plate descends under the leading edge of the Eurasian Plate. For billions of years, hydrothermal vent fields have been delivering super-heated 700-degree Fahrenheit water into isolated habitats within the 1,550-mile-long, forty-mile-wide gorge. Laden with minerals, the volcanic discharge from these "black smokers" has coalesced about a mile off the bottom, forming a ceiling of soot which effectively insulates and seals off the frigid waters of the abyss. More than sixty feet thick, this hydrothermal plume is further stabilized by the steep walls of the trench's submarine canyon, creating a temperate zone in an unexplored realm located at the bottom of the western Pacific Ocean.

Prior to 1977, scientists were convinced life could not exist in the depths without sunlight. Once they actually investigated their claims aboard the *Alvin* submersible, they were shocked to find a vast food chain, all originating from tube worms—eight-to-ten-foot-long invertebrates that seemed to be feeding off the hydrothermal vents. In fact, the *Riftia pachyptila* actually existed on the bacteria living inside their own bright red nutritional organs. In a symbiotic relationship, the tube worms' bacteria were feeding off the toxic chemicals spewed into the sea by the hydrothermal vents—a process that became known as chemosynthesis.

In the depths of the Mariana Trench, giant albino crabs and shrimp fed off the tube worms; small fish fed off the crabs and shrimp, and larger fish fed off the smaller fish. Feeding off the larger fish were an exotic array of sea creatures, both modern and prehistoric, that had existed in this isolated temperate zone for hundreds of millions of years. While there were no whales or sea elephants in the Mariana Trench, there was still plenty of prey, all stemming from an ecosystem that flourished seven miles below the surface of the Pacific Ocean.

At the top of this food chain was *Carcharodon megalodon*.

* * *

The albino shark moved slowly through the pitch-dark canyon. At forty-eight feet and twenty-seven tons, the juvenile female Megalodon was already equal to her adult male counterparts—all of whom continued to avoid a confrontation, at least until her first fertility cycle.

Warm water streamed into her slack-jawed mouth, held open in a cruel, jagged smile. Just visible above the lower gum line were twenty-two razor-sharp teeth she used for gripping prey. The upper jaw held twenty-four—far larger, wider weapons designed by nature to puncture bone, sinew and blubber. Behind these front rows of teeth were four or five additional rows, folded back into the gum line like a conveyor belt. Composed of calcified cartilage, these serrated teeth—three to six inches long—were set within a ten-foot jaw that, instead of being fused to the skull, hung loosely beneath the brain case. This adaptation enabled the upper jaw to actually push forward and hyperextend in a gargantuan bite, wide enough to engulf a mini-van from the back end all the way up to the front windshield.

For most of the last thirty million years, Megalodon had dominated every ocean, feeding on the high-fat, high-energy yielding content of whales. Everything had changed two million years ago with the arrival of the last Ice Age. Warm water currents had been cut off, creating land bridges which altered whale migration patterns. While these factors did not significantly affect the Megalodon population, the rise of another species caused the giant sharks' numbers to plummet.

Orca.

Hunting in pods of thirty to fifty individuals, the Killer Whales decimated Meg nurseries. Within the span of a hundred thousand years, very few of Mother Nature's apex predators remained.

It would be the nurseries located along the coastline of the Mariana Island chain that prevented the species from going extinct. Driven from the shallows of the archipelago by Orca, the surviving Meg pups went deep, escaping the mammals and, in the process, discovering a warm water habitat in the deepest canyon on the planet.

* * *

The juvenile female continued on her southwesterly course, navigating around skyscraper-tall black smokers on a swiftly moving current that allowed her to expend little effort. Although there was no visible light in the trench, the Meg could still see. Adaptation and evolution equipped the shark's eyes with a reflective layer behind the retina that offered wisps of nocturnal vision. Normally black, the Megalodon of the Mariana Trench had developed blue-gray eyes, a common trait found among albinos. The loss of the species' lead-gray dorsal pigment had occurred over eons—an adaptation to an existence quarantined in perpetual darkness.

The female glided effortlessly through the tropical void, her massive torpedo-shaped body undulating in slow snake-like movements. As her flank muscles contracted, the Megalodon's caudal fin and aft portion pulled in a powerful rhythmic motion, propelling the shark forward. The immense half-moon shaped tail provided maximum thrust with minimal drag, while the fin's caudal notch, located in the upper lobe, further streamlined the water flow.

Stabilizing the Megalodon's forward thrust were her broad pectoral fins, which provided lift and balance like the wings of a passenger airliner. Her dorsal fin rose atop her back like a six-foot sail, acting as a rudder. A smaller pair of pelvic fins, a second dorsal, and a tiny anal fin rounded out the complement, everything synchronized and perfected over 400 million years of evolution.

The female inhaled her environment through two grapefruit-size directional nostrils, her brain processing an elixir of chemicals and excretions as traceable as smoke in a kitchen.

Ahead, moving through the canyon as one, were thousands of giant cuttlefish.

While the Meg had been tracking the school for weeks, there had been no urgency to feed. Feeding required hunting and hunting expended energy. With her core temperature approximating that of her environment, the huntress could go weeks without feeding—provided she remained in the balmy depths in a non-predatory state.

The *Sea Bat*'s sonic acoustics had disrupted the female's sensory organs, forcing her to attack. A dozen successive rushes had sent the shark up through the hydrothermal ceiling—the sudden shock of 33-degree water chasing her back before she could kill the source of the disturbance.

Energy had been expended, her reserves were running on low.

Now she had to feed.

With a flick of her massive caudal fin, the hungry female accelerated through the darkness, closing fast on her quarry.

* * *

In the ocean's pecking order it is size that matters. The cuttlefish of the Mariana Trench had adapted to their environment by growing large—eighteen to twenty feet from their finned heads to the tips of their eight sucker-covered arms and two feeding tentacles. Three hearts were required to pump their blue-green blood to these ten extremities while fueling a camouflage technique that allowed the squid to alter its skin color. Brilliant neon lights could lure prey or stun an enemy.

Intelligent creatures, the cuttlefish had learned to travel in schools, their perceived size scaring off potential enemies. Upwards of ten thousand cephalopods moved as one through the canyon, the school undulating like a quarter-mile-long sea serpent.

The cuttlefish tactic was clever, but it could not fool a Megalodon's senses. Located along the top and underside of the female's snout were sensitive receptor cells collectively known as the ampullae of Lorenzini. These deep jelly-filled pores connected to the shark's brain by a vast tributary of cranial nerves, allowing it to detect the faint voltage gradients and bio-electric fields produced by the cuttlefish as their skin moved through the water. So sensitive were the ampullae of Lorenzini that the Megalodon could distinguish an individual cuttlefish from the moving pack of thousands by the distinctive rhythm of its beating hearts.

* * *

The Megalodon stalked its quarry, moving parallel to the swarm.

Sensing the predator, the cuttlefish increased their speed while simultaneously illuminating their hides in phosphorescent greens and blues. The color pattern was a method of communication among the school as well as a warning to stay away.

The Meg's spine arched, forcing her pectoral fins to curl downward. Flushed in full attack mode, the juvenile killer was about to swoop in upon the moving mass of squid when she detected another presence lurking close by—a challenger.

* * *

At thirty-three feet and eighteen tons, the pliosaur was nearly as large as the megalodon, though it lacked the species' girth. The creature's head, nearly a third its length, resembled a crocodilian jaw overloaded with ten-inch dagger sharp teeth. Its skull sat atop a thick neck and stocky trunk, tapering back to a short tail. Snakelike movements were powered by four oversized flippers that propelled its streamlined body through the water.

A survivor of the Middle Cretaceous, *Kronosaurus* began its existence as a reptile. For more than 50 million years its ancestors dominated the seas—until 65 million years ago when an asteroid struck the Earth. The celestial impact filled the planet's atmosphere with debris which blocked out the sun, causing an Ice Age.

Reptiles are cold blooded animals, their body temperatures dependent on the warmth generated by their environment. As the oceans rapidly cooled, the plesiosaur order quickly died off, unable to generate enough body heat to survive. Inhabiting the seas off Australia, *Kronosaurus* were the only species of plesiosaur in proximity to one of the few warm spots on the planet that remained unaffected by the glaciation period.

Much as an alligator spends its days basking in the sun, members of the *Kronosaurus* species took to diving down to the hydrothermally heated depths of the Mariana Trench in order to survive. Over thousands of generations, this particular pliosaur group adapted to these extended dives by developing gills—an evolutionary feature that allowed them to permanently inhabit the warm abyss.

* * *

The male *Kronosaurus* glided silently through a vent field that spewed pockets of clear near-boiling water, the brackish sulfuric backwash causing acres of tube worms to dance. If Megalodon was the lion of this deepwater Serengeti then the *Kronosaurus* was its leopard. Though wary of the presence of a superior hunter, it too had to feed.

Pumping its powerful fore-fins, the pliosaur banked sharply around a black smoker, placing it on a direct intercept course with the river of cephalopods racing through the canyon like a six-story-high train more than three football fields long.

Detecting the charging *Kronosaurus*, the cuttlefish engaged their photochromic skin, igniting green and blue neon sparks of light in both directions in a flashing fast-changing pattern that appeared like the denticles of a massive sea snake.

The intimidated *Kronosaurus* veered away, its survival instincts momentarily overriding the need to feed.

And then, without warning, the formation suddenly burst—ten thousand phosphorescent bodies flushing red as they dispersed in a cascading explosion of brilliant blinding color—

—the stampede ignited by 54,000 pounds of rampaging shark. The Megalodon bulldozed its way through the center of the herd, the female's hyperextended jaws clamping down upon a mouthful of squirming cephalopod, its serrated teeth shredding tentacles into ribbons as its senses searched the chaos for the *Kronosaurus*.

The startled challenger darted away, twisting and turning, scorching its belly in the super-heated outflow of a vent as it was swept away in a frenzy of fleeing squid.

The Meg swallowed a succulent thousand-pound bite of cuttlefish as the squid circled back into formation, their skin flashing in rapid sequences as they twisted and looped again as one. The reforming mass of glowing bodies raced north through the submarine canyon, igniting the darkness like a slithering green-blue luminescent serpent.

The Meg circled the scraps twice, its senses searching the area for its challenger. The female detected the *Kronosaurus* several hundred yards away, moving along the sea floor as it followed the reorganizing school of cuttlefish.

Her appetite stimulated, the shark altered its course, homing in on both the cuttlefish and her fleeing nemesis.

6

Challenger Deep

JONAS'S EYES DARTED from the depth gauge to the viewport, the last five hours of fatigue disappearing in the adrenaline rush accompanying the extreme depths.

31,500 feet…

31,775 feet…

Debris rattled across the *Sea Cliff's* outer hull like hail on a tin roof. He eased up on the foot pedals, adjusting the submersible's rate of descent.

31,850 feet.

An object bloomed into view in the small reinforced porthole by his stockinged feet, the DSV's lights illuminating a swirling river of brown water. Jonas hovered the submersible fifty feet above the hydrothermal plume, fighting to adjust the trim against the rippling surge of the raging current.

STEVE ALTEN

"Wake up, gentlemen, we've arrived at the gates of hell."

Michael Shaffer shook Dr. Prestis awake. "You need to get a new tagline, Jonas. How about, 'Hey, Toto, I've got a feeling we're not in Kansas anymore.'"

Richard Prestis rubbed the sleep from his eyes. "That's not new, every lame movie uses that line. How about, 'Of all the deep water trenches in the world, she swam into mine.'"

"Can you imagine looking out the viewport and seeing a mermaid?" Shaffer said, readying the ROV for deployment.

"I prefer my mermaids with a D-cup or better," Prestis joked. "Any mermaids surviving down here would be flat-chested from all the pressure. Stand by, I'm powering up the *Flying Squirrel*."

Jonas smiled. "I meant to ask you guys—whose idea was it to name the ROV the *Flying Squirrel?*"

"Dr. Shaffer gets the credit on that one."

"What can I say; I'm an old Rocky and Bullwinkle fan."

Jonas struggled to control the DSV's pitch and yaw as the *Sea Cliff* tossed above rolling wakes of cold water hitting warm. "Maybe we should nickname Danielson and Heller, Boris and Natasha."

Prestis grabbed for a handle bar, closing his eyes against the turbulence. "Which one's Boris and which one's Natasha?"

Shaffer ignored him, reciting a quick prayer.

"Heller should be Natasha," Jonas responded, "he has nicer legs. Mike, you okay?"

The submersible's bow and tail teetered as if on a slow-moving see-saw. "Let's just finish this damn mission and get the hell out of Dodge. Deploying *Flying Squirrel*."

Roughly the size of a go-cart, the rectangular, canary-yellow ROV decoupled from the DSV's sled, its twin propellers rapidly moving it away from the submersible, its docking berth feeding out piano wire from a motorized spool, keeping the drone

56

tethered to the *Sea Cliff*.

"Engines—check. Lights—check. Infrared—check. Night vision—check. Forward camera—check. Rear camera—check. Grappler—check. Richard, try the vacuum."

"Vacuum's working. Send your *Flying Squirrel* into Jonas's hell hole and order it to bring back some juicy nuts."

Shaffer mumbled, "I'll settle for a dozen manganese nodules filled with Helium-3." Using a joystick, the scientist maneuvered the ROV into a steep descent, aiming for a dark spot on the hydrothermal plume now appearing on his monitor. "Tears in his eyes as he lines up this last shot. A Cinderella story, outta nowhere …a former greenskeeper, now about to become the Masters champion."

Jonas and Prestis looked at one another, grinning at their colleague's dead-on imitation of Carl Spackler from *Caddyshack*. Together, all three yelled out, "It's in the hole! It's in the hole!" as the ROV punched through the warm layer of swirling soot, its reinforced chassis buffeted by the volcanic debris.

For several minutes Shaffer's monitor remained a field of static—until the remote sub exited the hydrothermal ceiling and entered a placid sea.

"We're through. Switching to night vision."

The monitor changed from black to an olive-green tint, revealing dark brown billowing clouds rising from unseen chimneys. Schaffer worked the joystick, veering the mini-sub away from the volcanic haze, diving the craft toward the bottom.

"Michael, quickly—pull up!"

"It's okay, Jonas. I'm clear."

"Just do it. There's something big on sonar, heading for the ROV."

Shaffer yanked back on the joystick, sending the tethered sub retreating back toward the hydrothermal plume.

Richard's heart raced. "Jonas, what is it? How big?"

"You don't want to know."

Jonas powered off the *Sea Cliff's* underwater lights, allowing them to see through the occasional swath of clear water into the swirling flotsam of minerals below.

Reverberations—like bare feet slapping on wet concrete—built to a crescendo, and then the darkness suddenly ignited into a dazzling green and blue current of phosphorescent strobe lights, the life forms streaking two thousand feet below the hydrothermal ceiling, racing through the trench like an offspring of St. Elmo's Fire.

Forty seconds passed before the silent darkness returned.

Richard Prestis wiped beads of sweat from his temples. "That was unbelievable. Almost alien."

"I think I crapped an alien." Dr. Shaffer's heart was pounding so hard that it affected his breathing, each deep inhalation bordering on hyperventilation. Hands quivering, he popped a Valium. "Richard, I think I need you to take over."

"Do you need another Valium?"

"I need air."

"Slow deep breaths, pal, nice and easy. Jonas, can you adjust the blowers?"

"Done."

"Michael, tell us a joke. How about the …"

"Shh." Jonas stared hard at the ROV's sonar. "Richard, keep the *Squirrel* steady."

"What's wrong?" Both scientists looked up, their faces pale.

"Sonar's picked up a straggler. Only this one's different. It moves like a predator."

The three men huddled over the sonar screen as an orange blip moved lazily through the depths, cutting slow figure-eights below the ROV.

Jonas whispered, "It knows the robot's there."

"How?"

"Steel prop. It gives off electrical discharges. Better cut the robot's power."

Prestis and Shaffer exchanged glances, unsure.

"Do it. The tether will hold it in place."

Prestis powered the ROV off.

* * *

The Megalodon circled the intruder, her back arched and ridged as she prepared to launch an attack from below—when her intended prey abruptly disappeared.

For several minutes the big female continued to circle. Then, with a succession of powerful whip-like flicks of her tail, the shark resumed the hunt, gradually closing the distance on the multitude of cuttlefish as they trekked through the heated waters of the submarine canyon.

Aboard the *Tallman*
6 miles north-northeast of Guam

"Paul, you'd better look at this. According to *Sea Bat-I*, your monster just changed course."

Paul Agricola pushed one of the other scientists aside to join Captain Heitman at the ROV's sonar screen, his head and stomach in knots from the twenty foot seas. "I see several blips. Which damn blip is it?"

"The smaller one, here. This larger mass must be a school of fish. When the fish changed course, your shark changed course with them. Look, it just passed below us."

"Bring us about before we lose it."

"Helm, come about quickly to course zero-one-five. Watch your bow, keep it facing into the waves. Increase speed to ten knots."

"Aye, sir."

Paul tapped the plastic light table with his index finger, his eyes studying the charts. "How much longer until *Sea Bat-II* can launch?"

The captain picked up the phone by his station and dialed the extension to the utility room. "Doug, how much longer on *SB-II?*"

"Twenty minutes. Call me again and it'll be thirty minutes."

Paul grabbed the phone from the *Tallman's* skipper. "Doug, it's Paul. I need to know the maximum depth we can fire the transmitter dart."

"As long as the *Sea Bat's* above the hydrothermal plume she'll fire. As far as firing straight or penetrating the Meg's hide—hell if I know. My advice is to let your fish get real close, then say a prayer."

Paul slammed the receiver down on its cradle. "Twenty minutes, captain. Call me the moment we launch, I'll be in the head puking up my guts."

Lucas watched his friend exit the pilothouse. *Land lover. Just like his old man ...*

Challenger Deep

There are rules on the African Serengeti, a pecking order to the hunt. When the lioness stalks zebra, it is her field of play. Only after she partakes of the spoils can the wild dogs and hyenas move in to feed.

There is a similar order in the ocean. In surface waters, the sea lion kill is orchestrated by Orca; the buffet of a dead cetacean by the Great White shark.

In the Mariana Trench, it is *Carcharodon megalodon* that commands the feast. It begins with the stalking of the prey, a ritual designed to warn off other predators. Body language moves from a submissive to an aggressive posture—the Meg's spine arching, its pectoral fins pointing downward. A Megalodon may also mark its kill zone by urinating while circling its intended meal.

To cross this boundary is to challenge the predatory pecking order.

* * *

The male *Kronosaurus* needed to feed. The encounter with the Megalodon had caught the pliosaur by surprise, and the escape expended what little energy reserves the creature had left.

Swimming parallel with the school of cuttlefish, the eighteen-ton *Kronosaurus* suddenly turned upon the swarm, succeeding in separating several dozen squid from the pack. A lone cuttlefish was targeted and the hunt began.

The squid was quick, but its brain patterns had been forged by a pack mentality, its unexpected separation from the group leading to its undoing. Instead of distancing itself from the hunter, the squid sought only to rejoin its fleeing siblings, taking the most direct route despite the obvious danger.

Soaring in from behind a towering black smoker, the *Kronosaurus* cut off the cuttlefish's retreat. In one treacherous bite it snatched the squid's head within its jaws, igniting a furious response of tentacles which lashed out, its barbed suckers tearing at its unseen enemy's hide. But the cephalopod's life force was bleeding out and it quickly went limp in the pliosaur's mouth.

The *Kronosaurus* managed to swallow the cuttlefish seconds before its senses were alerted to the presence of a larger predator.

By attacking the cuttlefish the *Kronosaurus* had indirectly challenged the Megalodon. The young queen changed course to intercept the pliosaur—the need to conserve energy holding no sway over thirty million years of predatory instinct.

Still clenching the dead cuttlefish within its crocodilian jaws, the *Kronosaurus* swam off, serpentining through undulating fields of giant tube worms in an attempt to lose the huntress.

Owning the higher ground, the Megalodon accelerated in a steep descent, adjusting her angle of attack as she closed the gap, rendering escape impossible. The Meg's bull rush ended in a violent cloudburst of silt as the forty-eight foot prehistoric Great White crushed the *Kronosaurus's* neck in a horrific bite while simultaneously pinning its enemy against the sea floor. A resounding *thud* fractured two of the Meg's upper teeth, her snout disappearing beneath a cloudburst of minerals, soot, severed tube worms and blood.

The blood originated from the *Kronosaurus*. The creature's internal organs had burst upon impact, the splattered remains ejected out of the dead animal's esophagus behind the vertebrae-splintering force generated by twenty-seven tons of shark moving at eighteen knots.

Stunned by the concussion-inducing blow, the juvenile queen could not locate the crushed remains of its prey. Shaking her gargantuan head, the female circled away from the cloud of silt, attempting to reboot her overloaded senses.

Recovering slowly, the Meg detected a familiar high decibel sound that exacerbated the injury and inflamed her sensory array. Attempting to lose the annoying sensation, the female swam in a figure-eight holding pattern, while bloodied remains from her kill danced along the sea floor. The irritating blip …blip …blip continued to taunt her, driving the Meg into a frenzy.

Abandoning the mangled remains of the *Kronosaur*, the Megalodon ascended toward the swirling hydrothermal plume to intercept the *Sea Bat*.

7

Aboard the *Tallman*

THE PILOTHOUSE HAD BECOME an orchestra of organized chaos.

Paul Agricola was its conductor, the mission's maestro calling out instructions in response to a rapidly changing concerto playing out six miles beneath his feet.

Two *Sea Bat* drones were now being towed by steel cable: *SB-I* just over the hydrothermal plume, *SB-II* a half mile above it, the second drone's range limited by the length of the steel cable available on its winch.

That missing two thousand feet of line was proving to be a difference maker. While the Megalodon had chased *Sea Bat-I* above the hydrothermal plume, it had never exposed itself to the frigid waters above the warm layer for more than thirty seconds. Paul was hoping this was due more to the fact that they had been forced to stop *Sea Bat-I* from pinging above the plume to keep the drone from being eaten rather than the Meg's avoidance of the frigid water.

The new plan was to engage *Sea Bat-II's* active sonar the moment the shark emerged from the mineral layer, hoping the *Meg* would immediately go after the second drone, which was armed with a transmitter dart rigged to a motion sensor, its maximum range—sixty feet.

Doug Dvorak, the ship's engineer, lowered his walkie-talkie. "Paul, the deck crew is standing by at the winches. *Sea Bat-II's depth* is steady at 28,435 feet, *Sea Bat-I* hovering just above the plume. Both sonars are off, as ordered."

"Make *Sea Bat-I's* depth 32,700 feet."

"Paul, that's more than seven hundred feet deeper than the

63

plume. I don't advise that."

"I wasn't asking for your opinion, Douglas. Captain Heitman, the moment *Sea Bat-I* drops through the plume and reenters the *Challenger Deep*, prepare to increase our speed just enough to maintain a safe distance."

"You want to get your shark used to chasing the lure before you lead it out of the warm layer?"

"Exactly."

"It could backfire, Paul. A longer chase expends energy. The Meg could lose interest."

"The Meg's tiring, Luis. If we don't hit it with the tracking dart soon, it may stop leaving the warm layer altogether."

"Paul, *Sea Bat-I* is inside the plume. Sixty feet to *Challenger Deep* …thirty feet. Standing by to activate *SB-I* sonar."

Paul wiped sweat from his forehead. "Maybe you should wait on the sonar …let the ROV reach its new depth first."

The captain shook his head. "It's too risky. The creature's already homing in on the *Sea Bat*'s vibrations. I can't chance running blind; I need to know exactly where that creature is the moment the *Sea Bat* emerges from the plume."

"Skipper, *SB-I* has entered the warm layer."

"Activate sonar on *SB-I*."

"*SB-I* sonar is active. Target acquired. Range 520 feet. Speed …seven knots. Ten knots."

"Helm, increase speed to twelve knots."

"Range is four hundred feet …four-twenty …five hundred. Target speed holding at twelve knots."

"Helm, decrease speed to ten knots."

"Skipper, I'm picking up a surface ship on radar. Two miles to the south; we're heading right for her."

Paul glanced at the radar operator. "It's probably just a fishing trawler. Ignore it, captain."

"They're hailing us, Skipper. It's a naval ship. The USS

Maxine D."

Paul swore under his breath. "Sonar, where's the Meg?"

"Two hundred and thirty feet from the ROV and closing."

"Skipper, the navy says we're entering a restricted area. We've been ordered to change course."

"Paul, target has closed to seventy-five feet, speed—sixteen knots."

"Helm, match speed. Doug, restart the winch."

Dvorak yelled into his walkie-talkie. "Restart the winch. Bring her up!"

"Sir, target has followed *SB-I* into the plume."

* * *

Agitated by the incessant reverberations generated by the *Sea Bat's* pinging sonar, the Megalodon rose through the hydrothermal layer, intent on devouring the creature. She closed her mouth to restrict the flow of sulfurous debris from entering her gills and within seconds had passed through the plume, once more entering a cold alien world.

* * *

"Range to Naval vessel one-point-three nautical miles."

"Paul?"

"I'm thinking!"

"Sir, *Sea Bat-I* has exited the plume."

"There's nothing to think about, Paul. We need to change course."

"Quiet! Doug, shut down *SB-I* sonar. Go active on *SB-II*."

"Paul, I'm changing course. Heading west on course two-seven-zero."

"Sir, target has exited the hydrothermal plume."

* * *

The Megalodon emerged from the hydrothermal plume into near-freezing temperatures, the cold momentarily invigorating its overheated muscles. Homing in on the annoying pings coming from the second drone, the female continued to rise, ascending a thousand feet in less than a minute.

* * *

"Target is now homing in on *Sea Bat-II*. Range—275 feet and closing. Congratulations, Paul, looks like your plan worked."

"It's too early to be doing the victory dance, Doug. Captain, reduce your speed, we need to keep it interested enough in *Sea Bat-II* to come within sixty feet of the tagging device."

* * *

The sea was ice-cold, penetrating the Megalodon's energy-depleted muscles, causing the creature's blood vessels to constrict.

The female's caudal fin slowed. Her breathing became erratic.

Seventy-two feet from her prey, a half-mile above the churning hydrothermal layer and just twelve feet from triggering *Sea Bat-II's* tracking dart, the twenty-seven ton predator's swim muscles suddenly seized.

Slowly, majestically, the Megalodon sank head-first into the abyss, the annoying reverberations in the female's brain fading to a dull, distant echo.

Aboard the *Sea Cliff*

The Valium had kicked in quickly, soothing Michael Shaffer's rattled nerves like a warm blanket. Sleepy-eyed, he watched Richard Prestis maneuver the *Flying Squirrel* to the sea floor, guided by the ROV's built-in sonar and the laptop's night-vision monitor.

"Michael, I'm two hundred feet from the bottom. How do I access the coordinates from the last dive?"

"Hit F-7."

A red blip appeared on the laptop's navigation screen. "Got

it."

"Right click on it with your mouse and the auto-pilot will engage—"

"—guiding the *Squirrel* to our sack of nuts." Prestis laughed as he right-clicked the mouse.

Nothing happened.

"Something's wrong. The coordinates are up but the autopilot won't engage."

Shaffer closed his eyes to think. "Check your sonar, make sure it's running active."

"Jonas, are you listening? Switch from passive to active. Jonas?"

The *Sea Cliff* drifted to starboard—then continued rolling, pitching Prestis into Shaffer's lap.

"Taylor, wake up!"

Strapped in at his control station, Jonas Taylor's eyes snapped open, his legs desperately pumping the foot pedals to trim the ballast tanks.

The teetering submersible rolled to port, finding equilibrium.

"Sorry boys. I just can't seem to be able to keep my eyes open."

"Then take another dose of caffeine pills before you flip us."

"I can't, my heart's doing somersaults already."

"At least switch the ROV's sonar to active."

"Sorry Richard, we're not going active. Not with a large predator in the area."

"What you saw could have been anything."

"Richard, you don't need to ping for black smokers, the ROV's guidance system has a temperature setting that will steer the unit clear of any vents exceeding 225 degrees. Just use the joystick and fly the *Squirrel* to the collection site."

"I still need the sonar active in order to use the auto-pilot to map the bottom. Now turn it on."

Mike Shaffer looked at Jonas through bloodshot eyes. "Please."

Jonas hesitated before flipping the toggle switch on the control board to ACTIVE.

A low decibel *PING* could be heard in the distance, the audible reverberations registering in his overwrought nerves.

Challenger Deep

Unable to propel herself forward in order to drive water into her mouth, the Megalodon sank head-first through the abyss, suffocating in the frigid sea. For three thousand feet she plunged, her mouth agape, the sudden influx of seawater still not enough to engage her gills.

Reaching the plume the Meg dropped into the swirling river of soot, swallowing sulfur and minerals. The combination of toxins unleashed a spasmodic regurgitation reflex that shocked her system, forcing her stomach to regurgitate the toxins by popping out of her mouth like a pink balloon.

Reentering the warmth of the *Challenger Deep*, the female re-swallowed her stomach. Once more, water passed through her gullet—only this time her gills worked, processing oxygen. The warmth of the vented depths reheated her blood, stimulating her half-frozen muscles to move.

Regaining her ability to function, the Megalodon entered the flow of an easterly current, allowing the river to carry her through the canyon.

Aboard the *Maxine D*

Dick Danielson entered the radio room, his complexion

pale, his head pounding from the unrelenting seas. He took a headset from the radio operator and positioned it over his ears, his empty stomach curled in knots.

"Danielson. This better be important, Mr. Leiffer."

"Sir, we had ... an incident. I'm not sure quite how to explain it."

"Damn it, Leiffer, just tell me what happened!"

"It involves Rear Admiral Quercio and Commander Mackreides."

Danielson closed his eyes. "Go on."

"Mac ... he took the admiral and his party down to Marizo aboard one of the *Sea Kings*."

"In the middle of a typhoon?"

"The admiral was insistent. Anyway, a service was being rendered aboard the chopper at five hundred feet between the admiral and two local girls. Apparently there was a disagreement over monies owed for services rendered. The admiral refused to rectify the matter, so the women tossed the admiral's clothing out the cargo door."

"Oh, sweet Jesus."

"It gets worse. Mac landed the chopper at Andersen Air Force Base ... in the middle of a ceremony honoring the governor. The admiral ... well, he was buck naked at the time, sir."

"Oh my God."

"There's more. One of the local television crews reporting weather conditions at the airfield got a few choice shots before MPs cleared the area. It's a shit-storm, sir. Admiral Gordon is flying in personally to oversee the investigation as soon as the weather clears."

"Where's Mackreides?"

"He's being held at Andersen for questioning. Fortunately, the bad weather has kept the media away."

"Listen carefully, Leiffer. I want you to go through Mackreides's personal belongings. Remove anything that might implicate any officer and stow it in my office."

"Sir, isn't that considered tampering with evidence?"

"That's why I'm having you confiscate everything, so no one tampers with it! Danielson out."

Aboard the *Sea Cliff*

His eyelids were heavy, his brain zapping in and out of consciousness. The voices of the two scientists became dull rhythmic chants, the swaying submersible a hammock.

Jonas laid his head back, slipping into yet another two-to-three minute catnap—each torturous tease of rest rendering him edgier, his body demanding REM sleep.

Without warning, a swell kicked up from the hydrothermal plume and broadsided the *Sea Cliff*, levitating it fifty feet as it rolled the submersible onto its port side.

Jonas snapped awake, his limbs pumping furiously at the controls even as the two scientists collided in a heap atop the sonar monitor. Sparks greeted the sudden darkness, until the back-up batteries powered on and the sub again found its equilibrium.

"Damn it, Jonas, stay awake!"

"Tell it to my brain, Richard."

Dr. Shaffer examined the damaged sonar monitor. "Looks like the *Flying Squirrel's* flying blind. Now what?"

Dr. Prestis checked his controls, zooming in on the sea floor using the ROV's forward camera. "We've loaded seventy-two pounds of manganese nodules. I say we finish with this patch and call it a day."

His colleague looked worried. "Washington wants samples from at least three patches."

"What am I supposed to do, Michael? Without sonar, we could smash the ROV head-first into a black smoker. No, I'm vacuuming up everything I can see, then we're retrieving the *Squirrel* ... assuming our pilot can stay awake."

"Jonas!" Shaffer shook him.

Jonas opened his eyes, the geologist's face blurry. "Where's Maggie?"

"Who?"

"My wife. I left her on the beach with Bud, just before the wave hit."

Shaffer glanced at Prestis, shaking his head. "He's cuckoo for Cocoa Puffs. Maybe we ought to bring the *Squirrel* back now."

Strapped into his seat, Jonas leaned forward so that his face was inches from the bottom viewport. The *Sea Cliff's* exterior lights were focused on the hydrothermal plume, casting its glow upon the swirling layer of soot like a full moon obscured behind clouds. Every so often a break in the murky water appeared, allowing the beacon to illuminate the inky depths of the *Devil's Purgatory*.

Jonas followed the ray of light through the parting plume cloud, his eyes detecting movement. There was something circling in the warm layer a hundred feet below the *Sea Cliff*—something ghostly-white and as big as a public transit bus.

Challenger Deep

As the current carried the energy-starved Megalodon through the trench, its senses had locked on to the telltale vibrations coming from another creature.

Homing in on the reverberations, the female left the current and ascended warily.

Like the school of cuttlefish, the light that flickered down from the hydrothermal plume glowed brightly, the Meg's unseen prey hovering just above the ceiling of hot minerals.

The big shark hesitated. While she needed to feed, the last foray into the cold had nearly killed her.

The cloud of soot thickened, cloaking the light.

Instinct took over—the creature was escaping.

Locking onto the *Sea Cliff's* churning propeller, the female once more ventured through the hydrothermal plume to attack.

8

JONAS RUBBED HIS EYES, watching in fascination as the glow rose higher. His heart pounded as the white haze appeared to morph into a triangular head, the creature's widening jaws as big as the door of his garage.

It was a Great White, ghostly pale and twice the size of the *Sea Cliff*.

Teeth, tongue and pink gill slits suddenly filled the viewport between his feet, the sub's beacon illuminating the monstrous shark's gullet.

Adrenaline surged through Jonas's body like a jolt of electric caffeine, igniting every neuron in a flight or fight response dating back to prehistoric man. Lunging for the red EMERGENCY handle, he nearly tore the device from its socket as an immense set of jaws snapped down upon the ROV's launch platform, sheering the metal hutch from the sub's chassis.

Then they were rising, soaring away from the nightmarish head as the 58,000 pound submersible jettisoned twelve percent of its mass. A dozen five-hundred-pound steel plates rained down upon the Megalodon's snout, glancing off the stunned shark's pectoral fins before disappearing through the hot mineral clouds below.

Jonas tumbled sideways out of his harness amid voices cursing and alarms beeping and body parts colliding. A veil of purple haze clouded his vision.

His eardrums popped, muting all sound.

Must have bit through the back-up battery ... took out the pressurization system ... that wobble in your ears is the titanium sphere ... we're losing internal pressure ... drain every air tank ... overcompensate by filling the chamber with pressurized air before we implode!

Fumbling in the darkness, Jonas stood, his hands groping along the curved ceiling, orienting himself. A whimpering body tumbled across his feet as he located the valve, his thoughts scattered.

Is this another nightmare or is it real? Doesn't feel real...

He wrenched open the valve as cold air tinged with water blasted into the cabin.

Jonas screamed at death, but the implosion never arrived.

Just condensation ... not seawater.

The darkness groaned, splattering him with warm droplets of slime. One of the scientists was hemorrhaging; the other was calling out his name, cursing his existence.

Aboard the *Tallman*

Paul Agricola cursed as the blip fell away from the sonar screen. "What the hell just happened? We were so close, then it retreated."

"Sir, I've got another object on sonar, rising fast."

"It's back! Doug, go active on *Sea Bat-I*. Luis—"

"Sir, it's not the Meg."

Heads turned.

"What do you mean it's not the Meg? Is it another creature? How big is it?"

"Half the size, only it's not a biologic, it's a submersible. I can hear the engines. It's at 28,550 feet and rising very fast."

Paul Agricola glanced at his friend, Lucas Heitman. The *Tallman's* skipper appeared shaken. "That's why the Navy's here. They're diving the *Challenger Deep*."

"Doug, retrieve the *Sea Bats*. I think it's time we headed south to flee the storm."

Aboard the *Sea Cliff*

Eight thousand feet, and they were running out of air.

Jonas couldn't see the sphere spinning but he felt the effects of the vertigo in his gut. He collapsed to his knees and retched, then gasped, unable to catch his breath. The sphere became his skull, the compressed weight crushing his brain, squeezing his lungs. As he gasped for air in a fetal position, a bottle rolled against him.

Water bottle? Attached to a piece of rubber ... a rubber mask?

Pony bottle!

Strapping the gift of life to his face, Jonas popped the release valve and breathed.

Aboard the *Maxine D*

In the swaying fury of the storm, Captain Richard Danielson entered the command center, his mind gripped by the developing consequences of his actions. "What happened down there? Why the emergency ascent?"

"Sir, we don't know. Commander Taylor hasn't responded, but they're coming up very fast … too fast, sir."

"Alert Dr. Heller and make sure he has the recompression chamber ready. What's the sub's surface ETA?"

"Ten minutes."

"Get a dive team standing by on deck."

* * *

Petty Officer Second Class Gustave Maren hooked his harness to the aft rail and held on as twenty foot swells tossed the *Maxine D* like an amusement park ride. It had been six weeks since Maren's secret rendezvous with Benedict Singer, five weeks since the billionaire's money arrived by wire into his Swiss bank account. The ten thousand was only an advance of course, the real money would come after he delivered the rock.

Not rock, asshole. Manganese nodule.

Gustave Maren had little interest in rocks or manganese or anything to do with the ocean, but he took great pride in the fact that his fourteen-year-old son was an expert on all these things. First in his class and an I.Q. that could not be traced to any genetic branch on the Maren family tree.

Gus was doing this for Michael.

Thoughts of money danced in the sailor's head. Yes, he was doing this for Michael, but the truth was that his son was already receiving offers to attend Ivy League schools. A scholarship meant Gus could save on his only child's tuition, using the profits from this minor theft to pay off the mortgage, perhaps even buy a new car.

The divers in the wild sea beckoned. The sub was rising. A belch of bubbles and foam and there it was, swaying on the surface like a drunken whale, the divers fighting with Typhoon Marian to capture it.

Harnesses in place, the A-frame kicked back, hoisting the

Sea Cliff out of the Pacific just as the swirling gray storm clouds opened up and the drenching began. Danielson appeared on deck, a fool playing to his men, his face ashen. The *Sea Cliff's* pilot, Taylor, was well-liked. This accident—or whatever they were witnessing—had been foreseen by everyone.

The captured sub swayed in the grayness of an angry dusk, the ship's deck lights revealing the rain ... and one other item.

Trailing the dripping *Sea Cliff* was a cable, taut with a weight still submerged.

Danielson pounded on Gustave's rain gear with his open palm. "Once the *Sea Cliff* is secure, I want your crew to retrieve that ROV! See to it, sailor."

"Aye, sir."

Gustave waited for the fiberglass hull to touch down, then he traced the ROV's cable to its docking station situated in the bow of the *Sea Cliff's* sled.

Jesus, what happened to it?

Using his flashlight, he located the exterior controls and attempted to reverse the winch, but the power was out.

"Wismer, Beck! We'll need a portable generator and some cables." Maren looked up as the sub's hatch was opened. Seconds later, a body was pulled from the submersible—a white-haired scientist. Dr. Prestis was followed by a corpse, pale except for the dead man's head wound, splattered dark with blood.

The third man out was Taylor. He was rushed with the first man to the infirmary below decks—leaving Gustave and his crew alone to tend to the ROV.

* * *

Jonas opened his eyes to a bright light that shifted from pupil to pupil, accompanied by waves of needle-like pain in his joints and the condescending voice of Frank Heller.

"Shaffer's dead. Prestis suffered what appears to be a major stroke about ten minutes ago. Before it hit he told me you lost it down there, that your actions endangered the mission and the crew. He said you put the sub into an emergency ascent which blew out the pressurization system."

Jonas shook his head, the pain becoming unbearable. "Shark attacked us. Big as a house, ghostly white. Bit the sled."

"A shark? That's your excuse? There are no sharks in the trench, Taylor. You imagined it." He signaled to the two orderlies. "Get him inside the recompression unit."

* * *

Gustave Maren waited for his crew to leave before turning his attention to the catch basket. The lid was sealed, the rocks having been collected and stored inside the porous steel bin by way of the interior vacuum assembly.

Lying on the swaying deck, Maren disconnected the vacuum and reached his hand up through the suction tube until his entire arm was inside the hose. He felt a nodule, the hard wet surface covered in slime. As a teen he had used a similar technique to steal cans of soda out of a vending machine, his crime spree ending when his arm had gotten caught.

He momentarily panicked as the deck shifted and the weight of the basket pinned his wrist inside the housing; mercifully the ship rolled again and he was able to yank the pineapple-size rock free.

He shoved it into his jacket as the crew returned with the portable generator.

* * *

"A shark?"

Frank Heller nodded at Danielson from behind his desk, his face red with anger. "He swears it was white and as big as a house."

"Could this shark have damaged the sub?"

"Wake up, Danielson, there was no shark. Taylor obviously imagined the whole thing. It's called aberrations of the deep.

Prestis said Jonas lost it down there." Heller unlocked a desk drawer, removed a bottle of whisky and motioned to his friend.

"No. And you shouldn't either."

"Don't pull rank on me now. We should have never allowed him to dive, he wasn't fit for duty. The two scientists ... they were friends. Prestis won't make it through the night. What do I tell Shaffer's wife and kids?"

"What about Taylor? How'd he manage to survive?"

"Seems he found a pony bottle before the air ran out."

"So he caused the accident, but managed to cheat death."

"I certified him fit for command."

"You also were an eyewitness to Prestis's account of what happened down there. What did you call it? Aberrations of the deep? Taylor was trained to handle these things and he failed."

"We should have sent the back-up pilot."

"Taylor wouldn't allow it, he said Royston wasn't ready. That was his fault, not ours." Danielson poured himself a shot and drained the liquid heat. "Frank, there will be an investigation. Taylor's finished as a submersible pilot. He's navy, but he's a flash-in-the-pan, destined for civilian life. You and me—we're career servicemen, we've put in our time. You want to lose everything because some rock star choked under pressure?"

"There's blood on all our hands, captain." Heller took a swig of whiskey, then resealed the bottle. "Prestis said he lost it down there. I'll testify to that. I'll also state that Taylor said he felt more qualified to handle the dive than his back-up. Will that do it for you?"

"That, and one last detail. Recommend Taylor undergo a three month psychiatric evaluation following his discharge."

"What for?"

"Credibility. Years from now, when he decides to write a memoir slamming the navy, I want to make sure the world knows that Jonas Taylor was deemed a nutcase by the medical establishment."

* * *

The *Maxine D* was underway, her bow rising and falling as it met the onslaught of twenty-five foot waves, the boat racing Typhoon Marian back to Guam.

Alone on deck, Captain Danielson made his way to the *Sea Cliff*, using his flashlight to inspect the damage before the ship's engineers could get a look back at the naval base.

The seas caused the submersible to teeter, its weight balanced awkwardly on its chassis. Danielson shone his light on the damaged sled, inspecting the back-up batteries and the air tanks, one of which had imploded.

A fourteen inch section of the reinforced fiberglass housing had been peeled back, leaving a gaping hole.

What the hell could have done that?

He knelt by the assembly, his light revealing a triangular white shape lodged in the mangled air tank—an object that clearly didn't belong there. Danielson gripped and twisted it free, its sharp serrated edges tearing the flesh of his right palm.

For a long moment he stared at the object, his bleeding hand cleansed by the rain. Then, concealing the six inch weapon under his jacket, he walked toward the stern rail.

The ship's twin propellers churned the dark waters into a trail of foam. Glancing around to make sure no one was watching, Danielson tossed the white Megalodon tooth into the Pacific Ocean, returning it to its rightful owner.

EPILOGUE

"THE HEARING WAS A JOKE. My JAG officer essentially told me my career was over, that the best deal I could make was to accept the dishonorable discharge and complete a three month psychiatric evaluation. I actually felt relieved this morning when I got the note that you finally wanted to see me. Guess I was lucky the hospital was in San Diego. At least my wife can visit."

"And does she?"

"Does she what?"

"Visit you. It's been a month. Has she been back since the men in the white suits brought you in?"

"She's been busy. She just started working weekends at a local television station."

"Which leaves Monday through Friday."

"What are you implying?" Lying on the leather sofa, Jonas Taylor sat up and gazed at the psychiatrist. The man had his bare feet propped up on the oak desk, the drab white wall at his back harboring framed diplomas and a few naval photos—none resembling the psychiatrist.

"Implying? Nothing. In fact, it's common for spouses of dishonorably discharged officers to distance themselves at first. Same thing happens with drunk drivers who kill innocent bystanders. Forgiveness takes time."

"Now that I think about it, Maggie seemed more upset about me losing my commission than killing those two scientists."

"Women ... Actually though, I was talking about you. I've been watching you since you got here. You're angry. You feel used. Abandoned by the navy, your brothers-in-arms. You also feel guilty about what happened on the dive. You're a moral guy. We need to work on that."

"What's that supposed to mean?"

"It means if you can't deal with death then don't become a mortician or enlist in the military. No sane person dives the Mariana Trench; those two eggheads knew the risks just as every soldier knows the risk when he enlists. Two guys died on your watch. Deal with it. I've been in combat and I've killed other human beings. It's a sucky, clouds-of-doom feeling, and even though it's true, the whole 'doing it for God and country' business still doesn't heal the wound."

"What does?"

"For starters, instead of moping around, try doing something nice for a stranger. Help others who are less fortunate than you. You're staying in a hospital, how about visiting some sick people? There's an entire ward of kids with cancer here—teach 'em how to play poker. God will judge you when He's ready; use the time you have left to give Him as many positives on your resume as you can. At the same time, stop being such an all-American patsy. You should have told Danielson and his piss boy, Heller to take that last dive order and shove it up their asses."

"You don't sound like any shrink I've ever met."

James Mackreides grinned. "That's because I'm more of a life coach."

"Hey coach, how come you're not in any of the family photos on your desk?"

"We'll discuss that in the EVAC chopper."

"EVAC chopper?"

"The one on the roof. We're taking it to tonight's 49ers-Cowboys game."

"You have tickets?"

"Hell, no. I figured we'd worry about that after we stole the chopper."

"Makes sense."

For the first time in as long as he could remember, Jonas Taylor smiled. Then he followed his new friend and fellow inmate out the door to steal a helicopter.

The end of
MEG: ORIGINS

The story continues in
MEG: A Novel of Deep Terror

MEG:

A Novel of Deep Terror

Originally published in July 1997

Rewritten & republished in January 2015

MEGALODON

Late Jurassic—Early Miocene Period
The Coast of the Asiamerica-Northern
Landmass
(Pacific Ocean)

FROM THE MOMENT the early morning fog had begun to lift, they sensed they were being watched. The herd of Shantungosaurus had been grazing along the misty shoreline all morning. Measuring more than forty feet from their duck-billed heads to the end of their tails, these reptiles, the largest of the hadrosaurs, gorged themselves on the abundant supply of kelp and seaweed that continued to wash up along the shoreline with the incoming tide. Every few moments the gentle giants raised their heads like a herd of nervous deer, listening to the noises of the nearby forest. They watched the dark trees and thick vegetation for movement, ready to run at the first sign of approach.

Across the beach, hidden among the tall trees and thick undergrowth, a pair of red reptilian eyes followed the herd. The Tyrannosaurus rex, largest and most lethal of all terrestrial carnivores, towered twenty-two feet above the forest floor. Saliva oozed from the big male's mouth; its muscles quivering with adrenaline as it focused on two duckbills venturing out into the shallows, isolating themselves from the herd.

With a blood-curdling roar the killer crashed through the trees, its eight tons pounding the sand and shaking the earth with every step. The duckbills momentarily froze, then rose on their hind legs and scattered in both directions along the beach.

The two hadrosaurs grazing in the surf saw the carnivore closing in on them, its jaws wide, fangs bared, its bone-chilling trumpet drowning the crash of the surf. Trapped, the pair turned

87

and plunged into deeper water to escape. They strained their long necks forward and began to swim, their legs churning to keep their heads above water.

Driven by hunger, T. rex crashed through the surf after them. Far from buoyant, the killer waded into deeper waters, snapping its jaws at the incoming swells. But as it neared its prey, the T. rex's clawed feet sank deep into the muddy sea floor, its weight driving it into the mire.

The hadrosaurs paddled in thirty feet of water, safe for the moment. But having escaped one predator, they now faced another.

The six-foot gray dorsal fin rose slowly from the sea, its unseen girth gliding silently across the dinosaurs' path. If the T. rex was the most terrifying creature ever to walk the earth, then *Carcharodon megalodon* was easily lord and master of the sea. Sixty feet from its conical snout to the tip of its half-moon-shaped caudal fin, the shark moved effortlessly through its liquid domain, circling its outmatched prey. It could feel the racing heartbeats of the hadrosaurs and the heavier *thumpa, thumpa* of the T. rex, its ampullae of Lorenzini—gel-filled sensory pores located beneath its snout—detecting the pounding organs' electrical impulses. A line of neuro-cells along its flank registered each unique vibration in the water, while its directional nostrils tasted the scent of sweat and urine excreted from its floundering meal-to-be.

The pair of hadrosaurs were paralyzed in fear, their eyes following the unseen creature's sheer moving mass which circled closer, creating a current of water that lifted and dragged the two reptiles into deeper waters. The sudden change panicked the duckbills—the beasts quickly reversing direction, paddling back toward the beach. They would take their chances with the Tyrannosaurus.

Legs churning water, they moved back into the shallows, feeling the mud swirling beneath their feet. T. rex, in water up to its burly chest, let out a thundering growl, but could not advance, the predator struggling to keep from sinking farther into the soft sea floor.

The duckbills neared the reptile's snapping jaws, then suddenly broke formation, striding in separate directions, passing within a few harrowing feet of the frustrated hunter. The T. rex lunged, snapping its terrible jaws, howling in rage at its fleeing prey. The duckbills never stopped, bounding through the smaller waves until they staggered onto the beach and collapsed on the warm sand, too exhausted to move.

Still sinking, the Tyrannosaurus had to struggle to keep its huge head only a few feet above water. Insane with rage, it lashed its tail wildly in an attempt to free one of its hind legs. Then, all at once, it stopped and stared out to sea.

From the dark waters, a great dorsal fin was approaching, slicing through the fog.

The T. rex cocked its head and stood perfectly still, instincts telling it that it had wandered into the domain of a superior hunter.

The Tyrannosaurus felt the tug of current caused by thirty tons of circling mass. Its red eyes followed the gray dorsal fin until it finally disappeared beneath the murky waters.

T. rex growled quietly, searching through the haze. Leaning forward, it managed to free one of its thickly-muscled hind legs, then quickly freed the other.

On the beach, the hadrosaurs took notice and backed away—

—as the towering dorsal fin rose again from the mist, this time racing directly for the T. rex.

The reptile roared, accepting the challenge, its jaws snapping in anger.

The wake kept coming, the dorsal fin rising higher ... higher, while underwater, the unseen assailant's head rotated slightly, its jaws hyperextending seconds before it slammed into the T. rex's soft midsection like a freight train striking a disabled SUV.

T. rex slammed backward through the ocean, its breath blasting out of its crushed lungs, an eruption of blood spewing from its open mouth seconds before its head disappeared beneath the waves.

With a *whoosh* the dinosaur fought its way back to the surface, its rib cage crushed within the powerful jaws of its still-unseen killer, the T-rex choking on its gushing innards.

And then the fearsome land dweller vanished beneath a swirling pool of scarlet sea.

The hadrosaurs had watched the scene unfold. They waited for their stalker to reappear, their bladders releasing in fear. Long moments passed, the sea remaining silent. The spell of the attack broken, the duckbills abandoned the beach, lumbering toward the trees to rejoin their herd.

An explosion of ocean sent their heads turning as the sixty-foot shark burst from the water, its enormous head and upper torso quivering as it fought to remain suspended above the waves, the broken remains of its prey grasped within its terrible jaws. In an incredible display of raw power, the Meg shook the reptile from side to side, allowing its upper front row of seven-inch serrated teeth to rip through gristle and bone, the action sending swells of pink frothing water in every direction.

No other scavengers approached the Meg as it fed. The predatory fish had no mate to share its kill with, no young to feed. A rogue hunter, territorial by nature, the shark mated out of instinct and killed its young when it could, for the only challenge to its reign came from its own kind. An evolutionary marvel that had evolved over hundreds of millions of years, it would adapt and survive the natural catastrophes and climatic changes that caused the mass extinctions of the giant reptiles and countless prehistoric mammals. And while Megalodon's own numbers would eventually dwindle, some members of its species would manage to survive, isolated from the world of man in the perpetual darkness of the unexplored ocean depths …

THE PROFESSOR

JONAS TAYLOR STOPPED the projector as the image of the Megalodon feeding upon the T-rex began to pixelate on the big screen. The house lights came up, allowing the thirty-seven-year-old paleobiologist to look out at his audience of just under fifty attendees, most of the seats empty.

"I hope you enjoyed our little 'match of the titans.' For the record, T-rex and *Carcharodon megalodon* never actually shared the same time period on our planet. Tyrannosaurus rex lived during the late Cretaceous and died off about sixty-five million years ago after an asteroid struck Earth. The Megalodon's reign began during the Miocene period, about thirty-five million years later and lasted until the dawn of modern man. Other than that, the film is fairly accurate. Megalodon was a real monster, the prehistoric cousin of our modern-day Great White shark, only it was fifty to seventy feet long and weighed close to seventy thousand pounds. Its head alone was probably as large as a Dodge Ram pickup; its jaws could have engulfed and swallowed half-a-dozen grown men whole. And I haven't even mentioned the teeth—razor-sharp, six to seven inches long, each possessing serrated edges like a steel steak knife."

The former deep-sea submersible pilot loosened his collar and took a slow deep breath, knowing he had his audience's attention. Of course, lecturing in front of a sparse crowd was disappointing. Jonas knew his theories were controversial, that there were as many critics in the audience as there were supporters.

Still, just to be heard, to feel important again …

"Fossilized Megalodon teeth found around the world tell us the species dominated the oceans over most of the last thirty million years. Some experts believe the species perished about two million years ago as a result of the last Ice Age. Others have found teeth that date back a mere hundred thousand years. From a geological perspective, either estimate is just a tick of the clock, and there's little doubt our two species shared the planet at the same time. The big question, of course, is why did the most fearsome predator in Earth's history die-off at all? If the Great White shark survived the last Ice Age, why not its prehistoric cousin?"

Jonas loosened his collar a bit more. He rarely wore suits, and this eight-year-old wool jacket itched like hell.

"Those of you who read my book are aware of how my opinions often differ from those of most paleobiologists. Many in my field spend a great deal of time theorizing why a particular species no longer exists, while I prefer to focus my research on how a seemingly extinct species might still exist."

A broad-chested man in his mid-fifties stood from his seat in the first row, demanding to be heard. Jonas recognized Lee Udelsman. His former colleague at Scripps had become an outspoken critic.

"Professor Taylor, I spent twenty-nine ninety-five on your book and read it from cover to cover, I was left with the impression that you actually believe *Carcharodon megalodon* may still be roaming our oceans. Is that true?"

The audience murmured, waiting for the answer they had come to hear.

Jonas composed himself. *Be careful. The wrong quote will kill your credibility, not to mention book sales.*

"Do I believe vast numbers of Megs may still be roaming our oceans? Not at all, Professor Udelsman. I'm simply pointing out that, as scientists, we tend to take a rather short-sighted 'if we haven't seen it, it doesn't exist anymore' approach when it comes to declaring certain marine animals extinct. For instance, scientists once believed the coelacanth, a species of lobe-finned fish that thrived three hundred million years ago, had gone extinct over the last seventy million years. That so-called fact held up until 1938, when a fisherman hauled a living coelacanth out of the deep waters off South Africa. Now scientists routinely observe these 'living fossils' in their natural habitat."

Lee Udelsman held his ground. "Professor Taylor, we're all familiar with the discovery of the coelacanth. But I think you'll agree, there's a big difference between a five-foot bottom-feeder and a sixty-foot predatory shark."

Jonas checked his watch, realizing he was running behind schedule. "Yes, I agree. My point was simply that I prefer to investigate the possibilities of a species' survival rather than add to any unproven conjecture regarding extinction among marine dwellers. I often hear critics state that if Megalodon were still alive we'd have seen one by now—at least a dead one that washed ashore. The statement is ridiculous. First, the oceans are vast and sharks have no reason to surface just to show a passing boat their telltale dorsal fin. As far as the remains of a dead Meg washing ashore, it's a physiological fact that dead sharks don't float, they sink. Other predators devour the meat, leaving behind the cartilage, which dissolves in seawater. All that's left are the animal's teeth, which end up buried on the sea floor."

"Agreed. But you still haven't answered my question, Professor Taylor. Do you believe Megalodon is still alive?"

The audience applauded.

Jonas glanced at his watch. *Ten minutes late ... Maggie's going to be pissed. Toss Udelsman some red meat, sign a few books, then call it a night.*

"From strictly a logical scientific standpoint, yes, professor I believe it's possible. We know Megalodon's major food source—whales—was still quite abundant following the last Ice Age, so there was plenty to eat. As far as colder temperatures affecting the creatures, we know that the internal anatomy of larger sharks like the Great White functions like an internal heat factory. The Meg's moving muscles could channel gobs of hot blood into its extremities through a process known as gigantothermy, enabling it to adapt to even the coldest temperatures.

"The question is—what happened? Obviously there was a great die-off. In my opinion, Megalodon's thirty million year reign was terminated by the rise of the Killer Whale. Pods of Orca numbering twenty to forty adults decimated Meg nurseries, which were relegated to the shallows. Over time the adult sharks died off and the species bottomed out."

His former colleague wasn't through, turning Jonas's night into a two-man show. "You're contradicting yourself, Taylor. You just said Megalodon might still be out there."

"Correct. A decimated population doesn't necessarily equate to extinction. Orcas may be the wolves of the shallows but they can't inhabit the mid-waters of the ocean, let alone the abyss. Prior to 1977, many scientists—no doubt you among them—believed the abyss was actually barren; after all, how could life exist without light … without photosynthesis? When we actually bothered to take a look, we discovered hydrothermal vents—miniature volcanoes of life-giving chemicals—spewing mineral-rich waters at temperatures that exceed seven hundred degrees Fahrenheit. In some cases these minerals will level off about a half-mile or so above the sea floor, creating a layer of insulation that keeps in the heat, forming what we now call a hydrothermal plume. In essence, you have an anomaly of nature, a tropical oasis of life running along the very bottom of the ocean, separated from the surface by a frigid layer of water. These hydrothermal vents and their minerals anchor vast chemosynthetic food chains, some of which, could support a subspecies of Megalodon."

A middle-aged woman stood, her teenage son squirming in the seat next to her. "You'll be happy to know my son, Brandon agrees with you about Megalodon still being alive. However, as a middle school marine biology teacher, I'd like to know if you actually have any proof these monster sharks are residing in the abyss."

Jonas forced a smile while he waited for the crowd's applause to subside.

"Ma'am, let me show you something that was discovered in the abyss more than one hundred years ago." From a shelf inside the podium Jonas pulled out a glass case, roughly twice the size of a shoe box.

Inside was a triangular gray tooth that was as large as his hand.

"This is a fossilized tooth of *Carcharodon megalodon*. Scuba divers and beachcombers have turned up fossilized teeth like this by the thousands. Some are tens of millions of years old. This particular specimen is special because it's not very old. It was recovered in 1873 by the world's first true oceanic exploration vessel, the British *HMS Challenger*. Can you see these manganese nodules?" Jonas pointed to the black encrustations on the tooth. "Recent analysis of these manganese layers indicate the tooth's owner had been alive during the late Pleistocene or early Holocene period. In other words, this tooth is a mere ten thousand years old, and it was dredged from the deepest point on our planet, the Mariana Trench's *Challenger Deep*."

The teen pumped his fist. "Ha, told you, Mom! You owe me twenty bucks."

Jonas held up his hand, attempting to quiet a dozen side conversations as his eyes shifted to a beautiful blonde making her way carefully down the center aisle in stiletto heels. Tan and in her early thirties, she was wearing a topaz evening gown which hugged her flawless figure. Her male escort, also in his thirties, trailed behind, his long dark hair slicked back into a tight ponytail which contrasted with his conservative tuxedo.

Jonas waited for his wife and friend to be seated in the second row.

"Please, if you'll give me a minute I'll explain my theory, which is detailed in my new book, then I have to wrap things up."

Silence took the room.

"Following the last Ice Age two million years ago, Megalodon pups inhabiting the shallow water nurseries along the Mariana archipelago could have gone deep in order to escape pods of Killer Whales. Descending to the Mariana Trench, these juvenile sharks would have discovered warm bottom waters insulated by hydrothermal plumes. Given these variables, members of this Megalodon nursery might have chosen to remain in the deep, surviving to breed a new generation of deep-water monsters. Scientists may or may not agree with my theory, however any answer rendered without a scientific investigation behind it—meaning an actual expedition into the Mariana Trench is simply worthless conjecture."

"What nonsense!" Mike "the Turk" Turzman, a popular local radio talk show host specializing in cryptozoology stood from his tenth row seat, shouting to be heard. "There are no hydrothermal vents in the Mariana Trench. None!"

Jonas shook his head. He had heard excerpts of the Turk's recent interview with Richard Ellis, a painter and self-proclaimed expert on all things nautical who had lambasted Taylor's research.

"You're wrong, Mr. Turzman. The Ocean Exploration Ring of Fire Expedition recently used satellite aperture radar to survey the Mariana Trench. They discovered more than fifty underwater volcanoes, ten of which possessed active hydrothermal systems. These hydrothermal systems were quite different from those found along the mid-Atlantic Ocean ridges, potentially harboring all sorts of exotic life forms. So maybe the next time one of your guests decides to publicly critique my research over the airwaves, you'll do some fact checking of your own."

A smattering of applause escorted "the Turk" back to his seat.

"Professor Taylor, an important question—"

He looked up, searching the auditorium for the woman calling out his name.

It was an Asian-American beauty in her late twenties. Her long jet-black hair was pulled into a tight bun, her white blouse tied around her midriff, revealing a taut stomach, her jeans—torn at the knees—ending in Gucci heels.

I know her from somewhere…

"Yes, go on please."

"Before you began studying these Megalodons, your career was focused entirely on piloting deep-sea submersibles. I'd like to know why, at the peak of your career, you suddenly quit."

Jonas was taken aback by the directness of her question. "First, I didn't quit, I retired. Second, my reasons are my own. Next question?" He searched the audience for another raised hand.

"Pretty young to retire, weren't you?" Heads turned as the Asian beauty approached from one of the side aisles. "Or maybe it was something else? You haven't been in a submersible for what? Seven years? Did you lose your nerve, professor? Inquiring minds want to know."

The audience chuckled. No one was leaving—this was getting good.

Jonas felt trickles of sweat drip from his armpits. "What's your name, miss?"

"Tanaka. Terry Tanaka. I believe you know my father,

Masao, CEO of the Tanaka Oceanographic Institute."

"Tanaka, of course. In fact, I think you and I met several years ago on a lecture circuit."

"That's right."

"Well, Terry Tanaka, since your inquiring mind insists on violating my privacy, let's just say, after almost ten years with the navy, I felt it was time to stop risking my life piloting deep-sea submersibles. And so I went back to school to pursue my doctorate degree in order to research prehistoric species like the Megalodon."

Jonas collected his notes. "Now, if there are no other questions …"

"Dr. Taylor, please." A balding man in his fifties wearing bi-focals and a UCLA hooded sweatshirt stood in the third row off to his left. "You mentioned the Mariana Trench as a potential habitat for any surviving Megalodon. Has the trench ever been explored?"

"Unfortunately, no. There were two manned expeditions back in 1960, but in both cases the bathyscapes merely went to the bottom and resurfaced. It's important to understand just how big this gorge is and how dangerous it is to access. We're essentially talking about a fifteen hundred mile long canyon that is over forty miles wide, located seven miles below the surface. The water pressure alone is sixteen thousand pounds per square inch. We actually know more about distant galaxies than the bottom of our own oceans."

"Well stated. But professor, aren't you forgetting about a few more recent descents into the Mariana Trench, specifically the *Challenger Deep?*"

Jonas stared at the man, red warning flags fluttering in his head. "I'm sorry?"

"Come now, professor, you made several dives there yourself. Seven years ago, to be exact, before your so-called-retirement from the navy."

Jonas felt the blood drain from his face as a buzz of excitement took the sparse crowd.

From the front row, Maggie motioned impatiently at her watch, her eyes tossing daggers his way.

"I'm not sure where you're getting your information, but I have another engagement and—"

"I'm getting my information from the same source that told me you were dishonorably discharged from the navy following a three month stint in a mental ward. Something about post-traumatic stress brought on by the death of two civilians aboard a deep-sea navy submersible … a submersible you were piloting in the Mariana Trench."

"You son of a bitch—that information's classified!"

Chaos broke out as the audience yelled out questions and three photographers rushed forward to snap photos, blinding Jonas with their purple flashes as he searched for his wife, who was already making her escape back up the center aisle with his friend.

Climbing down from the stage, he attempted to chase after them, only to be cut off by students calling out questions and Mike Turzman demanding answers. He was forced to sign three books as he apologized for having to run, then managed to squeeze his way up the aisle before the Asian beauty intercepted him at the auditorium doors.

"We need to talk."

"Call my literary agent, Ken Atchity. He's in the book."

Pushing past her, he exited through the lobby to the street, banging his knee as he jumped in the back seat of an awaiting limousine.

MAGGIE

THE LIMOUSINE RACED along the Coronado peninsula.

Jonas sat across the aisle from his wife, his back to the driver. Maggie was seated next to Bud Harris, who was concluding a business transaction on his cell phone. He watched as his former roommate at Penn State University absentmindedly fingered his ponytail like a schoolgirl before glancing at Maggie.

Maggie Taylor looked very much at home on the wide leather seat, one tan slender leg slipping out from the side slit in her dress, a glass of champagne balanced in her fingertips.

Jonas allowed his mind to wander, imagining her in a bikini, tanning herself on his millionaire friend's yacht. "You used to be afraid of the sun."

"What?"

"Your tan. You used to say you were afraid of skin cancer."

She stared at him. "I never said that. Besides, it looks good on camera."

"What about your sister's melanoma—"

"Don't start with me, Jonas. I'm not in the mood. This is probably the biggest night of my career, and I had to practically drag you out of that lecture hall. You've known about this dinner for a month, and look at you—why the hell are you wearing that piece-of-shit suit? I should have tossed that in the Goodwill bin years ago."

"Hey, lighten up. This was my biggest book signing event, and you came prancing down the aisle like Madonna—"

"Whoa, guys, time-out." Bud powered off his cell phone. "Everybody take a deep breath and let's all just calm down. Maggie, this was a big night for Jonas too, maybe we should have just waited in the limo."

"A big night? Are you serious? Bud, you know how long I've waited for this opportunity, how hard I had to work while I watched my husband flush his career down the toilet? Do you know how many times we've had to refinance the house, live off credit cards, all because Professor Taylor here insisted on studying dead sharks for a living? Now it's my turn, and if he doesn't want to be here, that's fine by me. Let *him* wait in the limo. You can be my escort tonight—at least you're dressed for it."

"Oh, no, keep me out of this," Bud said, reaching for his drink.

Maggie frowned and looked out the window, the tension hanging in the air.

After a few long minutes, Bud broke the silence. "Hey, uh, I spoke with Henderson. He thinks you're a shoo-in for the award. This really could be the turning point in your career, Maggie, assuming you win."

Maggie turned to face him, managing to avoid looking at her husband. "I'll win," she said defiantly. "I know I'll win. Now pour me another drink."

Bud obediently filled Maggie's glass, then offered the bottle to Jonas.

Jonas shook his head and sat back in his seat, staring absently out the window at the passing scenery, wondering who the blonde stranger was seated across from him.

* * *

Jonas Taylor had met Maggie Cobbs eleven years earlier in Massachusetts during his deep-sea pilot training at the Woods Hole Oceanographic Institute. Maggie had been in her senior year at Boston University, majoring in journalism. The petite blonde had at one time vigorously pursued a modeling career, but lacked the required height. Upon entering college, she had reset her sights on making it as a broadcast journalist.

Maggie had read about Jonas Taylor and his adventures

aboard the *Alvin* submersible. She knew the former college football star was a celebrity in his own right and found him physically attractive. Under the guise of doing an article for the university press, she approached the naval commander for an exclusive interview.

Jonas Taylor was amazed that anyone like Maggie Cobbs would be interested in deep-sea diving. His naval career had left him little time for a social life, and when the beautiful blonde showed signs of flirting, Jonas asked her out on a date. The following week he invited Maggie to the Galapagos Islands during her last spring break. She accompanied him on one of his dives in the *Alvin* submersible, after which things got hot and heavy.

Maggie was impressed by the influence Jonas wielded among his navy peers, and loved the excitement and adventure associated with ocean exploration. Ten months later they married. The couple moved to San Diego, where Jonas began training for a top-secret naval mission in the western Pacific.

For the small-town girl from New Jersey, California proved to be the land of opportunity. With Jonas's help, Maggie was hired as a correspondent at an ABC flagship station. Within three years she branched out into investigative journalism.

And then disaster struck.

Jonas had been training to pilot one of the navy's deep-sea submersibles into the Mariana Trench. On his fourth dive in thirty-five thousand feet of water, the veteran pilot had panicked, surfacing the sub too quickly. Pipes had burst, causing pressurization problems that led to the deaths of the two scientists onboard. Jonas had survived—barely—only to learn his commanding officer blamed him for the incident. The official report called it "aberrations of the deep," and the incident ended Jonas's career in the navy. Worse, it permanently scarred his psyche.

Three months in a mental hospital were followed by a

dishonorable discharge and a severe bout of depression. A year of private psychiatric sessions eventually helped refocus the goal-oriented former naval officer, who decided to pursue advanced degrees in paleobiology. Jonas would earn his doctorate degree, eventually writing a book on the subject of extinction among deep-water species.

Without Jonas's naval income, Maggie's lifestyle quickly changed. The San Diego position turned out to be a dead-end job, and her life was suddenly thrust into that of the mundane.

Then, by chance, Jonas ran into Bud Harris, his former roommate at Penn State University. Harris had recently inherited his father's shipping business in San Diego. He and Jonas took in a few football games, but the paleobiologist was constantly doing research, leaving Maggie to entertain her husband's new best friend.

Bud used his father's connections to get Maggie part-time work as a writer for the San Diego Register. In turn, Maggie convinced her editor that Bud's shipping business would make an interesting article for the Sunday magazine. It was the excuse she needed to follow the bachelor millionaire around the harbor, with trips to his facilities in Long Beach, San Francisco, and Honolulu. She interviewed him on his yacht, sat in on board meetings, took a ride on his hovercraft, and spent many an afternoon learning how to sail.

The article she wrote became the Register's cover story and was syndicated across North America. Bud Harris's charter business boomed. Not one to forget a favor, Bud helped Maggie secure a weekend anchor spot with a San Diego television station, doing two-minute fillers for the ten o'clock news. It wasn't long before she was promoted, producing weekly features on California and the West Coast.

While Jonas Taylor floundered as an author, Maggie Taylor was becoming a local celebrity.

* * *

Bud climbed out of the limo, extending a hand to Maggie. "Maybe I ought to get an award. Whaddya think? Executive producer?"

"Not on your life," she replied, handing her glass to the chauffeur. The alcohol had settled her down a bit. She smiled at Bud as they ascended the stairs of the Hotel del Coronado, Jonas lagging behind. "If they start giving you awards, there won't be any left for me."

They passed through the main entrance beneath a gold banner announcing "The 15th Annual San Diego MEDIA Awards." Three enormous crystal chandeliers hung from the vaulted wooden ceiling of the Crown Ballroom. A band played softly in the corner while well-heeled guests picked at hors d'oeuvres and sipped drinks, wandering among tables draped with white-and-gold tablecloths.

Jonas suddenly felt underdressed. Maggie had told him about the gala a month ago but had never mentioned it was a black tie event.

He recognized a few television people in the crowd, provincial stars from the local news. Harold Ray, the fifty-four-year-old co-anchor of Channel 9 Action News at Ten smiled broadly as he said hello to Maggie. Ray had helped secure network funding for Maggie's special about the effects of offshore oil drilling on whale migrations along the California coast, and now the piece was one of three competing for top honors in the "Environmental Issues Documentary" category.

"You just may take home the Eagle tonight, Maggs, Ray said, his eyes wandering over her tantalizing cleavage.

"What makes you so sure?" she cooed back.

"For one thing, I'm married to one of the judges." Harold winked, then turned to Bud. "And this must be Jonas. Harold Ray—"

"Bud Harris, friend of the family," Bud replied, shaking his hand.

"Bud's my … executive producer," Maggie said, smiling. She glanced at Jonas. "This is Jonas."

"Sorry, big guy, honest mistake. Say, didn't we do a piece on you a couple years ago? Something about dinosaur bones in the Salton Sea?"

"You may have. There were a lot of news people out there. It was an unusual find—"

"Excuse me, Jonas," Maggie interrupted, "I'm just dying for a drink. Would you mind?"

Bud pointed a finger in the air. "Gin and tonic for me, J.T."

Jonas looked at Harold Ray.

"Nothing for me, Doc, I'm a presenter tonight. One more drink and I'll start making the news instead of reporting it."

Jonas forced a polite smile, then made his escape to the bar. The air was humid in the windowless ballroom, and Jonas's wool jacket felt prickly and hot. He asked for a beer, a glass of champagne, and a gin and tonic. The bartender pulled a bottle of Carta Blanca out of the ice. Jonas cooled his forehead with it and took a long draft.

He looked back at Maggie, who was still laughing with Bud and Harold.

"Another beer, sir?"

Jonas looked at his bottle, suddenly realizing he had emptied it. "Give me one of those," he said, pointing at the gin.

"Me too," a voice said behind him. "With a lime."

Jonas turned. It was the balding man from the book signing and lecture.

He looked at Jonas, peering over his wire-rimmed bifocals with the same tight grin on his face. "Funny coincidence, meeting you here."

Jonas regarded him suspiciously. "Did you follow me?"

"Hell no," the man replied, scooping up a handful of almonds from the bar. He gestured vaguely at the room. "I'm in the media." He offered his hand. "David Adashek. Science Journal."

Jonas ignored it. "You're playing a dangerous game, Mr. Adashek."

"How so?"

"What is it you want?"

The man finished a mouthful of almonds, washing it down with a swig of his drink. "My source told me you made the Mariana Trench dives; what he didn't tell me was what you were looking for."

"Who's your source?"

"Former navy guy, just like you." Adashek slipped another almond into his mouth, chewing it noisily like a stick of gum. "Funny thing, though. I interviewed the fellow about it four years ago. Couldn't get a word out of him. Then last week he calls out of the blue, says if I want to know what happened I ought to talk to you ... Did I say something wrong, Doc?"

Jonas's brown eyes blazed at the shorter man. "Be careful; I wouldn't want to see you choke on your nuts." He turned, locating Maggie and Bud at their table.

From the other side of the room, a pair of dark Asian eyes followed Jonas Taylor as he made his way across the ballroom, watching as he took a seat next to the blonde.

* * *

Four hours and half a dozen drinks later, Jonas found himself staring at the Golden Eagle now perched on the white tablecloth, a TV camera clutched in its claws. Maggie's whale film had beaten out a *Discovery Channel* project on the Farallon Islands and a Greenpeace documentary on the Japanese whaling industry. His wife's acceptance speech had been largely a passionate "save the whales" plea. Her concern for the cetaceans' fate had inspired her to make the film, or so she said.

Jonas wondered if he was the only one in the room who didn't believe a word she was saying.

Bud had passed out cigars. Harold Ray made a toast. Fred Henderson stopped by to offer his congratulations, adding that if he wasn't careful Maggie would get snapped up by a major station in Los Angeles. Maggie feigned disinterest. Jonas knew she'd heard the rumors ... she had started many of them herself.

They were all dancing now. Maggie had taken Bud's hand and led him onto the floor, knowing Jonas wouldn't object. How could he? He didn't like to dance.

Jonas sat alone at the table, chewing the ice from his glass and trying to remember how many gins he'd downed in the last few hours. He felt tired, had a slight headache, and all signs pointed to a long evening still ahead. He got up and walked to the bar.

Harold Ray was there, picking up a bottle of wine and a pair of glasses.

"So how was Baja, professor?"

Jonas wondered if the man was drunk. "Baja?"

"The cruise."

"What cruise?" He handed his glass to the bartender, nodded for a refill.

Ray laughed. "I warned her three days was no vacation. Look at you, you've already forgotten."

"Baja? You mean ... last week." Then it hit him. The business trip to San Francisco. The tan. Bud Harris.

"Too many margaritas, professor?"

Jonas stared for a long moment at the glass in his hand, then scanned the dance floor for his wife. The band was playing "Crazy," the lights dimmed low, the couples dancing close. He located Maggie and Bud, clinging together like a pair of drunks. Bud's hands were caressing her back, working their way down.

Jonas watched as his wife repositioned his hands to her buttocks, kissing him on the lips.

Blood rushed into Jonas's face, the veins in his neck throbbing. He slammed his drink down, then made his way awkwardly across the dance floor.

Oblivious, Maggie and Bud continued to grind their groins against one another, lost in their own world.

Jonas tapped Bud on the shoulder. "Excuse me, pal, but I think that's my wife's ass in your hand."

Maggie and Bud stopped dancing, a look of apprehension coming over the millionaire's face. "Easy big guy, I was only—"

The right cross was a glancing blow, but still had enough force to send Bud crashing into another couple, all three sprawling to the dance floor.

The band stopped playing.

The lights came up.

Maggie looked at Jonas, aghast. "Are you crazy?"

Jonas rubbed his sore knuckles. "Do me a favor, Maggie. Next time you take a cruise to Baja, don't come back." He turned and left the dance floor, the alcohol spinning the room as he strode toward the exit.

* * *

Jonas stepped out the front entrance and ripped off his tie. A uniformed valet asked him for his parking stub.

"I don't have a car."

"Would you like a taxi, then?"

"He doesn't need one. I'm his ride." Terry Tanaka stepped out the door behind him.

"Man, when it rains it pours. What is it you want, Tracy?"

"It's Terry, and we need to talk."

"You talk, I need to puke." He staggered down the block, searching for a trashcan, settling for the back of a dumpster.

Terry turned her back as he heaved his dinner. She searched

her purse, then tossed him a pack of gum when he finished. "Now can we talk?"

"Look, Trixie …"

"Terry!"

Jonas sat on the curb and combed his fingers through his hair. His head was throbbing. "What is it you want?"

"Following you here … it wasn't my idea. My father sent me."

Jonas glanced back at her. "Masao's an old friend. Find me on Monday, we'll talk. This isn't exactly a good time …"

"Ever hear of UNIS?"

"Is that your sister? No wait … it's some kind of deep ROV, isn't it?"

"Unmanned Nautical Informational Submersible. UNIS. Our institute holds the patents. They're made for deep-water assignments, their hulls able to withstand 19,000 pounds per square inch of pressure."

"I'm happy for you. Now I need to find a cab and a bottle of aspirin."

She removed a manila envelope from her purse and shoved it in his face. "Look at this."

He opened the envelope and pulled out a black-and-white photograph taken underwater. The image was of a UNIS, lying on its side, its hull crushed almost beyond recognition.

Jonas looked back at the woman. "Where was this drone deployed?"

"The Mariana Trench."

UNIS

THE DODGE CARAVAN sped along the rain-slick streets of San Diego. Terry was at the wheel, the rental car challenging every yellow traffic light. Jonas laid back in the passenger seat, the window open, the cool breeze soothing his headache and sore knuckles. His eyes remained open and on the road—the woman's driving was making him nervous—but he kept studying the photograph in his mind.

Taken 35,000 feet beneath the surface of the western Pacific, the black-and-white photograph showed a spherical remote-sensing device resting near a dark canyon wall. Jonas was somewhat familiar with these remarkable robotic devices, having followed their development in science journals. He had heard rumors that JAMSTEC, the Japan Marine Science and Technology Center, was involved with the Tanaka Institute in a joint project.

"My father agreed to deploy twenty-five UNIS drones into the *Challenger Deep* in exchange for financing for our whale lagoon in Monterey," Terry told him as they reached the freeway. "The UNIS array is essentially an earthquake early warning system designed to monitor tremors along a 125-mile stretch of the underwater canyon where the Philippine Sea Plate meets the Pacific Plate. Within days of the system's deployment, our surface ship, the *Kiku*, began receiving a steady stream of data, and seismologists on both sides of the Pacific were eagerly studying the information.

"Then something went wrong. Three weeks after the array was up and running one of the drones stopped transmitting data. A week later, two more units shut down. When another one stopped a few days after that, JAMSTEC cut off our funding, demanding my father repair the array."

Terry looked at Jonas. "He sent my brother, D.J., down in the Abyss Glider to video one of the damaged units."

"Alone?"

"D.J.'s the most experienced pilot we have, but I agree with you. In fact, I argued with Masao to allow me to escort him down in the second glider."

"You?"

Terry glared at him. "You have a problem with that? I happen to be a damn good pilot."

"I'm sure you are, but at thirty-five thousand feet? What's the deepest you've ever soloed?"

"I've hit sixteen thousand twice, no problem."

"Not bad," Jonas admitted.

"You mean, not bad for a woman?"

"Easy, Gloria Steinem, I meant not bad for anyone. Very few humans have been down that deep."

She forced a smile. "Sorry. It gets frustrating, you know. My father is strictly old-fashioned Japanese; his grandmother was a geisha. Women are to be seen and not heard. It drives me crazy."

"Finish the story. What happened with D.J.? I assume he took this photo?"

"Yes. The photo came from his sub's night vision camera."

Jonas glanced again at the photograph. The titanium sphere had been cracked open, its tripod legs were mangled, a bolted bracket torn off. The hull itself looked battered beyond recognition.

"Where's the sonar plate?"

"D.J. found it forty feet down-current. He managed to haul it to the surface—it's back at the Institute in Monterey. That's why I tracked you down. My father needs you to take a look at it."

Jonas stared at her skeptically. "Why me?"

"He didn't say. You can fly up with me in the morning and ask him. I'm taking the Institute's plane back at eight."

Lost in thought, Jonas almost missed his house. "There—on the left."

She turned down the long, leaf-littered driveway, then parked in front of a single story Spanish Colonial buried in foliage.

Terry switched off the engine. Jonas turned to her and narrowed his eyes. "Masao sent you all this way, just so I could render an opinion on scrap metal?"

"My father needs advice about redeploying along the *Challenger Deep*."

"You want my advice? Stay the hell out of the Mariana Trench. It's far too dangerous to be exploring, especially in a one-man submersible."

"Everything's dangerous to a man who's lost his nerve. D.J. and I are good pilots, we can handle this. What the hell happened to you anyway? I was only seventeen when we first met, but you were different. I still remember your piss-and-vinegar attitude. I was actually attracted to your swagger."

"Swagger leaves you when you grow old."

"You're not old, but you are afraid. What are you so afraid of? A sixty-foot prehistoric Great White shark?"

"Maybe I'm afraid of Asian women with too much swagger."

She smirked. "Let me tell you something – the data we collected during those first weeks the UNIS array was functioning was invaluable. If the earthquake detection system works, it'll save thousands of lives. No one's asking you to dive the *Challenger Deep*, we simply want your opinion on why the UNIS was damaged. Is your schedule so damn busy that you can't take a day to fly up to the Institute? My father's asking for your help. Examine the sonar plate and review the video that my brother took and you'll be home to your darling wife by tomorrow night. We'll pay you for your time, and I'm sure Dad will even arrange a personal tour of our new whale lagoon."

Jonas took a breath. He considered Masao Tanaka a friend, a commodity he seemed to be running short of lately. "When would we leave?"

"Meet me tomorrow morning at the commuter airport, seven-thirty sharp."

"The commuter ... we're taking one of those puddle jumpers?" Jonas swallowed hard.

"Relax. I know the pilot. See you in the morning."

Jonas exited the van and watched her drive away. "What the hell are you doing, J.T.?"

* * *

Jonas shut the door behind him and switched on the light, feeling for a moment like a stranger in his own home. The house was dead quiet. A trace of Maggie's perfume lingered in the air. *She won't be home until late. Ah, who are you kidding, she won't be home at all.*

He went into the kitchen, pulled a bottle of vodka from the cabinet, then changed his mind and turned on the coffeemaker. He replaced the filter and added some coffee, then filled the slot with water. He ran the faucet, sucked cold water from the spigot, and rinsed out his mouth.

For a long moment he stood at the sink, staring out the back window while the coffee brewed. It was dark out back, all he could see was his reflection in the glass.

A favorite *Talking Heads* song kept replaying in his mind ...

And you may tell yourself, this is not my beautiful house, and you may tell yourself, this is not my beautiful wife. Same as it ever was ... Same as it ever was ... Same as it ever was ...

When the coffee was done, he grabbed a mug and the pot of coffee and went into his study.

Sanctuary. The one room in the house that was truly his own. The walls were covered with contour maps of the ocean's continental margins, mountain ranges, abyssal plains, and deep-sea trenches. Fossilized Megalodon teeth cluttered the shelves of a glass bookcase, sitting upright in their plastic support holders like small, lead-gray stalagmites. A framed photo of a Great White shark hung above his desk, sent to him by Andrew Fox, son of Rodney, the famous Australian photographer who had nearly been bitten in two by a similar creature many years ago. Now the entire Fox family made a living taking pictures of the very animal that had scarred Rodney for life... and had given him a new livelihood.

Jonas set the coffee mug down beside his computer, then positioned himself at the keyboard. A set of jaws from a twelve-foot Great White gaped at him from high above his monitor. He punched a few keys to access the Internet, then typed in the Web address of the Tanaka Oceanographic Institute.

Jonas sipped the hot coffee as he waited for the Web site to upload. He typed in the word "UNIS."

UNIS: Unmanned Nautical Informational Submersible

Designed and developed by the Tanaka Oceanographic Institute to track seismic disturbances along the sea floor. The UNIS system is composed of a three-inch-thick titanium outer shell. The unit is supported by three retractable legs and weighs 935 pounds. UNIS is designed to withstand pressures of 19,000 pounds per square inch and communicates information back to a surface ship by way of fiber-optic cable.

Jonas reviewed the engineering reports of the UNIS systems, impressed by the simplicity of the design. Positioned along a seismic fault line, their tripod legs burrowing deep into the ocean floor, the UNIS remotes could detect the telltale signs of an earthquake or an impending tsunami, providing, as Terry had said, an invaluable early warning system.

Southern Japan had the misfortune of being geographically located within a convergence zone of three major tectonic plates.

Periodically, these plates ground against one another, generating about one-tenth of the world's annual earthquakes. One devastating Japanese quake in 1923 had killed more than 140,000 people.

Masao Tanaka had been desperately seeking a bank to underwrite his dream project, a man-made cetacean lagoon located off the coast of Monterey. JAMSTEC had agreed to fund the Tanaka Institute in exchange for the completion of the UNIS early warning system.

Now the system's breakdown was pushing the Tanaka Institute toward bankruptcy, and Masao needed Jonas's help.

He drained his coffee cup.

The Challenger Deep. Submersible pilots referred to it as "hell's antechamber."

Jonas just called it hell.

* * *

Six miles away, Terry Tanaka, freshly showered and wrapped in a hotel bath towel, sat on the edge of her queen-size bed at the Holiday Inn, her blood pressure still elevated. Jonas Taylor had really irked her. The man was obstinate, with strong chauvinistic ideas. Why her father had insisted their team seek his input was beyond her.

Pulling out her briefcase, she decided to review the personnel file on Professor Jonas Taylor.

She knew the basics by heart. Bachelors of Science from Penn State University, advanced degrees from the University of California, San Diego and Scripps Institute of Oceanography, trained at the Woods Hole Oceanographic Institute as a submersible pilot and now had just published a controversial book on paleobiology. At one time, Jonas Taylor had been considered one of the most experienced argonauts in the world. He had piloted the *Alvin* submersible seventeen times, leading multiple explorations to four different deep-sea trenches. And then, seven years ago, for some unknown reason, he had simply given it all up.

"Doesn't make sense," Terry said aloud. Thinking back to the lecture earlier that evening, she remembered the balding man who had revealed that Jonas had piloted a naval expedition into the Mariana Trench. Her father knew this of course, it was the reason he had sent her to bring Jonas into their council.

The three month stay in a mental ward, however, was news to her.

Terry powered up her laptop. She entered her password, then accessed the Institute's computers, searching for "Mariana Trench."

MARIANA TRENCH
LOCATION: Western Pacific Ocean, east of Philippines, close to island of Guam.

FACTS: Deepest known depression on Earth. Measures 35,827 feet deep (10,920 m), over 1,550 miles long (2,500 km), averages 40 miles in width, making the trench the deepest abyss on the planet and the second longest. The deepest area of the Mariana Trench is called the *Challenger Deep*. Note: A 5 pound bowling ball dropped from the surface would require more than an hour of descent time to reach bottom.

EXPLORATION (MANNED):
On January 23, 1960, the U.S. Navy bathyscaphe *Trieste* descended 35,800 feet (10,911 m), nearly touching the bottom of the *Challenger Deep*. On board were U.S. Navy Lt. Donald Walsh and Swiss oceanographer Jacques Piccard. In the same year, the French bathyscaphe *Archimede* completed a similar dive. In each case, the bathyscaphes simply descended and returned to the surface ship.
EXPLORATION (UNMANNED):

In 1993, the Japanese launched *Kaiko*, an unmanned robotic craft, which descended to 35,798 feet before breaking down.

Terry skimmed through the file, skipping the recent reference to the UNIS deployment. *Nothing about Jonas Taylor here, or the naval dives seven years ago.*

She signed off and closed the laptop, thinking back to the lecture.

Her first meeting with Jonas Taylor had been ten years ago at a symposium held in San Francisco, sponsored by the Tanaka Oceanographic Institute. Masao had invited the deep sea navy pilot to speak about his dive into the Puerto Rican sea trench. At the time, Terry was fresh out of high school. She had worked closely with her father, organizing the symposium, coordinating travel and hotel arrangements for more than seventy scientists from around the world. She had booked Jonas's ticket and met him at the airport herself. She recalled developing a schoolgirl crush on the deep-sea pilot with the athletic build.

Terry looked at his picture again in her file. Tonight, Taylor had clearly lacked the confidence of their earlier meeting. He was still a physical specimen, possessing a handsome face, bearing a few more stress lines around the eyes. The dark brown hair was turning gray near the temples. Six foot three, she guessed, about 195. But something was missing on the inside.

What had happened to the man? And why had her father insisted on locating him? As far as Terry was concerned, Jonas Taylor's involvement was the last thing the UNIS project needed.

* * *

Jonas woke up on his office sofa, his wool suit jacket serving as a blanket. A dog was barking somewhere in the neighborhood. He squinted at the clock: 6:08 a.m.

He sat up slowly, his aching head pounding, his foot knocking over the half-empty coffeepot, staining the beige carpet brown. Computer printouts from the overflowing catch tray were scattered around him. He rubbed his bloodshot eyes, then glanced at the computer. His screen saver was on. He tapped the mouse, revealing a diagram of the UNIS remote, glowing on screen. His memory came flooding back.

The dog stopped barking. The house seemed unusually quiet. Jonas got up, went into the hallway, and walked down to the master bedroom.

Maggie wasn't there. Their bed hadn't been touched.

THE LAGOON

TERRY TANAKA SPOTTED Jonas as he crossed the airport tarmac from the parking lot. She jogged out to meet him.

"Good morning, professor" she said, just a little bit too loud. "How's your head?"

"Don't ask." He shifted his carry-on bag to his other shoulder. "Talk softer, and stop calling me professor. It's Jonas or J.T. Professor makes me feel old." He eyed the waiting plane. "Kind of small, isn't it?"

"Not for a Beechcraft."

The plane was a twin-turbo, with a whale logo and "T.O.I." painted on the fuselage. Jonas climbed aboard, tossed his bag behind him, then looked around. "Okay, where's the pilot?"

She gave him a mock salute.

"You? No way—"

"Hey, let's not start that chauvinistic crap again. I'm licensed and qualified, and if it makes you feel any better, I've been flying for six years."

Jonas nodded uneasily. It didn't make him feel better.

"Are you all right?" she asked as he fumbled with his seat belt. "You look a little pale."

"Low blood sugar."

"In back's a small cooler, might be some apples. If you'd rather sit in back there's plenty of room to stretch out. Barf bags are in the side pocket." She smiled innocently.

"You're enjoying this."

"In all honesty, I never imagined an experienced deep-sea pilot like you would be so squeamish."

"Just fly the damn plane," he said, his eyes compulsively scanning the dials and meters on the control panel. The cockpit was a little tight, the copilot seat felt jammed up against the windshield. He searched for a level to adjust his leg room.

"Sorry, that's as far back as it goes."

He swallowed dryly. "I need a glass of water."

She noticed his trembling hands. "In back."

Jonas got up and struggled into the rear compartment.

"There's beer in the fridge," she called out.

Jonas unzipped his bag, found his shaving kit, and took out a prescription bottle filled with small yellow pills.

Claustrophobia. His doctor had diagnosed the problem after the accident, a psychosomatic reaction to the stress he had endured. A deep-sea pilot with claustrophobia was as useless as a high diver with vertigo. The two just didn't mix.

Jonas chased down two of the pills with a bottled water. He stared at his trembling hand, then closed his eyes and took a long, deep breath. When he reopened them he was no longer shaking.

"You okay?"

Jonas looked up at her. "I told you, I'm fine."

* * *

It was a two hour flight to Monterey. The pills eventually took effect, allowing Jonas to relax. They were following the coastline north, flying over Big Sur, one of the most dramatic landscapes on the planet. For seventy-two miles violent Pacific waves crashed against the foot of the Santa Lucia Mountains, all bordered by California's scenic Highway 1, a mountainous roadway with harsh grades, twin bridges, and blind turns.

Terry spotted a pod of whales migrating south along the shore. "Grays," she said.

"Cruising to Baja," he mumbled, thinking of Maggie.

"Jonas, listen ... about the lecture. I didn't mean to come off so harshly. It's just that my father insisted I find you, and frankly, I didn't see the purpose of wasting your time. I mean, it's not like we need another submersible pilot."

"Good, because I wouldn't be interested."

"Good, because we don't need you!" She felt her blood beginning to boil again. "Maybe you could convince my father to allow me to follow D.J. down in the second Abyss Glider?"

"Pass." He gazed out his window.

"Why not?"

"First, I've never seen you pilot a sub—"

"I'm piloting this plane."

"It's totally different. You're dealing with harsh currents, perpetual darkness and unnerving water pressure."

"Pressure? You want pressure? Hold on." Terry pulled back on the wheel.

Jonas grabbed the dash in front of him as the Beechcraft rolled into a series of tight 360s, then dropped into a nauseating near-vertical nosedive.

Terry righted the plane at 1,500 feet.

Jonas grabbed an airsick bag and puked.

San Diego

David Adashek adjusted his wire-rimmed bifocals, then knocked on the double doors of Suite 810. No reply. He knocked again, this time louder.

The door opened, revealing a groggy Maggie Taylor, wearing nothing but a white robe. It was loosely tied, exposing one of her tan breasts.

"David? Christ, what time is it?"

"Nine a.m. Rough night?"

She smiled, still half asleep. "Not as rough as my soon-to-be ex-husband's. Come in before someone sees you."

Adashek entered. She pointed to a pair of white sofas that faced a big-screen TV in the living area. "Sit."

"Where's Bud?"

Maggie curled up on the far sofa opposite Adashek. "He left

about an hour ago to play golf. You did a nice job of harassing Jonas at the lecture."

"Is all this really necessary, Maggie? He seems like a decent enough guy—"

"So you marry him. After ten years, I've had enough."

"Why not just divorce him and get it over with?"

"It's not that simple. Now that I'm gaining traction as a local celebrity, my agent says we have to be very careful about the public's perception. Jonas still has a lot of friends in this town. He has to come off as a lunatic. People have to believe that his actions brought this divorce on. Last night was a good start."

"The mental ward thing was a low blow."

"I play to win. Where's Jonas now?"

Adashek pulled out his notes. "He went home with the Tanaka woman."

"Jonas? With another woman?" Maggie laughed hysterically.

"It was innocent. Just a ride home from the awards. I followed him to the commuter airport earlier this morning. They're headed to Monterey. My guess is to that new whale lagoon the Tanaka Oceanographic Institute is constructing along the coast."

"Keep me informed. By the end of the week I want you to go public with the navy story, emphasizing the fact that two innocent civilians were killed. Once the story gains traction you'll do a follow-up interview with me, then I'll push for the divorce, public humiliation and all."

"You're the boss. Listen, if I'm going to be following Jonas, I'll need more cash."

Maggie pulled a thick envelope out of her robe pocket. "Bud says to save the receipts."

Yeah, thought Adashek, *I'm sure he needs the write-off.*

Monterey

"There it is." Terry pointed to the coastline as they descended toward Monterey Bay.

Jonas sipped the coke, his stomach still jumpy from Terry's little air show. His head pounded, and he had already made up his mind to leave immediately after meeting with Masao. As far as he was concerned, Terry Tanaka was the last pilot he'd ever recommend to descend to the bottom of the *Challenger Deep*.

Looking down, he saw an empty white shell stretched out like a giant bathtub on a five-square-mile parcel of land just south of Moss Landing. From the air it looked like an emptied oval-shaped swimming pool. Lying parallel to the ocean, the structure was just over three-quarters of a mile in length and a quarter mile wide. From having read articles on its construction, Jonas knew it was over one-hundred-and twenty feet deep, its underwater viewing area, located along its southern end, featuring galley windows three stories high. A concrete canal intersected the western section of the lagoon and merged with the deep waters of the Pacific.

The lagoon held no water. If and when it was ever finished, the massive steel doors located at the canal entrance would open and the lagoon would fill with seawater, rendering it the largest man-made aquarium in the world.

"Impressive. If I hadn't seen it with my own eyes, I wouldn't have believed it," Jonas said as they prepared to land.

Terry nodded. "My father's dream. He designed it to be a living laboratory, a natural yet protective environment for its future inhabitants. Each winter tens of thousands of whales migrate along California's coastal waters to Baja. Masao is convinced we can coax a few pregnant females inside to give birth."

Jonas nodded. "Marine science meets family entertainment."

* * *

Forty minutes later, Jonas found himself in the Tanaka Institute's empty parking lot, the lagoon's owner and CEO exiting a set of glass doors to greet him.

"Taylor-san!" Masao Tanaka strode across the tarmac to shake Jonas's hand. The tall Japanese man was in his early sixties, his gray hair tucked behind a San Francisco Giants baseball cap, his goatee white, contrasting with his tan complexion. The almond eyes were full of life.

"Let me look at you. Ah, you look like shit. Smell like it too. What's wrong? You don't like flying with my daughter?"

"No, as a matter of fact, I don't." Jonas gave the girl a look to kill.

Masao glanced at his daughter. "Terry?"

"His fault, Masao. It's not my problem if he can't handle the pressure. I'll be in the projection room." She headed inside the building, leaving them to talk.

"My apologies, Taylor-san. Terry is very head-strong, she is somewhat of a free spirit. It is difficult raising a daughter without a female role model."

"Forget it. I really came up to see you and your whale lagoon. Looks amazing from up there."

"I'll give you a tour later. Come, we'll get you a fresh shirt. Then I want you to meet my chief engineer, Alphonse DeMarco. He is reviewing the video D.J. took in the trench. Jonas, I really need your input."

Jonas tossed his bag over his shoulder and followed Masao inside.

The lobby was unfinished, the floor still bare concrete. There were abandoned scaffolds by the drywall, canisters of plaster and paint half-covered with a drop cloth.

Masao led him past empty twenty-foot-high cylinder-shaped saltwater tanks to a souvenir shop. Using a pocketknife, he cut open a box labeled XXL and tossed Jonas a tee-shirt. "Your pay for the day."

"Thanks." Jonas stripped off his soiled shirt and pulled on the cotton tee-shirt, the front emblazoned with an artist's rendition of gray whales inside the Tanaka Lagoon.

A stairwell led them downstairs. A long maintenance corridor harbored the massive filtration systems that would one day hum to life.

At the end of the hall was a media room.

A short man with dark curly hair and a wrestler's physique was seated before a control console, a large projection screen taking up most of the forward wall. Terry occupied a leather wrap-around couch facing the screen.

"Jonas Taylor, this is my chief engineer Alphonse DeMarco. Al, this is the submersible pilot I've been bragging to you about."

Jonas shook the man's hand, which was heavily calloused and felt like it could crush steel.

"Have a seat, Commander Taylor. We were just looking at footage D.J. took of the damaged UNIS."

Avoiding Terry, Jonas sat down in a folding chair as DeMarco dimmed the lights.

The video was shot using a night-vision lens, giving the footage an olive-green tint. The UNIS was lying on its side, its exposed flank crushed like a beer can.

Masao took the empty chair on Jonas's right. "D.J. found it fifty yards south of its original position. These systems weigh close to half a ton. They are lowered into position using a large A-frame mounted in our surface ship. For the current to have moved this half the length of a football field ... impossible."

Jonas rose from his seat and approached the screen. "What do you think happened?"

DeMarco zoomed in, revealing the scarred titanium surface.

"The simplest explanation's always the best. The robot got caught in a seismic event. The subduction zone can be pretty violent."

Jonas examined the sonar plate Tanaka's son had retrieved on his last dive, the section of titanium lying on an oak work table. He touched the dented metal surface. "The titanium casing's three-inches thick. I've seen the stress-test data—"

"Once the UNIS's shell loses its integrity, the water pressure takes over and the titanium might as well be aluminum."

"But again, what would cause it to lose its integrity?"

DeMarco zoomed out on the video. "You tell us, that's why we brought you here."

Jonas stared at the video footage, his mind drifting back to his last dive in the trench. He had never seen the *Challenger Deep* sea floor, his mission confining him above the hydrothermal plume. He looked back at DeMarco. "What about the other three damaged robots? Were they crushed the same way?"

"We've only accessed this one unit, so it's impossible to say."

Jonas turned toward the monitor. "You've lost four units. Isn't it pushing the limits of probability to say they've all been destroyed by seismic activity?"

DeMarco removed his reading glasses and rubbed his eyes. He'd had this argument with Masao more than once. "The purpose of the array is to detect seismic activity. To detect seismic activity required us to distribute the UNIS 'bots along a fault line. Three of the four downed systems were all located in the same sector of the *Challenger Deep*. I'd say those factors even out the probability odds significantly."

Masao stood. "Jonas, the future of this facility depends on our ability to determine what happened to these robots and correct the situation immediately. We've located the last UNIS, the only one of the four not located directly along the fault line. I've decided we must retrieve this robot. The job requires two

127

subs working together: one to clear debris from the O-ring used to hoist the unit topside while the other pilot attaches the tow cable."

"I'm going, Masao," Terry said. "I've trained for this, I can get it done."

Masao was about to reply when Jonas yelled, "Stop the tape." He pointed to the screen. "Al, go back about twenty seconds."

DeMarco rewound the video.

"Good, that's good. Let it play again from there."

They stared at the screen, seeing nothing new.

"There—can you freeze that frame?"

DeMarco complied.

Jonas pointed to a tiny white fragment lying beneath the tripod legs. "Can you blow that up?"

The engineer punched some buttons and a square outline appeared on screen. Moving a joystick, he positioned the square around the object, then pulled it out so that it filled the entire screen.

The object appeared triangular and white, still a bit too out-of-focus to identify.

Jonas stared at the screen. "It's a tooth."

DeMarco moved closer to the screen, scrutinizing the image. "A tooth? You're nuts."

"Al," commanded Masao. "Show the proper respect to our guest."

"Sorry, Mas, but what our professor here's saying is impossible. You see that?" He pointed to a bolt dangling from a titanium strut. "That bolt is three inches long. That would mean this tooth, or whatever it is, would be twice that length ... at least six, maybe seven inches long."

He looked at Masao. "There's no creature on Earth with teeth that big."

MASAO

THE SURFACE OF THE PACIFIC OCEAN sparkled like diamonds beyond the western bleachers; a cold wind howled through the barren canal.

The man-made lagoon was spread out before them like God's bathtub. Massive drains were set along its walls, part of a massive filtration system. A glint of sun reflected off the acrylic windows situated along the southern wall twenty feet below the main deck, the gallery accessible from inside the arena.

The arena itself provided bench-style seating for 10,000.

Jonas was awestruck by the lagoon's sheer size. "To see a pod of gray whales inhabiting this waterway, or better yet a few Humpbacks ... you could watch them for days on end and not be bored."

Masao Tanaka nodded, warming his face in the late afternoon sun. "This lagoon has been my dream since I was six years old. Forty million dollars, almost seven years of planning, four years of construction, Jonas. I did all I could, gave it everything I had."

He turned and faced him. "I fear, my friend, that we will never see her open."

Terry was straddling a rail five rows down, her back to them.

Masao lowered his voice. "Taylor-san, with all due respect, I don't see how this object on the video could possibly be a tooth."

"It's a bottom tooth. You can tell the difference; the upper teeth are much wider, they were used for crushing whale bone. The bottoms are narrow, designed to puncture and grip prey."

"The object was white, Jonas. There are no white Megalodon teeth."

"Mas, white indicates it's not a fossil, that the creature who owned it may still be alive. It's the reason we have to retrieve that tooth. It proves my theories."

"Your theories?" Terry slid down from the rail and approached. "Are those the same theories that landed you in a mental ward for three months? The theories that earned your dishonorable discharge? Here's a reality check for you, *professor*—there are no giant prehistoric Great White sharks in the Mariana Trench or any other trench, for that matter. And even if there were, since when do sharks eat titanium robots?"

"They don't," Jonas snapped, "unless the titanium robots happen to be transmitting electrical signals, like your UNIS." He turned to Masao. "Years ago, I was hired by AT&T to investigate problems they were having with a fiber-optic cable system. They had just laid cable along the ocean floor in six thousand feet of water, the line encased in stainless-steel mesh, and yet the sharks were still attacking it, tearing it up, costing the company millions of dollars in repairs. The sharks' ampullae of Lorenzini were attracted to the electronic booster signals originating in the fiber-optic bundles."

130

"Ampullae of who?" Terry sneered.

"Lorenzini," Jonas shot back. "It's a cluster of sensory cells located along the underside of the shark's snout. Masao please, I need D.J. to recover that tooth; it's very important to me."

"What if I offered you an opportunity to collect the tooth yourself?"

Terry's almond eyes blazed. "No, no, no. If anyone's descending with D.J., it'll be me!"

"Enough." Masao looked at his daughter, the old man's eyes fierce. "I will speak to my guest about this; for you, this discussion is over."

Terry glared at Jonas then stormed off.

Masao closed his eyes, taking a few slow, deep breaths through his nose, exhaling from his mouth. "You will stay with us tonight as my guest. My daughter is a very good cook."

Jonas looked at his friend. "I'm sure she is. I just might need a food taster to make sure she didn't drop arsenic into my serving."

Masao smiled and breathed deeply again. "Jonas, you smell that ocean air? Makes you appreciate nature, eh?"

"Yes."

"My father ... he was a fisherman. Back in Japan, he would take me out on his boat almost every morning before school. My mother, Kiku Tanaka, died when I was only four. There was no one else to take care of me. Just my father.

"When I was six, we moved to America to live with relatives in San Francisco. Four months later, the Japanese attacked Pearl Harbor. All Asians were locked in detention camps. My father ... he was a very proud man. He could never accept the fact that he was in a prison, unable to fish, unable to live his life. One morning, my father just decided to die. He left me all alone, locked in a prison in a foreign land, unable to speak or understand a word of English."

"You must've been pretty scared."

Masao smiled. "Very scared. Then I saw my first whale. From the prison gates, I could see them leap. The humpbacks, they sang to me, kept me company at night, occupied my mind. My only friends." He closed his eyes for a moment, lost in the memory. "They bussed us out to Idaho a week after my father died. The Minidoka War Relocation Camp. This is where I learned to speak English.

"You know, Taylor-san, Americans are funny people. One minute you feel hated by them, the next loved. After eighteen months, I was released and adopted by an American couple, Jeffrey and Gay Gordon. I was very lucky. The Gordon family loved me, supported me, put me through school. But when I felt depressed, it was always my whales that kept me going."

"Now I understand why this project means so much to you."

"*Hai*. Learning about whales is very important. In many ways they are superior to man. But capturing and imprisoning them in small tanks, forcing them to perform stupid tricks so they can receive their rations of food, this is very cruel. This lagoon, it will allow me to study the whales in a natural setting. The lagoon will remain open so the whales can enter and exit of their own free will. No more small tanks. Having been locked up myself, I could never do that. Never."

"The lagoon will open, Masao. JAMSTEC won't hold the money back forever."

Masao shook his head. "Unless we can get the array working again, the project is cancelled."

"What about finding another funding source?"

"I tried, but my assets are already heavily leveraged and no bank will support my venture. Only JAMSTEC. But they don't care about building lagoons, they just want the UNIS array to monitor earthquakes. The Japanese government will not back down, there are political careers at stake. We either fix the array or declare bankruptcy."

"You'll finish the lagoon, Masao. We'll figure out what happened."

"Jonas, you and I are friends. I tell you my story, now you tell your old friend Tanaka the truth. What happened to you in the Mariana Trench?"

"What makes you think—"

Masao smiled knowingly. "We've known each other … what? Ten years? Do not underestimate me, my friend. I have contacts in the navy as well in the Pentagon. I read a report filed by your commanding officer, Richard Danielson. Now I want to hear your side."

Jonas rubbed his eyes. "Okay, Masao, for some reason it seems the story's being leaked anyway. First off, Danielson wasn't my C.O., he was assigned to Guam when our mission began, then ended up overseeing the dives as they were in his waters. I had trained for the mission for several years along with three other pilots, two of which eventually dropped out.

"The sub was called the *Sea Cliff*, the navy having refitted her to handle the *Challenger Deep*. Three teams of scientists were flown out to supervise the mission. I was briefed with some bullshit story about measuring deep-sea currents in the trench in order to determine if plutonium rods from nuclear power plants could be safely buried within the subduction zone. Funny thing—when we descended on that first dive the eggheads were suddenly no longer interested in currents, what they came for were rocks."

"Rocks?"

"Manganese nodules. Don't ask me why they wanted them, I haven't a clue. My orders were to pilot the sub down to the hydrothermal plume and remain there while the geologists operated a remotely-controlled drone designed with a vacuum."

Jonas closed his eyes. "The first dive went okay; the second was three days later and by the time I had surfaced again I was seeing double."

"What about the other pilot?"

"He wasn't ready. I made a third dive four days later, and then a storm front moved in.

"The eggheads decided the last patch of rocks was the Holy Grail and demanded one last dive. It was barely forty-eight hours after my last dive and I wasn't fit enough to operate a TV remote, let alone a submersible. But with a little prodding from Dick Danielson the ship's physician, Frank Heller, certified me ready."

Masao shook his head. "Go on."

"I managed to get us to the plume. The scientists were busy conducting tests when sonar picked up a school of squid. There must have been a river of them ... they passed beneath us like a freight train. Then sonar picked up another biologic, only this one was clearly a predator. It circled and then moved off. Anyway, two hours later I was gazing out the porthole, staring down at the swirling hydrothermal plume when I thought I saw something big circling just below the layer."

"What can you see in darkness?"

"I'm not sure, but the sub's light reflected off something large and white. At first I thought it could be a whale, but I knew that was impossible. Then it just disappeared. I figured I had to be hallucinating."

"What happened next?"

"I ... to tell you the truth, Masao, I'm not sure. I was so tired, I could barely keep my eyes open ... but suddenly this huge triangular head emerged out of the hydrothermal ceiling. It was monstrous, as big as a truck, its jaws filled with huge teeth. I don't remember much after that. They say I panicked, dropped every weight plate the sub had and rocketed toward the surface. We ascended way too fast, and something went wrong with the compression system. The two scientists died. I was rushed inside a recompression chamber and woke up in a hospital three days later … never knew what happened."

"And the mental ward?"

"A parting gift from Danielson. Actually, the rest did me good. But the dive left me with a bit of an anxiety issue."

"What makes you think this biologic was a Megalodon?"

"Mas, before this accident happened I didn't know a Megalodon from a Mastodon. It was only after … it was after I saw a psychiatrist that I started piecing things together."

"But the monster … it never pursued you to the surface?"

"Apparently not. Like I said, I blacked out, but it could have overtaken us at any time. My guess is it wasn't interested in being in that cold layer, where the water temperature's barely above freezing."

"Two men died on your watch. Knowing the kind of man you are, that karma must have been hard to live with."

"Still is. Not a day goes by I don't think about it." Jonas looked to the horizon. "The truth is, it's been so long, I've begun to doubt my own memories of the event."

Masao sat back in his chair. "Jonas, I believe you saw something, but I don't think it was a monster. You know, D.J. tells me there are giant patches of white tubeworms located all along the bottom. D.J. says these worms reflect the light so it appears like they are glowing. You never did make it to the very bottom of the trench, did you?"

"No."

"D.J. made it. That boy loves deep-sea exploration, says it's like being in outer space. Jonas, I think what you saw was a patch of tubeworms. I think the currents pushed them in and out of your sight line, your submersible's exterior light catching their glow. That's why they seemed to disappear. Remember, you were exhausted, staring into the darkness. The navy worked you too hard, three dives in eight days is not safe, a fourth is criminal. Were you falling asleep?"

"Like I had terminal narcolepsy."

"Given the circumstances, what is the more likely event—that you were attacked by an extinct species of shark or that you dreamt the attack and panicked when you awoke?"

Jonas sat in silence, tears clouding his vision.

Masao placed his hand on Jonas's shoulder. "My friend, I need your help. And I think maybe it's time to face your fears. I want you to return to the Mariana Trench with us and make the dive with D.J., but this time you'll make it all the way to the bottom. You'll see these patches of giant tubeworms for yourself. You were once a great pilot, and I know in my heart you still are. You can't live in fear your whole life."

"What about Terry? She wants to make the dive—"

"She's not ready. Too head-strong. No, I need you. And you need to do this, so that you can get on with your life."

Jonas nodded. "Okay ... I'll go back."

"Good. And when all of this is over, you will come work with me at the Institute, yes?"

"We'll see." Jonas choked back a laugh. "Boy, your daughter is going to be pissed at me."

Masao nodded. "She will be upset with us both. Let's skip the home-cooking; I think it best we eat at a restaurant tonight."

THE KIKU

THE AMERICAN AIRLINES JUMBO JET five hours
out of San Francisco, soared 36,000 feet above the blue
carpet of the Pacific Ocean, five hours out of San Francisco.

Terry rose from her business-class seat and headed back
toward the plane's restroom. Alphonse DeMarco was seated in
the row behind her next to Jonas Taylor.

The former naval submersible pilot had a briefcase-sized
Abyss Glider-II flight simulator on his lap, a dark visor over his
eyes. The simulator's dual joysticks allowed Jonas to practice
coordinating yaw and pitch with speed and stabilization while
focusing on underwater images appearing in his visor.

For a contraption he had labeled a "kid's video game," the
experience turned out to be quite intense.

Removing the head gear, he took a break to rest his eyes.
There'd be plenty of time for more practice. It was a twelve-hour
flight across the Pacific to Guam, not counting a stopover in
Honolulu for refueling.

Terry's attitude toward Jonas had gone from cold to ice. She
was visibly hurt that her father had ignored her qualifications to
back up her brother, D.J., and felt Jonas had lied to her about not
being interested in piloting the sub into the Mariana Trench. She
flatly refused to help train Jonas on the simulator.

Having been at it for three straight hours, Jonas opened his
sleep pod to take a break. Staring out the window at the night sky,
he thought about his last conversation with Masao Tanaka.

Despite seven years of self-analysis, it had never occurred to
Jonas that he could have been focused on a cluster of tubeworms.
According to D.J. Tanaka, vast expanses of *Riftia* grew along the
bottom of the *Challenger Deep*. If true, then it was possible he had
been staring at a worm cluster through the swirling debris of

137

minerals, fallen asleep, and dreamt the triangular head.

The thought made Jonas ill. Two men had died for his mistake, two families shattered. At least the Megalodon defense had served to lessen his guilt. Coming to grips with this new evidence which suggested he may have imagined the entire threat was not sitting well with his psyche.

Jonas knew Masao was right; he had to face his fears and return to the trench. If a white Megalodon tooth could be found, it would justify seven years of research. If not, so be it. One way or the other, it was time to get on with his life.

* * *

Fifteen rows behind Jonas and DeMarco, David Adashek closed the hardback *Extinct Species of the Abyss* by Jonas Taylor, Ph. D. He removed his bifocals, positioned his pillow against the window, and fell asleep.

Western Pacific Ocean

The naval transport helicopter soared two hundred feet above the waves, its co-pilot glancing over his shoulder at Jonas and DeMarco in the second seat. "She's just up ahead."

"About time," DeMarco said. He turned to wake Terry, who had been sleeping in the third seat since they'd left the naval station in Guam.

Jonas trained his eyes on the horizon, a faint line separating the gray ocean from the gray sky. He couldn't see anything.

Maybe I should have slept. He was certainly tired enough. They'd been traveling for more than fifteen hours.

Moments later he saw the ship, a flat speck quickly growing larger in the distance.

The deep-sea research vessel, *Kiku,* was two-hundred-and-seventy-four feet long with a forty-four foot beam and was outfitted with labs, machine shops, and accommodations to support a dozen scientists and a crew of eighteen for extended voyages. The ship was also equipped to launch submersibles, a reinforced-steel winch and A-frame towering over its stern deck. Behind the winch was a massive spool containing more than eight miles of steel cable.

Approaching from the north, the helicopter hovered high over the *Kiku's* helipad but did not attempt to land.

DeMarco peered out of his window, then motioned to Terry.

An athletic man wearing a black and neon-green wetsuit was kite-boarding along the port side of the ship. The wind was gusting at forty knots, the swells twenty feet high, generating ideal conditions to achieve radical lifts.

Glancing overhead, the kite-boarder saw the hovering chopper. Executing a heel turn jibe, he quickly reversed his direction, creating incredible tension on the lines. Feeling a gust of wind take the kite, he edged his board as he headed into an incoming fifteen foot swell, then released the built-up kinetic energy and soared over the top of the wave, becoming airborne.

As the helicopter passengers watched, the kite launched its rider eighty feet into the air. Defying gravity, the daredevil whipped his body into a tight one-eighty, hovering high over the *Kiku's* bow. For the next twelve seconds he pirouetted into the wind, then, bleeding air from his kite, he dropped onto the aft deck and skidded to a halt.

Terry beamed proudly at Jonas. "D.J."

* * *

Twenty-four-year-old D.J. Tanaka was lean and tall like his father, his body taut with muscles, his skin a deep Asian tan. He hugged his older sister as she stepped off the chopper, ushering her to a quiet location away from the helicopter's dying overhead rotors to talk.

Jonas grabbed his carry-on bag and joined them. With their

black hair, dark eyes, high cheekbones and identical smiles the siblings could almost pass as twins.

"D.J., this is Jonas Taylor. Don't call him professor, it makes him feel old."

D.J. shook Jonas's hand. "My sister's a pistol, huh?"

"A real delight."

"So, I understand we're going to be descending together into the *Challenger Deep*. Sure you're up for it?"

"I'll be fine," said Jonas, sensing D.J.'s competitive nature. "I would like to do a few practice runs. Where are the subs?"

"Come on, I'll show you."

Jonas followed D.J. and Terry aft to where the two Abyss Gliders were lying horizontally, secured to the deck in their dry mounts. The vessels were ten feet long by four feet in diameter and resembled fat glass torpedoes with small mid-wings and a tail assembly.

Working on one of the undercarriages was a man in his late thirties, only his grease-stained sky-blue jumpsuit visible.

D.J. slapped his hand on one of the sub's clear plastic nosecones. "Lexan. The plastic's so strong, it's used as bulletproof glass in presidential limousines. The entire escape pod's made of the stuff, rendering the craft neutrally buoyant. Technically, the chamber is one big escape pod. If the Glider gets into trouble, simply pull the lever located in a metal gear box along your right side and the interior chamber will separate from the heavier chassis. It's like being in a buoyant bubble. You'll rise right to the top."

The mechanic crawled out from beneath the sub's chassis, wiping his hands on his pants. "I'll give the tour, kid. After all, I did redesign the damn things."

Jonas's face broke into a broad smile. "Mac! What the hell are you doing here?"

James "Mac" Mackreides turned to his friend. "I should be

asking you the same question. I called Vegas this morning; the line on you actually showing up was six-to-one."

"How did you bet?"

"You know me, always go with the underdog."

The two men embraced.

Terry looked at her brother. "Did you know they knew each other?"

He shook his head. "Mac never said a word."

Jonas stood back, taking in his friend. Mac's navy-regulation crew-cut had grown out into a mop of dirty-blonde hair, his hawkish hazel eyes sporting a few more stress lines since their shared three month stay together in the mental ward where they had met seven years ago. The boyish twinkle was still present.

"You look good." Jonas patted Mac's stomach. "Glad to see you're eating well."

"That's bought and paid for, pal."

"Just like your women."

"You misjudge me, Commander Taylor. I'm no longer delivering V.I.P.s to tropical island bordellos."

"That's because Dick Danielson shut you down."

"Danielson didn't do dick. Some hotshot Congressman decided to use his wife's VISA card to pay for services rendered. When the missus found out, she went on a rampage. Doesn't matter. I work for Masao now, keeping his ship and submersibles running and his bar replenished with the finest kind of beer and shine."

D.J. hesitated. "I was just about to explain about the advantages of having a neutrally-buoyant sub."

"Go for it."

"When you construct a sphere out of titanium, you lose half your battery power just trying to pilot the sub, not to mention your lack of speed and maneuverability."

Mac looked at D.J. "At least explain to him how the mission will go."

"Look beneath the belly of the sub," D.J. instructed Jonas "There's a retractable mechanical arm with a claw. When we make our descent, you'll take the lead. I'll follow in my sub, which will have a steel cable attached to my glider's claw. The damaged UNIS has several eye bolts located along its outer casing. Once you clear the debris away from the UNIS, I'll attach the cable and the *Kiku's* winch will haul the unit back to the surface."

"Doesn't sound too bad."

"It's a walk in the park, but it's still a two-man job," said D.J. "I tried to attach the cable on my first descent, but I couldn't maintain the claw's grip on the steel cable and clear the debris. I finally tried letting go of the cable; the next thing I know the hydrothermal plume dragged it two miles to the south."

"Maybe you were just nervous," Terry teased. "You told me it's kind of scary down there. Being cramped in a pod the size of a phone booth, knowing that you're seven miles down, surrounded by thousands of pounds of pressure. One mistake, one crack in the hull, and your brains implode." She glanced at Jonas, looking for a reaction.

"Ah, you're just jealous," said D.J., who turned to Jonas, his face full of animation. "Truth is, I loved it down there. What a rush, I can't wait to go back. I thought bungee jumping and kite surfing were cool, but this beats the hell out of them."

Jonas stared at the young man, recognizing traits from his own youth. "You consider yourself an adrenaline junkie?"

D.J. calmed himself. "Me? No, sir ... I mean, yeah, I'm an adrenaline junkie, sure, but this is different. The *Challenger Deep* ... it's like being the first person to explore another planet. There are these huge black smokers everywhere, and the weirdest fish you ever saw. But why am I telling you? You've been on dozens of trench dives before."

Jonas tugged on one of the glider's red vinyl flags emblazoned with the Tanaka logo. "I've piloted more than my share of dives into deep-sea trenches, but I've never been to the bottom of the *Challenger Deep*."

"Then tomorrow morning we'll pop your cherry."

"What about my practice dive?"

"No practice dives."

They turned as a large dark-skinned man in a red knit cap approached, accompanied by two Filipino crew members.

"Jonas Taylor," D.J. said, "Leon Barre, the *Kiku's* captain."

Jonas shook the French-Polynesian's hand, his thick palm as padded as a catcher's mitt.

"Welcome aboard," he said, his baritone voice booming. Barre tipped his hat to Terry. "Mademoiselle," he said reverently.

DeMarco joined them, slapping the big man across his shoulder. "You're putting on a little weight, Leon?"

Leon's face darkened. "The Thai woman, she fattens me like a pig."

DeMarco laughed, turning to Jonas. "The captain's wife's a hell of a cook. We could all use a little of that, Leon. We're starving."

"We eat in an hour, but no practice dives. Bad weather is two days out; I want to be back in port before it hits."

Jonas turned to Mac. "What about a quick surface dive?"

"Sorry, pal. The A-frame's generator is being repaired; we need to save the back-up unit's juice just in case we need it for tomorrow's dive. But stick around and I'll prep you as best I can."

Jonas waited until the two Tanaka siblings followed DeMarco and the captain into the ship's infrastructure. "Mac, you haven't been speaking to Masao or anyone else about our little vacation in the crazy bin?"

"No."

"But you knew I was coming."

"I knew Masao was going to offer you the dive; I honestly didn't think you'd take the gig... not with Frank Heller on board."

Jonas felt the breath squeeze out of his chest. "Heller's part of this expedition?"

"Masao never told you?"

"You think I'd be here if he did?"

"Stay calm. Heller's Masao's physician, his presence has no bearing on your dive this time around."

"Where is he?"

"Probably in sick bay. That's on C-Deck."

Jonas turned and walked away.

FRANK HELLER

JONAS ENTERED THE SHIP'S infrastructure and ascended one flight of stairs to C-Deck. Following signs posted on a corridor wall, he located sick bay and entered without knocking.

A gaunt man in his early fifties with short gray hair and heavy, black-framed glasses was bent over a computer keyboard. He glanced up at Jonas, his moist blue-gray eyes swollen behind the thick lenses, then turned back to his monitor. "Another fishing expedition, Taylor?"

Jonas paused a moment before he answered. "That's not why I'm here, Frank."

"Why are you here?"

"Masao asked for my help."

"The Japanese have no sense of irony."

"Like it or not, we're going to have to work together. The only way to find out what's going on down there is to haul up the damaged UNIS. D.J. can't do it alone—"

"I know that!" Heller rose quickly and crossed the room to refill his coffee cup. "What I don't understand is why you should be the one to go with him."

"Because nobody else has been down there in the last thirty years."

"Oh yes they have," Heller said bitterly. "Only they died making the trip."

Jonas broke eye contact. "Look, there hasn't been a day that's gone by in the last seven years that I haven't thought about the *Sea Cliff*. To be honest, I'm still not sure what really happened. All I know is that I believed I saw something rise up from the bottom to attack our sub, and I reacted."

"Reacted? You panicked like it was your first day at boot

camp." Heller moved to Jonas, standing nose to nose. His eyes burned with hatred. "Maybe your little confession makes everything all right in your book, but it changes nothing with me. You were daydreaming, Taylor. You hallucinated, and instead of reasoning, you panicked. You killed two of our team. Mike Shaffer was my friend; I'm godfather to his kid. Shaffer's family lives with your mistake every day."

"And what about your contribution to the accident?" Jonas yelled back. "You were the physician of record. You assured Danielson that I was medically fit to make a fourth dive, despite the fact that I had vertigo and was suffering from exhaustion. Four descents in nine days! Do you think that decision may have had anything to do with my ability to function?"

"You were a naval commander. You're supposed to be a cut above the rest. Ultimately, it was your decision whether you piloted the sub or your back-up."

"He wasn't ready. You and Danielson knew it, which was why the two of you set me up to be the fall guy ... just to cover your own asses."

"What is it you want from me, Taylor? I can't absolve you of your actions any more than I can render an excuse for my own. Danielson was my commanding officer, but he was being pressured by the Pentagon. Did you want him to disobey a direct order because his lead pilot was tired? The navy's not interested in hearing excuses, they want results."

"And if you could turn back the clock to that morning, what would you do?"

"I don't know. The truth is, you were a damn good pilot—maybe that influenced my decision to let you go as well. But let's just make sure that the reason you're making this dive with Tanaka's kid is to assist him and not to go off looking for some tooth."

Jonas headed for the door, then turned to face Heller. "I

146

know my responsibilities, Frank. I hope you remember yours."

* * *

An hour later, having showered and changed, Jonas entered the galley where a dozen crewmen were noisily feasting on fried chicken and potatoes. He made himself a plate and grabbed a bottled water from a cooler.

Mac signaled him over to his table.

He sat down, listening to D.J., who was involved in a heated debate with DeMarco and Captain Barre.

Heller's absence was conspicuous.

"Doc!" D.J. sprayed half his mouthful of chicken out with the word. "You're just in time. There's a rumor going around the ship that you spent three months in a looney bin after you blamed a submersible accident on one of those prehistoric sharks you wrote about. Is that true?"

The chamber fell quiet.

Jonas no longer felt hungry.

Mac flicked a potato at D.J. with his fork.

"Dude … really?"

"Jonas and I met at that facility seven years ago. What you call a looney bin was actually a clinic that cared for disabled vets. So be careful; as a fellow lunatic-turned-submersible mechanic, your accusation may cause me to accidentally forget to charge your emergency batteries."

D.J. smiled, but it was forced.

"We have a right to ask, Mac," Terry interjected. "One of the guests at Jonas's lecture claimed two people died as a result of your friend's actions. I spoke to Frank Heller; he wouldn't come out and say exactly what happened, but he did tell me Jonas received a dishonorable discharge from the navy following the incident."

D.J. looked Jonas squarely in the eye. "Doc?"

All eyes were on Jonas, who pushed his tray away. "It's true.

147

STEVE ALTEN

Only Frank left out a few things … like I was exhausted from
having completed three deep dives prior to the fourth, all amassed
within a nine day period. As far as tomorrow's dive is concerned, I
made a commitment to your father to complete the mission and I
intend on doing so. And for the record, I've piloted more
submersibles on deep-sea missions than you've had birthdays,
D.J. Now, if you'll excuse me," Jonas stood up to leave, "I think
I've lost my appetite."

D.J. grabbed his arm. "No, wait, Doc, come on now. Tell
me about this shark. I really want to know. After all, how will I
recognize it if we happen to run into one tomorrow?"

"You'll know right away," Terry said. "It'll be the one with
the missing tooth."

Laughter cascaded around them.

Jonas sat back down. "Okay, kid, you really want to know
about these monsters, I'll tell you. The first thing you have to
realize about sharks is that they've been around a lot longer than
us, about four hundred million years. Our ancestors only fell from
the trees two million years ago. And of all the species of sharks
ever to have evolved, Megalodon was the undisputed king. We're
not just talking about a shark; we're talking about a formidable
killing machine, the apex predator of all time—a sixty-foot, forty
ton version of a Great White shark. The Meg wasn't just big, it was
endowed with senses that could track prey from miles away. It
could smell and taste you, it could feel your heart beating and
sense the electrical impulses generated by your moving muscles.
Blood or urine in the water? You might as well have lit up a flare.
And if it ever got close enough to see you, then you were already
dead."

Leon Barre shook his head. "How do you know so much
about a dead fish nobody's ever seen?"

The room quickly quieted, awaiting Jonas's response.

"For one thing, we have their fossilized serrated teeth. An

148

inch of tooth equates to about ten feet of shark. The biggest teeth we've found were just over seven inches in length, so do the math. The bottom teeth were narrow, used for gripping their prey while the uppers were massive, designed to puncture whale bone and saw through muscle and sinew."

"I want to know more about these senses," said D.J., now truly curious.

Jonas gathered his thoughts. "All right. Just like its modern-day cousin, *Carcharodon megalodon* possessed eight sensory organs that allowed it to search, detect, identify, and stalk its prey. Let's start with the ampullae of Lorenzini. These jelly-filled capsules located beneath the snout could detect the faint electrical field of another animal's beating heart or moving muscles from many miles away. That means if the Megalodon was circling our ship, it could still detect a whale calf in distress off the shoreline of Guam.

"Almost as amazing as the ampullae of Lorenzini was the Megalodon's sense of smell. Unlike man, the creature possessed directional nostrils which not only could detect one part of blood or sweat or urine in a billion parts of water, but could also determine the exact location of the scent. That's why you see Great Whites swimming with a side-to-side motion of their heads. They're actually smelling the water in different directions. And a full-grown adult Megalodon's nostrils ... they were probably the size of a cantaloupe.

"Now we come to the monster's skin, a sensory organ and weapon combined in one. Running along either side of the Meg's flank was its lateral line, a canal that contained sensory cells called neuromasts. These neuromasts were able to detect the slightest vibrations in water, even the flutter of another fish's heartbeat. The skin itself was made up of denticles, which were essentially layered scales, sharp as scalpels. Rub your hand against the grain and your flesh would be sliced to ribbons."

Al DeMarco stood up. "You'll have to excuse me. I've got work to do."

"Ah, come on, Al," said D.J. lightheartedly. "There's no school tomorrow. We'll let you stay up late."

DeMarco gave D.J. a stern look. "Tomorrow happens to be a big day for all of us, especially you and Mr. Shark Tales here. I suggest you get some rest."

"Al's right, D.J." agreed Jonas. "Besides, I've already mentioned the best parts."

"One thing you didn't mention, Taylor, is how these sharks of yours could exist in depths where the water pressure reached 16,000 pounds per square inch."

"Water pressure effects mammals and subs because they both have air cavities. Sharks, being fish have no air cavities to squeeze. Megalodon also possessed an enormous liver that probably constituted one-fourth of its entire weight. Besides serving the creature's normal hepatic functions and storing fatty energy reserves, the liver would have allowed the Megalodon to adjust to any changes in water pressure, even at depths as great as those in the *Challenger Deep*."

"All right, professor," said DeMarco, feeling baited, "let's assume, just for shits and giggles, that these Megalodon sharks do exist in the trench. Why haven't they surfaced? There's got to be a lot more food up here than down there."

"Fleas in a jar."

"What's that supposed to mean?" Terry asked.

"If you place fleas in a jar without the lid, they'll all jump out. Leave the lid on a week, then remove it and the fleas will still remain inside. The reason is conditioning. The hydrothermal plume insulates the warm bottom layer from six miles of freezing-cold water. Megalodons that survived in the Mariana Trench were conditioned over eons to remain in the warm depths—there'd be no impetus to surface."

"Food's an impetus," said DeMarco, the cynicism rising in his voice. "What food source would be available in the Mariana Trench that could sustain a colony of predators the size of a sixty-foot Great White?"

"Giant Cuttlefish, squid—who knows what else might be down there. The lower oxygen content in the trench no doubt slows the creatures' metabolism while decreasing their appetites. Being territorial predators, the Megs would probably thin out their numbers by devouring any weaker members of their own species. Every habitat has its food chain; the *Challenger Deep* is no exception."

"What nonsense."

Heads turned as Frank Heller entered the galley. "Don't listen to him, D.J. Taylor's sole reason for becoming an academic was to justify his actions seven years ago in the *Challenger Deep*. I made the mistake of certifying him as fit to dive. I won't make that same mistake again."

Jonas felt his pulse jump. "What are you saying, Frank?"

"I'm saying you're off the dive. As Masao's chief medical officer I'm declaring you mentally unfit. Terry will accompany her brother into the trench."

"Yes!" Terry hugged D.J.

Jonas glanced at Mac. Humiliated, he exited the galley and headed out on deck.

DESCENT

JONAS AWOKE SOMETIME BEFORE DAWN. His cabin was pitch-black, and for a moment he didn't know where he was.

The second series of knocks had him fumbling for the light switch. Dressed in a navy blue and white Penn State sweat suit, he made his way to the stateroom door and unlocked it.

Mac was standing in the corridor, holding a black and red neoprene body suit and matching footwear. "Masao's en route from Tokyo. He just reamed out Frank on the radio. Terry's benched, you're back in the game."

He handed Jonas the garment. "This is a bio-suit, it allows us to monitor your vitals during the dive. Get dressed, grab some breakfast, then do whatever you deep-sea divers do to purge your bowels, you launch in ninety minutes."

Jonas closed the door, his heart racing.

Damn ...

* * *

The dawn sky was a fierce tapestry of gray, gusting with thunderclouds that blew whitecaps across the roiling sea.

A forty knot wind assaulted Jonas as he stepped out onto the main deck in his bio-suit and rubber boots. He had forced down a light breakfast of scrambled eggs and toast, needing to put something in his stomach before popping two of his yellow pills for the descent. In his left shoulder pouch were four more tablets. Despite the medication, he still felt anxious.

Mac's launch team was busy attaching canvas harnesses to each of the Abyss Gliders. D.J.'s sub would be hoisted into the sea first, the end of the steel cable clipped to the folded mechanical arm secured beneath the sub's undercarriage. The cocky young pilot was huddling with his older sister, who was wearing a wetsuit.

Seeing Jonas, she approached the submersible pilot. "You can still back out."

"Give it a rest."

"Why are you really doing this? Is it ego?"

"It's something I just have to do. A piece of me died down there, maybe this is the only way to make myself whole again."

"And did you pack your little yellow pills, Dr. Feel Good?"

She grabbed his arm as he tried to walk away. "D.J.'s my brother, Jonas. When our mother died, I practically raised him. So if you screw up down there … if anything happens to him, don't bother surfacing."

Without waiting for a reply she returned to D.J. They talked for a minute, then she hugged him and joined three other divers who were pulling on their scuba gear.

Mac stood by Jonas. "You do have a way with the women. Speaking of which, how are things going with that wife of yours … you know, the one who refused to visit you in the mental ward?"

"She's screwing my old college roommate."

"Ouch."

"Any other painful subjects you wish to broach before I pilot this glass coffin seven miles beneath the Pacific?"

"Still listen to my boy, Tom Jones?" Mac held up a *Best of Tom Jones* CD.

"The Abyss Glider has a CD player?"

"No, but there's one in the command center linked to your radio."

The two men watched as D.J. crawled head-first through the rear hatch of his glider. Moments later, the big A-frame powered up, lifting the torpedo-shaped vessel off the deck, over the stern rail, and into the sea, the winch feeding out steel cable.

Alphonse DeMarco's booming voice faltered in the wind.

"Let's go, Taylor, we're burning daylight."

Mac muttered, "As if you'll need it where you're going."

Jonas punched knuckles with his friend before ducking down on all fours to climb through the open rear hatch of his submersible, straining his back as he sealed the Lexan pod behind him.

The interior was tight but well-cushioned, the body hammock smelling of new leather. Jonas realized the sub *was* new, and the sudden thought of taking an untested vessel seven miles below the surface only added to his trepidation.

Securing himself in the hammock, he adjusted the padded elbow rests which were situated in front of and below his chest. Placing the headphones over his ears, he reached for the two joysticks, his left hand controlling the sub's thruster, the device in his right hand used to steer. He did a quick inventory of the storage areas, finding snacks, bottled water, and a urine bottle in one, a medical kit, a knife, and a pony bottle of air attached to a face mask in the other. In a Velcro pouch he discovered a pair of night vision goggles.

Small LCD computer screens mounted on a low forward rise provided him with sonar, radio, battery levels, and life-support readouts. As he ran through a pre-launch check list the sub suddenly lifted away from the deck, sending his equilibrium spinning.

Jonas's pulse raced as the big winch hoisted the Abyss Glider beyond the *Kiku's* rail, offering him a birds' eye view of the harsh Pacific. The A-frame rotated forward, lowering him to a team of divers waiting in the fifteen-foot swells—Terry amongst them. For several nauseating minutes he held on as the ocean lifted and dropped the buoyant submersible unmercifully while the team of frogmen detached the A-frame's harness. Finally, one of the divers knocked on the Lexan nose cone, giving the all-clear sign... followed by the middle finger.

"Love you, too, Terry." Jonas started the engine, pressed forward on the throttle, then adjusted the mid-wings, aiming his vessel underwater.

The glider responded at once, nose diving beneath the waves. The seasickness immediately subsided, yielding to smooth sailing. Jonas noticed the sub felt much heavier, perhaps even sluggish compared with the lighter weight surface model he had test-piloted nine years ago. Still, the Abyss Glider was a Corvette compared to the tank-like design of the *Sea Cliff.*

Jonas followed the thick steel cable down another thirty feet before spotting D.J.'s sub. The radio crackled, the young pilot's voice filtering through.

"Age before beauty, Professor. You take the lead, I'm right behind you."

Walk in the park...

Jonas moved the starboard joystick forward, sending his ten-foot glider into a steep forty-five-degree descent.

D.J. followed him down, the steel recovery cable in tow, the two subs looping downward in a slow spiraling pattern.

Within minutes the blue of the Pacific faded to a deep shade of purple, followed by pitch blackness. Jonas checked his depth gauge: a mere 1,250 feet. He searched a pad of toggle switches on his right, located the exterior lights, and flicked them on.

A column of light illuminated a patch of sea below, scattering a school of fish. Descending into nothingness was disorienting, and Jonas wondered if he'd be better off just focusing on his LCD readout. He checked his depth gauge again: 2,352 feet.

Relax and breathe. This is a marathon, not a sprint, J.T. You've got a long way to go.

* * *

The UNIS command center was located in the *Kiku's* bridge, the horseshoe-shaped bank of monitors and sonar arrays uploading data from the two Abyss Gliders. Alphonse DeMarco was tracking the descent; Mac keeping vigil over the subs' propulsion and life support systems.

Frank Heller sat facing two computer screens linked to the pilots' bio-suits. Vital signs were displayed in real time, with heart rate, blood pressure, body temperature, and breathing patterns falling into either a green, yellow, or red zone.

D. J. Tanaka's reading were all well within the green zone.

Jonas Taylor's were fluctuating within the yellow.

Heller looked up as Terry entered the bridge. Masao's daughter was dressed in a sweat suit, her hair still wet from the releasing the gliders.

"How are they doing, Frank?"

"Your brother's as calm as a frozen lake. Taylor … not so good. If his vitals go red, I'm scrubbing the mission. If your father doesn't like it then he can fire me."

Terry smiled, patting him on the shoulder.

* * *

Jonas popped a yellow pill into his mouth, washing it down with a swig of bottled water.

DeMarco's voice rattled his ear drums. "Jonas, I need you to switch off your exterior light, you're wasting battery power. Nothing to see down there anyway."

Jonas gritted his teeth as he flipped back the toggle switch, casting his existence into darkness, save for the soft orange glow from his forward console. He took a deep breath, trying to focus on the nothingness before him.

In the distance he saw a flash of light, followed by a dozen more. Luminescent sparks twinkled all around him, blinking in and out of existence, the green, blue, and red flashbulbs of color disorienting to look at.

Jonas had entered the ocean's mid-water region, a habitat enshrouded in perpetual darkness. Known as the twilight zone, the creatures inhabiting this vast domain had adapted by evolving their own bioluminescent light.

A scarlet vampire squid was caught surfing in his bow-wake. Turning itself inside-out, it cast a false glowing turquoise eye upon the sub, attempting to scare it off. When this tactic failed, it expelled a cloud of bioluminescent mucus, executing a magician's vanishing getaway.

Remembering the night vision goggles, he pulled them out of their pouch and placed them on—instantly transforming the sea into an olive-green world. A thousand shadows became bulbous eyes and jaws that unhinged, and bizarre fish with bioluminescent bulbs that dangled before their open mouths like bait. They were everywhere—Viperfish and gulper eels, Fangtooths and Dragonfish and Anglerfish with teeth that would put a piranha to shame, the underwater universe twinkling with ten thousand points of light.

The deeper he descended, the more curious the fish became. Schools of hatchet fish flew past his nose cone, staring at him with freakish eyes, their narrow bodies blinking blue by means of light-producing photophores. The glider descended past harvests of bioluminescent jellyfish, their transparent bodies filtering red in his sub's emergency keel light.

"Abyssopelagic animals," Jonas whispered to himself, reciting the technical name for these unique groups of fish, squid, and prawns. He watched as a four-foot gulper eel hovered in front of him, surfing on the nose cone's wake. Deciding to attack the larger sub, the eel spun around and opened its mouth, hyperextending and unhinging its jaws, revealing vicious rows of needle-sharp teeth. Jonas tapped the acrylic and the eel darted away.

To his left, a deep-sea anglerfish circled, an eerie light appearing over its mouth. The species possessed a rod fin that lit up like a lightning bug's tail. Small fish would mistake the light for food and swim straight toward it, right into the angler's wide-open mouth.

Even in the cold, perpetual darkness of the sea, nature had found a way to adapt.

Jonas hadn't noticed the cold creeping in on him. He glanced at the sub's external temperature gauge: *Forty-two degrees.* He adjusted the thermostat to heat the interior capsule.

The blast of Guns 'N Roses' *Welcome to the Jungle* caused Jonas to nearly jump out of his harness. Tearing the headphones from his ears didn't help, the pounding heavy metal was turned up way too loud to be ignored.

The wave of panic happened without warning. It was a desperate, empty, frightening feeling—a feeling of being trapped … of being squeezed beneath six thousand feet of water in a crawl space barely wider than a coffin.

Sweat poured from Jonas's body. His breathing became erratic, and he found himself hyperventilating. He fumbled for another pill, only to drop it beneath the console.

* * *

"He's losing it," Frank Heller announced, pointing to Jonas Taylor's vital signs, all readings deep inside the red zone.

Mac rolled his chair away from his console to look at Frank's monitor. "What the hell happened?"

DeMarco grabbed the radio. "Taylor, what's wrong? Taylor, answer!"

Mac glanced at Terry, who was watching from behind the horseshoe, her back to a wall panel stacked with communications equipment. That's when he noticed the volume level lights jumping on one of the CD players.

* * *

Jonas couldn't breathe. His heart pounded so hard his chest hurt, his limbs shaking so badly he could no longer pilot the sub.

Welcome to the jungle, we take it day by day. If you want it you're going to bleed, but it's the price you pay...

The music abruptly stopped, his ears still buzzing.

A moment of terror passed during the silence that followed, and then another song played at half the volume over the headphones...

Pussycat, Pussycat, I've got flowers and lots of hours to spend with you.
So go and powder ... your cute little pussycat nose—.

Jonas smiled. The tightness in his chest disappeared.

What's new pussycat? Woah woah...
What's new pussycat? Woah a-woah woah.

Retrieving the discarded headphones, he placed them back over his ears to listen to the Tom Jones romp.

* * *

Frank Heller watched, dumbfounded, as Jonas's vital signs returned to the green zone. "Son of a bitch..."

Terry glanced back at Mac, who was standing next to the CD player, holding the *Guns 'N Roses* CD in one hand, wagging his index finger at her with the other.

* * *

Eighteen thousand feet...

Jonas had settled into a nice groove when D.J. interrupted his music over the ship-to-ship frequency. "Doc, how are you holding up?"

"No problems to speak of. How are you doing?"

"Okay, I guess. This damn cable's all tangled around the mechanical arm. Kind of like my telephone cord gets."

Jonas cut his speed, allowing D.J.'s glider to come up along his starboard side.

The cable was badly twisted into tight loops beneath his chassis.

"D.J., if it's a problem, we should head back—"

"I've got it under control. When we get to the bottom, I'll flip the arm around a few dozen times and ease some of the tension."

Jonas called up to DeMarco. "D.J.'s cable is twisting around the mechanical arm. Can you do anything topside to relieve some of the pressure?"

"Negative. D.J.'s got the problem under control. We'll monitor him. You concentrate on what you're doing. DeMarco out."

Jonas checked his depth gauge: 19,266 feet. They had been descending now for forty minutes, and were still only a little more than halfway to the bottom. He rubbed his eyes and then attempted to stretch his lower back within the tight leather hammock.

The Lexan pod creaked. The water pressure surrounding him was 9,117 pounds per square inch. Jonas felt the telltale signs of claustrophobia creeping in again, his skin tingling, his face flushing.

The feeling reminded the former Penn State All-Big Ten conference tight end of the time he had to submit to ninety minutes' worth of MRIs after suffering a concussion during his junior year in a game against Ohio State University. The massive machine had been situated only inches above his head like a sword of Damocles waiting to crush his skull.

Only the soft glow from the Abyss Glider's control panel gave him a sense of direction, keeping him sane.

His eyes moved over the interior of the capsule, damp with condensation.

Why am I here?

Long minutes passed. The depth gauge numbers continued to mount: 23,850 ... 28,400 ... 30,560 ... 31,200 ... He stared out into the blackness, his hands trembling from nerves and fatigue. 33,120 ... 34,000...

Jonas felt a slight trace of vertigo, which he hoped had more to do with the rich oxygen mixture in the submersible than with his medicine. His eyes moved from the inky water to the control panel readouts. The outside ocean temperature was a frigid thirty-six degrees.

D.J.'s voice shattered his thoughts. "Okay, Doc, turn on your exterior light, you should be able to see the hydrothermal plume."

Jonas complied, the light cannon piercing the darkness, illuminating a steaming, swirling, muddy layer of soot sixty feet below.

"Doc, here's where it gets a bit rough. Best way to get through is to accelerate into a sixty-degree angle and don't stop until you've passed on through to the Land of Oz."

Jonas accelerated into the maelstrom, his heart racing as the glider shook, the sweeping black current slamming him sideways in his harness as gravel rained upon his tiny craft. Fear washed over him as he prayed to his maker, begging for the ship's acrylic seals to maintain their integrity beneath the weight of the ocean's depths. He recalled the words of wisdom offered by U.S. Navy Lt. Donald Walsh during a lecture when he initially began training as a submersible pilot. The first man ever to venture into the Mariana Trench had a rather simple philosophy regarding the dangers of the depths—"if you're afraid it's a good sign, it means you're still alive."

And then he was through, his craft flying through the crystal clear bottom waters as if he had entered the eye of a hurricane.

Jonas adjusted his night vision glasses, awestruck by the view. Below was a petrified forest of black smokers—towering chimneys of hardened mineral deposits, their open vents spewing thick brownish black clouds of superheated mineralized water into the abyss. As he drew closer to the sea floor he could make out acres and acres of tubeworms, their stalks ghostly-white, their tips blood-red in his sub's heavenly light. There were thousands of giant albino clams lying around the vents, along with countless crustaceans, albino lobsters and crabs, all glowing in the darkness of the abyss, all completely blind.

Life. The amount and variety within the trenches had shocked scientists, who had incorrectly theorized that no life form could exist on the planet without sunlight. Jonas felt awed at being in the *Challenger Deep*. In the most desolate location on the planet, nature had found a way to allow life to not only exist, but to thrive.

A wave of anxiety washed over him with the thought.

What else is down here?

CHALLENGER DEEP

D.J.'S VOICE SNAPPED JONAS BACK to the reality of their mission. "Okay, Doc, I'm through. My glider has a tracking device that'll guide me to the UNIS, so follow me. It's gonna get very hot as we pass above those black smokers, so be careful. You catch a geyser of superheated water full on and it could melt the seals on your sub's chassis."

"Thanks for the warning." Jonas checked his digital temperature readout: seventy-one degrees Fahrenheit and still climbing as they descended toward the bottom. *How hot could it go? How much could the Abyss Glider handle?*

He followed D.J.'s submersible as it wove its way through the blackness, the trailing steel cable occasionally slapping against his nose cone. Water billowed up at them from below, heavy in sulfur, copper, iron, and other minerals that seeped out of the seabed's cracks.

Jonas maneuvered his sub between two of the smoking towers, his temperature gauge momentarily rocketed past 230 degrees. He veered hard to port, the maneuver causing him to graze his left wing against the side of another black smoker.

He chastised his carelessness, his mind teetering on the border of fear and panic. *Locate the damaged UNIS, help secure the tow line, and get the hell out of Dodge.*

A chill ran down his spine as he recalled one of the dead scientists using the same phrase on their last dive together.

The glider passed over massive clusters of tubeworms flowing like clumps of spaghetti in the warm currents. Twelve feet long, five inches thick, the Riftia were being fed on by eelpouts and other small fish.

D.J.'s sub slowed up ahead. Jonas backed off, careful to maintain a safe distance from the trailing cable.

"We're almost there, Doc. Steady on course one-five-zero."

163

Jonas followed D.J.'s sub along the 200-million-year-old sea floor, maneuvering just above a winding highway-sized gulley.

"Doc, I'm getting hit by strong currents, better hold on." As if on cue, Jonas felt his vessel's aft end wagging like a dog's tail. The submersible pitched, its engine fighting to maintain course and speed.

"There it is." D.J. announced.

The shell of the crushed UNIS was buried beneath a pile of mineral debris from the surrounding hydrothermal vents. D.J. positioned his sub above the remains, shining his spotlight over it like a streetlamp. "It's all yours, Doc."

Jonas moved closer to the UNIS, aiming his own spotlight at the robot's hull as he searched the area for a glimpse of something white. He circled the pile of debris—and there it was!

"D.J., I can't believe it, I located that tooth!" Jonas could barely contain his excitement. He extended his sub's mechanical arm, aiming the claw above the six-and-a-half inch triangular object, carefully lifting it from the pile of minerals.

Bringing it into his beacon of light, Jonas gazed at the precious object he had traveled seven miles beneath the Pacific Ocean to obtain.

D.J. laughed. "Doc, that's not a tooth, it's an arm from a dead albino starfish."

Terry, Frank Heller, and Alphonse DeMarco filled his headphones with laughter.

Jonas could feel his blood pressure rising. For a long moment, he seriously considered ramming his submersible into the nearest black smoker.

"I'm sorry for laughing, man," said D.J., "but you gotta admit, that was pretty funny. The thought of a killer starfish crushing the UNIS—"

"Enough already."

"Okay, okay. Hey, wanna laugh at my stupidity? Take a look

at my sub's mechanical arm."

Jonas looked over at D.J.'s sub. The steel cable had wound in a dozen chaotic loops around the six-foot mechanical limb, so much so that the arm was barely visible. "D.J., that's not funny. You've got a lot of untangling to do before you can free yourself to attach the line."

"I can handle it. You work on clearing that debris."

Jonas lowered his sub's mechanical arm, forcing himself to focus on the task at hand. He felt his blood boiling, beads of sweat dripping down his sides. Within minutes, he had managed to clear a third of the debris from the UNIS, exposing several intact eyebolts.

"Nice job, Doc." D.J. was slowly revolving the mechanical arm in tight counterclockwise circles. Gradually, the steel cable began freeing itself from around the extended appendage.

"You need some help?" asked Jonas.

"No, I'm fine. Stand by."

Jonas hovered the Abyss Glider twenty feet off the bottom. Masao had been right, all of them had. He had hallucinated, allowed his imagination to wander, violating a major rule of deep-sea exploration. One mistake, one simple loss of focus, had cost the lives of his crew and his reputation as a submersible pilot.

What was left for him now?

He thought about Maggie. She'll want a divorce, and who could blame her? Jonas was an embarrassment. She had turned to Bud Harris, his own friend, for love and support while Jonas had built his new career on a lie. His triumphant return to the *Challenger Deep* had merely served as a wake-up call. He had wasted seven years of his life chasing an aberration, destroying his marriage in the process.

A starfish, for Christ's sake ...

Blip.

The sound caught him off-guard. Jonas located his sonar. A

red dot had appeared on the abyssal terrain, the source of the disturbance approaching from the west.

Blip.

Blip, blip, blip …

Jonas felt his heart racing. Whatever it was, it was big.

"D.J., check your sonar."

"My sonar? Whoa … what the hell is that?"

"DeMarco?"

The engineer had stopped laughing. "We see it too. Has D.J. attached the cable yet?"

Jonas looked up, the cable nearly free from the other sub's mechanical arm. "Not yet. How big would you estimate this object to be?"

"Jonas, relax," Terry interjected. "We know what you're thinking. Heller says sonar's merely detecting a school of fish."

"Heller's a doctor, and not a very good one. Whatever this is, it's homing in on our location."

Jonas took several deep breaths, forcing himself to think. *Homing in … it is homing in … on our vibrations.*

"D.J., stop twisting."

"Jonas, I'm nearly—"

"Shut down everything, all systems."

"You're crazy. It's just a school of fish."

"Maybe it is. But if it's not, it'll be homing in on the vibrations and electrical impulses from our subs. Kill your power now, dammit."

Jonas powered off his sub, then flicked off his exterior lights.

D.J.'s heart raced. He stopped twisting the mechanical arm. "Al, Jonas just shut down. What should I do?"

"Taylor's crazy. Attach the cable and get the hell out of there."

"D.J. …" The words caught in his throat, "we have

166

company."

D.J. stared into the darkness with his night vision goggles. Something was out there, moving back and forth along the periphery like a caged tiger.

Jonas drew a quick breath as D.J.'s sub went dark. He kept one hand close to the power switch, the other by his exterior light, both extremities shaking.

In the silent depths half a football field away he saw the predator.

There was no doubt. He could see the conical snout, the thick triangular head, the crescent-moon tail. He estimated the Megalodon to be forty-five feet long and 40,000 pounds. Pure white … an albino ghost, just like the giant clams, just like the tubeworms.

From its lean torso, Jonas guessed the shark was a male.

D.J.'s voice whispered across the radio. "Okay, Doc, I swear to you, I'm a believer. So what's your plan?"

"Stay calm. It's sizing us up. It's not sure we're edible. No movements, we have to be careful not to trigger a response."

"Taylor, report." Heller's voice ripped through the capsule.

"Frank, shut up," whispered Jonas. "We're being watched."

"D.J.?" Terry's voice whispered over the radio.

D.J. didn't respond. He was mesmerized by the frightening creature before him, paralyzed with fear.

Jonas knew they had only one chance; somehow they had to make it past the hydrothermal plume and back into the frigid open waters. The Meg wouldn't follow; at least he prayed it wouldn't.

It was getting warm. The subs were drifting, the bottom currents pushing them toward a patch of vents. Dripping with sweat, Jonas watched as the monster broke off from its holding pattern to investigate.

"Doc?"

"Let it come closer. When I say, blast it with your exterior lights, then head for the plume."

"Okay, good."

Jonas watched the creature move closer, its massive head moving from side to side, its mouth agape—

"Now!"

Jonas and D.J. ignited their exterior lights, blasting 7,500 watts into the creature's sensitive nocturnal eyes.

The male whipped its head sideways, retreating back into the darkness.

The concussion wave from the Meg's swishing caudal fin struck a second later.

D.J.'s glider twisted and spun, the steel cable going taut, preventing the mini-sub from drifting farther. Spinning around in a tight one-eighty, the pilot accelerated into a near-vertical ascent.

Untethered, Jonas's glider was swept backwards into the side of a three-story-high black smoker, the impact crushing the sub's propeller shaft and knocking its pilot woozy.

Jonas felt warm liquid ooze down his forehead seconds before he slipped into unconsciousness.

THE FEMALE

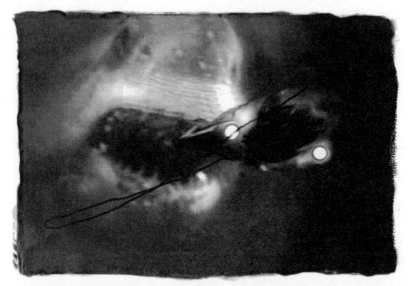

D.J. TANAKA ACCELERATED HIS Abyss Glider into a steep seventy-degree climb. He ignored the constant barrage of voices begging him to respond, choosing instead to focus on the race at hand. Blood pounded in his ears, but his hands were steady. He knew the stakes were high—life and death. The adrenaline junkie grinned.

He stole a quick glance over his left shoulder. The albino monster had banked sharply away from the sea floor and was now pursuing him like a guided missile. D.J. estimated he had a two-hundred-foot lead, the frigid waters still a good two to three thousand feet away.

It was going to be close.

His sonar beeped louder.

The depth gauge rose faster.

Sweat poured from his angular face. "Come on baby, climb!"

He saw the hydrothermal plume, the ceiling of soot swirling overhead like a maelstrom. The small glider burst through the minerals and debris, the current whipping him sideways as if he were caught by a tornado—and then he burst free into the frigid open waters.

D.J. looked back over his shoulder. The Megalodon was nowhere in sight. He checked his exterior temperature gauge. Thirty-two degrees.

Made it ...

The glow of the albino's hide in his light registered in D.J.'s vision a split second before the gargantuan mouth exploded sideways into the submersible. Spinning upside down, D.J. tried to scream, the sickening crunch of ceramic and Lexan popping in his ears as his skull imploded, splattering his brains across the shattering cockpit glass.

* * *

The Megalodon snorted the warm blood into its nostrils, its entire sensory system quivering in delight. It rammed its snout farther into the tight chamber, but was unable to reach the remains of D.J. Tanaka's upper torso.

Clutching its crippled prey within its jaws, the male descended back into the warm currents, guarding its kill.

* * *

Jonas Taylor opened his eyes. He was lying on his back, the glider upside-down. Seeing nothing, he fumbled around the inverted submersible until he located the night vision glasses.

One lens was cracked, the other intact. Through the olive-green world he saw tubeworms dancing around his Lexan bow like alabaster serpents. He attempted to move—stifled by a sharp pain that shot up his leg. His foot was caught on something. He worked it loose and turned his body. A warm liquid drained into his eye. He wiped it away, realizing it was blood.

How long have I been out?

Disoriented, he reached above his head and groped for the power switch, but nothing happened. He tried the radio … dead.

The enormity of his circumstances caused his body to convulse. He was trapped in a powerless sub, resting beneath 35,000 feet of water.

Then he remembered the Megalodon.

He saw something in the distance—a soft glow of light. The male was swimming slowly toward the sea floor, a dark object dangling between its upper jaw and snout.

"D.J. …" The crippled submersible was lodged in the predator's jaws, the light from the starboard mid-wing somehow still shining. He caught a glimpse of the steel tow line, the slack now looping and winding itself around the Megalodon's torso.

* * *

Frank Heller sat in his chair, staring at his monitors. "Taylor's bio signs just jumped. He's conscious again and his numbers are all in the red. I'm not getting any readings from D.J. Mackreides, what are you getting on the subs' diagnostics?"

"D.J.'s sub is running on emergency power, circling six hundred feet over the second glider, which is lying on the bottom, powerless."

Terry continued in vain to make radio contact. "D.J., can you hear me? Jonas, report."

DeMarco was speaking rapidly with Leon Barre over an internal phone line. The captain and his crew were stationed in the stern, manning the A-frame's massive winch.

"Frank, Leon says there's movement registering on the steel cable. D.J.'s sub is still attached."

Heller turned to Terry. "I'm guessing Taylor screwed up and got too close to a black smoker, frying his engine. Being the team player he is, D.J. refuses to leave him. But if he's on emergency power then we need to bring him up before his life support system shuts down."

171

"What are you suggesting?" Terry asked.

"We tow him up by the steel cable."

Mac spun around in his chair. "What about Jonas?"

"His primary batteries are intact. If he remembers how to engage the emergency pod, then he'll survive. If not, there's nothing we can do about it."

Terry looked to DeMarco, who nodded.

"Do it. Tow D.J. to the surface as fast as you can."

* * *

Jonas held his breath, watching as the male passed seventy feet directly overhead, its belly quivering as its jaws opened and closed. The ravenous predator continued to prod its snout into the remains of the submersible, but could not gain enough leverage to access the gushing meat wedged inside.

The creature's attention was focused on D.J.'s bloody remains, unaware that the cable was going taut, the slack being rapidly taken in from above.

Seconds later, the steel line bit into the monster's white hide, pinching back the shark's pectoral fins.

The cable's crushing embrace sent the male Megalodon into spasms. It spun its torso in a fit of rage, whipping its caudal fin to and fro in a futile attempt to free itself. The more it fought, the more entangled it became.

Jonas stared in helpless fascination as the Meg fought in vain, unable to release itself from the steel bonds. With its pectoral fins pinned to its side, it couldn't stabilize itself. Shaking its monstrous head from side to side, it released powerful concussion waves that rocked Jonas's sub.

After several minutes, the predator stopped thrashing, exhausted. Within the entanglement of steel cable, the only sign of life came from the occasional flutter of its gills. Slowly, the *Kiku's* winch began hauling the entrapped creature toward the frigid waters above.

The dying male thrashed again, its movements sending telltale signals of distress throughout the *Challenger Deep*.

Miles away, a much larger predator moved through the abyss, homing in on the vibrations.

* * *

The female had been stalking a school of squid when the vibrations had reached its lateral line. Instinctively, it knew it was the adult male—by its elevated heart beat and movements it appeared to be under duress.

Abandoning the squid, it went after its mate.

* * *

Jonas waited, lying in a puddle of his own sweat. The moment the Meg disappeared above the hydrothermal plume, he would activate the emergency release, causing small charges to detonate around the sub's chassis, separating his internal pod from the rest of his vessel. The buoyant Lexan egg would rise quickly, returning him to the surface in a few hours.

If he was lucky his air would not run out.

It appeared out of nowhere, sweeping directly over his inverted sub, its deathly glow illuminated by the emergency light situated along his keel.

The underside of a triangular snout appeared first, peppered with the dark pores of its ampullae of Lorenzini. The lower jaw was next, followed by the gill slits and the underside of the monster's massive pectoral fins, which revealed a nasty half-moon-shaped bite scar along the Megalodon's left limb—evidence of a violent act of reproduction. The distended stomach and the female's lacerated cloaca confirmed both the creature's sex and its unborn young.

The female was at least fifteen feet longer than its mate and possessed twice its girth, the monster weighing well over thirty tons. As she passed, a quick flurry from her caudal fin created a powerful concussion wave that sliced through the tubeworms and lifted the damaged sub off the sea floor.

Jonas braced himself as the AG II flipped twice before settling in a cloud of silt. He pressed his face to the nose cone and, as the muck settled, saw the female rise toward the male, which was still struggling to free itself from the steel cable.

The female circled warily, her nostrils inhaling the remnants of D.J.'s blood. Suddenly she turned, driving her hyperextended jaws around the soft underbelly of her former mate.

The colossal impact drove the smaller Megalodon fifty feet upward. Rows of six-inch serrated teeth ripped open the male's pale white hide, the female whipping its monstrous head from side to side until it tore away a seven hundred pound mouthful of flesh and muscle, exposing the mortally wounded male's stomach and intestines.

* * *

Terry ran out on deck in time to see her father's helicopter touch down on the helo-deck. She waited for him, then dragged him toward the A-frame.

From his daughter's expression Masao knew there was a problem.

"They made it to the UNIS when something appeared on sonar. We lost communication with both subs. D.J.'s bio-suit stopped working, but we know he was circling over Jonas's glider, which is lying powerless on the sea floor. D.J.'s primary batteries are out, but his mechanical arm is still attached to the cable; we're using it to tow him up to the surface."

Masao was about to ask about Jonas when Leon Barre pushed his way into the conversation. "She's coming up now. There's a lot of weight on the line; D.J. must have gotten entangled on something down there."

* * *

The *Kiku's* winch bit into the slack and dragged the dying male Megalodon toward the hydrothermal plume as its mate chewed and swallowed its flesh.

Jonas panted as he watched the spectacle through his cracked night vision glasses. The female refused to abandon her meal, circling her suddenly animated prey.

She struck again, the male reacting as if jolted by electricity. Burying her snout deep within the gushing wound, she gnashed and gorged upon succulent hot chunks of entrails.

The male's body spasmed as it rose through the hydrothermal plume. The female escorted it up, the hot blood of her mate bathing her in a soothing thick river of warmth as she rose out of the depths.

Free of the plume, she continued to feed, her murderous jaws entrenched deep within the wound, her teeth shredding the spleen and duodenum as hundreds of gallons of warm blood rushed into her open mouth and over her torso, insulating her from the cold.

* * *

Trapped in his sub, Jonas watched as the two creatures disappeared overhead. He waited several minutes, but the female did not return.

And yet Jonas refused to engage the emergency ascent. Huddled in the darkness, he waited while sixteen thousand pounds per square inch of pressure squeezed the sub's chassis, looking for a way in. He was beyond frightened, yet he knew he'd suffocate if he didn't act soon, his only shot at survival depended upon him jettisoning the sub's chassis and floating free in the Lexan escape pod.

But if he floated toward the surface, the movement would attract the female.

Suffocate or be eaten…

Jonas was drenched in sweat, beginning to feel dizzy again. He couldn't be sure if it was from loss of blood or the steadily diminishing supply of air. Waves of panic, accelerated by the claustrophobia, rattled his nerves. Seven miles of ocean sat on top of him! Seven miles!

Gotta breathe ... Gotta get outta here.

His fingers groped along the floor beneath his stomach, locating the small storage compartment. Leaning back, he pulled open the hatch, straining to reach the spare tank of air. He unscrewed a valve and released a steady stream into the pod.

Rolling over, Jonas strapped himself back into the shoulder harness. Suspended upside down, he felt along his right side until he found the metal latch box.

Gripping the emergency lever, he yanked back hard on the handle, his effort igniting a half dozen small charges that cracked open the Abyss Glider's engine mount, mid-wings, undercarriage and lights, releasing the Lexan egg.

The emergency pod rose horizontally, its terrified passenger fearful of whether he could make it through the swirling ceiling of soot ... and if he did, what would be waiting for him on the other side.

* * *

Masao held his daughter's hand. Mac, DeMarco, and Heller were close by, waiting at the stern rail as the winch strained to gather its submerged line. Every forty seconds or so the cable would suddenly appear to free itself of its burden, spinning wildly around the spool a dozen or more revolutions before re-catching its weight and slowing again.

Captain Barre stared at the iron O-ring that connected the pulley from the steel frame of the winch. It was straining under the weight of its load, threatening to snap apart at any moment.

* * *

Jonas heard the dull roar as the pod floated closer to the swirling silt-covered ceiling. The moment he entered the vortex he knew he was in trouble. The rapid current grabbed hold of the buoyant Lexan tube and whipped it around on its perpetual merry-go-round of gravel and soot and sulfuric gases.

Desperate, Jonas rolled the pod into an upright vertical position, managing to guide the vessel higher through the plume's dense layers until the torrent released its death grip.

He collapsed on his belly as the Lexan pod floated free, then searched the olive-green void using his night-vision glasses.

Nothing.

The internal temperature dropped quickly, plunging into the forties. It would be an hour or more before he reached the surface, and Jonas knew he had to concentrate on keeping warm. His clothes were soaked with perspiration. His teeth began to chatter.

Pulling himself into a fetal position, he closed his eyes and tried to remain calm.

* * *

The *Kiku's* crew stood by the stern guardrail, watching the steel cable emerge yard by yard from the heavy sea, waiting and hoping for D.J.'s submersible to peek out from under the swells.

Terry pressed her forehead to the cold rail and prayed.

Shouts caught her attention. She opened her eyes, crewmen pointing to the green surface waters as they began to bubble … gurgling with a bright pink froth.

Seconds later, the enormous head of an albino Great White shark broke the surface, the dead creature as large as a school bus.

Dangling from its horrible jaws, held fast by the cable was the remains of the mangled Abyss Glider.

Terry screamed; her father swooned.

Frank Heller dropped to his knees.

The creature kept rising, revealing its own ravaged lower torso. Steel cable held together hunks of partially eaten flesh, muscle, and internal organs. The behemoth had been gutted from its pectoral fins clear down to the base of its crescent-shaped caudal fin, its assailant even ravaging the male's twin claspers.

The shocked crew could only stare as the partially devoured monster was hauled out of the water and over the stern rail. As the forty-five foot shark struck the deck, the bloated, nearly unrecognizable remains of D.J. Tanaka poured out over the planks.

Mac caught Terry as she fainted.

* * *

The escape pod had been rising steadily in the darkness. Loss of blood and the bitter cold were pushing Jonas deeper into a state of shock. His shivering had ceased, yielding to a loss of feeling in his toes and fingers, and still he could see nothing but pitch-black water above his head.

Hang on, J.T. It's just a walk in the park ...

* * *

Ten foot swells had become twenty foot peaks, the approaching storm lifting the two motorized orange rafts onto its back before dropping them precariously into its next valley.

James Mackreides lowered his binoculars and scanned the seascape with his naked eye from the bow of the lead Zodiac. The high seas and blistering rain made it nearly impossible to see, let alone spot a three-foot red flag.

Mac's radio crackled to life. "You see anything, DeMarco?"

"Yeah, I can see the storm's getting worse. Your friend's dead, Mac, the bio-suit stopped transmitting his life signs thirty minutes ago. I feel for your loss, but we're risking a dozen lives in these seas looking for a corpse."

"He'll surface."

"Five minutes and I'm calling it."

"Are you close, Al?"

"Am I close to what?"

"Your balls. I was just wondering, because if you call this rescue mission before we find Jonas's escape pod I'll be introducing your boys to my Bowie knife and the three of you can sing soprano in the church choir this Christmas."

* * *

Terry Tanaka stood in the bow of the second Zodiac, her almond eyes searching the valley of waves ahead of her as another crewman wretched over the side. Until she found Taylor's escape pod there would be no grieving, no time for the pain gripping her heart. She had to locate the man whom she had ridiculed, and somehow she knew he was still alive.

"Wait—" Something had disappeared behind a swell … a flicker of color. She pointed off the starboard bow. "There! Head over there."

The red vinyl flag was just visible over the crest of an incoming wave. Terry guided them to the buoyant capsule. They could barely see Jonas's body through the fogged interior.

A team of divers jumped in as Mac's craft joined them. "Is he alive?"

Divers opened the rear hatch and reached in, grabbing Jonas by his legs. They hauled him out of the craft as it quickly filled with water and sank, disappearing beneath the waves.

One of the divers turned, signaling a thumbs-up.

AFTERMATH

FRANK HELLER COULDN'T FIGURE OUT how the news had spread so quickly.

It had taken less than three hours for the *Kiku* to reach the Aura Harbor naval base in Guam. Despite heavy winds and rain, two Japanese television crews and members of a local station were waiting for them on the dock, along with press reporters and photographers from the navy, the *Manila Times*, and the local *Guam Sentinel*. They surrounded Heller the moment he disembarked, bombarding him with questions about the giant shark suspended from the *Kiku's* A-frame, the dead pilot, and the surviving scientist who'd been airlifted ahead for medical treatment.

Heller read from a prepared statement. "The *Kiku* was on a humanitarian mission to repair damage to an earthquake early warning system deployed in the Mariana Trench. Two of our one-man submersibles were deployed to retrieve one of the array's damaged drones. During the course of this mission our subs were attacked by the creature you see before you. Jonas Taylor suffered a concussion and is being treated for hypothermia. The other pilot, D.J. Tanaka, son of oceanographer Masao Tanaka was killed."

"Dr. Heller, is this shark a Great White or a Megalodon?"

"I'm a medical doctor, not a marine biologist, but we suspect it's a Meg."

"Where will you take the shark?"

"It'll be stored in a refrigerated warehouse for examination. The remains will eventually be taken to the Tanaka Oceanographic Institute."

"What happened to the creature? Obviously, it was attacked."

"We're not certain at this point. The shark might have been ripped apart by the cable that entangled it, and drowned."

"It looks like it's been eaten," said a balding American with bushy eyebrows. "Is it possible another shark attacked this one?"

"It's possible, but—"

"Are you saying there are more of these monsters out there?"

"Did anyone see—?"

"Do you think—?"

Heller raised his hands. "One at a time." He nodded to an American reporter.

"Xavier Solis, Manila Times. Our readers will want to know if it's safe to go boating?"

Heller spoke confidently. "Let me put your fears to rest. If there are any more of these sharks in the Mariana Trench, six miles of near-freezing water stands between them and us. Apparently, it's kept them trapped down there for at least two million years. It'll probably keep 'em down there a few million more."

"Dr. Heller?"

Heller turned. David Adashek stood before him. "Isn't Professor Taylor a marine paleobiologist?"

Heller glanced furtively at the crowd. "Yes. He has done some work—"

"More than some work. His book justifies the existence of these Megalodon sharks in the deep-sea trenches. Was Tanaka's mission organized to test his theory? And if not, why would you risk—"

"We were salvaging a damaged drone designed to detect earthquakes. The Tanaka Institute has no interest in prehistoric sharks. Now if you don't mind, we've just lost a loved one, try to understand." Heller ignored the flurry of questions that followed him as he pushed through the crowd.

"Clear out, you vultures." Leon Barre's deep accented voice cut through the heavy weather as the captain supervised the transfer of the Megalodon carcass onto the dock. A four-story-high boom raised the creature off the stern deck, preparing to swing the netted remains over the pier and onto an awaiting flatbed truck.

A photographer pushed to the front and shouted, "Captain, could we get you in the shot for a little perspective?"

The big Filipino waved his arm at the crane operator, who stopped the boom. Momentum sent the Megalodon's head swaying to and fro, drenching the crowd with bloody seawater. Cameramen scrambled for an angle, but the carcass was so long it would not fit into the frame.

Leon Barre stood beside the giant head, the boat captain clearly unnerved to be so close to the mouth. He gazed inside the lower jaw line at the teeth, the front row standing upright, another five to six rows of replacement teeth folded neatly behind them, back into the gum line. Feeling his knees go weak, the burly sea captain backed away.

"Smile," someone shouted.

Barre turned, staring grimly ahead. "Just take the damn picture and let me be."

Aboard the Yacht: The *Magnate*

It was another gorgeous day in San Diego, the sky near cloudless, the temperature a balmy 78 degrees. San Diego's harbor was teeming with boaters, the catamarans racing beneath the Coronado Bay Bridge, the whale watchers moving farther out to sea, hoping to catch a close-up view of California's Gray Whales, twenty-five thousand of which were passing through San Diego's waters on their annual 7,000-mile migration from the Bering Sea to Baja California.

The ninety-seven-foot Abeking & Rasmusen super-yacht, *Magnate*, moved at a leisurely three knots, its course paralleling the

San Diego skyline. A sleek fortress of fiberglass and steel, she was white with pine-green trim, possessing a 25-foot beam and 9.5-foot draft. Her twin 1200 horsepower engines could drive her through choppy seas at an easy twenty knots, her lush interior making the ride a pleasure in any weather.

Bud Harris had purchased the yacht from the owner of a struggling Arena League football franchise. He had gutted the insides, redoing everything in polished teak and mahogany, the walls and cabinets in a deep cherry wood. The floors were blue sapphire marble, the bay windows tinted, running floor to ceiling in the master suite, which was complete with a small gymnasium, home entertainment center, and a Jacuzzi.

Maggie Taylor was lying topless in a padded lounge chair on the teakwood deck of the master suite's private sundeck, her oiled body glistening under the noon-day sun.

Bud watched her from his Jacuzzi, reading the *Los Angeles Times*. "You always said a tan looks good on camera."

Maggie shielded her eyes, squinting up at him. "This is for you, baby." She rolled over on her stomach to watch CNN on a wall-mounted television. "How about another drink? This is hard work."

"You got it." He climbed out of the tub, wrapped himself in a towel, and headed back inside the air-conditioned stateroom.

Crossing to the bar, he grabbed two glasses and a bottle of wine—

"Bud! Bud, get out here!"

Heart racing, he ran across the marble floor, nearly slipping. "What the hell, Maggie? I nearly broke my neck."

Maggie was clutching a towel to her breasts, staring openmouthed at the TV. "I don't believe it."

Bud hurried over, gazing at the Special News Report. "Jesus … is that thing real?"

The Megalodon's head and open jaws filled the screen, its

body dangling from a crane.

Bud turned up the sound:

"… experts believe could be *Carcharodon megalodon*, a giant prehistoric ancestor of the modern-day Great White. No one seems to know how the creature could have survived, but Dr. Taylor, who was injured in the capture, is an expert on these sharks and is expected to provide some answers. Taylor is recovering at the naval hospital in Guam …"

Bud lowered the volume. "Dr. Taylor? Maggie, you think they mean Jonas?"

"Who the hell else could they mean?" She rushed into the master suite, Bud shouting after her, "Hey? Where are you going?"

"I need to call my office." She grabbed her cell phone, dialing frantically. Her assistant answered. "It's Maggie. Any messages?"

"Mr. Henderson called twice, and I've got a dozen messages from media outlets looking for a quote. Something about your husband. Oh, and a David Adashek's been trying to reach you all morning."

"The rest can wait, give me Adashek's number."

Maggie scrawled the number on a cocktail napkin, hung up, then dialed the overseas operator to connect her to Guam. Several minutes later, the line was ringing.

"Adashek."

"David, what the hell is happening?"

"Maggie? I've been trying to reach you all night. Where are you?"

"Never mind that. I just saw the news report. Where did that shark come from? Where's Jonas? Has anyone spoken with him yet?"

"Slow down. Jonas is recovering in the Guam naval hospital. He's okay, but there's a guard posted at his door so no

184

one can speak with him. The Megalodon's for real. Looks like you were wrong about your husband."

Maggie felt ill.

"Maggie, you still there?"

"Shut up, I'm trying to think."

"Maggie, this could be the story of the decade. Jonas is a major player, you could still get to him before anyone else."

"That's true."

"Be sure to ask him about the other shark."

Maggie's heart skipped a beat. "What other shark?"

"The one that ate the one that killed the Tanaka kid. Everybody's talking about it, but the Tanaka Institute's people are refusing to comment. Jonas is the only one who knows what really happened down there. Maybe he'd talk to you?"

Maggie's mind raced. "Okay, okay, I'm coming to Guam. Now listen carefully: I want you to stay on the story. Try to find out what the authorities are going to do to locate this other shark."

"Maggie, they don't even know if it surfaced. The crew of the *Kiku* are claiming it never left the trench."

"Just stay on it, someone will talk. There's an extra grand in it for you if you can get me some inside dope about this second shark. I'll call you as soon as I land in Guam."

"You're the boss."

Maggie hung up.

Bud was standing next to her. "So?"

"Bud, I need your help. Who do you know in Guam?"

AURA NAVAL HOSPITAL, GUAM

The navy MP on duty outside Jonas's room at the Aura naval hospital rose to attention as Terry approached the door.

"Sorry, ma'am. No press allowed."

"I'm not with the press. My name's Terry Tanaka. I was

with—"

"Oh … excuse me." The MP stepped aside. "My apologies, ma'am. And … my condolences." He averted his eyes.

"Thank you." She knocked softly, then entered the private hospital room.

Jonas lay in bed, facing the window. A gauze bandage was wrapped around his forehead, an IV dripped into his left arm. He turned toward Terry as she entered, his face pale.

"Terry? I'm sorry."

She nodded. "How are you feeling?"

"Better. Just tired. Where's your father?"

"Making funeral arrangements. He'll be here in the morning."

Jonas turned toward the window, unsure of what to say. "This is my fault, I should have never—"

"You tried to warn us. We ridiculed you … especially me."

"I shouldn't have let D.J. go. I should have—"

"Stop it, Jonas," Terry snapped. "I can't deal with my own guilt, let alone yours. D.J. was an adult, and he certainly wasn't about to listen to you. He wanted to go, and so did I. We're all devastated … in shock. I don't know what's going to happen next. I can't think that far ahead—" Tears flowed from her almond eyes.

Moving to him, she sat on the edge of his bed, hugging him while she cried on his chest.

Jonas smoothed her hair, trying to comfort her.

After a few minutes, she sat up and turned away from Jonas to wipe her eyes. "You're seeing me in rare form. I never cry."

"You don't always have to be so tough."

She smiled. "Yeah, I do. I told you, my mom died when I was very young. I've had to take care of Dad and D.J. all these years by myself."

"How's your dad doing?"

"He's a wreck. I need to get him through this. JAMSTEC's not making that easy. The Japanese are flying in tomorrow morning, insisting on a meeting."

Jonas looked up at her. "Terry, you need to know something. There were two Megs in the trench. The one that the *Kiku* hauled up, it was attacked by a larger female. She was rising with the carcass ..."

"No, it's okay. Everyone on board was watching. Nothing else surfaced. Heller says the other creature, this female, couldn't survive the journey through the icy waters. You told us that yourself."

"Terry, listen to me." He tried to sit up, but the pain forced him down again. "The male's carcass ... there was a lot of blood in the water. Megalodons are like Great Whites. They're not warm-blooded like mammals, but they are warm-bodied."

"What's your point?"

"When the *Kiku* began hauling up D.J.'s sub, the male became caught in the steel cable. I saw the larger Meg, the female ... she was rising with the carcass, remaining within the warm-blood stream. I watched her disappear into the colder waters. I think the male's blood trail was keeping her warm."

"How do you know she didn't return to the trench?"

"I don't. But she wouldn't be so quick to abandon her kill. If the female remained within her dead mate's blood stream, she could have made it to the thermocline. She's much bigger than the male, sixty feet or more. A shark that size could probably cover the distance from the trench to the warmer surface waters—"

"Jonas, the second shark never surfaced, just the remains of the first ... and D.J." She wiped back tears. "I have to go. Try to get some rest."

She squeezed his hand, then left the room.

EVIDENCE

JONAS AWOKE WITH A START. He was in the Abyss Glider capsule, bobbing along the surface of the western Pacific. Sunlight glared through the Lexan Plexiglas sphere; waves washed over the escape pod's acrylic dome.

The *Kiku* was gone.

I've been dreaming. The rescue, the hospital…Terry—it was all a dream.

He stared at his hands, covered in dried blood. He felt the lump on his scalp.

How long have I been out? Hours? Days?

The water beneath him rippled with curtains of sunlight. He stared down into the deep blue sea, watching … waiting for the Megalodon to appear.

He knew she was down there.

He knew she was coming.

The white glow appeared first, then the snout and that demonic grin. The albino monster rose majestically beneath him, her sinister mouth widening, her jaws opening, revealing her pink upper gums as her front row of serrated teeth jutted forward, hyperextending … her widening mouth a black abyss—

* * *

"Ahhhh!"

Jonas awoke with a start. He was in bed, his hospital gown bathed in sweat. He was alone in his room. The digital clock read 12:06 a.m.

A dream? More like a nightmare.

He fell back on the damp sheets and stared at the moonlit ceiling, then forced a deep breath, exhaling slowly.

The fear was gone. Suddenly, he realized he felt better. The fever, the drugs … maybe it was the vindication. *I'm hungry*, he thought.

Wrapping a blanket over his shoulders, he gripped the I.V. drip's stand and wheeled it into the empty corridor. He found the MP at the nursing station flirting with one of the nurses.

"Mr. Taylor ... you're up."

"And I'm hungry. Where can I find something to eat?"

"Cafeteria's closed till six," the nurse said.

The MP fished through a brown paper bag. "I've got a sub ... a sandwich. You can have it."

Jonas stared at it, his mouth watering. "No, that's all right—"

"Go ahead. It's good stuff."

"All right, sure, thanks." Jonas took the Italian sub and began to eat. He felt like he hadn't tasted food in days. "This is great," he said between bites.

"Good subs are hard to come by out here," the young man said. "Only place I know is halfway around the island. Me and my buddies, we make the trip once a week, just to kind of remind us of home. I don't know why they don't open something closer to the base. Seems to me ..."

The kid continued talking, but Jonas wasn't listening. Something had caught his eye on the television. "Excuse me," he said. "Can you turn that up?"

The MP stopped talking. "Sure." He raised the volume.

"... fourteen pilot whales and two dozen dolphins beached themselves along Saipan's northern shore. Unfortunately, most of the mammals died before rescuers could push them back out to sea. In other news ..."

"Saipan. That's in the middle of the northern Marianas, isn't it?"

The MP nodded. "That's right, sir. Third island up the chain."

Jonas looked away, thinking. "Thanks for the sandwich."

He turned and headed back down the hall, wheeling his I.V.

Western Pacific
Eight Miles off the Coast of Saipan

The 455-foot cargo ship, *RMS St. Columba*, pushed through the dark waters of the western Pacific, her mass displacing 7800 tons. The vessel had set sail from the United Kingdom two months earlier, making her way to South Africa, the Ascensions, and the Canary and St. Helena Islands before continuing her voyage along the Asian coast. While most of her gross tonnage was devoted to cargo, she also carried seventy-nine passengers, the majority of them boarding in Japan, bound for the Hawaiian Islands.

Thirty-year-old Tehdi Badaut stood by the starboard rail, watching the moonlight dance across the surface of the Philippine Sea. The French-Portuguese officer had been assigned to oversee the transportation of six Arabian horses, caged in pairs in specially built stalls that were mounted in the forward deck. Two of the horses were studs, worth a small fortune, the others all national and Legion of Honor winners.

Tehdi approached the first stall, offering a carrot to a three-year-old black mare. He enjoyed caring for the animals, and the truth was, there were worse duties on board. "How's my lady tonight? Bet you wish you could run around this ship, huh? I'd love to take you out of that cage, but I can't."

The mare shook its head, agitated.

"What? Suddenly you don't like my carrots?"

The other horses started prancing in tight circles, rising up on their hindquarters. Within minutes they were all snorting and bucking, bashing their frames against their wooden stalls.

The officer pulled the radio from his back pocket. "It's Badaut, on the main deck, forward. Better send that horse trainer, something's wrong with the horses."

* * *

The female moved effortlessly through the thermocline, its torpedo-shaped body gliding with slow, snake-like movements perpetrated by the shark's powerful swimming muscles, which attached internally to her cartilaginous vertebral column and externally to her thick skin. As her flank muscles contracted, the Megalodon's crescent-moon-shaped tail pulled in a rhythmic, undulating motion, propelling the monster forward. The immense caudal fin gave the fish maximum thrust with minimal drag while maintaining a streamlined flow through the sea.

She was one of the last of her kind, and the first in more than 80,000 years to venture from the abyss. Hunger had driven her from her warm-water purgatory, and she had guarded her kill nearly to the surface, until the gray curtains of daylight had burned into her sensitive nocturnal eyes, forcing her retreat into the depths. She had remained two thousand feet below the surface in total darkness, her senses "seeing" everything. Her ampullae of Lorenzini knew the *Kiku* by the electrical impulses emanating from the ship's keel. The female had followed the ship to Guam, her primordial senses gradually becoming attuned to the magnetic variations in her new geography.

Although the Megalodon had no external ears, the female could "hear" sound waves as they struck sensory hair cells located in her inner ear. Carried by the auditory nerve, these signals not only alerted the predator to fluctuations within her environment, but allowed her to track the precise direction the disturbances were originating from.

Unlike the trench, there were disturbances everywhere. The female could feel deep, tantalizing heartbeats coming from distant pods of whales, and she could sense a cacophony of sounds created by the splashing of dozens of breaching dolphins. More alien acoustics and electrical fields teased her senses ... but she remained in the mid-water realm, waiting until the painful sunlight had diminished before rising once more.

Hitching a ride on an upwelling of cold, nutrient-rich water, the creature ascended, the oxygen-rich surface waters continuing to stimulate her hunger.

* * *

The horse trainer, a Floridian woman named Dawn Salone, watched helplessly as a half-Arabian pinto filly bashed its head against the wooden gate of its stable, the other horses following suit. "What the hell's spooking them? I've never seen anything like this."

"They're getting worse," said Tehdi. "Perhaps you should tranquilize them before they injure themselves. And those wooden gates ... they won't hold up too much longer."

The moon peeked out from behind a cloud formation, casting its glow upon the Pacific—

—illuminating a seven-foot-tall ghostly-white dorsal fin that had surfaced minutes earlier off the starboard beam.

The horses went into a frenzy, neighing and bucking, their coats lathered in sweat. A few of the taller stallions smashed their skulls against the fifteen-foot stable roofs.

Dawn had seen enough. "I'll get the tranquilizer gun, you stay with them." She headed aft, jogging along the starboard rail as she headed for the cargo ship's infrastructure.

Hitching a ride on the displacement current generated by the moving ship, the 62,000-pound shark continued gliding through a stream of surface refuse and human waste discharged by the steel vessel.

Detecting the vibrations of the panicking horses, the curious female did something her ancestors had once practiced while hunting close to shore—she raised her head above the surface and spy-hopped.

The Meg watched the moving landmass long enough to

determine she would not be feeding upon the giant. Descending once more, she headed inland toward the coastal waters off Saipan.

Saipan

The moon retreated behind a canopy of cirrus clouds. Small waves lapped along Saipan's deserted beaches. Somewhere at sea, a humpback moaned a distress call, the haunting cry blotted out by the thunder of the approaching airship.

The landing struts of the two-passenger Guimbal G2 Cabri helicopter bounced twice upon the dirt runway before settling down. The pilot glanced over at his lone passenger, who looked a bit shaken after the forty-five-minute flight.

"You okay, J.T.?"

"I'm fine, Mac."

"You don't look fine, you look pale."

"I'll be sure to work on my tan."

"Maybe you shouldn't have yanked out your own catheter."

"After the way you pulled out my I.V., I wasn't about to let you touch *that*."

Jonas took a deep breath as the chopper's rotor blades gradually slowed to a stop. They had landed on the perimeter of a makeshift airfield. A faded wooden sign read, "Welcome to Saipan."

"Okay, Mac, where's this fisherman friend of yours? I thought he was meeting us?"

"They usually keep the boats near the water. And he's not a friend; he's the brother-in-law of one of my former girls. So don't expect any favors; this is strictly a business transaction."

Jonas followed Mac down a path leading to the beach, the sounds of the crashing shoreline growing louder in the distance.

* * *

The last boat anchored in the shallows hardly looked seaworthy. Eighteen feet long, carrying a deep draft that left less than two feet of free board, the wooden vessel lay low in the water, its worn gray planks showing specks of red paint that dated back to the Korean War. Only one person was on board, a short, thick Filipino man in his mid-thirties, wearing a sweatshirt and jeans. He was busy repairing a crab trap when the two Americans appeared on the beach.

Mac waved.

The islander ignored him.

"John Paul, what's wrong, bro?"

"What's wrong? What's wrong is you still owe me money. Last time we do business you want three girls for those two congressmen from Texas, I get you three girls, you never pay me!"

"*Girls*, John Paul. You sent me livestock. The fat broad weighed more than me, and the older one had to be in her sixties—hell, she had no teeth."

"Ahh, forget you." The fisherman looked at Jonas. "You have money?"

"John Paul Chua, this is Jonas Taylor."

Jonas extended his hand.

John Paul ignored it, sniffing the night air. "Smell that? Dead whale, floating about two miles out. You want I take you there? Cost you one hundred American. Cash up front."

Mac shook his head. "Fifty, which is worth more than your whole damn boat."

"Eighty. You take it or leave it."

"Fine." Jonas turned to his friend. "Mac, pay the man."

"What? You don't have any money?"

"My wallet's back on the *Kiku*. Besides, you owe me twice that in bail money. Or did you forget our trip to Tijuana?"

"You remember that, huh?" Mac dug into his wallet, handing John Paul two twenty-dollar bills. "You'll get the rest if and when we make it back to the dock in one piece."

"Ahh."

Jonas and Mac climbed aboard, the boat rocking beneath their weight.

* * *

Jonas knew he needed some kind of evidence to prove the female had surfaced. The numerous whale and dolphin beachings weren't enough, but if John Paul Chua had really come across a dead whale and the female had killed it, then the oversized bite radius would be all the proof he needed.

The Filipino cut the engine as the dead whale's stench became overpowering. Handing Mac an oar, he had him paddle the last fifty yards.

"There she is, just like I said. Now give me the rest of my money."

Mac fished out another forty dollars, slapping the bills in the fisherman's hand. "I want a receipt."

"What you need a receipt for?"

"I'm sending it to your wife."

Jonas located a flashlight, using it to inspect the dead whale. It was a Humpback, a mature female, perhaps forty feet long. "Mac, there's blood pooling everywhere but I can't find the wound."

"Orcas like to attack the belly," John Paul said, counting his money.

Grabbing Mac's oar, Jonas used it to bob the carcass up and down in an attempt to flip it over, his effort causing the boat to teeter.

"Lose that oar, it cost you another twenty dollar."

"Easy, Crazy Eddie." Mac turned to Jonas. "There's thirty tons of whale there. You'll flip our boat before you roll that carcass."

"Agreed. John Paul, do you have a diving mask?"

"A diving mask? Jonas, are you crazy? What are you going to do? Stick your head underwater for a quick peek? With all that blood in the water, there must be a dozen sharks down there, waiting for a dumbass like you to join the buffet."

"Actually Mac, I haven't seen a single shark. Have you?"

Mac aimed his light at the water. "You're right."

Jonas stopped to think about that when something illuminated in Mac's flashlight beam. "Wait. Shine your light near that flipper, that's it, right there."

The beacon settled on a jagged object jammed into an exposed section of the whale's ribcage just above the waterline.

"Mac, I can't be sure but I think that's a tooth."

"Again with the tooth?"

"If it is a tooth and it's white that's all the proof I'll need. Can you bring us in closer?"

Taking the oar, Mac paddled on the starboard side of the boat.

Jonas reached out, feeling the rough edges of the root. "It's definitely a tooth, but its point is wedged tight inside the Humpback's ribcage. Mac, I need something to pry it out with."

"Who do I look like? *Mr. Goodwrench*?" Mac turned to the fisherman. "Where's your tools?"

"Ten dollars."

"Sonuva bitch…" Mac tossed him his last twenty. "I want change."

John Paul grinned, pointing to a storage bin.

Mac searched through the foul-smelling wooden box. Locating a hammer, he handed it to Jonas. "Don't drop it or Happy Harry here will be asking for the shirt off my back."

Jonas leaned out over the side, attempting to pry the tooth loose using the back end of the hammer.

Mac grabbed the oar, pressing the paddle to the blubber to keep the unstable boat close.

"Steady ... a little bit more—"

The six inch alabaster tooth pulled loose, flipping high into the air.

Jonas caught it—as a massive ivory-white snout, jaw, and upper row of teeth gracefully broke the surface along the far side of the whale's remains, the creature's lower jaw emerging right below Jonas as the submerged Megalodon clamped down upon the dead humpback's torso, dragging the entire carcass below.

Mac and Jonas stared at the surface, pie-eyed.

John Paul crossed himself, muttering in Hiligaynon.

Before they could speak, the dead humpback floated back to the surface, this time belly-side up, revealing a nine-foot-wide, three-foot-deep jagged crater-shaped wound.

John Paul's mouth hung open. "That no Orca bite ... that's a demon."

"Okey-dokey. Jonas, we good?"

Jonas felt his throat constrict. "Leaving now would be a really good thing."

John Paul gunned the engine. It flooded, coughing blue smoke as it died. Grabbing the hammer from Jonas, the Filipino tore off the outboard's hood and proceeded to whack the motor, the loud blows reverberating across the deck.

Jonas yelled, "John Paul ... no!"

A stark-white seven foot dorsal fin rose from the black sea, slowly circling the boat.

Mac shoved John Paul aside and hurriedly checked the spark plugs. He tried the engine again.

It spewed more smoke and died.

The dorsal fin changed course, the shark moving toward the boat to investigate.

* * *

The female had been so focused on feeding that it had not sensed the wooden craft. Detecting these new vibrations, the Meg nudged the boat's keel with its snout, jolting the craft with enough force to knock Jonas and Mac off their feet.

John Paul fell backwards over his crab trap and landed in the water.

Jonas grabbed the oar. "Start the engine, I'll help John Paul."

The fisherman surfaced.

Jonas extended the oar to the splashing Filipino—as the Meg's ghostly white head rose straight out of the sea, engulfing the man whole in one swift ascent.

Jonas staggered back.

Mac grabbed John Paul's hammer and started smashing it against the motor as he tried to turn it over—

Miraculously, the engine started.

Veering away from the carcass, Mac executed a tight one-hundred-and eighty degree turn that nearly tossed Jonas overboard.

Lights appeared in the distance, Saipan's shoreline beckoning two miles away.

Jonas sat down next to Mac, visibly shaken. "Christ, that poor bastard."

"Yeah. At least he died a wealthy man."

Jonas's eyes widened as he glanced over his friend's shoulder. "Mac, we have company."

A ten-foot-high wake was racing after the boat, an unseen luminous mass pushing it.

Mac zigged and zagged, but the wave continued closing the distance. "Okay, professor, I'm open to suggestions."

"She's homing in on our engine."

"No shit? You went to college for that?"

As they watched, the wake disappeared, the monster going deep.

"Thank God."

Jonas looked around. "No, Mac... this isn't good. She'll come up from below."

"How do you know that?"

"Don't you ever watch *Shark Week* on the Discovery Channel? It's what they do!"

Mac veered hard to port as they nearly sideswiped the first in a series of marker buoys, the boat's wake causing its bell to toll.

"Okay, Mac … radical idea time."

* * *

The female descended, her lateral line locked in on the engine's vibrations. Pumping her tail harder, the agitated predator suddenly ascended, her soulless gray-blue eyes rolling back an instant before—

Wa-boosh! The sea erupted as the Meg smashed straight up through the keel of John Paul's boat, splintering it into kindling.

Flopping sideways back into the sea, the female moved back and forth through the debris field, searching for prey. A chorus of dull *gongs* accompanied her thrashing caudal fin, the marker buoys' bells renting the night air—save for one.

Jonas and Mac hugged the nearest buoy, the two dripping wet men balancing precariously on either side of its steel frame. Jonas's right hand gripped the bell, silencing it.

Thirty feet below, the white glow passed beneath them, heading back out to sea to continue feasting on the Humpback.

OPTIONS

TERRY TANAKA ENTERED the Aura naval hospital and glanced at her watch—8:40 a.m. That gave her exactly twenty minutes to get Jonas to Commander McGovern's office, assuming he was in any condition to travel. She walked down the empty hallway, the navy MP no longer on duty.

Jonas's door was ajar.

Inside, a woman with platinum blond hair was ransacking a chest of drawers. The bed was empty. Jonas was gone.

"Can I help you?" Terry asked.

Maggie jumped. "I'm … I'm looking for my husband."

"You won't find him in a drawer. Wait … you're Maggie?"

Maggie's eyes narrowed. "That's right, I'm Mrs. Taylor. Who the hell are you?"

"Terry Tanaka."

Maggie eyed her up and down. "Well, well…"

"I'm a friend. My brother … he was the one who was killed. I stopped by to drive Dr. Taylor to the naval base."

Maggie's disposition changed. "Sorry … about your brother. Did you say naval base? What does the navy want with Jonas?"

"There's a hearing. Exactly what are you doing here?"

"My husband was nearly killed. Where else would I be but by his side?"

Terry frowned. "Not that it's any of my business, but—"

"—but you're right," said Maggie, "it's not your business. Anyway, since Jonas obviously isn't here, he must already be at the meeting, so maybe you can take me?"

* * *

The hearing at Guam's naval base took place in a refrigerated warehouse that had once been used to "hold" the

200

bodies of deceased soldiers awaiting transport back to the States. Under three sets of mobile surgical lights lay the remains of the male Megalodon. Two Japanese men, both scientists from JAMSTEC, were busy examining the enormous jaws of the ancient predator.

An MP greeted Terry and Maggie, handing each woman a lined coat as they entered the cooler.

A conference table and chairs had been set on the far side of the room. Frank Heller and Al DeMarco were consoling Masao, who wore dark sunglasses to obscure his red-rimmed eyes. Terry embraced her father, then introduced Maggie.

Commander Bryce McGovern, a silver-haired veteran of two wars, entered the warehouse, followed by an aide and a Frenchman in his late forties. "I'm Commander McGovern. This is Andre Dupont of the Cousteau Society."

"I'm Tanaka," Masao said. "My daughter, Terry."

The commander nodded. "Our condolences. We'll try to make this briefing as painless as possible. Mr. Tanaka, is everyone present?"

"Dr. Tsukamoto and Dr. Simidu have just arrived from the Japan Marine Science and Technology Center. But Jonas Taylor is not here. Apparently, he left the hospital late last night."

McGovern grimaced. "Our only real witness. Anyone know where Dr. Taylor went?"

Terry pointed to Maggie. "There's his wife. Ask her."

Maggie flashed a smile. "I'm sure Jonas will show up eventually. Studying these creatures was such a big part of our lives."

Terry rolled her eyes.

"Let's get started," said McGovern, taking his place at the head of the table. "If everyone can find seats ... including the two gentlemen by the shark." The commander waited. "The Mariana Trench is under United States jurisdiction. As such, the United

States Navy has assigned me to investigate the incident that occurred in the *Challenger Deep*. With all due respect to the bereaved, my rules are simple: I'm going to ask the questions and you people are going to provide me with the answers. First question," he pointed toward the Megalodon carcass, "would somebody please tell me what that thing is over there?"

Dr. Simidu, the younger of the two Japanese, replied. "Commander, JAMSTEC has examined the teeth of the creature and compared it with those of *Carcharodon carcharius,* the Great White shark, and its extinct prehistoric cousin, *Carcharodon megalodon.*" Simidu unfolded a towel, revealing one of the male Megalodon's teeth. "This is an upper tooth. As you can see, the tooth has a chevron, or scar, above the root, identifying it as a Megalodon. Its existence in the Mariana Trench is shocking, to say the least."

"Not to us, Dr. Simidu," replied Andre Dupont. "The disappearance of the Megalodon has always been a mystery, but the *HMS Challenger's* discovery in 1873 of several ten-thousand-year-old fossilized teeth dredged from the floor of the Mariana Trench made it clear that some members of the species may have survived."

McGovern paused, allowing his stenographer to catch up. "How many more of these creatures are down there, and is there a danger to the local island population?"

"There's no danger." All heads turned to Frank Heller. "Commander, the shark you see here attacked and killed the pilot of one of our deep-sea submersibles, then became entangled in our cable and was attacked by another one of its kind. These creatures have been trapped in a tropical layer at the bottom of the Mariana Trench for God knows how many millions of years. The only reason you even see this specimen before you is because we accidentally hauled it up to the surface."

"So you're telling me at least one more of these ... these

Megalodons exists, but it's trapped at the bottom of the trench."

"That's correct."

"You're wrong, Frank." Jonas entered from the rear door, followed by Mac, their clothing still damp. Jonas stopped as he laid eyes on his wife. "Maggie? What are you doing here?"

She looked up innocently. "I came as soon as I heard."

"Yeah, I'll bet you did."

"Dr. Taylor, I presume?" McGovern was losing patience.

"Yes, sir. And this is James Mackreides, a friend of mine."

McGovern's eyes blazed. "Yes, the captain and I know one another." He signaled to the MP. "Get these men some coats."

"There was a second shark, Commander, a female, much larger. She followed the male's blood trail out of the abyss. She's hunting in our surface waters as we speak."

Masao looked incredulous.

"It's true, Commander," said Mac, "and I've got the stained skivvies to prove it. Jonas, show him the tooth."

Jonas passed the tooth he had taken from the humpback whale's carcass to McGovern. The commander compared it to the tooth Dr. Simidu had handed him. The female's was an inch and a half larger than its deceased mate's.

Masao shook his head. "My God ... Jonas, how big was this second shark?"

"The tooth measures just over six inches. Figure ten feet of shark for every inch of tooth, so about sixty feet. But she's also a female, and female sharks are much bulkier than their male counterparts."

McGovern shook his head. "A predator that size in these coastal waters, it'll be a human smorgasbord."

Dr. Simidu objected, "Megalodon hunted whales, Commander, not humans."

Mac mumbled to Jonas, "And the occasional Filipino fisherman."

McGovern massaged his brow, clearly out of his element. "Dr. Taylor, since you seem to be the closest thing to an expert on these creatures and you were present in the trench, perhaps you can tell me how this monster managed to surface. Dr. Heller seems convinced these creatures were trapped below six miles of frigid water."

"They were. But the first Meg, the male, was bleeding badly. The second, this female, was ascending within its dense blood stream. As I tried to explain yesterday to Terry, if the Megalodons are like their cousins, the Great Whites, their blood temperatures will be about twelve degrees higher than the surrounding ocean water, or, in the case of the hydrothermal layer of the trench, about ninety-two degrees. The *Kiku* hauled the first Meg topside and the female followed her kill straight up to our warmer surface waters, protected by a river of hot blood streaming out of her mate."

Andre Dupont interrupted. "Dr. Taylor, you keep referring to this second shark as a female. How do you know for sure?"

"Because I saw her cloaca as she passed over my sub while I was in the trench. She's much larger than this first shark ... and she's pregnant."

Conversations broke out across the conference table.

Mac looked at Jonas. "How the hell do you know she's pregnant? Did you perform a gynecological exam while you were down there?"

McGovern banged his palm on the table for quiet. "What else do we need to know about this ... female?"

"Like its mate, it's an albino. This is a common genetic adaptation to its deep-water environment, where no light exists. Its eyes will be extremely sensitive to light. Consequently, it won't surface during the day." He turned to Terry. "That's why no one on board the *Kiku* saw her rise. She would have stayed deep enough to avoid the light. And now that the shark has adapted to our surface waters, I think she's going to be very aggressive."

"Why do you say that?" Dr. Tsukamoto spoke for the first time.

"The deep waters of the Mariana Trench are poorly oxygenated compared to our surface waters. The higher the oxygen content, the more efficiently the Megalodon's system will function. In its new, highly oxygenated environment, the creature will be able to process and generate greater outputs of energy. In order to accommodate these increases in energy, the Meg will have to consume greater quantities of food. And, I don't need to tell you, sufficient food sources are readily available."

McGovern's face darkened. "Our coastal populations could be attacked."

"No, Commander, these creatures are too large to venture into shallow water. So far, the female has only attacked whales—"

"And D.J." Heller reminded him.

"That was actually the male, which this female killed." Jonas retorted. "In my opinion, we shouldn't have been down there."

"And if this female eats a group of divers? Will you make the same excuse?"

"There's another concern," said Masao. "This female's presence could potentially affect one of the whale migrations along the Asian coast."

"Whale migrations?" McGovern looked perplexed.

"*Hai*. Whale migration patterns began millions of years ago. Some scientists theorize the mammals first migrated into colder polar waters not just to follow the food, but to escape Megalodon attacks. I'm not saying one creature could change the annual southern migration now occurring along the Asian coastline, but if this large female's presence led to whale beachings in Saipan, then technically there is the potential to create an alternative route. When you consider the amount of plankton, krill, and shrimp required to feed thousands of whales, then even a slight deviation could affect the species of fish that share the same diets as these mammals. The sudden competition for food could affect salmon and tuna runs, altering breeding patterns while playing havoc with the local fishing industry for years to come."

Dr. Simidu and Dr. Tsukamoto whispered to each other in Japanese.

Commander McGovern waited for quiet. "Let me be sure I'm understanding this situation correctly. Essentially, we have an aggressive sixty-foot version of a Great White shark on the loose, a pregnant female, no less, whose mere presence could indirectly affect the fishing industry of some coastal nation. Does that about sum it up?"

Masao nodded.

"So how do we deal with the situation?"

"Commander, why must you do anything?" Andre Dupont asked. "Since when does the United States Navy concern itself with the behavioral patterns of a fish?"

"And what if this 'fish' starts devouring small boats or scuba divers? What then, Mr. Dupont?"

"Dr. Taylor," said Dr. Tsukamoto, "if this creature's presence alters the migration patterns of whales along Japan's coast, our entire fishing industry could suffer a major setback. JAMSTEC therefore officially recommends that this creature be found and destroyed."

McGovern nodded. "I happen to agree. I don't think nature intended to release these monsters from the abyss. Despite Mr. Dupont's assurances, I can't take the chance that this ... female might venture into populated waters. And what if she has her pups along our coasts? Christ, we could be looking at dozens of these monsters in the next decade. What then?"

"There's no precedent for this," Dupont retorted. "At the very least, we're dealing with an endangered species on the brink of extinction, at the most, the scientific find of the century. You declare war on this shark, and everyone from PETA to the Cousteau Society will be picketing your naval base starting tomorrow."

Masao turned to Jonas. "In your opinion, in which direction will this Megalodon head?"

"Difficult to predict. She'll follow the food, that's for sure. Problem is, there are four distinct whale migration patterns heading south from the Arctic Circle as we speak. The Asian coastline is closest, but right now she's moving east. There are two major runs occurring off the coast of Hawaii, plus the big California-Baja migration that intersects with your whale lagoon. Of course, if she ended up there…"

"What is it, Taylor-san?"

"Maybe you don't have to kill her. Masao, how close to completion is the Tanaka Lagoon?"

"Two weeks, but JAMSTEC cut off our funding. Jonas, you're not thinking of capturing this creature?"

"Why not? The lagoon's certainly big enough to hold one Megalodon. You could study the creature while drawing huge crowds. Within a few months you'd be debt-free."

"Tanaka-san," Dr. Simidu asked, "is this option feasible?"

"Simidu-san, *hai*, it is possible, assuming we can locate this female."

Terry stood, Masao's daughter furious. "Father, what are you thinking? One of these monsters killed D.J. Our actions allowed this female to surface. We need to kill it before it hurts anyone else, or starts laying eggs, or having babies … or whatever the hell these things do to breed."

Masao turned to his daughter, removing his sunglasses. "Kill? Is that what I've taught you? Do you know what this creature is, Terry? It is not a monster, it is a work of nature, the culmination of four hundred million years of evolution. Killing this majestic animal is out of the question. Its capture, however, would bring great honor, great meaning to D.J.'s death. It is what your brother would want."

"It's not what I want!" Terry stood and headed for the exit, slamming the warehouse door behind her.

Maggie smiled. "Temperamental little thing, isn't she?"

The two representatives from JAMSTEC were talking rapidly in Japanese. When they were finished, Dr. Simidu turned to Masao. "Tanaka-san, I have the authority to release funding to your institute and will do so if you really believe you can capture this female."

Masao looked to Jonas. "Taylor-san?"

"The lagoon would have to be finished quickly, the *Kiku* refitted. If we could locate the creature, we could tranquilize it, then drag it in using nets and inflatable buoys."

"Inflatable buoys ..." Maggie was scribbling notes. "And why do you need them exactly?"

Jonas turned to his wife. "Unlike whales, sharks don't float. Being inherently heavier than seawater, if they stop swimming they'll sink. Once we tranquilize the female, she'll sink and drown unless we can keep water pumping through her gills."

Mac mumbled. "Oh, is that all."

"Tanaka-san," said Dr. Tsukamoto, "you have lost a son to these creatures. With respect, if you so desire to capture this female, we will agree to underwrite the project and allow you to complete the lagoon. Of course, assuming you are successful, JAMSTEC will expect full access to the captured Megalodon, as well as our agreed-upon financial share of the lagoon's tourism trade."

Masao paused, tears welling in his eyes. "I think D.J. would have wanted this. My son dedicated his life to the advancement of science. The last thing he would want is for us to destroy this unique specimen. Jonas, will you help us capture the Megalodon?"

"Of course he will," said Maggie, jumping in.

"Hold it gentlemen ... and lady," said Commander McGovern, rejoining the conversation. "Mr. Tanaka, just so we understand each other, the navy cannot support any of these efforts. My recommendation to my commanding officer will be to use gunboats to patrol the island shorelines. Should you manage to capture the shark first, so be it. Personally, I hope you're successful. Officially, however, the navy cannot recognize this course of action as being a viable option."

McGovern stood, signaling an end to the meeting.

STRATEGY

THE OFFICER'S GALLEY onboard the *Kiku* had been converted into a war room. On one wall Jonas had mounted a large map illustrating the global whale migration patterns. Red pins indicated the location of the whale carcass off the coast of Saipan and the whale and dolphin beaching. Although it was too early to establish a pattern, at first glance it appeared as if the Megalodon was heading east, away from the Philippine Sea and the Asian continent.

Next to the whale map hung a large diagram illustrating the external and internal anatomy of the Great White shark, along with a list of its sensory organs.

Maggie was onboard. Jonas's spouse had convinced her network to sponsor the expedition in exchange for complete access to the ship and crew. As chief correspondent, Maggie and her cameraman, Fred Barch, would film raw footage and crew interviews which they would then upload to her producer back in California. The segments would be edited down and broadcast on the evening news in San Diego and their affiliate stations.

It was a huge career break, but it required Maggie to keep up appearances with her soon-to-be-celebrity husband. When she showed up with her suitcase in his stateroom aboard the *Kiku*, fully expecting to bunk together, Jonas quickly set her straight. "You've been having an affair with Bud Harris; story at eleven!"

Maggie did not take this unexpected rejection well.

Then there was Terry. As if one angry woman on board wasn't enough, Jonas had to deal with Masao's daughter, who openly blamed him for having the audacity to suggest they capture the monster that had devoured her brother. Never mind the fact that it had actually been the male Megalodon which had killed D.J.; as Mac reminded Jonas, neither facts nor logic held any bearing on a woman, especially one in grief. For his part, Masao assured Jonas that Terry would eventually come around, but the anger in her eyes told him a different story.

Mac was quick to point out that angry women came in threes; the third being a sixty foot, seventy thousand pound female shark.

Capturing that angry lady was going to be a bitch.

* * *

Terry and Masao filed into the galley, taking seats opposite DeMarco and Mac. Maggie and her cameraman were situated in the back of the room. Frank Heller was the last to arrive.

Masao addressed the group, Maggie's cameraman filming everything. "As you know, I've appointed Jonas to head this expedition. If there's anyone in the room who has a problem with that, speak now." He glanced at his daughter and Frank, neither of whom made eye contact. "Jonas?"

Jonas stood. "Before I review my plan to capture the female, it's important everyone knows exactly what we're dealing with." He pointed to the anatomical chart. "Megalodon's no ordinary predator. It's intelligent, it can sense vibrations in the water miles away, and it can detect the electrical impulses of its preys' beating hearts. Its nostrils are directional, allowing it to target one particle of blood or urine in billions of particles of seawater—"

"Yes, we know all this," Terry said. "We'll all make sure we use the bathroom prior to hunting her down."

Jonas shot her a look, then walked to the back of the room to a pneumatic drill. Loosening its vise, he attached the female's tooth to the hammer end, then held up a square piece of 3-inch titanium from a UNIS robot. "Megalodon teeth are among the hardest substances ever created by nature. Each tooth is serrated, like a steak knife, designed to puncture whale bone."

Positioning the titanium plate beneath the tooth, Jonas

flipped on the drill's power switch. When the air pressure indicator pointed to green, he hit the ON switch.

The tooth instantly punctured the titanium plate, its tip protruding from the other side. He powered off the machine and returned to his seat.

"That was 10,000 pounds per square inch of pressure. The female's jaw probably exerts twice that force. Now imagine a mouth the size of a small bus filled with hundreds of these teeth—a jaw big enough to swallow our mini-sub whole."

In the back of the room, Maggie's eyes widened as an idea came to her. "Jonas, let's say we wanted to film her capture underwater."

Terry scoffed. "Are you suicidal or just stupid?"

"I'm talking to my husband, *sweetheart.*" She turned to Jonas, her cameraman filming the exchange. "How large would a shark cage have to be in order to prevent the Meg from swallowing it?"

Fred Barch stopped filming. "Hey, I'm not getting in any cage."

"A shark cage would be crushed," Jonas replied. "However a Lexan tube, say twelve feet in diameter and cylindrical, would be too large and slippery for the female to expand its jaws around."

"I'm still not getting in any tube," said the cameraman.

Maggie ignored him, jotting down notes.

"Let's talk about something more important," DeMarco said, pointing to the map. "How are you going to find one fish in all that ocean?"

Jonas nodded. "It's not going to be easy. We know she needs to feed … that her favorite prey will be whales. Her eyes are too sensitive to surface during the day, which means she'll do her hunting at night, attacking whales close to the surface. Mac's equipped the helicopter with a thermal imager and monitor, which will assist us in spotting both the Megalodon and the whale pods in the dark. I'll be riding shotgun, using a pair of night-vision binoculars. The Meg's hide is white, making her easier to locate, so that helps. It also helps that whale carcasses float. After a certain number of kills we should know how often she surfaces to feed and her average speed—variables that will allow us to anticipate where she'll surface."

"Then what?" Frank Heller asked.

"Then we tag her." Jonas held up a homing dart the size of a magic marker. "This transmitter dart fits into the barrel of a high-powered rifle. If we can inject the homing dart within twenty feet of the Megalodon's heart, we'll not only be able to track her, we should be able to monitor her pulse rate."

"What good will that do?" asked DeMarco.

"Once we tranquilize the Meg, the next step is to harpoon her. These are not whaling harpoons, they're hollow tubes with explosive back ends designed to inject a mixture of pentobarbital and ketamine into the shark's bloodstream. The pentobarbital will depress the Meg's cerebral oxygen consumption; the ketamine is more of a nonbarbiturate general anesthetic. The Meg's heart should slow significantly once the combination of drugs take effect, however there may be an initial reaction that we need to watch out for. That's why monitoring her heart rate is so important."

Mac looked up. "I'm a little fuzzy on the whole 'initial reaction' thing. Maybe you can elaborate?"

Jonas nodded. "The pentobarbital could cause some initial hyperactivity."

"What the hell does that mean?" asked DeMarco.

Mac slapped both palms on the table. "It means she's gonna be one mighty pissed off fish just before she goes into la-la land."

Masao stared at the whale migration map. "Jonas, once we tranquilize the creature, how will you bring it to the lagoon?"

"That's the tricky part. The harpoon gun will be positioned at the *Kiku's* stern. We'll use the steel cable that's wrapped around the big winch as its line. The harpoon won't remain fastened very long in the Meg's hide, so it's important that we get the harness around her as quickly as possible. The harness itself is basically a two-hundred-foot fishing net with inflatable buoys attached every twenty feet along its perimeter. Inflate the buoys and the net should level her out. As the *Kiku* tows the net, the forward momentum will channel seawater into her mouth, forcing her gills to breathe. After that, it's just a matter of towing her into the lagoon."

Terry looked skeptical. "And how do you propose we secure the net around a thirty-ton sleeping shark?"

"Once her heart rate slows, I'll enter the water in the shallow water version of the Abyss Glider and use the sub to align the net into position."

Terry looked at Jonas, incredulous. "You're going back in the water with that monster?

"I'll be fine. Remember, we'll be monitoring the Megalodon's heart rate and I'll be in constant communication with the *Kiku*. If the Meg begins to awaken, her pulse rate will increase rapidly as a warning. We can then inject her with more pentobarbital and ketamine. Believe me, I have no desire to play the hero. The Meg will be knocked out long before I enter the water in the glider."

Jonas looked over his team. "There's a sense of urgency here. The Coast Guard has been patrolling the area over the last few nights with no dead whales reported. Tonight will mark seventy-two hours since Mac and I located the whale carcass off the coast of Saipan. It's vital we locate another kill as soon as possible. The longer it takes, the wider the search perimeter grows. And let's not forget the Meg is pregnant, she's feeding for two … or maybe twenty-two, who knows how large a Megalodon litter is."

Masao nodded. "Better get some rest; it could be a long

night."

* * *

Seven hours later, Maggie stood at the stern rail with her cameraman. The sun was beginning its descent along the western horizon, the shadow of the two-story-high A-frame creeping across the main deck toward the bridge.

Jonas approached. "You said five o'clock. Let's get this over with. I still have a lot to do before we go on patrol."

The cameraman clipped a dime-size microphone to the lapel of Jonas's jumpsuit. He handed him the battery pack. "Slip that into your pocket, then count backwards from ten, I want to do a quick sound check."

Jonas counted while Maggie checked her hair again. The wind was wreaking havoc, despite having used a third of the contents of her can of hairspray.

The cameraman framed the shot, the setting sun to his back, washing Maggie and Jonas in its golden hue. "Looks great. Any time, Maggie."

Maggie smiled, pouring on the charm. "So Jonas? How does it feel to be vindicated after all these years?"

"It doesn't change anything."

"Of course it does. It changes the public's perception about Jonas Taylor."

"Meg or no Meg, two men died under my command. Their families have to live with that every day."

"It was an accident, Jonas. Life goes on." She gazed at the sunset. "So beautiful, isn't it? Reminds me a little of our honeymoon."

Jonas stared at her perfect profile. "What happened to us, Maggie?"

"Cut! This is an interview, Jonas, not a venue to air our dirty laundry."

"Then why the honeymoon remark? Are you attempting to manipulate the public's perception of our marriage?"

STEVE ALTEN

She looked at her cameraman. "Fred, give us a minute."

"Okay, but we're losing the light."

She waited until he walked out of earshot. "Jonas, we're so beyond this."

"Just answer the question."

"Okay, if you really need to know. The man I fell in love with was a cocky navy commander with an ambition that matched my own. You knew you were the best, and that turned me on."

"And after the accident?"

"The Jonas Taylor who surfaced from the Mariana Trench was bitter and angry. I came to realize you weren't the same man I fell in love with."

"Shit happens, Maggie. People change."

She touched his cheek, her eyes all business. "I don't. But listen, life goes on, right? I put up with a lot over these last seven years. You're in a position now to either help my career or destroy it, that's up to you. You want to hold onto your anger, then do it, but you're only hurting yourself. Me? I'm a survivor. Bitterness doesn't put food on the table or Emmys on my bookshelf, only hard work can do that."

Jonas nodded. "You're right. I have been angry ... it was me who pushed you away. At the same time you haven't exactly been the supportive wife."

"Agreed. We're both at fault and this marriage is over. So, do you want to finish the interview? Or would you rather burn our relationship to the ground?"

Jonas signaled the cameraman to return. "I'll give you what you want, Maggie, only don't play me. I know it was you who fed that reporter the story about my dives into the trench. Trust me, there are people in Washington who wouldn't be happy if that story grew legs."

She saw Terry Tanaka watching them from the starboard rail. Taking his hand, she held it as she whispered in his ear. "Okay, Jonas. We'll keep our relationship professional."

216

ATTACK

THE FULL MOON REFLECTED off the windshield of the helicopter, illuminating the interior of the small compartment. Jonas was up front in the passenger seat, using the night vision binoculars. Seated in back directly behind him was Terry, who was holding the high-powered rifle and a backpack full of transmitter darts. If they could locate the Megalodon, it would be Terry's job to tag it, allowing the *Kiku* to track it and move into range of the harpoon gun.

Maggie was seated next to Terry, holding the heavy video camera mounted on a steady-cam. The chopper only held four passengers, and she was not about to allow Fred Barch to hog her glory.

Situated between Jonas and Mac was a monitor wired by cable to an Agema Thermovision 1000 infrared imager. Mounted below the helicopter was a small gyrostabilized platform that held the thermal imager pod in place. The device was designed to detect objects in the water by the electromagnetic radiation the object emitted. The internal temperature of a warm body would appear on the monitor as a hot spot against the image of the cold sea. The warm-blooded whales were easily detected; the Megalodon's internal temperature would be slightly cooler.

For nearly five hours, Mac had flown his chopper along a thirty-mile perimeter of ocean, hovering two hundred feet above the black Pacific. They had located a dozen pods of whales without seeing a trace of the Megalodon, and the initial excitement Jonas had felt was quickly fading into boredom as he realized just how difficult their task was going to be.

"This is crazy, Jonas," Mac shouted over his headphone's mouthpiece. "It's worse than looking for a needle in a haystack."

"How are we set for fuel?"

"Another fifteen minutes and we'll have to turn back."

Jonas refocused his ITT Night Mariner Gen III binoculars on the Pacific. The bifocal night glasses penetrated the darkness by improving light amplification, turning the black sea a pale shade of gray.

In the back seat, Maggie had drifted off to sleep. Terry watched her as she quietly unzipped her backpack. From a hidden compartment she removed a 20 mm explosive bullet. Gently popping open the high-powered rifle, she swapped the lethal bullet for the tracking device.

Jonas spotted another pod of whales. "Mac, eleven o'clock. Looks like humpbacks. Let's follow them a while, then we'll turn back."

"You're the boss." Mac changed course to intercept the pod.

Jonas was growing worried. With each hour that passed, the search perimeter extended an additional ten miles. Soon there would simply be too much ocean to cover, even with their sophisticated tracking equipment.

Exhausted, the former submersible pilot felt himself becoming mesmerized by the moonlight dancing across the ocean, barely noticing the white blur streak across his peripheral vision. The moon had illuminated something below the surface. For a moment it had seemed to glow.

"See something, J.T.?"

"Huh? No … I don't know—maybe." He focused the night glasses on the whale pod, locating three spouts. "I can make out two bulls, a cow and her calf … no, make that two cows, five whales total. Get us on top of them, Mac."

The helicopter hovered above the pod, keeping pace as the whales changed direction, turning north.

Jonas searched the sea to the left and right of the fleeing mammals; his heart suddenly jumping in his chest, "There!"

Behind the pod, a white glow appeared, streaking beneath the surface like a giant luminescent torpedo.

Terry leaned forward, staring at the infrared imager's monitor. "What is it? Is it the Meg?"

"Affirmative."

"What's she doing?" Maggie asked, fixing the camera to her shoulder.

Jonas looked at Mac. "I think she's stalking the calf."

* * *

One hundred feet below the dark Pacific, a deadly game of cat and mouse was taking place. The humpbacks had detected the hunter's presence miles back, the mammals altering their course repeatedly to avoid a confrontation. As the albino predator closed to intercept, the two cows moved to surround the calf, the larger bulls taking positions at the front and rear of the pod.

The Megalodon slowed, circling to the right of her quarry, sizing up her prey while marking the position of the calf. Faster than the whales, the female darted in and out, testing the reaction time of the two bulls.

As the shark crossed in front of the lead male, the forty-ton bull broke from the group and made a run at her. Although the humpback whale possessed baleen instead of teeth, it was still quite dangerous, able to ram the female with its enormous head. The male humpback's charge was sudden, but the Meg was far too quick, accelerating away from the cetacean before circling back to taunt the bulls again.

* * *

"What do you see?"

Jonas was peering through the night glasses. "Looks like the lead bull is chasing the Megalodon away from the pod."

"Wait a minute, did you say the whale's chasing the Meg?" Maggie chuckled. "I thought this Megalodon of yours was supposed to be fearsome?"

"Sure, you can say that now," said Mac. "Try hanging from a buoy, you'll change your tune real fast."

Jonas turned to Terry. "You ready with that tracking dart?" She nodded.

* * *

Once more the pod altered its course, heading southeast in yet another attempt to evade the relentless hunter. The Megalodon compensated, selecting an alternative approach, this time targeting the massive bull guarding the rear. This angle presented a different problem for the shark, which instinctively feared the humpback's powerful fluke.

The Megalodon remained parallel with the bull, darting closer, pulling away, trying to entice it to leave the pod and attack. The female grew bolder with each foray, snapping at the humpback, once even biting at its enormous right pectoral fin.

The bull finally turned upon the Meg, chasing it from the rest of the pod. Only this time the female retreated to the rear, doubling the bull's distance from the safety of the pack.

As the male humpback turned to rejoin the others, the albino hunter circled back with a frightening burst of speed and launched her 62,000 pounds at the retreating humpback's exposed flank. Her upper jaw hypertended away from her skull, her teeth sinking deep into the whale's lower belly close to the base of its fluke, the Megalodon holding on, shaking her head like a pit-bull.

The bull spasmed, the pain paralyzing. Writhing in agony, its wild contortions only served to aid the Meg's serrated teeth, which sawed cleanly through the humpback's gushing grooves. An agonizing, high-pitched moan reverberated from the bleeding rorqual as the albino predator shook itself loose, gnashing upon a thousand pound mouthful of blubber.

* * *

"What the hell was that noise?" yelled Mac.

"I can't be sure," said Jonas, the night glasses pressed

against his eyes, "but I think the Meg just attacked one of the bulls."

"The pod's moving off."

"Forget the pod, Mac. Stay with the wounded bull."

* * *

Hot blood gushed from the gaping wound as the crippled humpback feebly attempted to propel itself forward with its massive lateral flippers.

The Megalodon circled below its struggling prey, allowing it to settle before launching its second attack—this one even more devastating than the first.

Seizing the baleen-fringed edges of the dying creature's mouth within its six-and-a-half inch fangs, the Meg ripped and tore apart an entire section of the humpback's throat, whipping its enormous head to and fro until a long strip of grooved hide and blubber peeled away from the mammal's belly like husk from a ripe ear of corn.

Helpless and in agony, the tortured humpback slapped its fluke repeatedly along the bloody surface as it wailed a death song of warning to its fleeing pod.

The Megalodon circled below the whale, waiting for it to die.

That's when the female's lateral line detected the heavy vibrations coming from the surface.

* * *

Maggie aimed her camera out her portside window. "Jonas, can you describe what's happening down there for my viewers?"

"Hard to tell, there's so much blood in the water. What's your thermal imager picking up, Mac?"

"Just a lake of hot blood. It's pooling along the surface so fast, it's camouflaging everything."

"Bring us in closer," Maggie yelled over her headphones.

Mac descended to fifty feet. "How's that?"

Maggie focused through her viewfinder. "I still don't see the Meg, just that damn whale."

Terry aimed the barrel of her rifle out the open section on the starboard side of the cockpit. She stood in her seat, looking down through the night scope. She could just make out the Megalodon's white hide, circling below the dying whale. Her finger slipped around the trigger. She took a breath ... *this is for you, D.J.*—

—as the blur suddenly disappeared. "Damn fish ... it just went deep again. Mac, we need to be lower."

Mac adjusted the airship's altitude, dropping another twenty feet.

Jonas's heart raced. "Something's not right. She wouldn't just go deep, not with her kill so close."

"Probably scared her off," said Maggie, shifting sides of the cramped backseat, dropping to one knee beneath Terry's gun. "Oh yeah, that's much better. God, look at that whale bleed. Now if only the guest of honor wasn't such a wimp."

Jonas felt sweat pouring down his face. "She has to sense the chopper's vibrations. I wonder if she perceives us as a threat? Mac, I've got a bad feeling about this. Take us higher."

"Higher? But I—"

"Dammit, Mac, higher—now!"

The sea exploded in a bloody froth as the Megalodon launched its girth out of the water at its challenger. The conical snout struck the helicopter's undercarriage, shattering the thermal imager, the midair collision sending the chopper caroming sideways.

Jonas's cockpit door popped open, his right foot losing its grip on the floorboard as the G-force of the copter's roll pushed him out, the seat belt all that was preventing him from falling into the gaping mouth.

Maggie and Terry wrestled for position, the blonde reporter attempting to keep her camera steady, the Asian beauty fighting to aim the rifle, her index finger inadvertently pulling the gun's trigger too soon.

The 20 mm shell just missed the Meg's left pectoral fin, exploding as it struck the surface below.

The cabin spun, Mac yelling, "Come on!" as he clutched his control stick with both hands, the ocean racing at him in his peripheral vision as he fought a thirty-degree down angle, the airship and albino monster falling toward the water at the same rate.

A thunderous wallop blasted a hole in the sea as the sixty thousand pound behemoth plunged sideways into the Pacific.

Mac felt his rotors catch air. He pulled the chopper out of its dive as a wall of water smashed into the open right side of the cockpit, drenching the cabin and its stunned occupants.

Maggie screamed, believing they had crash-landed—until she realized the helicopter was climbing.

Mac groaned with relief. "God-damn, Jonas, I think I just shit my pants."

Jonas fought to catch his breath. His limbs quivered, his voice abandoning him. After a good minute, he forced the words out of his parched throat. "She's ... she's a lot bigger than I thought."

Terry gritted her teeth, saying nothing.

Maggie stared at her. "What was that explosion?"

"I wouldn't know."

"Bullshit!"

Jonas reached back and grabbed Terry's backpack. A quick search revealed two more 20mm explosive shells. "Nice."

Mac wiped seawater from his fuel gauge. "We're low on fuel. I'll radio the *Kiku* to rendezvous. Hopefully we won't have to ditch."

The three passengers looked at him, the blood rushing from their faces.

Mac smiled to himself, not bothering to mention his reserve tank.

HAWAII

THE *KIKU* WAS BERTHED next to the *USS John Hancock*, the 563-foot Spruance class destroyer that had arrived in port earlier that morning. Under pressure from animal rights activists, Commander McGovern had personally arranged the docking space for Masao Tanaka's vessel, while he secretly recruited a makeshift crew to report to Pearl Harbor for a "special assignment."

These actions were precipitated by Maggie's helicopter footage of the Meg attack, which had aired nine days earlier on her network in San Diego and its NBC affiliates. The ratings were through the roof—unfortunately for the budding blonde media star, the first sighting had been the last.

A break had come four days earlier when a Coast Guard chopper spotted a Gray whale carcass floating thirty-seven miles west of the island of Oahu. The *Kiku* had spent the next seventy-two hours patrolling the area, but there were no other sightings or kills.

* * *

Captain Barre stood on the *Kiku's* stern deck, overseeing the installation of a harpoon gun behind the ship's massive A-frame. Jonas was with Mac, who was repairing a bad set of batteries on the Abyss Glider-I. The sub was a smaller, sleeker version of the deep-sea craft Jonas had piloted in the Mariana Trench. Designed for speed, the one-man vessel weighed a mere 462 pounds, with the majority of that weight located in the instrument panels in the Lexan nose cone.

"The AG-I was a prototype," Mac explained. "It was only designed for depths up to two thousand meters. This hull's made

225

of pure aluminum oxide, extremely sturdy, but positively buoyant. She can move faster, turn on a dime, and has enough thrust to leap ten feet straight out of the sea."

Jonas inspected a small tank anchored by the vessel's tail fin. "It would take a rocket to out-jump the Meg."

"Actually, it has one. That auxiliary tank you're looking at is filled with hydrogen. Look inside the nose cone; see that lockbox on the left side of the pilot's control console? Inside that box you'll find a lever. Turn it a half-click counterclockwise, then pull it toward you, and it'll ignite the fuel."

"How long of a burn?"

"Fifteen seconds, maybe twenty. Enough to free you if you ever got stuck in a fishing net or kelp forest where using the prop would just get you tangled worse. Once the sub's freed, she'll float topside, just like her deep water sister."

"Hey, Jonas—check this out." DeMarco was standing by the portside rail, pointing at two tugboats pushing an antiquated nuclear submarine into an empty berth. A dozen crewmen stood on the sub's deck, proudly standing by with ropes to tie the ship off.

Jonas stared at the insignia SSN-571 as if seeing a ghost. "Son of a bitch, that's the *Nautilus*. I thought they put her out to pasture in Groton?"

Mac nodded. "It's McGovern. He's in way over his head, fighting a losing publicity battle with the animal rights lovers. Bottom line: If you're ordered to kill a fish, kill it with a legend. The public loves the *Nautilus*. McGovern had her refit for one last sail into the sunset. His orders are to make sure your shark stays clear of the Hawaiian islands."

* * *

On September 30, 1954, the *Nautilus* became the United States Navy's first commissioned nuclear powered ship. The submarine would shatter all submerged speed and distance records and became the first vessel to travel beneath the ice floe to reach the geographic North Pole. After serving the navy for a quarter of a century, the famous submarine was eventually decommissioned, but only after having logged nearly a half million miles at sea.

As Jonas watched, two officers showed themselves in the sub's conning tower. "Holy shit. It's Danielson. Can you believe this?"

"My former CO? Yeah pal, I already knew. A friend stationed on Guam told me Danielson volunteered when he heard you were involved. In fact, it was his suggestion to McGovern to use that old tin can to go after the shark."

As the *Nautilus* passed the *Kiku*, United States Navy Captain (Ret.) Richard Danielson squinted in the sunlight, stealing a glance at Mac and the former deep-sea pilot.

"Hi, Dick, how's it hanging?" muttered Mac, a smile plastered on his face.

"He probably heard you."

"Danielson can kiss my big hairy ass. The guy not only destroyed your career, he locked you up in a loony bin for three months. He should be publicly apologizing to you, not leading a mission. This is strictly damage control."

"Somehow I don't think Danielson volunteered so he could apologize to me in person. Megalodon or not, the guy blames me for killing two men and tarnishing his record."

"J.T., no living person on this planet would have done any different than you if they had seen what we saw coming at us in that chopper. And I told that to Heller."

"What'd he say?"

"Heller's an asshole. If I had served with him in combat, he'd have been a casualty of friendly fire." Mac looked toward the stern. "When's that big net of yours due to arrive?"

"This afternoon."

"Good. Hey, you should've heard the old man ripping Terry a new one this morning. He wanted her put ashore and she flatly told him no. I think she feels bad about what happened."

"She's a hellcat."

"Speaking of which, what's going on with you and the old lady? I saw you two eating breakfast together."

"I don't know, Mac. I know she cheated on me but there's a part of me that still loves her."

"Yeah, and we know which part that is. Remember, this is the same woman who refused to visit you during your stay at the mental hospital. Let her go, move on. Let this prick Harris deal with her. Trust me, he'll be bankrupt within a year."

Jonas stared at the horizon, a line of storm clouds building in the distance. "Looks bad. What do you think?"

"No hunting by chopper tonight, I'd say."

Jonas nodded. "Hope the Meg agrees with you."

* * *

Frank Heller stood on the pier, watching two crewmen secure the submarine's thick white bow lines, carefully lining the slack up along the deck of the *Nautilus*. Moments later, Captain Richard Danielson emerged from the forward section of the hull. He waved at Heller, slapping the "571" painted in white along the black conning tower before heading down the gangway.

The two men embraced. "Well Frank, what do you think of my new command?"

Heller shook his head. "I'm just amazed this old barge still floats. Why the hell would McGovern assign a decommissioned sub to hunt down this shark?"

Danielson led him across the open gangway. "My idea. McGovern's in a tough position. The negative publicity's killing him. But the *Nautilus*, she's a different story. The public loves this old boat. She's like an aging war hero, going out with one last victory. McGovern went crazy for the idea."

"I don't like it. You have no concept of what you're dealing with, Richard."

"I read the reports. One tube in the water and this overgrown shark is fish food."

Frank was about to respond when he saw a tall officer exit the sub, a big smile planted on his face.

"Denny?"

"Hey, big brother." Chief Engineer Dennis Heller came bounding down the ramp and bear-hugged Frank.

"Denny, what in the hell are you doing aboard this rusty tin can?"

Dennis glanced at Danielson. "I'm due to retire this year. Turns out I'm thirty hours shy on active duty. I figured, why not serve them aboard the *Nautilus* with my first CO. Besides, shore leave in Honolulu beats the hell out of Bayonne, New Jersey."

"Sorry to disappoint you, Chief," interrupted Danielson, "but all shore leaves are cancelled until we fry this Megala … whatever Taylor calls it. By the way, Frank, I saw him on board your boat this afternoon. Honestly, I can't stomach the man."

"Turns out he was right. Why not just leave it alone."

"So he was right. His actions still killed two men. You and Shaffer were close, weren't you?"

"We went to the same high school, our families knew each other." Heller lowered his voice. "I should have never allowed you to talk me into pushing Taylor on that last dive."

"He was fine."

"He was exhausted, unfit to pilot that sub."

"Those geologists wanted one last dive. The Pentagon was calling the shots. You and I … we were just following orders."

"Whose orders were you following when you pushed for his dishonorable discharge? Face it, Richard, Jonas Taylor was the best deep-sea pilot in the navy and we made him a scapegoat to cover our asses."

"You're out of line, doctor." Danielson's neck was turning red.

"Whoa, Frank, Captain, take it easy." Dennis moved between them. "Come on, Frank, I'll take you out for a quick bite. Skip, I'll be back at sixteen-thirty hours."

Danielson stood in silence as the two men headed into town, the first drops of rain echoing against the outer steel casing of the antiquated nuclear submarine.

North Shore, Maui

The towering swells, rising into walls of water six to eight stories high, rolled on to the rocky beach, carrying quarter-size chunks of whale blubber and debris. None of that seemed to bother the thousands of onlookers who had braved rain, no parking, and a long hike down private back roads to witness the Jaws-Maui leg of the annual *Billabong XXL Global Big Wave contest*. Spectators lined the shore and surrounding cliffs. Professional photographers were strapped to the open doors of helicopters or the rails of boats bobbing and weaving just beyond the break. A constant flow of competitors were being towed out by brave friends on jet-skis while judges watched from their covered tents.

Pe'ahi, more commonly known as Jaws, was the biggest big wave surfing break in Maui. It takes a variety of conditions to form big waves, the two most important factors being the distance a swell travels over deep water and the effect created when it hits the shallows. Jaws-Maui possessed a uniquely shaped underwater ridge along with a dramatic depth change from one-hundred-and-twenty feet to just under thirty, the combination creating waves that rose into seven story giants. Because the waves are moving so fast, wave runners must tow the surfers into the path of these powerful swells, with rides lasting as long as thirty seconds ... and wipeouts sometimes fatal.

* * *

The big-name competitors had been at it all day, Laird Hamilton, Pete Cabrinha, Dave Kalama, and Buzzy Kerbox. Now, as the sun began to set, the youngsters moved in to try their luck.

Twenty-two-year-old Wade Maller had been cutting waves since he was twelve. He was joined by his younger brothers, Dylan, a defenseman on the University of New Hampshire ice hockey team, and Austin, a freshman at Florida State. The Maller boys had only recently begun training on the big waves, but with the *Billibong* finals in town the three brothers were more than game, especially with an audience of spectators and cameras present.

Dylan pulled on his black and purple wet suit while Wade and Austin studied the break. As he headed for the water with his board, the twenty year old circled around a group of girls he recognized from his early teen years living in South Florida. Kelsey Danielle caught his eye and gave him a quick wave, the knockout blonde jump-starting his heart. Confidence brimming, he caught up with his brothers—only to see they had been joined by another surfer.

Surfing is a spiritual release, with everyone watching out for one another, especially when it comes to riding the big waves. Michael Barnes was driven strictly by ego, which was why none of the big surfers on the circuit wanted anything to do with the gang banger, who was reputed to carry a small arsenal of weapons in his van.

Austin was on his wave runner, waiting in the shallows. Wade pulled Dylan aside. "Barnes is going to join us; just let it go."

Dylan was about to object when the muscular heavily-tattooed twenty-seven year old pushed his way into their conversation. "She's out of your league, faggot."

"Huh?"

"The blonde. Don't even bother." Barnes ran through the surf and paddled out to hitch a ride on Austin's tow rig.

"Asshole." For a moment Dylan debated whether to leave. The skies were darkening, the crowd beginning to thin. He saw Austin waving them out and knew Kelsey was watching ...

Wade put his arm around his younger brother's shoulder. "Forget him. Let's just get one good ride."

Bellying up on his board, Wade dove into the surf, Dylan paddling behind him.

Minutes later, the three surfers and their Jet Ski tow were waiting beyond the breakpoint for the next incoming set. They were a good half-mile out, in water more than one hundred feet deep.

* * *

The female moved lazily along the sea floor, digesting the remains of her last meal. Nestled within her swollen oviduct were live young, each six to seven feet long, weighing upwards of five hundred pounds.

Almost sixteen months had passed since the violent act of copulation that had impregnated the female. As embryos, her unborn offspring had been sheathed in a protective, transparent capsule, nourished by an external placenta-like yolk sac attached to their gut. Over time these capsules had ruptured, exposing the developing Megalodon sharks to a womb whose liquid world was far different from the chemistry of the ocean. As the day of their birth rapidly approached, their mother's uterus steadily regulated their ion-water balance, preparing the unborn young for their emergence into the sea.

For all its life-giving chemicals, the depths of the *Challenger Deep* were not equipped to sustain a large colony of apex predators, so it was left to nature to balance the scales and thin the herd. Undernourished, the unborn Megs at first subsisted on ovulated, unfertilized eggs. But as they grew larger, the pups instinctively turned to cannibalism, the larger infants feeding upon their smaller, less fortunate siblings.

What had begun as a brood of seventeen was now down to three.

For the big female, inhabiting the abyss meant longer gestation periods than her surface-breeding ancestors had to endure, her internal anatomy delaying contractions until her pups could achieve greater size. This evolutionary feature, designed to increase the pups' rate of survival in the wild, was taking a toll on their mother, forcing the female to expend greater amounts of energy during these final weeks of pregnancy.

Expending more energy meant an increase in feeding.

Since leaving her abyssal habitat, the female had stalked more than a dozen different whale pods. Most of these earlier attempts had failed, but the Meg was learning, having succeeded in her last three tries.

Failure or not, the whale pods around Hawaii were spooked by the hunter's presence. Haunting warning calls from humpbacks and gray whales reverberated through miles of ocean. Almost as one, the pods began altering their migratory course, skirting west away from the island chain. By morning of the third day, very few whales could be found in Hawaiian waters.

The Megalodon sensed the departure of its prey, but did not give chase. Gliding through the thermocline, the boundary between sun-warmed waters and the ocean depths, it headed toward the shallows, its senses enticed by a strange new stimulus.

* * *

The three Maller brothers and Michael Barnes waited impatiently for their first set of waves to arrive. The sun was going down, the air had turned chilly, and they were losing their audience as the weather began gusting.

Austin was the first to register the arriving swells. "Here we go. Wade and Barnes are first up; Dylan I'll be back for you in three minutes."

The wave runner took off with the two surfers in tow, leaving Dylan behind.

The first wave struck the underwater ridge, channeling its force vertically into a majestic deep blue mountain of water five-and-a-half stories high. Wade was on the inside as the fifty-four foot crest broke from right to left. He was in a zone, a mind space where his only focus remained at the front of his board and a hundred feet down the line. Rooted within this tunnel vision, he never saw what was happening behind him.

Barnes had just made his turn, pulling into the wave's tube for what he knew would be an "insane" ride. For a quick second, he stole a glance toward the beach, hoping to see the blonde—his peripheral vision catching a bizarre wall of white water emerging on his right.

Never seeing the creature break through the wave, Michael Barnes surfed right into the Megalodon's open mouth!

The gangbanger was slingshot into darkness, smashing headfirst into an arching wall of cartilage. He bounced across an undulating tongue as rows of serrated white teeth gnashed his surfboard and tossed him about, spraying him with fiberglass splinters.

Disoriented, unable to catch a second to reason, Barnes was convinced he was underwater, being pummeled by the wave's fury, the lacerations now flailing at his wet suit and skin caused by the sharp ridges of coral along the bottom.

He attempted to swim against the current to reach the surface as the Meg's opening and closing jaws searched for his flesh, its hideous tongue pushing him towards chomping rows of teeth … and suddenly, he knew!

Michael Barnes heard himself scream — as his existence was crushed into scarlet oblivion.

* * *

Austin Maller circled on his wave runner, searching for Barnes. As the roar of the breaking wave passed, he heard shouts coming from the beach, the crowd waving frantically—pointing.

Turning, he saw the white dorsal fin—as tall as a small sailboat. Gunning the engine, he raced after Wade.

* * *

Her appetite primed, the female circled the kill zone, gnashing her teeth as she swam. Beneath her thick skin along either flank was a thin canal that contained sensory cells called neuromasts. Mucus contained in the lower half of these two canals transmitted vibrations from the seawater to these sensitive cells, giving the predator a spectacular "vision" of her surroundings through echolocation.

Somewhere close was more prey, and her senses were isolating it.

* * *

Dylan Maller shivered from the cold, waiting for Austin to

come back out and get him. The swells were pushing him closer to the breakpoint, but were still moving too fast to catch.

What's taking him so long?

Something struck his leg, causing him to look down.

"What the hell?" Small bits of bloody flesh clung to his surfboard. He felt vomit rising in his throat and swallowed hard to keep it down.

Then he spotted the dorsal fin. It was impossibly tall and pure white … gliding straight for him. Dylan pulled his legs onto his surfboard and froze, willing his muscles and nerves to be still, Looking down, he saw his board was quivering in the water.

The Megalodon rose to the surface, the sheer mass of its moving girth creating a current that towed the surfboard and its hijacked passenger out to sea. Beyond the dorsal, the upper section of a half-moon-shaped tail lashed back and forth along the surface. Stretching higher than Dylan's head, it swatted past his face, missing him by mere inches.

Dylan felt something lifting him. His heart fluttered, anticipating the bloody mouth and rows of fangs. But the shark was still swimming away from him; the pressure had been caused by a swell. The next waves were coming in, fast and furious, and he needed to catch one.

He turned around, the monster already a good sixty feet behind him.

Go!

Dylan rolled onto his stomach and paddled, stroking as fast as he could, his pounding heart threatening to explode from his chest.

The Megalodon turned, zeroing in on these new vibrations. The female's peppered white snout broke the surface thirty feet behind him, snorting sea like a Brahma bull.

Dylan slammed the left side of his face against the board, simultaneously gripping the outer edges with his ankles as he plunged his arms into the water, double-stroking furiously. He screamed as he registered the monster's nostrils along the soles of his bare feet, and then he fell over the edge of a cliff.

Plunging down the rolling mountain of water, Dylan somehow managed to remember to pop up at the last moment on his exhausted legs, feet wide, crouching low. He reached back with his right hand, the sixty-six-foot wave roaring at him like a tornado, its whitewater crest twenty feet above his head, threatening to bury him beneath the sea floor.

Dylan cut hard to his right as the Megalodon burst through the wave, missing him by two board lengths, its forward momentum sending it momentarily airborne. The surfer stole a quick glance then dug in, looping over the monster's head as the crashing wave consumed the beast and spit Dylan out its pipeline.

Refusing to be tossed, the trembling youth rode the dying wave another fifty yards. The ride was over, the shoreline a good seventy yards away.

The dorsal fin surfaced, the shark searching for him.

He heard the outboard and turned to see his Austin on the jet-ski, older brother Wade waving frantically, instructing him to get ready to jump.

Austin never slowed. With the monstrous shark less than twenty feet behind Dylan, he cut across its path, racing past his brother, who leaped onto the wave runner's tow rig—Wade grabbing him before he could roll over the side.

The jet-ski shot through the shallows and straight onto the beach, the delirious crowd chanting, "Dylan, Dylan, Dylan …"

Austin leaped off the wave runner and joined Wade, who was hugging Dylan, slapping him on the back as the crowd swelled—parted by an official from the *Billabong XXL Global Big Wave Contest* who presented him with a trophy, congratulating him on the ride of the day.

Dylan was exhausted, shaking with fear, the burst of

adrenaline nearly forcing him to puke. He caught himself as Kelsey appeared, a huge smile stretched across her face, tears in her blue eyes as she hugged him.

"Are you okay?" she asked. "You scared the hell out of me."

Dylan cleared his throat and took a breath. "Yeah…it's cool." Then, seeing his opening, he flashed a crooked smile. "So Kelce, you doing anything tonight?"

BATTLE AT SEA

THE COAST GUARD HELICOPTER hovered two hundred feet above the breaking swells. Spotting the predator's alabaster hide, the airship followed the female as she headed out to sea, radioing her position to the naval base at Pearl Harbor.

Within minutes, both the *Nautilus* and the *Kiku* had put to sea, racing north past Mamala Bay. By the time the *Kiku* reached Kaena Point, the incoming storm had reached gale-force proportions, the raging night fully upon them.

Jonas was in the bridge when the door leading to the outer stairwell was wrenched open against the howling wind and Mac slipped into the dry compartment, dressed in a yellow slicker. He slammed the hatch closed behind him.

"Copter's secured. So's the net and harpoon gun. We're in for a rough one."

"This may be our only chance. If we don't tag the female before she heads into open water, we may lose her for good."

They joined Masao, who was standing over a crewman seated at the sonar console. He looked grim. "The Coast Guard broke off its pursuit because of the weather." Masao turned to the crewman. "Anything on sonar yet, Nash?"

Without looking up, the technician shook his head. "Just the *Nautilus*."

Everyone grabbed a console as a twenty-foot swell lifted and tossed the research vessel from one side to the other.

Captain Barre stood at the helm, his sea legs giving naturally with the roll of his vessel. "Hope nobody had a big dinner. This storm's gonna be a bitch."

* * *

Life on board the world's first nuclear-powered submarine was relatively calm as the ship entered Waimea Bay one hundred

239

feet below the raging storm. Though refitted several times during its life span, the sub still possessed a single nuclear reactor that created the superheated steam necessary to power its twin turbines and two shafts. It was an antiquated system, far from battle-ready.

Commander Danielson, too, felt far from battle-ready, but the semi-retired naval man was more than game. "Anything on the sonar, Ensign Raby?"

The sonar man was listening with his headphones while watching his console. The screen was designed to give a visual representation of the difference between the background noise and a particular bearing. Any object within range would appear as a light line against the green background. Because they were searching for a biologic, sonar was actively pinging the area every three minutes, Raby looking for return signals. "Lots of surface interference from the storm. Nothing else yet, sir."

"Very well, keep me informed. Chief of the Watch, what's our weapons status?"

Chief Engineer Dennis Heller, six years younger than his brother Frank, yet still one of the oldest members of the sub's makeshift crew, looked up from his console. "Two Mark 48 AD-CAP torpedoes ready to fire on your command, sir. Torpedoes set for close range, as per your orders. A bit tight, if you don't mind my saying, sir."

"Has to be, Chief. When sonar locates this monster, we'll need to be as close as possible to ensure an accurate solution."

"Captain Danielson!" The radioman leaned back from his console. "Sir, I'm receiving a distress call from a Japanese surface vessel. Hard to make out, but it sounds as if they're being attacked."

"Navigator, plot an intercept course, ten degrees up on the fair-weather planes. If this is our friend, I want to kill it and be back at Pearl in time for last call at Grady's."

* * *

The Japanese ship rolled with the massive swells, rain, sea, and wind pelting her crew mercilessly. For two days the storm front had chased the ship east, bringing it into Hawaiian waters. The captain had no desire to be this far from home, but his ship was riding low in the water and he couldn't risk his crew … or their valuable cargo.

The vessel was a whaler, its hold dangerously overloaded with its illegal catch—the carcasses of eighteen Gray whales. Two more had been lashed to the port side of the ship with a cargo net.

A pair of lookouts held on to the main mast, disoriented by weather and darkness. The two sailors had been assigned the hazardous duty of making sure the valuable whale blubber remained firmly secured during the storm. Unfortunately for the exhausted men, their searchlight hardly penetrated the maelstrom. Sporadic flashes of lightning afforded them their only real vision of their precious cargo.

Flash. The ocean dropped from view as the ship rolled to starboard, the cargo net groaning with its keep. The sailors hung on as the poorly ballasted vessel rolled back to port.

Flash. The sea threatened to suck them under, the net momentarily disappearing beneath the waves.

Flash. The vessel rolled again to starboard, the net reappearing. The men gasped—a massive white triangular head had risen from the sea with the cargo!

Darkness returned as the whaler rolled back to port, its lookouts blind in the storm. Silent seconds passed before a fork of lightning lit the sky and the horrible head reappeared, its mouth bristling razor-sharp teeth.

The crewmen screamed, but the storm muted the sound. The senior mate signaled to the other that he would find the captain.

Flash. The unimaginably large jaws were tearing at the

241

carcass now, the head leaning sideways against the rolling vessel, its teeth gnashing at the whale blubber.

The ship rolled to starboard once more. The senior mate struggled to make it below deck, squeezing his eyes shut against the gale while holding tight to the rope ladder. He could lower himself only a rung at a time as the vessel ship back to port ... and kept rolling!

He opened his eyes, his stomach churning as the sea kept coming, an immense force pulling the ship onto its side and into the water.

* * *

"Captain, the whaler is two hundred yards ahead."

"Thank you, Chief. Take us to periscope depth."

"Periscope depth, aye, sir."

The sub rose as Danielson pressed his face against the rubber housing of the periscope and stared into darkness. The scope turned night into shades of green, but the storm and rolling waves severely reduced visibility.

Flash. The raging Pacific was illuminated, and for an instant Danielson caught the silhouette of the whaler lying on its side. "They're sinking. XO, contact the Coast Guard. Where's their nearest cutter?"

"The only surface ship within twenty miles is the *Kiku*."

The sonar operator called out, "Skipper, there's something else out there, circling that ship."

* * *

Robert Nash held the headset tightly against his ears, verifying the message once more. "Captain Barre, we're receiving an emergency call from the *Nautilus*. A Japanese vessel is sinking, twelve miles to the east on heading zero-eight-one. They say there may be survivors in the water, but no other surface ships are in the area. They're requesting immediate assistance."

Masao looked at Jonas. "The Meg?"

"If it is, we don't have much time."

"Get us there quickly, captain."

* * *

The Japanese whaler lay on her port side, the buoyant vessel refusing to sink as she rose and fell with the twenty-foot swells. Within the bowels of the ship, eleven men struggled in darkness to escape a chamber of death in which they could not tell which way was up. The cold ocean hissed from all directions, battering the keel, searching for a way inside the battened-down ship.

Below the waves the Megalodon tore at the remains of the whale meat lashed to the cargo net. It was her physical presence in great part that supported the vessel from below, keeping the dying ship afloat.

The senior lookout had been thrown overboard when the ship had toppled. Somehow he had managed to climb back on board, and now he struggled to hold on. From within, he heard the screams of his shipmates. Kicking open one of the sealed hatches, he shone his flashlight inside. Four crewmen crawled out from below, joining him on the tilting main deck.

* * *

"Skipper, I can hear ambient sounds," reported the *Nautilus's* sonar tech. "There are men in the water."

"How far away is the *Kiku?*"

"Six minutes," Chief Heller called out.

Danielson tried to think. What could he do to distract the Megalodon, keep the monster from the survivors? "Chief, continuous pinging, loud as you can. Sonar, watch the creature, tell me what happens."

"Continuous ping, aye, sir."

Ping … ping … ping.

The metallic gongs rattled through the hull of the *Nautilus*, the deep throb of the reverberations radiating acoustically through the sea.

* * *

The deafening *pings* reached the female's lateral line in seconds. The dense sound waves overloaded her senses, sending her into a rage—an unknown creature was challenging the female for her kill.

Abandoning the whale meat still entangled within the cargo net, the Megalodon circled below the sinking whaler, her head and lateral line throbbing. Descending beneath the ship, the shark homed in on the source of the annoying vibrations.

* * *

"Captain Danielson, I've got a bearing on the biologic. Six hundred meters and closing. You've definitely got its attention."

"Chief, ready a firing solution."

"Four hundred meters and closing."

"Chief?"

"I've got a temporary solution, sir, but the explosion could harm the crew of that whaler."

"Two hundred meters—"

"Helm, change course to zero-two-five, twenty degrees down-angle on the planes. Dive the boat to eight hundred feet; make your speed fifteen knots. Let's put some ocean between this fish and that ship."

The sub accelerated in a shallow descent, the Megalodon in pursuit. The female measured less than half the *Nautilus's* length, and the submarine, at three thousand tons, easily outweighed her. But the female was faster and could outmaneuver its adversary; moreover, no adult Megalodon would allow a challenge within its domain to go unanswered.

The female accelerated at the sub's steel hull like a berserk sixty-foot locomotive.

"Seventy meters…. Thirty meters… brace for impact!" The sonar man ripped off his headset.

Whomp!

The thirty ton creature struck the *Nautilus* along its starboard flank, the solid impact crushing several steel plates while rolling the sub hard to port. The collision sent crewmen hurtling from their posts. The power died, darkness momentarily taking the sub until red emergency lights flickered on.

Powerless, the sub listed at a forty-five-degree angle.

The Megalodon circled, measuring her challenger. The collision had caused a painful throbbing in her snout. The female shook her head, several broken teeth falling out. In time they would be replaced by those lying behind them in reserve.

Captain Danielson felt warmth seep into his right eye. "All stations report," he yelled, wiping the blood from his forehead.

Chief Heller was the first to call out. "Engine room reports flooding in three compartments, sir. Reactor is off-line."

"Radiation?"

"No leaks found."

"Batteries?"

"Batteries appear functional and are on-line, Captain, but the stern planes are not responding."

"Son of a bitch." Danielson was fuming ... how could he have allowed a fish to cripple his boat? "Sonar, where's the creature now?"

"Circling, sir. Very close."

"Skipper, damage control reports one screw is out, the other should be on-line within ten minutes. Emergency batteries only, sir."

"Torpedoes?"

"Still ready, sir."

"Flood torpedo tubes one and two sonar, I want a firing solution."

The hull plates groaned ... followed by a bizarre scratching sound.

Danielson looked around, baffled. "Raby, what the hell is

that noise?"

The sonar man looked up, fear in his eyes. "Skipper, I think the Megalodon's attempting to bite through our hull."

* * *

The *Kiku* arrived at the last known coordinates of the Japanese vessel, but without the support of the Meg pushing from below, the ship had gone under without a fight.

Jonas and Mac, wearing life jackets and secured to the main deck by life lines around their waists, stood at the stern rail by the harpoon gun. Mac manned a searchlight while Jonas held the rifle loaded with the tracking dart, his right arm looped inside a life ring secured to the rail.

They held on as the *Kiku* rose again and fell, the thirty foot swells threatening to send both men head-first into the sea.

"There!" Jonas pointed to starboard. Two sailors clung to what was left of the whaler's mast.

Mac aimed the light, then called Barre on his walkie-talkie. "Two men in the water, fifty yards astern."

Jonas handed the rifle to Mac, then tossed the life ring toward the sailors. With the sea breaking in peaks and valleys and the *Kiku* bucking like a wild bronco, he could not tell whether the men could even see the flotation device, let alone reach it.

"Forget it, J.T., you'll never reach them!"

Jonas continued scanning the surface as the bow dropped thirty feet, another swell rising ten yards away. They rose again and Jonas saw the beacon of light flash on the men. One was waving.

Retrieving the floatation device, he untied the rope around his waist and connected it to the life ring's rope, doubling its length.

"What are you doing?"

As the bow dropped, Jonas looped his right arm through the life ring and placed one foot on one the rungs of the rail.

When the ship rose again, he leaped into the maelstrom with all his might. Propelled by the rising deck, he launched high into the air, falling beyond the next incoming swell.

Cold water shocked his body, driving the breath from his chest, sapping his strength. He rose with the next wave but was unable to see anything, then swam as hard as he could in the direction he prayed was correct, the life ring encumbering his progress but keeping him afloat, the wind howling in his ears.

Without warning, Jonas found himself falling into a valley between two swells. Swimming was not an option: he was being hurled up and down mountains of water. Rolling onto his back, he kicked with his legs and stroked with his left arm, his heart pounding with the effort.

* * *

The Meg couldn't tell if the creature was alive, its piercing vibrations having ceased. She circled back, attempting to gnaw on the object, taste buds located in her rostrum telling her the strange fish was inedible.

And then the Meg detected vibrations along the surface … the floundering movements accompanied by the rapid heartbeats of prey.

* * *

"It's moving off, skipper. She's heading back to the surface."

"Engines back on-line, Captain," reported Chief Heller. As if in response, the *Nautilus* leveled out.

"That's my girl. Helm, bring us around; make your course zero-five-zero, up ten degrees on the planes. Take us to four hundred feet. Chief, I want a firing solution on that monster. On my command, start pinging again. When she descends to attack, we'll hit her with both torpedoes."

Heller looked worried. "Sir, engineering warns the ship can't withstand another collision. I strongly suggest we return to

Pearl and—"

"Negative, Chief. We end this now."

* * *

Jonas let out a yell as something grabbed him by his collar and hung on.

A Japanese sailor pulled Jonas onto the fallen mast and sputtered something incomprehensible, the man terrified.

Jonas looked around—the second sailor was gone.

He felt a strong tug on the life ring; Mac and his men were pulling him back.

Taylor instructed the sailor to hang on to the floatation device. Seconds later they were dragged backward along the violent surface toward the *Kiku*.

* * *

The Meg locked in on the electrical impulses generated by the two men's beating hearts. It could smell blood in the water, their floundering movements rendering them easy prey—

Ping…ping….ping—

Incensed, the albino monster broke off her attack, descending on an intercept course with the *Nautilus*.

* * *

"Here she comes, skipper. Six hundred meters and closing quickly."

"Chief Heller, do we have a firing solution?"

"Aye, sir, we do."

"On my command …"

"Three hundred meters."

"Steady, gentlemen."

"One hundred and fifty meters."

"Let her come closer …"

"Skipper, she's changing course."

Danielson ran to the console, sweat mixed with the blood dripping down his face. "Where is it?"

Sonar was bent over, cupping his ears, trying to hear. "She went deep. I can barely hear her. Wait—Oh shit, she's coming up below us."

"Evasive maneuvers! Hard to starboard, all ahead full."

The crippled submarine lurched forward, struggling to reach a speed above ten knots—as the Megalodon rose from below, her snout striking the hull at twenty knots. This time the casing gave way, spreading a gap between the steel plates, venting the engine room to the sea and rupturing the submarine's aft ballast tanks.

* * *

Seaman Anthony Gonzalez tumbled backwards, the engineer's head slamming hard against a control panel, knocking him unconscious.

Lieutenant Peter Suarez found himself pinned under a collapsed bulkhead, his left ankle caught. As the engine room filled with water, he managed to free himself and crawl up into the next compartment, sealing the watertight door behind him seconds before the sea could rush in.

* * *

"Damage report!"

"Engine room's flooded. I can't raise—"

A loud wail was followed by flashing red lights.

"Core breach," Heller yelled. "Someone's got to shut it down."

"Helm, high-pressure air into the ballast tanks, put us on the ceiling. Dennis?"

"On my way." Chief Heller ran through a tilting maze of chaos. He squeezed past crewmen attempting to staunch the flow of seawater spraying from a thousand leaks. At least half of the electrical consoles looked down.

He found Lieutenant Suarez outside the engine room frantically throwing switches, shutting down the nuclear reactor.

Heller joined him, shutting off the alarm. "Report, Lieutenant."

"Reactor's gone, but at least we averted a meltdown. Everyone and everything aft of the engine room is underwater."

"Radiation?"

The officer looked at his friend. "Denny, this ship's over forty years old. We've lost the integrity of the hull, the steel plates are falling off like shingles. We'll drown before any radiation kills us."

* * *

Jonas and the Japanese sailor were hauled out of the sea and onto the *Kiku's* stern deck. Frank Heller escorted the whaler's lone survivor to sickbay, Mac leading Jonas up to the bridge.

Terry Tanaka wrapped a blanket around him as he entered the command center. "Diving in the sea like that—are you insane?"

"Technically, Mac and I did spend three months together in a mental ward."

She shot Jonas a look to kill. "Don't ever do that again."

"Terry, quiet," Masao called out. "We're receiving a distress call from the *Nautilus.*"

Bob Nash cupped his ears, trying to hear. "They're surfacing. No power … major breach. They need our assistance immediately."

Captain Barre barked orders to change course.

The *Kiku* turned, fighting against the relentless swells.

* * *

Anthony Gonzalez had regained consciousness. The engineer's face was pressed hard against the watertight door where a small pocket of air remained. The chamber was bathed in red emergency lighting. Blood gushed from his forehead.

As the *Nautilus* rose, debris began seeping out of the gap in the hull and into the Pacific.

The Megalodon ascended after the sub, snapping its jaws at anything that moved. Smelling Gonzalez's blood, the Meg jammed her head into the engine room breach, separating the already loose steel plates, enlarging the gap in the hull significantly. Her white hide illuminated the dimly lit flooded compartment, catching the engineer's attention.

Holding his breath, he ducked underwater and looked down.

The monster's ten-foot-wide jaws opened and closed below him, the upper jaw pushing forward and away from the creature's head like something out of a 3-D horror film, the hideous triangular teeth less than five feet away.

Gonzalez felt his body being sucked into the vortex. He surfaced and tore at the door, his screams muffled by the rising sea. Unable to escape, he chose an alternative death, ducking his head underwater, inhaling the salt water deep into his lungs, struggling to kill himself before the mouthful of teeth could reach him.

The female inhaled the heaving body into her vacuous gullet, crushing and swallowing her prey in one gulp. The warm blood sent her into a renewed frenzy. She shook her head, freeing herself from the opening, then circled the *Nautilus* again as its bow burst through the surface.

* * *

"Abandon ship! All hands, abandon ship!" Captain Danielson barked his orders over the ship's intercom as the *Nautilus* tossed hard to starboard against the incoming swells.

Three hatches exploded open, releasing the crew. Pink phosphorescent flares pierced the blackness. Three yellow rafts inflated instantaneously and were lashed to the side of the boat. Survivors rushed to board, struggling to maintain their balance against the raging sea. The *Kiku* was close, her spotlight now guiding the rafts.

251

Danielson was in the last life raft. Bolts of lightning lit the seascape as he looked back at the *Nautilus*. Within seconds, the submarine was overcome by the waves. Her bow rose, only to be swallowed by another swell which drove the ship toward her final resting place at the bottom of the Pacific.

Flash. The first raft reached the *Kiku*. Fifteen men scrambled up a cargo net draped along her starboard side. A swell slammed against the ship, lifting the research vessel before dropping it thirty feet.

Flash. The force of the wave tossed some of Danielson's crew back into the sea. Like insects they scrambled to reach the net, climbing once again.

Jonas aimed the spotlight into the swell, locating a seaman. It was Dennis Heller.

Frank saw his younger brother struggling to stay afloat less than fifteen feet from the *Kiku's* cargo net. He tossed a ring buoy as the second raft closed in from behind.

Dennis grabbed at the life preserver and held on as his brother pulled him toward the *Kiku*. The survivors in the second raft were already scaling the cargo net, the last group now within ten feet of the ship.

Dennis reached the net and began climbing. He was halfway up when his shipmates from the third raft joined him.

Frank Heller held on to the starboard rail, one hand holding the metal pipe, the other extending toward his brother, now only two body-lengths away. "Denny, give me your hand!" They touched momentarily—just as another swell washed over the starboard rail, battering the ship.

Heller panicked; Denny was gone. He searched the dark sea, littered with flailing seamen.

Flash—

The albino creature's head rose out of the swell, grasping Dennis Heller in its jaws.

"No, no!" Frank screeched at the monster, its massive throat wobbling as it chomped down upon his brother's gushing remains.

Another swell rolled over the albino devil, and it was gone.

Having witnessed the scene, Danielson and the other men still holding onto the net climbed with reckless abandon.

The Meg reappeared, the bloody remains of Dennis Heller still shredded within its front row of teeth as it rose with the next thirty foot swell which washed over the cargo net, delivering the shark to the bounty of human morsels floundering along the side of the *Kiku*.

The wave lifted Danielson away from the net. He kicked and strained to reach the starboard rail—screaming as he turned to see the Megalodon's open mouth right behind him—

The searchlight ignited over his head, Mac directing the intense beam of light at the shark's left eye, scorching the organ's sensitive ocular tissue like a laser.

The monster reeled sideways into the sea, its assault on Richard Danielson and the *Nautilus's* survivors terminated.

The captain and his men climbed over the rail and collapsed onto the teetering deck where they were met by the *Kiku's* crew and led inside the ship's infrastructure.

Frank Heller remained on his knees by the starboard rail, his eyes tightly clenched, his frail body trembling.

Jonas reached for him, only to have the physician push him away.

Dragging himself off the deck, the physician cried out into the night, his words deadened by the wind. "You're dead, monster, you hear me? You … are … dead!"

LOST & FOUND

THE MEG DISAPPEARED. No telltale whale carcasses, no sightings by chopper ... nothing. Many speculated the creature had gone deep ... never to return.

Nine members of the *Nautilus's* crew were missing, along with fourteen sailors from the Japanese whaler. A ceremony honoring the dead had taken place at Pearl Harbor. Two days later, Captain Richard Danielson re-retired from the navy.

Commander Bryce McGovern was in the hot seat. Who had authorized the United States Navy to hunt the Megalodon? Why had McGovern selected the *Nautilus* to complete the mission, knowing the decommissioned submarine was far from battle-ready? The families of the deceased were outraged, an internal investigation ordered. Many believed Commander McGovern would be the next naval officer to be "retired."

Frank Heller was a raging bull; his hatred for the Megalodon all-consuming. He informed Masao he was through, stating that he had his own plans for the "white devil." After the ceremony in Oahu, he flew home to San Francisco, and no one had heard from him since.

Days turned into a week; the weeks into a month. Leaving Hawaiian waters, the *Kiku* continued its trek east toward California, not so much because Jonas believed the Megalodon would be enticed by the thousands of whales migrating along the coast—he simply wanted to end the voyage and go home.

Maggie rode the wave of high ratings for about a week. But as the empty days mounted and the futility of their mission became apparent her producers back in San Diego cut back her broadcasts from once a day to once a week before they finally terminated the project.

Jonas learned she was leaving when he found her waiting by

the helipad with her cameraman, her suitcase packed.

"So, this is it, huh?"

She nodded. "We live and die with each new news cycle."

"I meant our marriage."

"I already filed for divorce; Bud's attorneys are handling it. You can have the house, we're upside-down on the mortgage. Bud already moved my stuff out."

"He's an efficient guy."

"Don't be bitter, Jonas. We had a nice run. Thankfully, there are no rug-rats to complicate our lives."

"That's because you never wanted any." He looked to the east as the chopper approached. "What about Bud? Does he want kids?"

"Bud wants me." She noticed Terry watching from the bridge. "She likes you."

"Who? Terry?"

"Don't act so innocent. I saw the two of you playing darts the other day. You were smiling. That's the first time I've seen you smile in seven years."

The thunder of the approaching chopper grew louder.

Maggie stood. Reaching up to Jonas, she kissed him hard on the lips, leaving behind a trace of Vaseline. "Bye."

He watched her board the helicopter with the cameraman and then she was gone.

When he turned, Terry was by his side. "Will you miss her?"

"We've both moved on." He looked around, realizing the *Kiku's* chopper wasn't there. "Where's Mac?"

"He flew my father to the institute to meet with JAMSTEC. The opening ceremony is in two days and there's still a lot to be done."

"He left you behind?"

"I told him we were involved in a serious dart tournament." She slipped her hand in his. "I think it's time we upped the stakes."

Tanaka Oceanographic Institute
Monterey, California

The crowd was sparse, numbering less than a hundred—no doubt reflecting the long odds of the public ever seeing the Megalodon captured. Having committed another seven million dollars of JAMSTEC money to finish the lagoon, Dr. Tsukamoto and Dr. Simidu now feared that they had made a mistake that would probably cost them their jobs.

Both men kept smiles on their faces as the ceremony began.

Masao Tanaka stood by a podium set up in the southern end of the arena. "Dear friends, thank you for coming. You see before you the culmination of a dream. Whether the D.J. Tanaka lagoon one day harbors a prehistoric shark or Gray whales seeking a habitat to birth their young, this facility honors my son, D.J. Tanaka, who dedicated his life to the advancement of the marine sciences."

Masao removed a small gold hammer hanging from a ribbon around his neck and struck a ceremonial gong standing on the podium.

With a thunderous *clap*, the towering eighty-foot-high steel doors located at the end of the canal were opened, venting the lagoon to the Pacific Ocean.

Within minutes the empty tank had become a glorious blue lake. For several minutes the host and his guests simply stared at the ebbing and flowing waters, and then the press turned on Masao, engaging in a media version of a feeding frenzy.

"Mr. Tanaka, it's been a month since the Megalodon was last seen. Many experts believe the creature has returned to deep water. What are the Institute's plans?"

"As long as we're funded, we'll continue the search."

"A lot of people have died, including your own son. If you could turn back time, what would you have done differently?"

"You cannot control karma, it is either good or bad. Our mission in the trench was honorable, our karma bad. Perhaps it will change, I don't know."

As the barrage of questions continued, one news reporter turned to face his cameraman. "And so the Tanaka Lagoon opens. The real question now—where is its 60,000-pound guest of honor? In Monterey, Joel Van Egbert, CNN Headline News."

Turtle Bay, Bahia Tortugas
Baja, California

The coastal outpost of Bahia Tortugas and the cove known as Turtle Bay lie just south of Punta Eugenia, the elbow in the middle of Baja, California's west coast. More accessible by sea than land, Bahia Tortugas is one of the few places for hundreds of miles where diesel fuel and gasoline can be purchased, rendering this protective out-of-the-way cove a common rest stop for boaters traveling up and down the Baja coast.

Jason Frost had gotten lost. Driving from Bakersfield, California to his best-friend's wedding in Los Cabos, the forty-two-year-old book store employee had made the mistake of asking for directions in broken *Spanglish* from a gas station attendant in Guererro Negro. He had driven forty-five miles south, then a hundred and fifteen miles west off of the Baja Highway when he found himself on a narrow road at ten-thirty at night, utterly lost.

Exiting his jeep to pee, he could hear the ocean close by. Deciding it best to rest here for the night, Jason grabbed his sleeping bag, his cell phone, and the remains of a taco he had left from lunch and made his way on foot down to Turtle Bay.

* * *

Jason opened his eyes. The predawn sky was gray, the sun still an hour away. Waves lapped along the shoreline, teasing him to close his eyes again.

Then he heard the sound—a deep, bellicose groan that he knew could not be human. Climbing out of the sleeping bag, he stood on the dunes facing the ocean, his heart pounding with excitement.

They were laid out along the coastline of Turtle Bay like the black keys on a piano. He counted thirteen whales and stopped, then ran down to the shallows to inspect the dying mammals.

He could find no wounds nor reason the cetaceans would have beached themselves en masse—and yet he knew the reason … the question was how to get the most bang from his buck.

Searching for a signal on his cell phone, he found the phone number of the television studio in San Diego.

"Yes, this is Dr. Jason Frost, and I'm a … an amateur marine biologist. I need to speak with Maggie Taylor."

San Diego

Maggie Taylor felt her blood pressure rising as she waited impatiently for Fred Henderson to get off his phone. Finally, she stood over her producer's desk and snatched the receiver out of his hand. "He'll have to call you back," she said into the mouthpiece, and hung up.

"Maggie, what the hell do you think you're doing? That was an important call—"

"Important my ass, you were talking to your bookie."

"All right, you have my undivided attention. Speak."

"The whale beaching in Baja was my story. Why'd you give it to David Lindahn?"

"First, because he speaks Spanish; second because he was already in Baja and this Frost fellow was putting the story out to other news agencies so we had to move fast."

The station manager put his feet up on his desk. "I know you want to get back into the game ... so wow me."

"What if I got you underwater footage of the Meg, I mean the real McCoy, scary as hell."

"I'm listening."

"I spent all day going through Jonas's office. Did you know these Megs used to proliferate along the California coast? Jonas has boxes filled with small fossilized teeth from a local spot he labeled an ancient Megalodon nursery."

"And this is important why?"

"Because the female's pregnant! Do you ever watch your own news features, Fred?"

"Get back to the underwater shots."

"I think the Megalodon is working its way back to this ancient nursery to give birth. What if I was there, waiting for it ... in a shark tube."

"You're nuts."

"Just listen to what I have to say."

For the next ten minutes she briefed her station manager about her plan to film the Megalodon.

When she was through, Henderson leaned back in his leather chair. "You've got some set of balls, lady, I'll say that for you. Okay, I'm sold. Tell me what you need."

* * *

Bud was reading the paper in his Mercedes convertible when Maggie opened his door, climbed onto his lap and buried her tongue in his mouth.

"Bud, he loved it. We called the network and they agreed to back me on everything ... the equipment, the crew—everything but the boat."

"Which is why you need me."

"No, Bud Harris. I need you because I love you ... because

you're my present and future. You and I are going to be the biggest power couple in California. This story makes me a star … the next Katie Couric. And you'll be there with me. Bud Harris, executive producer."

Bud smiled, enjoying the con. "Okay, Maggs, just tell me what you want."

THE CANYON

SITUATED LESS THAN TWO HUNDRED yards
from the open steel doors of the Tanaka Lagoon's canal and
fanning out over sixty miles of sea floor, the Monterey Bay
Submarine Canyon runs deeper than the Grand Canyon,
possessing channels that plunge 11,800 feet. An anomaly of
nature, this unique underwater geology was created by the
subduction of the North American plate. Originally located in the
vicinity of Santa Barbara, the entire Monterey Bay region was
pushed ninety miles northward over millions of years, carried
along the San Andreas fault zone on a section of granite rock
known as the Salinian Block. The canyon itself is a confluence of
varying formations; steep and narrow in some places, as wide as a
Himalayan valley in others. Sheer vertical walls can drop two miles
to a sediment-buried sea floor that dates back to the Pleistocene.
Closer to shore, twisting chasms, some as deep as 6,000 feet, reach
out from the main artery of the crevice like fingers of a groping

hand.

Home to kelp forests and krill, Humboldt squid, and a plethora of fish and marine mammals, the area is one of many protected sanctuaries in the area, extending as far west as the Farallon Islands.

* * *

The Megalodon moved through the pitch-black depths of the Monterey Bay Submarine Canyon, following the steep walls of the C-shaped crevasse. Millions of years ago, these same Pacific waters had been a favorite habitat of the creature's ancestors—until pods of Orca had raided their nurseries and forced the adults away from the surface and the staple of their diets ... whales.

Blinded in her left eye, the pregnant female had fled the coast of Hawaii. Coming across a warm current flowing southeast along the equator, the injured Meg had ridden the river just as a Boeing 747 rides an airstream.

Crossing the Pacific, the predator's senses detected the faint but alluring pounding of tens of thousands of beating hearts and moving muscles. Homing in on the cetacean migration, she arrived in the waters off Baja, California. Ignoring the tempting shallows where mother Grays were birthing their young, the albino monster followed the coastline to the north—her presence causing pods of Gray whales to beach.

Despite the bountiful offerings she had not fed, her internal organs undergoing changes ... preparing her for labor.

Following the sea floor, she had descended into the extreme depths of the Monterey Bay Canyon.

Something seemed familiar. Perhaps it was the hydrothermal vents or the steep canyon walls, the water pressure or salinity. Territorial by nature, the sixty-foot female claimed the area as her own, an expanse of ocean awarded by her mere presence as its supreme hunter. Her senses indicated there were no other adult Megalodons in the area to challenge her rule. The territory therefore became hers to defend.

Her young grew active, demanding she feed. For three hours, the predator had been stalking the blue whale and its calf. They were moving just below the surface, the Meg shadowing them in the darkness. The female waited to attack, refusing to venture into the daylight.

Nightfall was coming …

The Red Triangle

The Ana Nuevo and Farallon Islands are a series of windswept rocks situated twenty-six miles west of San Francisco's Golden Gate Bridge. Uninhabited by people, one marine mammal dominates its barren landscape—the northern elephant seal.

Reaching lengths of more than fifteen feet and weighing upwards of six thousand pounds, the northern elephant seal is the largest pinniped in the world and the most sexually dimorphic, with an alpha bull mating with as many as four dozen females. Winters are spent onshore at rookeries where the mammals mate, birth, and fight for dominance. Each spring and summer they return to the Farallons to laze about the rocky beaches, playing, sleeping, and molting.

The presence of these massive creatures entices another species to visit the remote island chain: *Carcharodon carcharius*, the Great White shark. The seals are the predator's favorite delicacy, and the predators circle these islands en masse, their presence giving this expanse of sea the nickname *The Red Triangle*.

* * *

The super yacht, *Magnate* was anchored in six hundred feet of water, her freeboard reflecting golden flecks of sunlight. On her main deck, a weary crew of cameramen and technicians were forced to tolerate the God-awful stench coming from the excrement of hundreds of sea elephants and thousands of California seals and sea lions. The herds were stretched out upon the rocky landmasses, the annoying creatures incessantly barking and snorting.

Of all the documented attacks by Great Whites worldwide, more than half occurred in the Red Triangle. Jonas believed the Farallons had once been a Megalodon nursery; if true then Maggie reasoned the pregnant female might be drawn to the area, if only to feast on the succulent fat of the islands' elephant seals.

For three days her film crew had waited patiently for the creature to show up. Underwater video cameras, audio equipment, and special underwater lights littered the ship's deck, along with cigarette butts and candy wrappers. A community laundry line had been hung along the upper deck, dangling sweatshirts and towels.

Now the long hours of boredom, sun, and the occasional nausea associated with seasickness had finally gotten to the crew. And yet even these conditions would have been tolerable had it not been for the overwhelming smell that hung thick in the chilly Northern California air...a stench different than the islands' accumulation of poop.

Trailing the yacht on a thirty-foot steel cable was the buoyant carcass of a dead humpback whale. The pungent smell seemed to hover over the *Magnate* as if to mark the heinous deed, for killing a whale in the Monterey Bay National Marine Sanctuary was indeed a criminal act. No matter: with his influence and deep pockets Bud Harris had managed to arrange for two local fishermen to deliver a whale carcass to their location, no questions asked.

Now, after thirty-eight hours of the wicked stench, the *Magnate's* crew were ready to mutiny.

"Maggs, listen to reason," begged Perry Meth. "Twelve hours of shore leave, that's all I'm asking. It could be weeks, months before this Megalodon even ventures into these waters. All of us need a break, even a fresh shower would be heaven. Just get us off this smelly barge."

She pulled her director aside. "Stop whining, Perry! This is the story of the decade, and I'm not about to blow it because you and your cronies feel the need to get drunk in some sleazy hotel bar."

"That's not fair—"

"No, what's not fair is that it's my ass on the line. Do you have any idea how difficult it was to organize all this? The cameras? That huge shark tube? Not to mention that hunk of whale blubber floating behind us?"

"Speaking of that, whatever happened to your campaign to protect the whales? I would have sworn that was you I saw onstage accepting a Golden Eagle on behalf of the Save the Whales Foundation."

"Grow up, Perry, I didn't kill the damn thing, I'm just using it as bait. I mean, cut me some slack. There are ten thousand of them migrating along the coast." She tossed her blonde hair, causing strands of it to stick to her oiled bare shoulders.

Perry lowered his voice. "The crew's not happy, Maggie. They're cold and tired and they feel you're grasping at straws. Honestly, what are the chances of that Megalodon actually showing up in the Farallons? No one's reported seeing the shark since the attack in Hawaii. And those beachings down in Baja mean nothing."

"The Meg will show, believe me, and we'll be the ones to get the footage."

"In what ... that hunk of plastic?" He pointed to the ten-foot-high Lexan shark tube which stood upright on the main deck, rigged to a winch. "Christ, Maggie, you'd have to be suicidal—"

"That hunk of plastic is two-inch-thick bullet-proof

Plexiglas. Its diameter is too wide for the Meg to get its mouth around." Maggie laughed. "I'll probably be safer in there than you guys will be on the *Magnate*."

"There's a comforting thought."

Maggie ran her fingers across her director's sweaty chest. She knew Bud was still in bed, sleeping off another hangover. "Perry, you and I have worked very hard together on these projects. Hell, look how much good our whale documentary did for those beasts."

He smirked. "Tell that to your dead humpback."

"Forget that already. Think big. I thought you wanted to direct movies?"

"I do."

"Then see this project for what it is, a door-opener into Hollywood, the story that puts us both on top. How does executive producer sound to you?"

Perry thought for a moment, then smiled. "It's a start."

"It's yours. Now, can we forget about the dead whale for a moment?"

"Fine. But as your executive producer I highly recommend we do something to create a little diversion; idle time is making things worse."

"I agree, and I've got an idea. I've been wanting to do a test run on the shark tube. What do you say we get it into the water and I'll shoot some footage."

"That's not a bad idea. It will give me a chance to position the underwater lights." He smiled. "Maybe you'll be able to get some nice footage of a Great White. That alone might be worth a few minutes on the weekend wrap-up."

She shook her head. "See, that's your problem—you think way too small."

Bending over to pick up her wet suit, Maggie's sweatshirt rolled up, rewarding Perry with a glimpse of her tan, thonged behind. "One last thing. Do me a favor and don't mention anything to Bud about being my executive producer." She smiled sweetly. "He gets jealous."

Monterey Submarine Canyon

The Meg ascended cautiously, wary of any lingering traces of sunlight. When the surface vibrations grew stronger and the sea remained dark, the female grew excited.

It was time to feed.

The ghost-like hunter circled three hundred feet below the Blue whale and her calf, mother and offspring feeding on krill.

Detecting the danger, the eighty-three-foot-long adult nudged her young, ending the feast. Remaining in a tight formation, the two cetaceans propelled their bodies just below the surface, the moving mass of the one-hundred-and-eighty-ton Blue whale creating a current which towed its newborn faster than it could possibly swim.

But not nearly fast enough.

Closing to within two body lengths of her prey, the Megalodon targeted the adult Blue whale's smallish pectoral fins, each feint designed to lure the cow away from its offspring.

Gnawing at the mother's belly finally caused the whale to charge, the sudden descent spinning the calf out from the displacement current.

The Meg circled back quickly, its jaws opening to engulf the calf—

—when suddenly the albino was seized by internal cramps that sent her back and pectoral fins arching in an uncontrollable spasm.

Forced to abandon her prey, the Meg descended rapidly to the canyon floor. Her muscles quivered with contortions, forcing her to swim in tight circles. Finally, with a mighty shudder that shook her entire girth she expelled a cloud of blood from her cloaca—along with the head of a Megalodon pup.

It was a female, pure white and seven feet long, weighing nearly three hundred pounds. The pup's teeth were sharper than its mother's, its senses fully developed, enabling it to hunt and survive on its own. Wiggling like a tadpole, it freed itself from its mother's oviduct, its soulless blue-gray eyes focused on the adult, instinct warning the pup of imminent danger.

With a burst of speed, it glided south along the canyon floor.

Still circling in convulsions, the female shuddered again, expelling a second pup—another female—from its womb. Slightly smaller than its sibling, the pup shot past its mother, barely avoiding a mortal, reflexive bite from the jaws of its cold, uncaring parent.

Minutes passed. With one last convulsion, the Meg birthed her third and last pup in a cloud of blood and embryonic fluid. The runt of the litter, a five-and-a-half-foot male, twisted out of its mother's orifice and twirled toward the bottom, righted itself, then shook its head to clear its vision.

With a flick of her powerful caudal fin, the Meg pounced upon the runt from behind, snapped her jaws shut around its lower torso, severing its caudal fin and genitalia in one vicious bite.

Convulsing wildly, the dying pup writhed to the bottom, trailing a stream of blood.

Giving chase, the female inhaled the runt down its gullet, swallowing its remains.

For several minutes the Megalodon hovered near the bottom, exhausted from the efforts of labor. Opening her mouth, she allowed the canyon's current to circulate through her gill slits, which fluttered as she breathed.

Water passed in and out of her nostril passages, feeding

information to her brain. It moved along the underside of her snout, plugging her in to the faint electrical fields generated by the swimming muscles and beating hearts of her offspring and her escaping Blue whale quarry. It ran along her lateral line, stimulating her neuromast cells, allowing her to "feel" the ocean's currents and the presence of all biologics within her domain.

The female heard every sound, registered every movement, tasted every trail, and saw every sight, for *Carcharodon megalodon* did not just move through the sea, the sea moved through the Megalodon.

Her half-moon shaped caudal fin swung back and forth as she glided slowly over the canyon floor, her massive head rotating from side to side, her nostrils flaring as they channeled water.

The predator quickened her pace, detecting an intoxicating scent.

Needing to feed, she turned to the north—passing within thirty feet of the steel doors guarding the canal entrance that connected the Tanaka Lagoon with the Pacific Ocean.

Farallon Islands

They came without warning; their presence energizing the disgruntled crew. Bradley Watson, the *Magnate's* captain spotted the first lead-gray dorsal fin twenty feet off the yacht's starboard bow. Within minutes, two more fins appeared, cutting back and forth through the blood slick seeping out of the towed Humpback whale carcass.

Perry Meth found Maggie pulling on her fluorescent yellow wetsuit.

"Okay, Maggie, you wanted some action. How about a test dive with three Great White sharks?"

Maggie felt her heart race. "Sounds like fun. Is everyone ready?"

"Reach-pole cameras and their operators are in position, underwater lights are on, and the plastic tube's all set. Your handheld camera is charged and ready to go."

"Where's Bud?"

"Still asleep."

"Good. He's been on the rag this whole trip. Now remember, when you start filming, I want it to look like I'm all alone in the water with the sharks. How much cable's attached to my tube?"

"Two hundred feet. We'll keep you within seventy to maintain the light."

She pulled the wetsuit's hood in place and zipped up. "Let's do it. I want to be in and out of the water before Bud wakes up."

She followed him to the main deck.

The crew had already lowered the Lexan shark cylinder over the side. The porous, clear container had been custom-made for Maggie from a design originally developed in Australia. Unlike a steel-mesh shark cage, the shark tube could not be bitten or bent, save for its buoyancy tanks, which were anchored to its top hatch. It would maintain positive buoyancy forty feet below the surface, affording its diver an unobstructed view of the underwater domain. A steel cable served as a leash, running from the top of the cylinder to a winch on board the *Magnate*.

Secured to reach poles were two underwater cameras linked to monitors on deck. While Maggie was in the tube filming, the crew would be filming Maggie. If the lighting worked properly, the shark tube would remain invisible in the water, giving the terrifying appearance of seeing the diver exposed and alone in the water among the circling sharks.

Two crewmen helped her down the ladder. The *Magnate* had eight feet of freeboard and she climbed down carefully, balancing on the bobbing cylinder's buoyancy tanks. Perry handed her a flipper, then the other, then climbed halfway down the ladder to hand her the thirty-seven pound underwater camera. He waited while she fixed her dive mask to her face. It was a bulky contraption that wrapped around her chin, allowing her to breathe through her nose and mouth while communicating with the ship via a speaker and headphone embedded in the mask.

"You ready?"

She nodded and took a quick glance around to confirm the location of her subjects. Satisfied she was not about to be attacked, Maggie squatted on the edge of the hatch and then lowered herself into the flooded tube.

Reaching up, she sealed the clear door.

She sank into the center of the plastic tube, adjusting her buoyancy vest so she didn't have to tread water. Maggie had been diving for ten years, though rarely at night. The practice would do her good.

The current was moving away from the yacht. Perry instructed his team to release steel cable, the underwater cameras focusing on the tube as it sank beneath the keel and drifted away from the *Magnate*.

"Stu, how are your remotes functioning?"

Stuart Schwartz looked up from his dual monitors. "Both cameras are working well. We'll keep Remote A in the stern and locked on to the bait. Remote B's perfect to starboard. I can zoom right up on that tube. Too bad Maggie didn't wear her thong."

The sound woman, Stuart's wife, Abby, slapped the *Phillies* baseball cap off her husband's head. "Focus on your job, *Spielberg*."

* * *

Maggie shivered from the potent combination of adrenaline and fifty-eight-degree water. Her world was now shades of grays and blacks, visibility poor. She could see the *Magnate's* keel in the distance and wondered how she looked.

"Hello? Can you guys hear me?"

"Loud and clear," reported Abby, her voice filtered.

Maggie looked around. Moments later, the first predator entered her arena.

It was a male, fourteen feet from snout to tail, weighing a full ton. Its head and dorsal surface were lead gray, blending perfectly with the water. It circled the plastic tube warily, and Maggie rotated to compensate.

Her eyes detected movement from below as a much larger nineteen foot female rose out of the shadows, catching the newswoman totally off guard. Forgetting she was in a protective tube, Maggie panicked, frantically kicking her fins in an effort to get away. The shark's snout banged into the bottom of the tube just as Maggie's head collided with the sealed hatch above. She smiled in relief and embarrassment at her own stupidity.

Stuart Schwartz was also smiling. The footage looked incredible, and scary as hell. Maggie appeared totally alone in the water with the three killers. The *Magnate's* artificial lights were just bright enough to highlight Maggie's fluorescent-yellow wetsuit. The effect was perfect. Viewers would not be able to detect the protective tube.

"Perry, this is great stuff," he announced. "Our audience will be squirming in their seats. I gotta admit, Maggie really has a knack for the work."

Perry stood behind Stuart, watching the monitor that was focused on the humpback carcass. One of the sharks had bitten onto the waterlogged remains and was tearing away a mouthful.

"Film everything, Stu. Maybe we'll be able to convince her to quit before this Megalodon actually shows up."

But Perry had a hard time believing that himself.

8 Miles North Of Santa Cruz

They had followed the coastline north past Big Sur, the

helicopter passing dramatic cliffs and the crashing Pacific surf. Minutes later they were soaring over the Tanaka Lagoon and Monterey Bay, the lights of San Francisco appearing in the distance.

Jonas held the night binoculars with two hands, steadying them against the herky-jerky motion of the helicopter. A new thermal imager had been purchased to replace the damaged unit, but after four weeks without a Megalodon sighting, it was the last money JAMSTEC would be laying out for the expedition.

Every few miles a blotch of bright color would appear on the thermal imager's monitor representing another pod of whales moving south along the coastline.

"Mac, I can't recall ever seeing so many whales in one place," said Jonas, attempting to make conversation.

Mac stared at Jonas with a burnt-out look. "We're wasting our time. That fish of yours could be back in Baja, or a million miles from here."

"The Coast Guard's well deployed over Baja. If they sight the Meg or anything resembling a kill we'll return."

Jonas continued returned to scanning the ocean. He knew Mac was thinking about calling it quits, and would have weeks ago if it hadn't been for their friendship. He couldn't blame him. Money was tight and paychecks were being held. If the female had been feeding in these waters, there would've been traces of whale carcasses washing ashore. None had been reported, just the beachings in Baja.

Mac's right, Jonas thought to himself. How many years of my life have I wasted chasing this monster? What do I have to show for it? A marriage that fell apart years ago, a struggle to make ends meet ...

"More whales," Mac said, pointing at the thermal imager's monitor.

Jonas stared at the monitor. Was he seeing things, or were

the whales changing course? "Mac, look at the pods; they're leaving the coastline and veering sharply to the west. Maybe they're changing course to avoid something?"

Mac shook his head. "You're grasping at straws. I say we land in San Francisco, then hit Chinatown for some dim sum ... your treat."

"Mac ..."

Mac looked down again at the thermal imager. If the Meg was heading north along the coast, it would be logical for the pods to avoid her.

"Okay, J.T., one last time." The helicopter banked sharply, changing course.

Farallon Islands

Maggie checked her camera. She had plenty of film left but only another twenty minutes of air. The shark tube had drifted beneath the humpback carcass, allowing for a spectacular view. But Maggie knew footage of Great Whites feeding had become commonplace. She was after much more.

I'm wasting film, she thought. She turned to signal the *Magnate* to pull her in, then noticed something very troublesome.

The three Great Whites had all vanished.

* * *

Bud Harris kicked the silk sheets off his naked body and reached for the bottle of *Jack Daniel's.* Empty.

"Dammit!" He sat up, his head pounding. It had been two days and still he couldn't get rid of the nagging sinus headache. "It's that damn whale," he said aloud. "The smell's killing me."

Bud staggered to the bathroom, picked up the bottle of aspirin and struggled to get the childproof cap lined up correctly. "Screw it," he yelled, tossing the bottle into the empty toilet. He looked at himself in the mirror. "You're miserable, Bud Harris,"

274

he said to his reflection. "You're too rich to be miserable. Why do you let her talk you into these things? Well, enough's enough!"

He slipped on a crushed velvet sweat suit and docksiders, then left his master suite and headed down the circular stairwell to the main deck.

"Where's Maggie?" he demanded.

Abby Schwartz sat on deck, monitoring the audio track. "She's in the tube. We're getting some great footage."

"Where's that director guy?"

Perry looked up. "Right here, Bud. What do you need? I'm kind of busy."

"Pack up, we're leaving."

Perry and Abby looked at one another. "Maybe you ought to speak with Maggie—"

"Maggie doesn't own this yacht, I do." He grabbed the makeshift laundry line and tore it down. "This isn't the *SS Minnow*. Now where's Maggie?"

"Take a look." Perry pointed to the row of monitors.

"Christ ..." A smile broke on Bud's face. "That looks pretty cool."

"Hey!" Stu Schwartz held up his hand. "Something's happening out there. My light meter just jumped. It's getting brighter."

* * *

Maggie saw the glow first, illuminating what remained of the humpback carcass. Then the head appeared, as big as her mother's mobile home and totally white. She felt her heart pounding in her ears, unable to comprehend the size of the creature that was casually approaching the bait. The snout rubbed against the offering first, tasting it. Then the jaws opened. The first bite was a nibble, the second took her breath away—as the jaws opened into a tunnel, slamming down on a three-ton chunk of blubber.

The mammoth head shook itself loose from its meal, sending a flurry of oil-laced debris swirling in all directions. As the monster chewed, the movement of its powerful jaws sent quivers down its gill slits, ruffling the loose flesh along its neck.

Maggie felt herself drifting to the bottom of the shark tube, unable to move. She was in awe of this magnificent creature, its power, its nobility and grace. She raised her camera slowly, afraid she might scare it off.

* * *

"Christ, pull her back in!" Bud ordered.

"Are you crazy? This is what we came here for." Perry was excited. The whole crew was excited … or scared. "What a monster. Goddamn, this is amazing footage!"

"Pull her back in now, Meth," Bud warned, "or you'll be joining her."

Bud's crew closed ranks around him. The boss meant business.

"Okay, okay, but she's gonna be mighty pissed off." The director signaled to his assistant, who activated the winch.

The steel cable snapped to attention as it began dragging the shark cylinder through the water.

* * *

The Meg stopped feeding, its senses alerted to the sudden movement. Being plastic, the shark tube had not given off any electronic vibrations, and so the predator had ignored it. Now the big female abandoned the carcass, sculling forward to examine this new stimuli.

Maggie's heart fluttered as the tube suddenly jerked backward through the water. "Hey? What the hell are you assholes doing?"

Bud's voice came over her headpiece, filtered. "Maggie, you okay?"

"Bud Harris, if you have any desire to touch my naked body

again, you'd better stop what you're doing. Now!"

The Meg rubbed its snout along the curvature of the shark tube, confused. Its head swayed, allowing it to focus on her with its good eye.

It sees me ...

The tube stopped moving.

The Meg's enormous mouth opened and closed, almost as if it was speaking to her. Then its jaws opened wider, its upper lip receding to reveal a band of pink gums and frightening front rows of teeth, which the monstrous shark attempted to use to bite down upon the cylinder.

The smooth plastic surface slid harmlessly away.

Maggie smiled. "What's wrong, gorgeous? Too big for ya?"

Regaining her swagger, she repositioned the camera, filming down the shark's cavernous gullet. "Can you say Ahhh—cademy Award?"

Applause filtered through her headpiece.

Maggie held up her hand, acknowledging the crew's appreciation.

The Megalodon turned and disappeared into the darkness. Maggie caught a flicker of its caudal fin on film before it vanished into the lead-gray periphery. She took a breath, all smiles.

* * *

"It moved off," confirmed Perry.

"Thank Christ," said Bud. "Okay, get her out of there before it comes back."

"Ohhhh shit!" yelled Stu, who impulsively backed away from the monitors.

The Meg had circled. It was accelerating at the tube.

277

Maggie screamed, paddling backwards until her air tank banged against the inside of the tube.

The head of the 62,000-pound prehistoric Great White rotated sideways to align its hyperextended jaws with the tube seconds before—

Whomp!

The bone-jarring impact sent Maggie's face mask smashing into the interior forward wall of the tube, her head spinning from a concussion wave that would have shattered her skull had she not been underwater.

The cylinder was driven backwards, pinning her to the plastic curvature—all that separated her from being swallowed whole. It smashed against the *Magnate's* keel, giving the enraged Megalodon enough leverage to wrap its mouth around its elusive prey, the tips of a few of its teeth catching onto the cylinder's drainage holes.

The Meg had established a grip, but it could not generate

enough power from its hyperextended jaws to crush the maddeningly wide tube.

Frustrated, the beast drove its kill to the surface, the plastic cylinder still locked sideways in its mouth. Swimming away from the *Magnate*, which it perceived as another challenger, it pushed the tube along the surface, plowing a ten-foot wake.

The spool of steel cable unwound six feet a second, then the entire assembly was wrenched away from the decking. It smashed through the mahogany guard rail and splashed into the sea.

The Megalodon's upper torso rose vertically out of the Pacific, then, in an unfathomable display of brute strength, it lifted the Lexan tube above the waves.

Water streamed out of the tube's vent holes, lightening the load as the creature's head shook it back and forth, left, then right.

Maggie couldn't hold on. Flopping one way then the next like a lone ball in a tennis can, she smashed sideways into the hatch, the collision denting her air tank.

The effort of supporting the shark tube and its passenger quickly wore down the Megalodon. The female shook her teeth free of the cylinder. The porous tube refilled with water and sank slowly beneath the waves with its badly shaken occupant.

* * *

Mac's helicopter soared over the Farallon Islands, hovering high above the luxury yacht anchored off one of the jagged coastlines.

Jonas looked through the night binoculars, zooming in on the deck of the ship. "Wait a minute ... I know that yacht. That's the *Magnate*, Bud Harris's ship."

"The guy banging your wife?" Mac circled the yacht. "Let's see if we can take out his satellite dish with my tool chest."

Jonas pulled the glasses away from his face. "Something's going on down there, the crew's in a panic."

* * *

Chaos reigned on board the *Magnate*. Captain Watson had started the engines, then shut them down, afraid the noise would attract the Meg. Perry was excited, yelling orders to cameramen to climb to the highest point of the yacht to film. Bud was watching by the starboard rail in a state of shock as Stuart and Abby Schwartz continued to try to communicate by radio with Maggie.

When the helicopter appeared, Bud had panicked, thinking it was the Coast Guard, afraid the authorities had come to arrest him because of the humpback carcass.

"Bud!" Captain Watson yelled from the pilothouse, "some guy in that helicopter wants to speak with you. Says his name is Jonas."

"Jonas?" Bud ran up to the bridge and snatched the radio. "Jonas, it's not my fault. You know Maggie, she does whatever she wants!"

"Bud, calm down," commanded Jonas. "What're you talking about?"

"The Meg. It took her. She's trapped in that damn shark tube."

* * *

Mac spotted the Megalodon. It was circling in deep water, three hundred yards off the *Magnate's* starboard bow.

Jonas focused with the night glasses. He could just make out Maggie's yellow wetsuit. "I think I see her. Bud, how much air's left in her tank?"

Perry Meth's voice filtered over the radio. "No more than five minutes. If you guys can distract the Meg, we could get her out of there."

Jonas tried to think. *What would draw the monster's attention away from Maggie? The copter?*

Then Jonas noticed the motorized raft on the *Magnate's* deck.

"Bud, the Zodiac, get it ready to launch," ordered Jonas.

"I'm coming aboard."

* * *

Maggie fought to keep from blacking out. Everything hurt, but the pain was good, it kept her conscious. Her face mask had a hairline crack and was leaking seawater into her eyes. The earpiece was buzzing with static. Her ears were ringing, and it hurt to breathe.

The Megalodon continued circling, watching her with its one functional basketball-size blue-gray eye. The glow from its hide cast an eerie light, illuminating Maggie's wet suit. She checked her air supply again: down to three minutes.

I've gotta make a break for it, she told herself, but refused to uncurl from her ball.

* * *

Jonas clipped the end of his harness to the hoist cable rigged to the chopper's winch, a radio transmitter and receiver looped around his neck.

Mac passed him the transmitter rifle. "For the record, are you doing this outta love, greed, or some bizarre sense of guilt?"

"Does it really matter?"

"Not at all, I just wanted to know what to say at your funeral." Mac activated the winch, lowering Jonas to the helo-deck.

Captain Watson ran over to Jonas as he touched down. "Zodiac's ready to launch. What do you want us to do?"

"I'll distract the Meg. Once she follows me, get your yacht over to Maggie's location and get her the hell out of there —fast."

Watson led Jonas to a motorized raft suspended over the starboard rail. He secured his rifle inside, then climbed in, the captain lowering him eight feet into the sea.

Bud joined them, a headset in his hand. He dropped it over the rail and into the Zodiac. "We've reestablished contact with Maggie."

Jonas positioned it over his ears and then gunned the engine. The rubber raft skimmed across the surface, its outboard engine gurgling a high-pitched whine. He shouted over the headset, "Maggie, can you hear me?"

"Jonas? Is that you?"

"Hang in there, baby, we'll lead the Meg away. How deep are you?"

"I don't know, maybe ninety feet. Jonas hurry, my mask cracked, the pressure's unbearable, and I'm almost out of air."

Jonas cut the distance to Maggie's tube in half, then switched headsets. "Mac, can you hear me?"

The helicopter was hovering a hundred feet above the Zodiac. "Barely. I'm guessing the Meg hears your engine. She stopped circling ... she's rising. Jonas, hard to starboard!"

Jonas veered the rudder hard to his right as the Meg's head and upper torso punched up through the surface, its snapping jaws just missing the raft.

Adjusting his course, Jonas headed for the nearest island.

The albino dorsal fin raced after him, its presence sending elephant seals and sea lions leaping out of the water onto the rocks.

* * *

The *Magnate* sprang to life, her twin engines growling as they pushed the yacht ahead.

Unable to breathe, Maggie unlatched the tube's hatch. Grabbing the underwater camera, she released her weight belt, her buoyant empty air tanks carrying her to the surface as she exhaled slowly, bleeding any nitrogen bubbles from her system.

* * *

Mac yelled over the headphones as the creature's snout collided with the back of the Zodiac, "Jonas, move! Zig-zag or something!"

Jonas cut back hard to port, racing for the shallows, nearly shredding the raft's skin on a jagged rock formation, the seals barking encouragement.

He stole a quick glance over his shoulder.

The fin was gone.

"Mac, where is she?"

"I don't know. She must have gone deep."

* * *

Maggie's pulse pounded in her ears as she ascended, the surface within view, yet still so far away. She kicked with lead legs, her free hand ripping the mask from her face to save precious seconds.

Finally her head broke the surface and she gasped a deep life-giving breath.

The *Magnate* was bearing down on her and she waved, treading water as the ship slowed, its port flank coming toward her. She leaped for the aluminum ladder and grabbed hold of a rung, but it was too slick and the boat was still moving too fast to hold on to and she fell away.

The yacht finally stopped moving twenty yards away. Dragging the heavy camera in one hand, she paddled awkwardly with the other to cheers from her production crew.

"Way to go, champ," yelled Perry.

She paused at the ladder to wave at one of her crew who was filming her from the bow.

"Maggie, get in the goddamn boat!" screamed Bud.

She unlatched her buoyancy vest, allowing the bulky air tank to fall off her shoulders. Unable to climb wearing her flippers, she pulled them off one at a time, then attempted to place her bare right foot on the bottom rung.

Bud was hanging over the side, reaching down. "Dammit, Maggie, come on!"

Maggie felt a wave of exhaustion. "The camera's too heavy."

"Then drop it."

"Not a chance." Reaching up, she held it over her head, forcing Bud to climb down the ladder to retrieve it.

Grabbing hold of the dripping case, he retreated back up the ladder and handed the underwater camera to Abby Schwartz, who grabbed it in both hands ... and dropped it to the deck, the blood rushing from the sound operator's face.

Maggie was levitating along the side of the boat as if possessed—her body rising above the mahogany rail, followed by the Megalodon's ghostly white head right beneath her.

Disoriented, Maggie looked down, shocked to realize she was standing in the creature's mouth, her bare feet on the sandpaper-like surface of its tongue.

"Bud?"

Caught between the yacht and the creature's upper torso, the millionaire slipped his body behind the ladder and held on, fighting to keep his trembling body from making contact with the glistening white hide.

The night spun in her vision, the surreal ride peaking as she glanced below at the shocked, horrified faces of her production team.

She was about to chastise her cameraman for having stopped filming when the lower jaw steadily closed in on her midsection, its semi-circle of white, sharp teeth puncturing her wetsuit, which instantly sprouted a warm scarlet blanket of liquid.

With a sudden terrifying lurch, she felt the creature drop like an elevator as a dozen unseen six inch butcher knives punctured her back and ribs and spleen, her lungs heaving hot blood up through her esophagus, gagging her scream as the Meg slipped back into the sea.

Bud was paralyzed in fear, his limbs no longer his to control. Afraid to move, he could only hold on to the ladder and look down.

The keel's underwater lights illuminated the Megalodon's head, which remained ten feet beneath the surface. Held within its half-closed jaws was the woman he loved, her face pale in death, her lifeless eyes open, her blonde hair rinsed pink in a crimson bath.

The shark was draining Maggie, inhaling her blood deep into its gullet, the residue streaming out its gills.

Bud choked on his own vomit—until he realized the creature's was staring ... *at him!*

The presence of more prey broke the spell. The Meg opened its mouth wider as it rose, creating a vacuum that sucked Maggie into its black vortex and out of sight, expelling a car-size burp of air and blood.

Bud squeezed his eyes shut and waited to die.

Once more the Megalodon's head broke the surface, its jaws opening to pluck the morsel from its perch—

The heavenly light smashed through the darkness as if guided by the hand of God, the helicopter's beacon scorching the Meg's remaining good eye, blinding the female as it sent white-hot waves of pain flooding into her optic lobe.

Convulsing in spasms, the Meg whipped its massive head sideways, bashing it against the port-side of the *Magnate,* crushing fiberglass—just missing the ladder and Bud Harris.

Standing in the Zodiac, Jonas aimed the rifle and fired, the transmitter dart burying its barbed end into the creature's snow-white belly.

The agitated beast slammed its head back into the water, generating a tremendous wake which flipped the Zodiac and tossed Jonas overboard. He surfaced, climbing quickly up the aluminum ladder, dragging Bud with him.

The two men were helped onboard, Bud taken below.

Jonas watched Mac's helicopter as it headed south, the spotlight illuminating the white dorsal fin until it submerged, the

MORNING MOURNING

HE AWOKE IN A STRANGE BED in a musky room. Daylight framed heavy curtains drawn over a window situated above an air conditioner vent.

His head hurt. He couldn't remember when he had last eaten, but the empty beer cans which littered the floor filled in the blanks.

He jumped at the knock on the door. The chambermaid was quick with the pass-key, the chain lock denying her entry. "Housekeeping?"

"Go away!"

The door pulled shut.

He rolled out of bed. Found his way to the bathroom and relieved his bladder. Rinsed his mouth out in the sink, then took stock of his reflection in the mirror.

The three-day-old growth and dark circles under his eyes aged him ten years. He thought about shaving.

Instead, he fished through the small refrigerator.

Most of the good snacks were gone. He debated recalling the chambermaid; instead he settled for a Ginger Ale and a bag of Oreos and climbed back into bed.

Locating the remote, he turned on the television.

Channel 9 Action News was showing Maggie's underwater footage taken from the Lexan cylinder.

"... Maggie Taylor gave her life to her profession, leaving these incredible scenes as her lasting legacy. A public service will be held on Thursday, and Channel 9 will be presenting a two-hour special tonight at eight honoring Mrs. Taylor.

"In a related story, a federal judge ruled today that the Megalodon has officially been listed as a protected species of the Monterey Bay National Marine Sanctuary. We bring you live to the steps of the Federal Court Building."

Jonas turned up the volume.

"Mr. Dupont, were you surprised today how quickly the judge ruled in favor of protecting the Meg, especially in light of the recent attacks?"

Andre Dupont of the Cousteau Society stood next to his attorney as microphones were pressed to his face. "No, we weren't surprised. The Monterey Sanctuary is a federally protected marine park designed to protect all species, from the smallest otter to the largest whale. There are other marine predators in the park—Orcas, Great Whites. Each year, we see isolated attacks by Great White sharks on divers or surfers, but these are rare occurrences. Humans are not the staple of the Great White's diet, and we certainly are not the preferred food source of a sixty-foot Megalodon. Of greater importance will be our effort to immediately place *Carcharodon megalodon* on the endangered species list so it is protected in international waters as well."

"Mr. Dupont, what is the Cousteau Society's opinion of the Tanaka Institute's plan to capture the Megalodon?"

"We believe all creatures have a right to exist in their natural habitat. However, in this case, we are dealing with a species that nature may have never intended to interact with man. The Tanaka Lagoon is certainly large enough to accommodate a creature of this size, therefore we agree it might be best if the Megalodon was captured."

The Channel 9 anchor reappeared.

"We had our field reporter, David Adashek, conduct an unofficial street poll to gauge public opinion. David?"

Jonas stared at the familiar face framed by the bushy eyebrows, and shook his head. "God, Maggie, what did I ever do to make you so bitter?"

"Trudy, opinions seem to favor capturing the monster. Personally, I feel the creature is a menace. I've spoken to several marine biologists who believe that it's possible for sharks to acquire a taste for humans. If true, then we can expect more gruesome deaths, especially in light of today's federal court ruling. This is David Adashek reporting for Channel 9 News."

Another knock sent him searching for his tee-shirt. "Hold on!" *Make sure she stocks the fridge with those little vodka samplers...*

He opened the door, daylight burning into his eyes.

"Masao?"

"Taylor-san, let me in."

Jonas stood aside. "How did you find me?"

"You charged the room to your credit card. Mac did the rest." He looked around, stepping over empty beer bottles and liquor samplers. "You have coffee? Never mind, I see it." Masao went into the kitchenette and filled the empty glass pot with water.

"What time is it?"

"One-twenty. No more alcohol, okay? It will rot your liver." Masao sat at the small kitchen table. "I am truly sorry about your wife. She died a noble death, doing what she believed in."

"Death is death. As for our marriage, that was over long ago. She died on her lover's boat." Jonas shook his head, taking a seat across from him. "I'm sorry, Masao, I can't do this anymore."

"What can't you do?"

"There's been too much death. Let the authorities handle the Meg."

"Authorities? I thought you were the authority? Jonas, we have a responsibility as marine biologists. I feel it. I know you do as well." Tanaka looked into Jonas's eyes, bloodshot and exhausted. "A tired mind should not make decisions, but we are running out of time."

"I already made my decision. I'm through."

"Hmm. Taylor-san, you are familiar with Sun Tzu?"

"No."

"Sun Tzu was a great warrior, he wrote *The Art of War* more

289

than twenty-five hundred years ago. Sun Tzu said, 'If you know neither the enemy nor yourself, you will succumb in every battle. If you know yourself but not the enemy, for every victory gained you will also suffer a defeat. But if you know the enemy and know yourself, you need not fear the result of a hundred battles.' Do you understand?"

"No … I don't know, Masao. I can't think right now."

Masao placed his hand on Jonas's shoulder. "Jonas, who knows this creature better than you?"

"This is different."

Masao shook his head. "The quarry remains the quarry; the enemy is yourself. It has been for the last seven years; it will be so for the next seven." He stood. "No matter. My daughter can handle what must be done." He stood, checking on the coffee.

"Terry? What's Terry going to do?"

"Pilot the Abyss Glider, of course. Someone must secure the net around the creature once it has been sedated. The transmitter you implanted is functioning; we just need a sighting to bring the *Kiku* within range of the signal."

"But Terry—"

"Terry is a competent pilot who is not afraid." He poured a cup of coffee, setting it on the table in front of Jonas. "The *Kiku* is docked inside the lagoon; I gave the crew seventy-two hour shore leave while we resupply the ship and test the net. We set out to complete the job tomorrow morning at ten, should you change your mind."

Masao patted him on the shoulder, then headed for the door.

"Masao…"

"Do not worry yourself. The Tanaka clan will finish this business ourselves."

He waved to Jonas, then left.

San Diego

Bud Harris stood by the port rail, watching the sun set over a placid sea. The millionaire always loved this time of day— a brief reprieve from the stress of work; an opportunity to meditate and recharge his batteries for the night ahead.

Not anymore.

He winced as the *Magnate's* underwater lights came on, illuminating the yacht's keel. He stared below, his limbs trembling, his breathing rapid and shallow. He was all alone and he knew that was a bad thing.

The sky darkened; the wind picked up.

And then the whispers came, tickling his ear. "Bud? Baby, where are you?"

"Maggie? Maggie, is that you?" Bud leaned over the rail, searching the black sea.

"Bud, please help me; I don't know where I am."

Hot tears rolled down his cheeks. "Maggie, sweetheart … you're dead."

"I'm not dead, Bud."

"Maggie, I saw you … I saw—"

"Stay there, Bud. I'm coming for you."

Bud's flesh tingled. He stared at the lit patch of water directly below the rail where he was standing. Then he saw the glow—a speck of white rising from the deep.

"Maggie?"

As he watched a snout materialized, followed by a massive triangular head.

"No … no, Maggie … stay away—"

The jaws opened, the Megalodon rising out of the sea…

"No!"

* * *

Bud shot up in bed, screaming, his right arm covered in

blood.

A Jamaican nurse entered the hospital room, followed by a male orderly.

"He tore his I.V. out again."

The nurse quickly slipped on a pair of rubber gloves. "It's okay, Mr. Harris," she soothed. "It was just another nightmare."

"A nightmare? Where am I?"

"You're in the hospital. You suffered a nervous breakdown."

The orderly opened a drawer and pulled out a set of Velcro straps. "Dr. Wishnov said if he pulls his I.V. out again we need to strap him down for the night."

"Touch me with those and your next job will be cleaning bed pans."

"I clean bed pans every day."

"Then I'll crap in bed and you can clean my ass!"

"Calm down, Mr. Harris—"

"I want out of here; I want my own doctor. Where's my goddam cell phone?"

The nurse signaled to the orderly to back off. "Tell you what ... let me fix your I.V. and we'll get you your phone."

He looked up at the nurse. "No straps?"

"As long as you stay calm."

He extended his left forearm, the veins bruised from repeatedly pulling out I.V. needles.

Unable to locate a clean vein, the nurse turned his hand over. Dabbing his flesh with an alcohol swab, she inserted the needle just below his index finger.

"Ouch! Where'd you go to nursing school? Haiti?"

Ignoring the comment, she taped down the needle and started the drip, then shot a syringe of sedative into the bag.

Bud's eyes grew heavy. He laid his head back, mumbling something as he passed out.

The nurse nodded to the orderly. "Strap this a-hole down."

* * *

The cab passed Jonas's house, continuing to the end of the block. The news vans were gone, but there were two SUVs parked a few houses away that looked suspicious.

Hunched low in the backseat, Jonas instructed the driver to turn down the next block.

He paid the driver, then cut through his neighbor's backyard and hopped the fence into his own yard. Locating the hide-a-key, he entered through his back door.

The house had been emptied. Paintings, furnishings, plants … Maggie's clothes—Bud's movers had taken it all. Even the pots and pans were gone.

She doesn't even cook … didn't cook … ah, geez.

He entered his office. Files were strewn everywhere, his laptop open. He wiggled the mouse, chasing away the screensaver. She had been Googling the Farallon Islands.

Jonas sat back in his chair, the image of the Megalodon's last attack burned into his memory. And yet every time he tested his emotional response, he kept imagining Terry.

Maggie had been right; Jonas found himself thinking about Terry all the time. Surrendering to their mutual lust, they had been together in his stateroom the night Masao had gone ashore. She had snuck out of his room just before dawn, winking to Mac who had seen her exiting his friend's cabin.

And then Jonas had pulled back, afraid things had gone too far.

Terry had misinterpreted his sudden coolness, believing Jonas still had feelings for his wife—either that or he felt like his actions had been disrespectful to her father. A woman scorned, she had treated him coldly after that—and deservedly so.

But it was neither Maggie nor Masao that caused Jonas to cool things off with Terry. The truth was that he was afraid.

Ever since the attack in Hawaii, Jonas had become convinced that he would not survive the mission. Premonitions of his own death came in the form of a recurring dream, one in which he found himself in the mini-sub, hovering along the surface, the Megalodon rising to attack from below, devouring him whole.

So realistic were these nightmares that, on several occasions Jonas woke up screaming.

Had this been an isolated experience, he would have chalked it up to the nature of their mission and the monster they were chasing. Only it wasn't isolated. Seven years earlier, Jonas had experienced a similar series of dreams while on board the navy transport, the *Maxine D*. It had been these night terrors that he secretly credited for saving his life on his last dive into the Mariana Trench. Despite Frank Heller's accusations, Jonas knew now that he hadn't panicked when the Meg had attacked the *Sea Cliff*. In fact, he had reacted with lightning-quick reflexes from hours of mentally rehearsing what he would do if the submersible had been threatened by the biologic they had first detected on sonar hours earlier ... a state of paranoia implanted by the dreams.

Seven years later the night terrors had returned.

The last one had been the worst. After Terry had left his cabin he had fallen back asleep. In a vivid dream he found himself in a suffocating, terrifying darkness. Trapped within this void, death had whispered into his ear.

With a blood-curdling scream, Jonas had shot up in bed, his entire body bathed in sweat.

Jonas had ended things with Terry Tanaka, not because he didn't care about her, but because he knew he was falling in love. Hers were the ties that kept him bound to the mission; their blossoming relationship would be his death knell.

* * *

The six-and-three-quarter-inch bottom tooth was a fossil.

Lead-gray and heavily serrated, it was worth at least a thousand dollars to collectors, though Jonas would never sell it. The Meg tooth had been a gift from Mac on his thirty-fifth birthday—a good-luck charm that had ushered in a book deal and a string of good tidings.

Jonas removed the tooth from its glass case. He ran his fingers absentmindedly along its sharp serrated edges as his thoughts returned to his last conversation with Masao.

Making up his mind, he carried the Megalodon tooth into his bedroom. Emptying his workout gear from a gym bag, he repacked it, sandwiching the tooth between a few days' worth of clothing.

Entering his bathroom, he located a razor and shaved, calculating the drive time to Monterey.

PAYBACK

BUD HARRIS GATHERED HIS BELONGINGS and stuffed them into a plastic bag provided by the orderly. Unshaven and badly in need of a shower, the once-proud entrepreneur had been reduced to a feeble shell of his former self. Deeply depressed after having witnessed his lover's death, Bud was also suffering from exhaustion brought on by a lack of REM sleep.

The millionaire no longer cared whether he lived or died. He felt alone and in pain, barely and was afraid to sleep. His doctors recommended he see a psychiatrist. Bud wasn't interested.

The nurse arrived to escort her patient out of the hospital with the traditional wheelchair ride. "Mr. Harris, is anyone meeting you downstairs?"

"No."

Two men strode up to the nurse. "We're here to meet Mr. Harris."

Bud looked up at them. "Who the hell are you?"

"Dr. Frank Heller. This is my associate, Richard Danielson." Heller held out his hand.

Bud ignored it. "Danielson? You're the asshole who got all those navy guys killed going after the shark. Should have killed the damn thing while you had the chance." Bud stood, walking away from the wheelchair, the orderly, and the two men. "I'll find my own way out."

"That's why we're here," Heller said, following him down the corridor. "My brother, Dennis, was butchered by the same monster that killed Maggie Taylor."

"Yeah? Well, I'm sorry for your loss, now if you'll excuse me—"

"Hold it," said Danielson. "This thing has killed a lot of people. We thought you'd want to be involved in a little payback." Danielson looked at Heller. "Maybe we were wrong."

The thought of killing the Megalodon seemed to set off a spark in Bud. He focused his eyes on Danielson for the first time. "What is it you need? Money? Weapons?"

"Just your boat."

Tanaka Oceanographic Institute

Jonas parked in the deserted lot, his dashboard clock reading 12:07 PM. Traffic in Los Angeles had cost him several hours, but he had managed to reach Masao by phone.

Grabbing his bag, he headed for the helipad.

Mac was waiting for him in the helicopter, his cheeks full from taking down a bacon cheeseburger in two bites. "Well, well, the prodigal son-in-law returns."

"Clever."

"While you've been camped out in your motel hide-a-way, I spent the better part of the last three nights flying up and down the coast searching for the Meg. The homing device you implanted seems to be functioning; unfortunately I had walkie-talkies as a kid that carried a better range. The Coast Guard's been helping out and we covered about four hundred nautical miles, but if she's in the canyon we may never find her." He tossed Jonas a fast food bag holding another bacon double-cheeseburger. "Lunch is on me. So Romeo, how long have you and the voluptuous Ms. Tanaka been sharing bodily fluids?"

"Just the one time, if you must know."

"Oh, but I must. It's all part of my responsibilities as your life coach."

"Seeing how my life has been going of late, maybe I should have fired you."

"Oh, boo-hoo." Mac strapped himself in, powering up the chopper. "I don't see anyone putting a gun to your head. Despite tossing yourself repeatedly and quite moronically, may I add, into the line of fire you're still very much alive. That's a lot more than we can say about D.J. and that two-timing wife of yours—my condolences, by the way. So, am I taking you to the *Kiku*, or not?"

"I've been having those dreams again, Mac. The ones I told you about when we first met—when I mistook you for a real shrink."

"More premonitions? Of what?"

"Being eaten by our friend."

Mac powered off the engine. "How long have you been having these new night terrors?"

"Since the *Nautilus* disaster."

"Maybe the dreams were warning you about Maggie?"

"I considered that. Only the dreams are clearly from my perspective. I'm in the Abyss Glider, powerless along the surface. It's daylight. Looking below, I see the Meg. She's rising from below. Her mouth opens wide … and in I go."

"When was the last dream?"

"The night I was with Terry … you know, afterwards."

"Jonas, if you're so convinced you're going to die on this mission, why the hell are you here?"

"Honestly, I wasn't going to show up. Then, I thought back to a story my father told me shortly after he was diagnosed with stage-four cancer. The story was about two men. The first was a Chicago native nicknamed, 'Easy Eddie.' Easy Eddie was Al Capone's lawyer. Despite his boss being a murderer and notorious gangster, Easy Eddie managed to keep Capone out of jail. To show his gratitude, Capone paid his attorney a lot of money. He set Easy Eddie and his family up in a huge mansion with live-in help. Made sure he had everything he could possibly want.

"Easy Eddie had a son that he loved more than anything in

the world. He gave his son everything … a good education, fancy clothes. Despite his own involvement with organized crime, Eddie even tried to teach his kid right from wrong. But there were two things Eddie couldn't give his son; he couldn't pass on a good name and he wasn't a good example of how to live your life.

"In an effort to cleanse his tarnished soul and restore some integrity to his name, Easy Eddie decided to testify against Al 'Scarface' Capone—as sure a death sentence as my father's cancer. He testified anyway.

"Capone died in prison, and within a year the mob killed Easy Eddie, who left this world giving his son the greatest gift he had to offer—his life.

"The second man my father told me about was Lieutenant Commander Butch O'Hare. Butch was a World War II fighter pilot assigned to the aircraft carrier *Lexington* in the South Pacific. On February 20, 1942, Butch and his squadron were sent on an important mission. After he was airborne, Butch realized his crew hadn't topped off his fuel tank, which meant he wouldn't be able to complete his mission and get back to the aircraft carrier. His flight leader ordered him to return to the ship.

"On his way back to the *Lexington*, Butch O'Hare spotted a squadron of enemy aircraft heading for the American fleet. The American fighters were gone, and the carrier fleet was all but defenseless. O'Hare had no way of alerting the *Lexington* in time, so he did the only thing he could, he dove into the enemy's formation with his 50 caliber guns blazing, taking out one plane after the next until all his ammunition was gone. Even then, he went after the remaining planes, attempting to clip them with his landing gear. In the end, he succeeded in diverting the enemy from the American fleet and made it back safely to the *Lexington*.

"The film from O'Hare's gun-mounted camera showed the extent of Butch's heroism and he became the navy's first Ace of World War-II and the first naval aviator to be awarded the Medal of Honor. A year later, at the age of twenty-nine, Butch O'Hare was killed in aerial combat. His home town decided to name their airport in his honor … Chicago's O'Hare airport. There's a memorial statue of Butch O'Hare located between Terminals 1 and 2."

"I never knew that. Why do you think your father told you about these two men?"

"Butch O'Hare was Easy Eddie's son."

Mac sat back, the story suddenly weighing heavier.

"When they found Easy Eddie's body, there were three possessions on him which the police gave to his son, Butch—a crucifix, a religious medallion, and a poem torn from a magazine. The poem read: '*The clock of life is wound but once, and no man has the power to tell just when the hands will stop, at late or early hour. Now is the only time you own. Live, love, toil with a will. Place no faith in time. For the clock may soon be still.*'

"The cancer took my father three months after he was diagnosed. To answer your question, Mac, I'm here because I have no control over my clock—none of us do. The only thing I can do is have faith and do the right thing. Take me to the *Kiku*."

"And the voluptuous Terry Tanaka."

Mac restarted the engine, then reached over and tossed Jonas's bacon double-cheeseburger out of the open cockpit. "Don't eat that stuff, it'll kill you."

Aboard the Whale Watcher: The *Cap'n Jack*

Four days had passed since the death of Maggie Taylor. Although surfing, jet-ski, and parasailing activities suffered, other businesses attracted out-of-towners to the Northern California coast like bees to honey.

At the top of the list were whale-watching excursions. Much like cage-divers yearning to photograph a Great White in the wild, the public was willing to pay good money for an opportunity to see a real live Megalodon shark ... albeit from the safety of a decent-size ship.

Within days, tour boat operators were offering special late afternoon and evening excursions to the Farallon Islands at triple the normal fares. Night trips sold out quickly, forcing the Coast Guard to announce it would be patrolling the area after dusk. Marine biologists from the Monterey Bay Aquarium reminded the public that the Megalodon had never surfaced during daylight hours and that the presence of hundreds of whales migrating south through the Monterey Bay Sanctuary without any noticeable changes in behavior served as a canary in the coal mine, rendering the odds of experiencing an actual Meg sighting on par with hitting the lottery.

* * *

Jason and Milisa Russell had driven from Covington, Washington to Monterey to catch "Meg-fever." Unfortunately, all of the evening tours were booked, and the few late afternoon openings on ebay were beyond their budget, so they settled on a late morning tour aboard the *Cap'n Jack*, a forty-two-foot sightseeing boat docked at the Monterey Bay wharf.

The skipper, an Iraqi War Vet named Robert Gibbons, greeted the Russells as they boarded the vessel. The couple located an empty bench in the stern next to a silver-haired woman and her red-headed teenage daughter.

"Hi, I'm Marilyn Rhea," the woman gushed, her southern accent heavy, "and this is my daughter, Shannon. Shannon, put the gosh-darn phone away."

"Ugh, you are so annoying."

Milisa forced a smile. "We're the Russells. I'm Milisa, this is my husband, Jason."

"Hey."

Marilyn rolled the collar of her sweater higher. "We're from

Tennessee; this is our first trip to California. Why is it so gosh-darn cold?"

Before Milisa could answer the boat's engines growled to life, its exhaust choking those passengers seated behind the pilothouse.

Captain Gibbons's voice squawked over the loudspeaker. "Welcome aboard the *Cap'n Jack*. I'm your skipper, Robert Gibbons, and we've got a great day in store for you. While I know many of you are hoping we'll come in contact with the Megalodon shark, we won't be venturing anywhere near the Farallon Islands this morning. We will, however, be looking to encounter the Meg's favorite food—whales. So keep your cameras ready, you never know what can happen."

Aboard the *Kiku*

Masao Tanaka was waiting by the helipad as Mac landed the helicopter. He smiled when he saw Jonas in the co-pilot's seat.

"Taylor-san, I am so glad to see you. Unfortunately, my daughter may not share these same feelings. When she heard you were returning, she went to her cabin to pack her belongings. Perhaps you could speak with her?"

* * *

Jonas knocked on Terry's door.

"Go away."

"Terry, give me five minutes and I'll be out of your life."

She yanked open the door. "Five minutes."

He entered her cabin. Her suitcase was on the bed, packed to the brim with clothes.

"Terry, why are you leaving?"

"I don't owe you an explanation."

"No, but I owe you one. The morning you left my cabin … I freaked out a little bit. See, I had this dream—"

"I don't care." She stuffed a toiletry bag inside the suitcase and zippered it closed.

"Terry, the reason I treated you coldly had nothing to do with Maggie. I do really care about you and—"

She wheeled around to face him. "You don't care about me. Your wife cheated on you and you used me to get even."

"That's not true. Yes, things were happening quickly between us, but that had nothing to do with Maggie … our marriage was over long ago. What scared me off wasn't you, it was these recurring nightmares about the Meg. I had these same premonitions seven years ago before I dived the trench for the navy. I knew if I stuck around that I'd probably die this time around, only I was falling in love with you."

"And so you pushed me away so you could leave without feeling guilty? That's a pretty lame excuse."

"Agreed. But I'm back."

"Why? So you can replace me on yet another dive? So you can save me from that big, bad shark? Well, guess what? I'm not some helpless damsel-in-distress that needs to be saved. As for these premonitions, did you ever stop to consider that maybe, if you had let me dive the Mariana Trench, things might have gone differently? Maybe it was your bad karma seven years ago that killed those men? Maybe, if I had gone with D.J. instead of you, my brother might still be alive."

Grabbing her suitcase, she pushed past him and left.

Aboard the Whale Watcher: The *Cap'n Jack* 14 Miles West of Santa Cruz

The Russells were sipping hot chocolate on the stern bench, the cold having chased Marilyn Rhea and her daughter, Shannon inside.

Jason was scanning the ocean with a pair of high-powered

binoculars when Captain Gibbons's voice came over the loudspeaker, "Folks, this is really exciting! On our port, or left side, is an unusually large pod of orca."

Everyone moved to the port side, cameras poised.

"Orca, also known as Killer Whales, are extremely intelligent hunters, able to kill whales many times larger than themselves. Looks like we're catching this pod in the middle of a hunt."

Jason focused his binoculars on the black dorsal fins moving parallel to the boat a good eighty yards away. There were at least twenty Orca, with three big males taking turns converging on a smaller object, the rest racing along the perimeter to ensure their prey would not escape.

As he watched, Jason saw what looked like an albino Great White shark, its three-foot dorsal fin bleeding as the wolf pack tore at its hide.

* * *

The Megalodon pup raced along the surface, prevented from submerging by the much larger predators below. The pod had tracked down the female as it hunted southeast of the Farallon Islands.

With frightening speed and power, the Orca bulls snapped at the shark, taking turns flipping its broken carcass high into the air, making a sport of the demise of the would-be future queen of Monterey Bay.

* * *

Ten minutes later the *Cap'n Jack's* engines powered off, leaving the boat to roll gently in three foot seas. The gray horizon ran unimpeded for miles in every direction, the sudden quiet magnifying the sensation of isolation.

"Folks, you're about to get your money's worth. Twenty yards off the starboard bow is a Gray whale cow and its calf. If we're lucky, they may come closer."

Marilyn and her daughter rejoined the Russells in time to witness the mother Gray whale's head break the surface, allowing a few passengers to reach over the rail and touch it.

"Wow, Shannon, did you see that?"

The teen ignored her, attempting to find a signal on her cell phone.

The Russells waited their turn, Milisa managing to take a picture of her husband reaching out to touch one of the gentle giant's barnacles.

The Gray whale submerged, its calf remaining close enough to the boat for passengers hovering by the starboard rail to snap selfies.

Without warning, something violently pounded the ship's keel, the multiple impacts rocking the vessel.

Jason watched as a patch of sea swirled below, the surface pooling a dark red.

"Is that blood?"

With a *whoosh*, the Gray whale breached ten yards behind the boat. Thrashing about, it slapped its fluke repeatedly against the surface before rolling onto its side—revealing a crater-shaped gushing wound the size of an open beach umbrella.

Pushing one another, the passengers rushed to the back of the boat to take photos.

"Maybe it's the Orca?"

"Can't be, the wound's too big. It has to be the Megalodon."

The Gray whale calf approached its mother, *chuffing* rapid exhalations.

Without warning, the Megalodon's stark-white head rose vertically from beneath the newborn, engulfing the newborn whole, slamming shut a second later like a steel bear trap, cetacean blood splattering the passengers.

Some screamed, others cheered.

The wounded Gray whale surfaced again, blood splashing everywhere.

A crewman raced inside the pilothouse to report to the captain. Seconds later, the engine restarted, joined by a sickening *clang* of metal as the dented propeller bashed against its crushed housing.

Feeding below, the Megalodon registered the annoying disturbance and rose to investigate.

Aboard the *Kiku*

Terry Tanaka entered the bridge to confront her father, who was standing over Alphonse DeMarco manning the radio.

"Masao, where's Mac? I need him to take me back to Monterey."

"Not now, Terry. The Coast Guard just picked up a distress call from a whale-watching boat not far from here."

"The female? In broad daylight?"

Jonas entered the bridge. "The attack on the yacht … Mac's light must have blinded her."

"The monster's blind? Taylor-san, is this a good thing?"

"Not if she's surfacing during the day. A shark losing its sight is a lot different than you or me going blind. She has other sensory organs that she'll be able to use to guide her. Considering daylight had been her Achilles heel, I'd say things just got worse."

Sonar operator Robert Nash pressed his headphones to his ears. "Masao, the Meg's transmitter signal just appeared on sonar. She's nineteen kilometers to the northwest on course two-seven-three."

Captain Barre adjusted their course and speed as Mac entered the bridge.

Masao turned, barking out orders. "Mac, the creature has surfaced. Refuel the chopper, then I want you in the air, Captain

306

Barre will feed you the coordinates. Alphonse, get to the harpoon gun. Jonas, I'll need you ready in the Abyss Glider."

"Change in plans, Masao. Terry's going to pilot the mini-sub. I'll work the winch."

Masao turned to his daughter. "You are okay with this?"

She glanced at Jonas, then nodded to her father. "I can handle it."

Aboard the Whale Watcher: The *Cap'n Jack*

The Gray whale's fluke had bent the *Cap'n Jack's* propeller when it had been attacked beneath the boat. The screw could turn, but not without chaffing metal on metal, creating a sound that irritated the Megalodon.

Each time Captain Gibbons attempted to move the boat, the sixty foot shark charged the stern—causing the twenty-seven passengers onboard to yell at the crew.

"Stop angering it!

"Here it comes again—hold on!"

Whump.

The creature plowed into the keel, the collision propelling the boat thirty feet, knocking Milisi Russell off her bench while sending the Meg's wake spilling over the transom, soaking her husband, Jason.

* * *

"Jonas, you read me?"

"Go ahead, Mac," Jonas yelled into his walkie-talkie. He and DeMarco were positioned at the *Kiku's* stern rail, ready at the deck-mounted harpoon gun.

"I'm about two hundred feet above the whale-watching boat. There's blood everywhere, looks like the Meg took out a whale. And the boat's just sitting there, dead in the water."

As Mac watched, a swell suddenly appeared sixty yards off

307

the boat's starboard flank, the albino creature charging the vessel.

Whomp!

The boat shuddered as it was plowed thirty yards to port, the passengers flailing across the deck.

To his horror, Mac saw a red-headed woman fall overboard.

"Jonas, what's your ETA?"

"Ten minutes."

"You'd better tell Leon to haul ass or this is going to turn into an all-you-can-eat human buffet."

* * *

Marilyn Rhea screamed as she saw her daughter flip head-first over the side.

Shannon surfaced forty feet from the still-drifting boat in water so cold it took her breath away. Barely able to tread water, still gripping her cell phone, she realized her clothing was stained in blood.

"Oh God, I'm bleeding."

Turning to her left, she saw the floating island of blubber and realized it was the Gray whale's blood, not hers. Relieved, she turned to her right—and screamed.

A four foot wake was rolling toward her. The monster was moving just beneath the surface, its open mouth visible within the swell, its mouth turning sideways to eat her.

Shannon bit down on her cell phone and then lunged to her left, desperately clawing and scrambling and pulling herself out of the sea and onto the back of the dying Gray whale.

The Megalodon rolled onto its side to consume its prey, its senses had been locked on the electrical impulses of Shannon's beating heart—which suddenly disappeared. The albino predator passed beneath the whale, its head rotating from side to side as it attempted to relocate the signal.

Shannon clung to the bobbing, bleeding whale as the swell rolled over her cetacean island up to her thighs.

When she looked up she saw a large ship racing towards the whale watching boat from the southeast.

* * *

Leon Barre cut the *Kiku's* forward speed in half as he attempted to come alongside the tour boat's portside beam, giving Jonas a clear shot.

Jonas spun the harpoon gun counterclockwise on its base and focused through its sight. "Mac, where is she, I still can't see her?"

"She just passed beneath the wounded whale."

"Okay, I see her. Al, warn them."

Alphonse DeMarco raised the megaphone to his lips. "Attention whale watcher passengers and crew. Get in the middle of the boat and take over."

* * *

The passengers were lying on deck, fearful of falling overboard when they looked up and saw the research vessel's bridge pass by, followed by the top of a steel A-frame and what appeared to be a harpoon gun.

Jonas fired.

The harpoon exploded out of the cannon, trailing smoke and steel cable. The projectile struck home, burying itself four feet deep into the Megalodon's thick hide, inches from the base of its dorsal fin.

The monster spasmed. Arching its back, it whipped its head sideways and submerged, jerking the steel line faster than its spool could unravel slack.

The *Kiku* lurched hard to starboard, its aft end smashing into the whale-watcher.

WHOMP!

The Meg rammed the *Kiku's* keel, the force of the blow bending steel plates, sending Jonas, DeMarco, and the two crewmen flopping to the deck.

* * *

"Hard to port," growled Captain Barre, picking himself up off the deck of the bridge. "Masao, when the hell's this shark of yours gonna fall asleep?"

"Just lead it away from that tour boat."

* * *

Hovering two hundred feet above the Pacific, Mac watched as the *Kiku* headed south, the enraged Megalodon circling back to ram the ship again. "Sweet Jesus. Jonas, you guys okay down there?"

"We're taking a beating. What's it look like to you?"

"Looks like I'm flying home alone. What happened to those drugs of yours?"

"My guess would be a bad reaction. Stand by." He changed frequencies. "Masao, what's the harpoon getting on the Meg's vitals?"

"I think we overdosed her. Her pulse just rocketed from seventy-seven to two hundred and twelve beats per minute."

"Hold on," yelled Nash, "she's breaching again!"

Wa-BOOM!

The *Kiku* shuddered, the impact sending books and charts flying.

"She's gonna tear my ship apart!" yelled Barre, grabbing the ship's internal phone. "Captain here … speak."

"Skipper, the engine room's taking on water. Another blow like that last one and we'll be swimming home."

"You think I don't know this? If it's leaking plug it, if it don't work fix it!" Barre slammed the receiver down, then turned his ship hard to port.

* * *

The Megalodon's brain was on fire, her blood boiling, her heart racing out of control. The predator's sensory system was overloaded by the madness brought on by the overdose of pentobarbital. Unable to reason, the creature was bound to her primordial instincts.

Dragging the steel cable to a depth beyond fifteen hundred feet, the Meg targeted its challenger, her senses homing in on the electrical impulses given off by the *Kiku's* steel hull moving through seawater. The crescent tail whipped back and forth, driving the monster back toward the surface as she rammed the ship again, smashing the forward compartment of the keel.

This time, the force of the blow knocked the giant predator senseless, stymieing her heart rate long enough for the pentobarbital and ketamine to take hold, shutting down the creature's central nervous system.

* * *

"Taylor-san, the creature's heart rate is plummeting. One-twenty … one hundred. Stand-by. Okay, it seems to be stabilizing … fifty-three beats per minute."

"We don't have much time. Al, take up the slack and release the net; I'll get Terry into the water."

He hurried to the Abyss Glider. The mini-sub was ready to launch, Terry waiting by its open rear hatch.

"You sure about this? It's not too late to change your mind."

"Shut-up," she said. Reaching for him, she buried her tongue in his mouth, the kiss more lust than passion.

Terry pulled away, her cheeks flushed, her eyes wide. "Okay, let's do this."

She crawled head-first into the sub, sealing the hatch from the inside as he started the A-frame's winch. The Abyss Glider was hoisted twenty feet off the deck.

Pivoting the A-frame aft caused the mini-sub to swing outward over the rail away from the *Kiku,* allowing Jonas to lower the craft into the sea.

* * *

311

The Meg was losing feeling in its tail. The female slowed, barely moving, dangling by the steel line almost twelve hundred feet beneath the surface.

DeMarco and h'is assistant, Philip Prousnitzer stood at the stern, watching the *Kiku's* winch strain to gather in steel cable.

"Phil, secure the winch at five hundred feet, then help me ready the net." He looked down as the Abyss Glider's saddle sunk beneath the mini-sub, freeing the buoyant craft.

Terry started the engine. The sub leaped forward, submerging into the vast blue world.

"Terry, can you hear me?" Masao's voice filtered over the radio.

"Loud and clear. I'm at five hundred feet. Visibility's good."

"The Meg's respiration rate is plummeting."

"Stand-by." Terry descended the glider, following the cable at a forty-five-degree angle. At eight hundred and sixty feet she saw the Meg.

The monstrous albino shark was suspended head-down, its tail thrashing uselessly. Unable to channel water into its mouth, the creature's gills could not function.

The Megalodon was drowning.

"Masao, the Meg's not breathing. You've got to tow her immediately. Do you copy?"

"*Hai.* Stand by."

The *Kiku's* engines restarted with a metallic, grinding sound. The line grew taut, and the Megalodon's head jerked upward at the sub. Terry circled the glider out of harm's way as the creature leveled off.

Keeping the submersible parallel with the shark's gills, she focused her attention on the five 15-foot long vertical slits. They remained pressed tight.

Moving ahead to the Meg's mouth, Terry realized the creature's jaws were clamped shut, perhaps a reflex action brought about by the drugs which targeted the shark's central nervous system.

Looping the glider into a tight three-sixty, she circled back and accelerated, smashing the mini-sub's Lexan nose against the Megalodon's mandible where the lower jaw hinged with the upper, the collision nearly tossing her head-first from her harness.

The Meg's lower jaw dropped open, seawater rushing in.

Seconds later, the gills began to flutter.

"Whatever you just did, Terry, it seems to be working. According to the harpoon's sensors, the creature's blood-oxygen levels are rising. Well done."

She beamed proudly. "Thanks ... Dad. You can tell Al to lower the net."

"Stand by."

Terry hovered by the Meg's right flank, marveling at the sheer size of the creature, its stark-white hide, its savage grace. For the first time she found herself looking at the Megalodon as something other than a menace that needed to be killed. The shark was a product of evolution, perfected by nature over hundreds of millions of years. It was the true master of the ocean, perhaps the last of her kind, and Terry felt better about not destroying it.

Looking up, she saw the Meg harness—a weighted cargo net, feeding out along the surface. Jonas had ordered flotation buoys attached along its perimeter, the inflatable devices designed to be operated from the *Kiku*. In this way, the Megalodon could be released safely once secured inside the lagoon, with the net simply dropping away as the devices were deflated.

Ascending to meet the sinking cargo net, Terry extended the glider's retractable arm, using it to grab hold of the lead marker buoy. Submerging, she dragged the net straight down on a ninety-degree descent, stretching out the rolled-up slack.

Passing the Megalodon's head, she leveled out, racing

beneath the creature's scarred belly and beyond its caudal fin.

"Masao … father, I'm in position. Inflate the harness."

"Stand by."

The net's perimeter buoys sprang to life, the compressed air causing the suddenly buoyant net to fit the contours of the Megalodon. The thirty ton shark rose, the tension releasing from the harpoon as it leveled off a hundred and sixty feet below the surface.

"That's perfect," Terry said. She descended beneath the half-moon tail, inspecting the netting supporting the Meg's belly.

"Uh-oh."

"Terry, what is it?"

"Masao, the female gave birth."

"Are you certain?"

"One hundred percent. Have Jonas stand by with the glider's saddle, I'm coming aboard."

"Terry, before you surface, Leon requests that you check the damage to the ship's keel."

"On my way." Terry accelerated past the captive female, moving beneath the boat's hull.

"Oh, wow…"

The multiple impacts by the Megalodon had taken out one of the ship's two propeller shafts and dented the other. Worse, a twelve-by-twenty foot section of steel plating had been crushed.

The boat was taking on water.

The *Kiku* was sinking.

DUSK

LEON BARRE POINTED TO A SECTION of the *Kiku's* keel on a computer program. "I counted seven bent plates," the captain said, "at least three of which are taking on water. They're right on the seam; no way to seal them while we're at sea. The starboard shaft's completely bent, it won't turn at all. The portside shaft's turning, but it's also damaged, making a helluva noise. Rev her any faster than six to seven knots and she'll tear loose."

"Will we sink?" Masao asked Captain Barre. The ship had taken on a tremendous amount of water, her decks were now listing at a fifteen-degree angle to starboard.

"Sink? Yes. Maybe not tonight, who knows, maybe not tomorrow. We sealed off the forward compartment and the pumps are running, but she's still takin' on water."

"How long until we arrive at the lagoon?" asked DeMarco.

"Pulling that monster out there, that's a lot of drag, lots of work for one screw. It's just after seven. I say we make it back tomorrow morning, just after dawn."

DeMarco looked at Jonas. "Will the Meg stay unconscious for that long?"

"I hate to add to all the uncertainty, but honestly, I don't know. There's no way of telling. I gave her what I thought was a sufficient dosage to keep her under twelve to sixteen hours."

"Taylor-san, can we inject her again?"

"We can, but it's dangerous. There's a risk of permanent damage to her nervous system. And we've already seen what happened before the drugs took effect. If she reacts that way along a populated shoreline like Monterey…"

Masao shook his head, unsure. "Not many options. Leon, how many crew members do you need to run the ship? Maybe we

315

should evacuate some of the men now—"

"No. With the damage to the screw and the sea knocking on the door, I need every hand I've got, plus some. We leave this ship, we're all gonna leave together."

"The problem is not the *Kiku*," Terry interjected, "it's the reliability of the Meg's cardiac monitor. Jonas and I can set up shifts to watch her in the Abyss Glider. If she appears to be waking up, we'll radio you to hit her with another injection. Maybe we can reduce the dose a bit and keep her under just long enough to make it inside the lagoon."

"Taylor-san?"

"It sounds like our best option."

"Very good. You and Terry set-up a schedule; begin the first shift at four AM. Alphonse, I want you and Philip Prousnitzer to set up similar shifts at the harpoon gun." Masao paused, listening to the sound of thunder rumbling in the distance. "Is that a storm front moving in?"

Mac entered the bridge, having just refueled his chopper. "Not thunder, Masao. That's the sound of helicopters. News choppers, five of em to be exact, and there's more coming. I'd say it's gonna be mighty crowded around here by dawn."

* * *

Frank Heller paused from his work, looking up at the television screen for the fourth time in the last hour to watch the latest news update:

"... two hundred feet below us, lying in a comatose state is the sixty-foot Megalodon, a monster responsible for at least a dozen deaths over the last forty-two days. From our view, you can clearly see the creature's snowy-white hide, its skin almost luminescent in the lunar light.

"At her present course and speed, the heavily damaged *Kiku* is expected to reach the entrance of the Tanaka Lagoon sometime around dawn. Channel 8 News will be keeping a vigil all night, bringing you the latest on this breaking story. This is Michelle Cylwa, KSBW-TV, reporting live from the ..."

"Turn it off already, Frank," yelled Danielson. They were aboard the *Magnate*, assembling a homemade depth charge in the yacht's exercise room. Danielson was hard at work, installing the fuse to the four-by-two-foot steel barrel. "Haven't you had enough? You've been watching the same story all night."

"You asked me to find out how deep the Meg is," Heller said in his defense. "Did you expect me to swim out with a tape measure? From the camera angle, I'd guess she's about a hundred and fifty to two hundred feet down. What kind of kill zone you rigging that charge with?"

"Enough to fry that fish and the rest of her kind. I've added extra amatol, which is rather primitive but highly explosive. The challenge will be getting close enough to make an accurate drop. We'll have to rely on Harris for that. Where the hell is he anyway?"

"Up on deck. Did you hear the guy screaming in his sleep?"

"Half of San Francisco heard him. I'll tell you something, Frank, I haven't been sleeping well myself."

"Relax, skipper, after tomorrow, you'll be sleeping like a baby."

* * *

Bud Harris stood by the starboard rail, staring at the reflection of moon on the black sea. The *Magnate* was anchored three hundred yards south of the Tanaka Lagoon, and in the lunar light, Bud could just make out the white concrete wall of the huge canal entrance.

"Maggie ..." Bud drained his beer as he watched small wakes lap at the hull. "Look what you've gotten me into. Hanging out with a bunch of navy bozos, playing war against some freakin' fish."

Bud tossed the empty can in the water and opened another. "Ahh, Maggs. Why couldn't you have just dropped the stupid

STEVE ALTEN

camera?" Tears rolled down his cheeks. "Well, don't worry, your man's gonna kill that monster and cut out its eyes." He turned, staggering past the grand spiral staircase to one of the guestrooms. Bud found he could no longer sleep in the yacht's master suite. Maggie's perfume still lingered, her presence too vivid. When the mission was over, he planned to sell the yacht and move back east.

Collapsing onto the queen-size bed, he passed out.

* * *

The three-foot albino-white dorsal fin cut the surface, circling the discarded aluminum can as it sank into the black waters of the sanctuary.

Aboard the *Kiku*

The *Kiku* crawled across the Pacific, listing twenty-eight degrees to port. All but two of the news helicopters had left, the others expected back by dawn as the ship moved within fourteen miles of the Tanaka lagoon.

Terry stood by the stern rail, staring at the soft white glow reflecting in the moonlight. Her hand caressed the switch controlling the air pressure feeding the net's inflatable buoys.

"Be easy to do, wouldn't it?"

Terry turned, surprised to find Jonas watching her.

"Release the net and she drowns. Been thinking about it myself. But it's not what your brother would want."

"Maybe it's what I want."

"Then do it."

Terry fingered the controls. Her hand quivered.

Jonas placed his hand over hers. "It won't bring him back."

She turned to face him and wept. Jonas hugged her to his chest.

* * *

The female ascended slowly, rising through the gray curtains of light that

318

could no longer harm her, her great caudal fin beating harder as she rose, her jaws agape.

At four hundred feet Jonas saw her rising through the blue underworld. The triangular head...the satanic grin. It was seven years ago and he was back on the Sea Cliff ... only this was different, this time there was no retreat, no escape.

I'm going to die...

* * *

"Ahhhh."

Jonas shot up in bed, bathed in sweat. Terry was next to him, wearing his grey Penn State tee-shirt. She had turned on the light and was now kneeling beside him.

"Are you all right?"

He nodded, struggling to find his voice.

"You screamed so loud, I thought I was going to have a heart attack. Was it the same dream?"

He nodded again, then reached for the open bottle of water by the bed, his hand trembling. He thought about popping one of his yellow pills, then changed his mind.

"What time is it?"

She looked at her watch. "Three-forty. The first shift starts in twenty minutes. It's mine."

"No."

"Jonas, if these nightmares really are premonitions—"

"The dream takes place in the Abyss Glider during the day. If you really want to help me then let me have the pre-dawn shift. We can switch at sunrise."

"Okay, that makes sense." She straddled him, removing his shirt.

"What are you doing?"

She smiled. "We still have twenty minutes."

* * *

Alphonse DeMarco loaded the injectable cartridge of

pentobarbital and ketamine into the harpoon, then checked his watch again. *Four-fifteen. Where was the man?*

Terry approached, smiling. "Morning, Al."

"Not yet it's not, but it will be soon. Where the hell is Jonas?"

"He's coming."

Jonas hustled out of the *Kiku's* infrastructure, zipping up his bio-suit. "Sorry. Forgot my good luck charm." He held up the lead-gray fossilized Meg tooth.

DeMarco shook his head. "Ever hear of a rabbit's foot?"

Jonas winked at Terry, fighting to take his eyes off her. For the first time in as long as he could remember, he felt happy.

He tucked the tooth inside a Velcro pouch over his chest, then he and Terry completed a visual inspection of the Abyss Glider. "Looks good. I'd better get going."

"Don't forget, I relieve you at sunrise." She squeezed his hand, then leaned in and whispered in his ear. "Jonas, what I said before about you bringing bad karma to the mission ... you know I didn't mean it."

"Yeah, you did. But karma can change. I think it usually takes about twenty minutes."

She smiled, watching him crawl inside the aft end of the glider.

DeMarco was standing by at the winch. He waited until Jonas sealed the hatch and gave a thumbs-up before reversing the cable, lifting the mini-sub off the tilted deck by its saddle.

Jonas held on as the A-frame swung him out over the *Kiku's* stern. For a long moment he swayed, DeMarco allowing gravity to rectify the awkward angle of the A-frame before lowering the glider into the dark waters of the Pacific.

Jonas activated the exterior light. He waited until the saddle sunk clear of his propeller, then powered up the engine and descended below the *Kiku's* keel for a quick inspection.

With the ship sitting lower in the water and listing hard to port, the damage looked far worse than Terry had described twelve hours ago. He circled below the slowly churning propeller, the wobbling blades caused by the bent shaft.

Descending to three hundred feet, he approached the Megalodon, the adrenaline causing his heart to race.

The creature's white hide reflected the mini-sub's exterior light, casting the gargantuan shark in a ghostly glow. Banking in a tight circle, Jonas maneuvered the AG-I along the right side of the unconscious monster's head, maintaining a twenty foot distance.

The lower jaw was agape, water passing through uninhibited. The Meg's lidless eye was involuntarily rolled backward in the shark's head, concealing the pupil. It was a natural response, the Meg's brain automatically repositioning the now-useless organ for its own protection.

"Jonas!" His heart jumped from his chest, his harness pulling hard against his shoulders. "Dammit, Terry, you scared the hell out of me."

He could hear her laughing through the radio. "Sorry. Hey, we're still steady at fifty-three beats per minute, though yours shot up to one-twenty. How's the Meg?"

"Sleeping like a baby. How close are we to the lagoon?"

"Six-point-three miles away. Leon predicts we'll be entering the canal right around seven-twenty."

Jonas smiled. "Sounds like the beginning of a great day."

Monterey Bay

They had been waiting all night, anchored close to shore—a pilgrimage gathered as if summoned by the creature itself. Some were marine biologists, others reporters, but most were simply curious tourists and thrill seekers, apprehensive yet prepared to face the risks in order to be a part of history. Their transports varied in size, from small outboards to larger fishing trawlers. Every whale-watching company within a fifty-mile radius was represented, their rates sufficiently inflated for the event.

And while they waited they partied. Music blared and beer flowed from kegs. Police boats patrolled the area, every once in a while issuing warnings. For a few minutes the sound decibel would drop, picking up again the moment the cops were out of range.

* * *

Andre Dupont had to lease the forty-eight-foot fishing trawler for the week, even though the Cousteau Society only needed the boat for the day. Leaning against the bow rail, the French marine biologist watched the northeastern sky through his binoculars as the gray haze grew lighter. Turning west, he followed the line of the horizon to the *Kiku*, the crippled research ship still a good three miles from the canal entrance.

He reentered the bridge, nodded to the captain, then pulled his American liaison, Kariane Philips aside, whispering to her in French. "Kariane, the *Kiku* is close now ... just over six kilometers away. How close to the Megalodon will our captain bring us?"

Kariane shook her head. "The captain refuses to leave the shallows until the Megalodon is secured in its pen. He won't risk the boat."

"I do not blame the man." Dupont gazed out the bridge windows, the predawn light revealing several hundred water craft. The Frenchman shook his head. "I fear that our other friends will probably not be as cautious."

* * *

Frank Heller sat in the *Magnate's* bridge, watching the *Kiku* crawl at its agonizingly slow pace through a pair of high-powered night binoculars. He shared none of Andre Dupont's exhilaration, only rage. In his shirt pocket was a photo of his brother, Dennis and his family. The side of his neck felt tight, throbbing with his rising anger. He imagined himself sitting down with his two nephews one day in the near-future, describing how he had killed the monster that took their father. The thought strengthened his resolve.

"It's time, Mr. Harris," he said, not looking away from the horizon.

Bud engaged the throttle. The *Magnate's* twin engines jumped to life, pushing the yacht toward their destiny.

* * *

The pre-dawn light filtered curtains of gray down through the depths.

Jonas watched as the creature's entire torso became visible, a lethal dirigible being led toward its new hangar. He brought the glider's Lexan nose cone within five feet of the female's right eye, the pupil still rolled back in its head, the light exposing a bloodshot white-yellow membrane.

"Jonas?" Terry's voice crackled over the radio. "Something's happening with the Meg. Her respiration rate is up and her pulse has been climbing steadily over the last few minutes. As we speak, it's at sixty-six. I think she's rousing herself, trying to come out of it."

"Jonas, DeMarco here. If the creature's heart rate reaches seventy-five, I want you back in the glider's saddle. As soon as you're back onboard, I'm hitting your monster with another harpoon full of drugs."

Jonas thought about arguing, but changed his mind.

DeMarco was right. If the Meg regained consciousness before the *Kiku* could get her safely in the lagoon, the ship and its entire crew would be in danger.

He stared at the creature's open jaws. Coursing through its DNA was four hundred million years of instinct. The predator would not think or choose; she would only react, each cell attuned to her environment, every response preconditioned. Nature itself had decided that the species would dominate the oceans, commanding it to perpetuate itself in the Mariana Trench, away from man.

Jonas whispered, "We should have left you alone."

Terry's voice pierced his thoughts. "Jonas, didn't you hear me?"

"Sorry, I—"

"Your friend's yacht is bearing down on us."

"You mean the *Magnate*? Is Bud on board? What's he doing?"

"I don't know, but they're within five hundred yards of the Meg and closing fast."

* * *

DeMarco focused his binoculars on the yacht, his line of sight drifting back to activity in the stern. Two men were balancing a large steel drum on the transom.

Four hundred yards...

DeMarco recognized a face ... "Frank?" He refocused on the steel drum and realized what he was witnessing.

"Mac, they've got a depth charge—get airborne! Jonas, they're trying to kill the Meg—get deep!"

* * *

Adrenaline pumping, Jonas rolled the sub beneath the Megalodon's massive pectoral fin and descended.

* * *

Mac pulled back on the joystick as he adjusted his foot pedals, sending the helicopter leaping off the *Kiku's* listing deck. Wary of the news choppers overhead, he stayed within twenty feet of the surface, racing to intercept the yacht.

"Morning, Bud. Hope you're in the mood for a...Mac attack!"

* * *

Bud looked up as a helicopter appeared out of nowhere,

bearing down on his bridge on a collision course. The millionaire yanked the wheel hard to port seconds before the platform supporting the chopper's thermal imager smashed into the *Magnate's* radar antenna, ripping it off of its aluminum base, the air raining shrapnel.

Reacting as if a grenade had just gone off above their heads, Danielson and Heller dove for cover, abandoning the depth charge.

As the yacht veered hard to port, the steel drum rolled over the transom and plunged into the ocean. Seawater rushed into the canister's six holes, filling the pistol chamber, sinking the bomb.

Cursing, Heller sat up, looking back in time to see the helicopter bank sharply, the pilot circling back.

"Lunatic..."

"Frank, the charge—get down!"

* * *

Mac pushed down on the joystick, a smile fixed on his face as he began a second run at the yacht.

Wa-BOOM!!

The underwater blast sent a geyser of sea rocketing skyward into the path of the helicopter, the rotor fighting to regain draft.

Mac fought his controls as the tail of his chopper swung out from behind him, smashing into the upper deck of the *Magnate*, shearing off the blades.

Before he could react, the copter slammed sideways into the ocean.

* * *

At three hundred and twelve feet, the depth charge's spring had released, thrusting the percussion detonator against the primer. The crude weapon had imploded, then exploded with a flash and subsonic boom. Although the lethal radius of the bomb measured only twenty-five feet, the resulting shock wave was devastating.

The invisible force of current caught the Abyss Glider broadside, rolling the craft wing over wing. Jonas pitched hard against the Lexan cone, cracking his head against the curved windshield, nearly knocking himself out.

* * *

Masao Tanaka had just exited the *Kiku's* bridge and started down the exterior stairwell when the blast had shaken the listing ship. Losing his balance, he tumbled head-first down the steel steps.

"Dad!" Terry ran to her father, DeMarco right behind her. Carefully, she rolled him over on his back, praying he hadn't broken his neck.

His head was badly bruised, his brow swollen and bleeding. He looked up at Terry with a far-away gaze that scared her more than his physical wounds.

"Al, we need to get a Medi-vac helicopter out here right away."

* * *

The frigid water snapped Mac awake. Opening his eyes, he was startled to find himself submerged upside down and underwater, the cockpit filling fast. Forcing himself to remain calm, he located the shoulder harness release and ducked out of the open side door, kicking toward the surface.

* * *

The power was out, the back-up batteries supplying just enough juice to keep the life-support system running.

Jonas swore to himself, then began rolling hard against the interior, gradually gaining enough momentum to rotate the sub right-side up. As he completed the maneuver, he could feel the natural buoyancy of the glider taking over as it gradually began to rise, tail-first, the heavier nose cone dropping.

"Terry, come in. *Kiku*, this is Taylor, can you read me?" The radio, like everything else on the sub, was down.

A glow loomed on his right, lighting up the interior. Jonas turned to find himself hovering within three feet of the female's basketball-size pupil.

The blue eye, now a foggy cataract gray, was open. Though blind, it was staring directly at Jonas.

The Megalodon was awake.

CHAOS

BUD HARRIS DRAGGED HIMSELF off the bridge's polished marble floor, unsure of what had just taken place. The *Magnate* was drifting, her twin engines down. He glanced out the tinted glass in time to see the helicopter's blades slip beneath the waves.

"Hope you die whoever you were," he muttered, then pressed the ON switch, attempting to restart the engines.

Nothing happened.

"Danielson, Heller? Where the hell are you two morons?" Bud headed out on deck, locating the two men standing by the transom.

"Well? Is the monster dead?"

Heller looked at Danielson. "Of course it's dead ... I mean, it has to be."

"You don't seem so certain."

"It's dead," said Danielson. "We had to release the charge a little earlier than we intended when that chopper showed up, but the blast was more than enough to kill it."

"We really should get out of here."

"Well, boys, that's gonna be a bit of a problem," Bud said, spitting over the side. "The engines are dead. Your damn explosive apparently loosened something, and I'm not exactly a licensed mechanic."

"Christ, we're stuck out here with that monster?" Heller shook his head, his jaws locked tight.

"Frank, it's dead. Trust me," said Danielson. "We'll be watching it float belly-up any second now."

Heller looked at his former commanding officer. "Dick, it's a shark. It's not going to float. If it's really dead, it'll sink to the bottom."

They turned in unison, a splashing sound to their left.

A hand appeared at the ladder, followed by Mac, who dragged himself on board the yacht, collapsing on a deck chair.

"Beautiful morning, isn't it, assholes?"

* * *

Jonas lay on his stomach, his head down, his claustrophobia causing shortness of breath. The lifeless Abyss Glider's left mid-wing had caught on the cargo net, keeping the sub eye level with the Megalodon. Jonas watched in fascination and horror as the female's cataract-gray eye continued focusing involuntarily on the tiny submersible.

She's blind, but she still knows I'm here. Don't move. Don't even breathe.

The caudal fin animated, swishing in labored, side-to-side movements, propelling the predator slowly ahead. The monstrous gill slits came into view, fluttering with labored breaths.

Still caught within the net, the Megalodon whipped its head back and forth—freeing the Abyss Glider. The powerless submersible rose tail-first as the most frightening animal on the planet became cognizant of its surroundings.

Jonas looked down, watching the Meg. The cargo net remained ensnared around her pectoral fins, restricting her movement. Enraged, she rolled once, then twice, twisting and tangling herself tighter within the trap.

The Abyss Glider tossed in the Meg's wake. The vessel spun away, causing Jonas to lose sight of the creature. Then, as the sub's nose cone drifted downward, he caught a glimpse of the shark, its upper torso completely entwined in the cargo net.

"She's going to drown," he whispered to himself. "Thank God."

* * *

The passengers aboard the flotilla anchored in Monterey Bay had witnessed the super-yacht break from the group to rendezvous with the incoming guest of honor. They had seen the helicopter intercept the vessel, only to end up crashing into the sea as the depth charge had detonated.

The onlookers grew anxious, wondering if the underwater explosion had killed the creature they had paid good money to see.

The owner of a cigarette racing boat gunned his engines, announcing his intentions.

Almost as one, the pleasure crafts, fishing boat owners, and tour ship captains weighed anchor, following the speedboat out to sea, everyone determined to get a close-up look at the captured Megalodon shark, be it dead or alive.

* * *

Nine media helicopters were hovering above the *Kiku*, continually shifting positions in their attempt to gain better camera angles. The underwater explosion had created a fresh twist on the story and for the first time in the last twenty-four hours there was actually something new to report. Network executives ordered their helicopter crews to lower their altitudes in order to assess whether the monster had survived.

David Adashek was in the back of an Action News copter, straining to see over his cameraman's shoulder. The creature's white hide was visible, but whether the shark was still alive was impossible to ascertain.

The pilot tapped David's arm, motioning him to look southeast.

Racing toward the Megalodon were dozens of boats.

* * *

From the tip of her snout to the base of her caudal fin, the Megalodon's skin contained fine, tooth-like prickles called dermal denticles. Sharp and sandpaper-like in texture, these "skin teeth" channeled water as the Meg swam, but when touched from back to front they could rip open leather, rendering the shark's hide yet another weapon in the predator's arsenal of evolutionary adaptations.

As the female twisted insanely within the cargo net, the dermal denticles sawed through the rope, slicing it to ribbons.

Jonas watched in horror as the Meg shook loose its bonds. His pulse pounded in his throat—compounded by the deep vibrations coming from the helicopters.

Desperate, he tried the power switch again—still dead—as the monster ascended past him, heading toward the surface to investigate.

* * *

DeMarco's eyes widened as he saw the Megalodon surface fifty yards to starboard, the semi-conscious creature swimming on its left side, a river of sea passing into her mouth as she exposed her glistening white belly to him.

It was too good of a target to pass up.

DeMarco aimed the harpoon gun, then released his breath, forced to wait until a speedboat raced by, its engines growling, its pilot completely oblivious to the fact that he had just passed the Megalodon.

DeMarco reset himself—
The Meg was gone.

* * *

The twenty-six foot Boston Whaler maneuvered past two other vessels to emerge from the pack of water craft racing out to the *Kiku.* Jani Harper was at the helm, her twelve-year-old son, Collin, standing beside her in the closed convertible cockpit, urging her on. Three of her friends were seated behind her on a vinyl wrap-around sofa, their husbands playing poker in the cabin below.

The sun peeked over the eastern horizon, bathing the Pacific in its brilliant golden hue—the light reflecting off the windshields of nine news helicopters that were trailing the *Kiku,* their presence no doubt marking the location of the netted creature. Jani could just make out the logo of the Tanaka Institute painted in red along the port-bow of the badly listing research vessel laboring a quarter mile ahead.

And then Jani Harper felt the blood drain from her face as the most frightening creature she had ever seen launched straight out of the sea behind the *Kiku,* its sixty thousand pound pure-white torso glistening in the sun, its snout nearly four stories high when it struck the landing gear of one of the low-flying news choppers.

The collision sent the helicopter careening sideways, initiating a domino effect that spiraled outward as eight terrified pilots simultaneously attempted to maneuver out of harm's way, sending eight sets of rotors climbing into the same airspace.

In a state of panic, Jani Harper veered her Boston Whaler hard to port—right into the path of another boat.

Stephanie Collins was operating her inebriated boss's twenty-three-foot cabin cruiser. She screamed at the Megalodon's shocking appearance—and then she went airborne as her employer's boat rode up a five foot swell and landed on top of the

Boston Whaler which had cut across her path seemingly out of nowhere.

The second wave of boaters swerved to avoid hitting the two disabled vessels, only to crash into one another, creating pile-ups similar to a multi-vehicle accident on a snow-covered highway, screams and swear words renting the chilly morning air.

* * *

Sweating profusely, Jonas could feel his claustrophobia building as he strained to reach the battery connections located in the aft compartment of his sub. Blindly, he groped at the terminals inside the rear panels, searching in vain for a loose connection.

* * *

The *Kiku's* crew assembled on deck, frantically donning orange life vests.

Terry Tanaka and Robert Nash stood over the registered nurse who had replaced Frank Heller as she tended to Masao, who was unconscious. "I can't be sure, Terry, but I'd guess your father fractured his skull. We need to get him to a hospital as soon as possible."

"At this rate we'll have sunk before that EVAC gets here." Terry glanced overhead at the four remaining news copters hovering several hundred feet above the Pacific. "Robert, get on the radio; try to get one of those news choppers to land on the *Kiku*. Tell them we have a serious injury."

"Yes, ma'am."

* * *

David Adashek focused his binoculars on the main deck of the sinking *Kiku* when he saw an Asian woman waving emphatically from the ship's helo-deck. "Hey, I know her, that's Tanaka's daughter."

"I'm getting a distress call from the *Kiku*," the pilot said. "They're requesting we transport an injured man to shore. Radioman says it's Masao Tanaka. Sounds serious."

"Land the copter," ordered Adashek.

The cameraman looked at him with a scowl. "My producer's screaming at me to get close-ups of the Meg. He'll have my balls for breakfast if we turn this chopper into a Medi-vac helicopter and leave the scene."

Adashek ripped the camera from the man's grip, holding it out his open door. "Choose now. We land or I feed this to the Meg."

* * *

The Megalodon circled beneath the *Kiku*. The ship's metal hull was generating galvanic currents—electrical impulses that stimulated the female's ampullae of Lorenzini like fingernails on a chalkboard.

* * *

The *Kiku's* crew gathered around the Action News chopper as it landed on the awkwardly tilting helipad, each sailor vying for passage off the sinking research vessel. When the men grew increasingly violent, Leon Barre removed his concealed sidearm and fired a warning shot in the air. "The chopper's for Masao; the rest of you can get on board one of the life boats."

The pilot of the news copter looked at Adashek and the cameraman. "Okay, boys, someone has to give up his seat for the old man. Which one of you is going to play the hero?"

The cameraman looked at Adashek with an evil grin. "Hope you can swim, tough guy."

David felt butterflies in his stomach as he exited the safety of the airship, allowing the *Kiku's* crew to load Masao on board.

Moments later, he stood on the lopsided deck, his heart in his mouth as the helicopter flew off toward the mainland. *Nice job, dumbass. You're supposed to report the news, not be a part of it.*

* * *

The sudden jolt rocked the *Magnate*, sending both men falling to the deck.

Richard Danielson stood painfully, then grabbed Frank Heller beneath his armpits and hoisted him to his feet. "Frank, do you hear that noise? It's the yacht's pumps. We must be taking on water."

Heller looked around. "Where are Harris and Mackreides?"

"They went below to try to fix the engine. Oh, crap—"

The white dorsal fin was circling the yacht.

"Any suggestions?"

"The Zodiac …" Heller pointed to the motorized raft.

"Frank, you really want to risk taking that tiny boat out versus staying aboard the yacht?"

"The yacht's sinking, Richard, and that tiny boat is fast. Give me a hand."

The two men released the catches to the pulleys supporting the bulky raft. It dropped to the surface with a muffled *splat*.

"You first, Frank, seeing how it was your idea."

Heller waited until the dorsal fin circled behind the boat, then swung his leg over the rail. Danielson followed him in.

The outboard whined to life. Heller gunned the throttle, the Zodiac skimming over waves, accelerating to the east in the direction of land.

Danielson kept an eye on their wake, praying silently that the Megalodon would remain with the *Magnate*. As the seconds turned to minutes and the yacht gradually disappeared from the horizon he began to feel better about their decision.

"Frank, head for those boats. Maybe we can—"

The inflatable raft exploded beneath him, the concussive force of the breaching behemoth tossing Danielson and Heller high into the air like ragdolls.

* * *

Leon Barre and Alphonse DeMarco stood by the *Kiku's* port rail in ankle-deep water, the two men watching the Zodiac race off to the east.

Seconds later they both gasped as the creature attacked from below.

"Man the lifeboats. We've got about five minutes before the *Kiku* sinks and the monster returns."

"Al, what about Jonas?"

"We can't help him, Terry. Wherever he is, he's on his own."

FEEDING FRENZY

RICHARD DANIELSON SURFACED, his heart racing, his chest constricting from the cold water which, accompanied by the sheer terror of his predicament, was causing him to hyperventilate. He had caught an inverted glance of the monster while tumbling through the air—now he was treading water in its kill zone.

He heard voices, saw a bizarre entanglement of boats forty yards away, and swam like hell for it.

* * *

Stephanie Collins stood in the bow of her boss's boat. The twenty-three-foot cabin cruiser was completely out of the water, rendered immobile by the larger Boston Whaler it was now using as a dry dock.

Between knowing the Megalodon was still on the loose and potentially very close, moving the Whaler's wounded onto their boat, and dealing with her irate boss, she was about to lose it.

Screw him. He doesn't pay me enough to handle his crap. And why'd I have to be the one to drive his stupid boat—is it my fault he had too much to drink?

The collective weight of the cabin cruiser and its wounded passengers had pushed the whaler three feet underwater, but the vessel was still quite buoyant. The boat's owner, Jani Harper stood in water up to her knees with her twelve-year-old son and eight volunteers from the two boats, all attempting to push the cabin cruiser back into the water. The task was proving impossible with so many people weighing Michael Roddy's boat down, and yet no one seemed to want to climb off the perched vessel.

And then, without warning, the Megalodon had breached fifty yards to the north, flipping over a motorized raft.

The creature's proximity sent the volunteers scrambling

back onto the cabin cruiser like rats fleeing a sinking ship—only every square foot of deck was now occupied by the Whaler's wounded, and the additional weight was causing the boat to teeter.

Michael Roddy, the boat's owner, was losing it. "Stephanie, what the hell were you thinking? Get these drunks off my boat so our people can get back on."

"Sir, they're hurt."

"And their blood is attracting the Meg." He pointed over her shoulder.

She turned to see one of the men from the raft swimming in their direction—followed by a five foot wake and six foot dorsal fin. "Oh, God, everybody move to the center of the boat—"

* * *

Richard Danielson felt the wave overtake him. As it rolled over his head his feet struck a solid object, causing him to tuck his legs to his chest.

Looking down, he saw an alabaster island rise beneath him, the Megalodon's head as wide as a bus, its hide as coarse as concrete. For a brief second of insanity he found himself straddling the creature's snout before he toppled backward into the sea.

The Megalodon's nose rose out of the water, its upper jaw jutting away from its skull, the horrendous bite slamming down on empty sea a second before the blind behemoth's head struck the two boats.

The impact freed the stacked vessels. It also tossed a dozen passengers into the Pacific, igniting a feeding frenzy.

* * *

The tail assembly of the powerless Abyss Glider bobbed just below the surface, its heavier nose cone pointing straight down at the ocean floor.

Jonas was standing upright in the mini-sub, his feet balancing on the shoulder harness while he worked on the battery.

Drenched in sweat, he had located the severed wire and had managed to peel away a section of rubber insulation. Carefully, he wrapped the exposed copper lead around the battery terminal and twisted the rusty wing nut into place—his actions generating an encouraging spark.

Twisting his body upside down, he slid back into the pilot's prone position, the blood rushing to his head. "Okay, baby, give daddy some juice."

He pressed the power button and was rewarded by the hum of the engine and a blast of cool air from the ventilation system. The revolving propeller leveled out the sub and Jonas quickly directed it to the surface.

He looked around, realizing he had drifted with the current.

A few pings from sonar revealed the *Kiku* and *Magnate;* the ships located a half-mile to the north. But it was the activity to the east that caught his attention.

* * *

The Megalodon may have lost its sense of vision, but the predator was far from blind. It could "see" its prey by the electrical impulses generated by their beating hearts, it could feel the vibrations of their churning muscles. Moreover, it could determine the weak from the strong by gauging the rapidity of its quarry's pulse, the efficiency of their movements, and the telltale scent of blood in the water.

To the Meg, the passengers thrown from the two boats were bizarre fish—their low fat content rendering them poor eating. At the same time they were easily consumed, requiring a low expenditure of energy, as opposed to taking on an adult whale. And they were now plentiful.

A methodical hunter, the creature knew to incapacitate the largest, strongest members of the pack first.

Michael Roddy may have been drunk, but the big man was still a good swimmer. Pushing his way past flailing arms and churning legs, he reached the aluminum ladder of his boat ahead of the others. Gripping a sun-warmed rung, he attempted to pull himself out of the water—only to discover that both his legs had been severed at the knees!

Dangling from the ladder by his arms, he screamed for help, his lower torso surrounded by a spreading pool of blood.

Richard Danielson was less than three feet from the Boston Whaler when his upper torso suddenly ignited with the insane sensation of a hundred surgeons' scalpels slicing his gut into ribbons. The blood drained from his face and neck, the soul from his body before the horrendous agony of being bitten in half ever had a chance to register as a last fleeting thought.

The Megalodon circled its feast from below, targeting its next prey—

Ping.

Ping … ping…ping.

The powerful burst of sound energy coming from the approaching Abyss Glider irritated the massive shark. Associating the high frequency echo with the *Nautilus,* the creature pinpointed the source, going after its challenger.

* * *

Jonas soared seventy feet below a surface tainted by two rapidly spreading pools of blood churned by a dozen or more people attempting to swim toward two boats.

The Meg's been busy … where is she?

Going active on sonar, he discovered the monster was bull-rushing him from below!

Accelerating to twenty knots, he maneuvered out of harm's way, the Meg chasing after him, forcing him to increase his speed.

Where to go? The lagoon's still too far away to maintain its interest. Better get back to the Kiku and let DeMarco drug it again.

Executing a wide turn, he altered his course, heading north.

* * *

Frank Heller had managed to swim to the Boston Whaler. Too weak to drag himself up the ladder, he clung to the side of the fishing boat, his eyes closed as he waited for death.

Minutes passed.

"Hey!"

Frank looked up, staring into the eyes of a twelve-year-old boy.

"My mom says we're leaving. She said either get your ass in the boat or get it bitten off."

"I c-c-c-can't move."

Collin Harper signaled to someone. A moment later a large hand reached over the side and grabbed hold of Frank Heller's life vest, dragging him out of the water.

* * *

The two-hundred-and-seventy-four foot long research vessel rolled to port and kept rolling, the *Kiku's* flooded hull finally pulling her beneath the waves.

Twenty-three crew members and David Adashek were packed into two lifeboats, the outboard motors of which remained dormant in fear that the disturbance might alert the monster.

Leon Barre had tears in his eyes as he watched the bow of his command slide silently into the Pacific. Terry Tanaka used the captain's binoculars to scan the surface for any sign of the Abyss Glider. David Adashek was visibly shaking, praying quietly, as were many of the crewmen, while Alphonse DeMarco waited for the albino monster to reappear, a loaded Colt .45 held in his quivering right hand.

"Terry, let me see the glasses."

She handed them to the captain, who focused in on the two boats now racing back to shore. "Sum bitch, do we start the motors or wait? Could be the Meg is following those boats. Maybe now would be the best time for us to leave. What do you think,

341

DeMarco?"

"How fast can these boats get us to land?"

"Overloaded like we are? Twenty-five … maybe thirty minutes."

DeMarco pinched the bridge of his nose, massaging out some of the tension. "I don't know. Jonas said this creature can feel the vibrations of an engine. Maybe we should wait, let the Megalodon clear the area."

"And what if it doesn't?" Robert Nash asked. "You expect us to just sit here and wait to get eaten alive like D.J.? Sorry, Terry, but I didn't sign on to this mission to end up as bait."

Murmurs of agreement.

"Okay, we take a vote," Leon Barre said. "All those who want to start the engines raise your hands."

All but two crewmen and Terry agreed.

"Okay then. Al, you follow me. We gonna head south away from those last two boats … just in case, then we turn east. Might take a bit longer but it's safer."

The two motors coughed to life, spewing thick clouds of carbon monoxide.

Terry used the binoculars, scanning the horizon.

Suddenly she stood, pointing to a five-foot wake heading in their direction, chasing an object running along the surface like a torpedo. "It's Jonas!"

Leon swore. "Sum bitch … he's bringing the monster right to us."

* * *

Jonas surfaced. He saw Bud Harris's yacht in the distance, but could not locate the *Kiku.*

Sonar found it sinking a hundred and ninety feet below the Pacific. Escorting the research vessel into the depths, he prayed no one was aboard—momentarily forgetting about the creature—his sonar warning him a split-second before he was nudged from behind with the force of a train tapping a Volkswagen Beetle.

Pulling back on his joystick, Jonas launched the Glider into a steep ascent, the mini-sub shooting out of the Pacific like a marlin being chased by Moby Dick. From his vantage he spotted the *Kiku's* two lifeboats heading east a moment before his vessel plunged belly-first back into the sea.

He descended quickly, his head on a swivel as he searched for the Meg. Unable to locate the creature, he engaged three more pings, waiting for the sound waves to return a reflected echo.

To his horror, the battery gauge suddenly dropped from 63% in the mid-green range all the way to 17% in the lower orange zone, the indicator very close to the red warning area.

Before he could react, the Megalodon appeared on his sonar monitor. The monstrous shark had changed course and was now chasing after the two lifeboats.

Damn it, Jonas ... what have you done?

* * *

The two lifeboats were just over three miles from shore when the alabaster dorsal fin rose out of the sea fifty yards behind Alphonse DeMarco's boat, its presence sending waves of panic among the *Kiku's* crew.

From the lead boat, Leon Barre frantically signaled to DeMarco to separate.

Barre turned south.

DeMarco continued to the east.

The Megalodon submerged.

Terrifying seconds passed; the two boatloads of survivors knowing the monster had descended to attack one of them from below.

"Faster ... go faster—"

"No, keep zig-zagging!"

A concussive explosion became a gyroscope of brilliant

blue sky, flailing bodies, and a towering white silo, all of which terminated with a shock of frigid water as DeMarco's boat was blasted apart from below.

Eleven men and a woman plunged into the sea. Seven heads broke the surface, gagging and moaning in pain, floating in their lifejackets among fragments of wood that, seconds before, had been a lifeboat. Three crewmen—Alphonse DeMarco among them—bobbed in their life vests along the surface, unconscious. Two were dead. Sonar tech Roberto Nash and crewman Chad Shahriyar had been seated on the bench absorbing most of the Megalodon's kinetic energy. Their spines had shattered on impact, their limbs torn away from their bodies.

Ten beating hearts remained.

Ten dinner bells.

The sixty foot prehistoric shark circled its killing field, its dorsal fin slicing through three foot seas as its owner sized up her next meal. The creature's sheer mass caught the unconscious DeMarco within its current, towing him along as the Meg homed in on a flailing body.

Petrified, Terry froze as the Megalodon surfaced, heading straight for her and one of the *Kiku's* cooks. Rolling onto its side, the monster opened its mouth, creating a vacuum which inhaled the screaming chef into its gullet.

"Oh, God... oh my God," cried Adashek. The terrified reporter attempted to drown himself by gulping seawater, only to puke.

With a bluster of coughs, Alphonse DeMarco opened his eyes. Unaware of where he was or what was happening, he started swimming toward Terry.

"Al, stay there. Don't swim … don't even move."

Terry fought to catch her breath as the Meg's gargantuan head broke the surface twenty feet away, revealing the peppered-black ampullae of Lorenzini beneath its hideous snout.

A pink band of upper gums widened, exposing a row of massive triangular teeth rooted in its upper jaw, the human flesh from its last snack still caught between several fangs.

Terry gritted her teeth, tears in her eyes as she readied herself for a gruesome end to her life. "Bitch … I should have drowned you when I had the chance."

The Abyss Glider leapt out of sea behind her, momentarily blotting out the sun before the six hundred and fifty pound submersible and its pilot landed on the Megalodon's snout, blood spurting from its wounded left nostril.

The AG-I stalled for a brief second. The moment its propeller caught water, Jonas slammed his palms down on both joysticks, whipping the mini-sub hard to port and away from the snapping jaws.

Like a mad bull, the Megalodon plunged below the waves to give chase.

The Glider's dying battery was costing him at least ten knots of speed, allowing the Meg to gain on him.

Where to go?

Lead her away from Terry, away from the others.

Jonas felt a bump from behind as the shark rammed his mini-sub's tail fin.

Banking hard to starboard, he shot to the surface, altering his angle of ascent a few seconds before the Abyss Glider corkscrewed out of the water like a Spinner dolphin—

—the leaping Megalodon right behind it, its jaws snapping empty air.

The predator flopped blindly back into the ocean, its thunderous splash rivaling that of the largest humpback whale. Unable to relocate the Abyss Glider, the Meg descended, searching for the telltale vibrations of its prey.

* * *

Terrified but suddenly given a survivor's chance in Hell,

Terry watched as a large trawler appeared in the distance.

It had taken a wad of cash and a signed agreement from Andre Dupont guaranteeing the Cousteau Society would pay for any damages to his trawler before the fishing boat captain agreed to head out to sea to rescue the *Kiku's* crew.

They had reached the crew aboard Leon Barre's lifeboat first, the *Kiku's* captain directing them to where their shipmates had been tossed into the sea. Several minutes later they arrived at the gruesome scene—nine survivors floating in lifejackets, the Meg nowhere in sight.

Terry Tanaka was pulled on board first. She tried to stand but the stress had sapped her strength and she collapsed on deck. David Adashek vomited from the stress. Alphonse DeMarco and several other shipmates fell to their knees, all thanking their maker for sparing their lives.

* * *

The Abyss Glider was powerless, the last leap having depleted the batteries, the indicator clearly in the red. Jonas's heart pounded as the Megalodon descended, searching for his craft.

It was eerily quiet, save for the sound of water lapping against the sub's buoyant tail assembly and its pilot's labored breathing.

A sickening feeling overcame him as the Lexan nose cone gradually dropped, the glider's horizontal status changing to an inverted vertical plane, causing the blood to rush to Jonas's head.

This isn't happening ...

Jonas stared into the deep blue depths, the blood pounding in his temples, his hands trembling.

Get out of the sub, J.T. Do something different ... change the dream. Move, damn you!

But he couldn't move—he was paralyzed in fear...defenseless. All he could do was stare at the flickering beams of sunlight filtering below, waiting for the angel of death to reappear.

And then Masao's words came back to him. *"If you know the enemy and know yourself, you need not fear the result of a hundred battles."*

"I know my enemy," he said aloud.

His hands shook as he deliberated.

Sometimes the best defense is a good offense. Do it, J.T. Don't wait for the Meg to attack, bring the fight to her.

Reaching to the sonar array, he pushed the active button, the sub's dead battery releasing one final, fading *PING*.

At four hundred feet she appeared … the stark white face, the satanic grin. It was seven years ago and he was back on the *Sea Cliff*...it was seven hours ago and he had dreamt this very moment—a premonition warning him about his impending, gruesome death.

Acceptance comes when there are no other options.

Two hundred feet.

Jonas reached forward with his right hand and grasped the lever, turning it counterclockwise.

One hundred feet …

The Megalodon's mouth hyperextended open.

Now.

Jonas bellowed a guttural, primordial yell as he pulled the lever toward him, instantly igniting the hydrogen fuel, transforming the powerless Abyss Glider into a rocket, blasting it straight down through the Megalodon's open gullet past fluttering gill slits and an archway of cartilaginous ribs before disappearing down a widening dark orifice into gelid blackness.

HELL

ANDRE DUPONT STOOD BY the fishing trawler's port rail, watching in awe and more than a bit of trepidation as the most fearsome animal ever to inhabit the planet ravaged the surface of the ocean a hundred and thirty yards to the east, the creature in obvious pain.

Terry approached the scientist, wrapped in a wool blanket, tears streaming down her cheeks. She had seen the fuel ignite, knew what Jonas had done. At that moment, she realized how deep her feelings had been for him … and now, like her brother, he was gone.

Leon Barre was arguing with the fishing trawler's owner in the pilothouse, warning him that the boat's engines would attract the monster. The older man swore at Barre, swore at Dupont, but decided it might be best to shut down the motor.

* * *

The Megalodon's digestive system was relatively short but infinitely flexible. After food entered its gullet, it passed through the esophagus where it reached a sphincter, a contractile ring of muscle that regulated what could and could not pass into the stomach. Almost everything that could pass through did, processed by powerful acids secreted from the stomach lining.

The Meg's stomach represented twenty percent of its entire girth. The muscular walls of the organ contained longitudinal folds which allowed it to expand or contract like an accordion. Another sphincter guarded the duodenum—the beginning of the small intestine. Located inside the duodenum were a series of folds known as the spiral valve. Similar in shape to a corkscrew, the spiral valve rotated within the Meg's small intestine like a *Slinky*, providing an immense absorption area for the shark to maximize the nutrients of its meal.

The unusual shape of the organ also served another purpose—anything that could not be properly digested could be regurgitated. During this violent act, the shark's stomach actually turned inside-out so that it protruded from the creature's mouth like a pinkish balloon, evacuating the contents of its digestive system to the sea.

* * *

The flames emitted from the Abyss Glider's hydrogen burn had blistered the female's gill arches. Circling rapidly, the Megalodon's jaws heaved open in a sudden, violent spasm, its insides attempting to vomit the eight-foot capsule from its stomach.

* * *

Jonas was slammed back into consciousness, the escape pod heaving in darkness, flipping again and again as the Megalodon's involuntary muscles attempted to regurgitate the capsule back out through its esophagus. But the opening was too narrow, the glider's nose unable to align correctly with the spasming sphincter. After a dozen attempts, the spiral valve retreated, the escape pod settling within its alien, pitch black confines.

Jonas trembled in the darkness, his hands searching through a zippered pouch by his left leg. Locating the flashlight, he aimed the powerful beam out the Lexan nosecone.

"Oh, Jesus … oh, God."

The light revealed the blistering pink insides of an organ swirling with partially-digested muck. Thick, hot, fist-sized chunks of mutilated whale blubber slapped across the acrylic cone. Jonas felt queasy, and yet he couldn't stop himself from looking. He could discern the remains of a porpoise's head, a sneaker, several pieces of wood, and then something that made him gag.

It was the upper torso of a human. The face was badly burned from stomach acid but it was still recognizable...

349

Danielson.

Jonas's belly gurgled, his scream cut off by the rising vomit. The walls closed in upon him, and he convulsed in fear. The sub shifted hard to one side, rolling with the sloshing remains of Taylor's former commanding officer as the host descended into the depths, attempting to quash its pain.

* * *

Bud Harris stood in ankle-deep water in his yacht's engine room, waiting impatiently while the chopper pilot who had attacked his vessel ran a compression test on one of the motors,

"You've been at this long enough, Mackreides. What's the verdict?"

Mac wiped grease on his damp jumpsuit's pant leg. "You've got no compression coming from your cylinders. The explosion must have damaged your head gasket."

"Can you fix it?"

"Not under these circumstances. Tell you what; if we live through this I'll give you a coupon for five free quarts of oil with your next engine."

"You're a funny guy. Restart the pump, funny man."

Mac flipped the toggle switch. The pump churned, vibrating the entire vessel as seawater was forcibly expelled from the floor of the engine room.

"Kind of loud, isn't it Harris? According to the husband of your former lover, noises like this could actually attract the Meg."

Mac turned to find himself staring at the business end of a .44 Magnum.

Bud pointed the gun at Mac's head. "Let's head out on deck and see if Jonas was right."

* * *

Jonas struggled to breathe, his nerves trembling amid horrific scenes of human carnage the likes of which could not be imagined. This was beyond claustrophobia, this was hell.

"Stop it! You're alive … you can reason. Find a way out."

He forced himself to slow his breathing, then used the flashlight to check the hydrogen fuel gauge.

Thirty-seven percent left … maybe enough for a five second burst. It's not enough to burn my way out, but I bet I can give it some serious indigestion.

He located the lever, held his breath, and pulled.

Nothing.

He pulled again and again, but was unable to ignite the remaining fuel.

Okay, okay, stay calm. There's fuel in the tank, the igniter must have come loose.

Releasing his harness, he twisted around in the escape pod, aiming the light outside the craft at the remains of the glider's tail assembly.

Sure enough, the hose connecting the igniter switch with the external tank had been pulled loose.

A calm resolve began to settle over Jonas. He had a plan—a lottery chance at surviving an impossible circumstance, but it was there, and it was more than Maggie had, more than Danielson.

Relax, J.T. It's just a walk in the park.

Rolling onto his side, he opened the two storage compartments below his hammock and removed the dive mask attached to a small pony bottle of air. He secured the mask to his face, then twisted open the cylinder, making sure he could breathe normally. Locating a pair of rubber gloves, he slipped them on to protect his hands.

He was ready.

Flipping around, he unscrewed the escape hatch, the rubber housing hissing as it lost its suction. Pushing the circular Lexan door open, he poked his head out of the opening, shining the flashlight into the darkness.

The mini-sub was lying in a confined chamber of smooth

muscle with no discernible top or bottom. Caustic digestive excretions designed to break down food into fuel were being secreted from an unknown source. Though he could not tell through the breathing mask, the smell had to be overwhelming.

Jonas crawled out of the glider, closing the hatch behind him. His rubber boots touched down on the stomach lining, giving him the sensation of stepping on a surface of molten putty. A thick hydrochloric acid oozed from unseen pores.

Wasting no time, he turned his attention to the sub's tail assembly.

* * *

Bud Harris pushed the barrel of the gun to the back of Mac's neck, forcing him up the steps and out to the main deck.

"Heller? Danielson?"

Mac pointed. "The Zodiac's gone. Looks like you chose the wrong bedfellows."

"I don't give a damn about those two idiots. That monster destroyed my life, took the one person I truly cared for. It continues to haunt me, preventing me from sleeping, preventing me from living. I could have ended some of that torture today, only you had to interfere."

Bud stepped back, motioning for Mac to walk toward the starboard rail. "Go ahead."

"Go ahead and what?"

"You wanted to save this monster, now you can feed it." Bud fired the Magnum, the bullet striking Mac in his right quadriceps muscle, blood oozing from the wound.

Mac collapsed to one knee in agony. "Are you crazy?"

"I want you off my boat. Get back in the water and bleed or I'll shoot you in the other leg."

Mac moved to the rail. He climbed over gingerly, attempting to stall. "This is called murder. You know what they do with murderers in the state of California, *Richie Rich*? They lock them up with guys like Charles Manson."

"Only the poor ones." Bud aimed the barrel of the gun at Mac's head. "Jump in or die."

Mac jumped.

Bud waited for him to surface. "Now start swimming."

Mac eyed the horizon—spotting a fishing trawler half a mile to the east.

Might as well be a million miles away ...

* * *

The captain of the fishing trawler had seen enough. The Megalodon was gone, and the Frenchman, his female assistant, and the Filipino boat captain could go screw themselves.

Restarting his vessel's engines, he headed for shore.

* * *

The female moved just beneath the thermocline, the colder, deeper water cooling the burning sensation within its inflamed gullet. Agitated, she attacked every motion that attracted her senses...a passing school of fish, a sea lion—

The surface vibrations sent ripples coursing along her lateral line. Locking onto the new stimulus, the Meg ascended in a steep vertical climb, targeting the disturbance.

* * *

Jonas managed to reattach the igniter hose to the hydrogen fuel tank when his feet were pulled out from under him as the Megalodon rose to the surface, its stomach rolling ninety degrees, catching him in an avalanche of partially-digested refuse.

Suddenly, he was sliding feet-first down a steep incline rendered slick by an abundance of whale oil. The undigested contents of the Meg's stomach piled up beneath and all around him. Aiming the light below, he saw to his horror that the muck was slowly draining down a three-foot-in-diameter expanding orifice.

The intestines! Get sucked down there and you're a goner.

Rolling onto his belly, he fought to stop his momentum, but was simply unable to establish a handhold on the oil-slick surface.

Making matters worse, the Abyss Glider was now on top of him, riding him down the slope.

A sickening feeling overcame him as he felt his feet enter the slime-covered sphincter all the way up to his knees. Desperate, he tore open the chest-pouch of his bio-suit and removed the six-and-a-half inch Megalodon tooth. Gripping it by its root, he stabbed it into the stomach lining above his head, praying it would hold.

The sharp point pierced the thick surface, the tooth's serrated edges forging a grip.

Hip-deep in the intestinal opening, Jonas stopped sliding.

The rest of the avalanche of undigested human flesh, whale oil and blubber did not, burying him alive. He held on as long as he could, the escape pod's weight pressing down on the back of his arm and skull, pinning him against the stomach lining.

* * *

Wrapped in a blanket, Terry stood alone by the port rail weeping for Jonas, when the fishing trawler's keel was suddenly struck from below, the bone-jarring impact rolling the boat thirty degrees to port, tossing her into the sea.

* * *

Jonas was about to lose his grip on the tooth when his surroundings went topsy-turvy again as the Megalodon descended, the hot wave of refuse washing over him like a receding tide.

For a bizarre moment he hung suspended upside-down, the sphincter muscle guarding the creature's intestines still suctioned tightly around his knees. But his bio-suit was drenched in whale oil and the lubricant, combined with his weight, was too much.

Jonas slipped free, plunging fifteen feet to the opposite end of the stomach, landing in a soft, molten pile of goop, his gloved hands fighting to keep from losing the flashlight and Meg tooth pinned against his chest.

The sub was close by, lying on its side. Regaining his feet, he gripped the Abyss Glider by its tail fins and managed to roll it back onto its belly.

Gasping deep breaths, Jonas rested against the damaged chassis, making sure the igniter hose was still connected to the hydrogen tank. He must have been anatomically close to the Megalodon's pectoral fins because he could feel the shark swimming, its side-to-side action orientating him to his surroundings. Turning to his left faced him forward in the direction of the Meg's head, which meant the esophageal opening had to be close.

Using his light, he located the sphincter designed to prevent food from escaping the stomach.

The idea came to him in an instant. Slogging through the refuse, Jonas pocketed the tooth, then reached beneath the escape pod and gripped the mini-sub's mechanical arm, using it as a handle to drag the Abyss Glider through the waist-deep muck to the esophageal valve.

Jonas tried to push his hand through to the other side but the muscle was far too strong, the seal too tight. He checked the pony bottle—only four minutes of air remained.

Somehow he had to pierce the gauntlet...

Reaching again for the Megalodon tooth, he used the serrated edges like a saw, the million-year-old fossil slicing surprisingly easily into the soft tissue.

* * *

Terry surfaced, shocked to see the trawler drifting sixty feet away from her. Having relinquished her lifejacket, it was all she could do to free herself of the wet wool blanket and stay afloat.

Andre Dupont was yelling at her. "...engine is down, you have to swim!"

Mac was halfway between the yacht and the fishing trawler when he saw the wave rolling toward him, the triangular white dorsal fin appearing a moment later.

He stopped swimming, the intense pounding in his chest accompanied by the deep vibrations of the Coast Guard helicopter approaching from the south.

"Okay, Lord, how's this for a deal: You rescue my sorry ass and I promise to ease up on the booze."

The wake rolled over Mac's head. He floundered underwater, fighting through the powerful current—and then he was free.

* * *

The Meg wasn't interested in the small creature bleeding along the surface; it was obviously wounded and required little effort to devour. What had lured it back to the yacht was the sound of the *Magnate's* pumps.

Shooting past Mac, the Megalodon circled the sinking ship.

Bud stood in the *Magnate's* bow, the gun in one hand, a bottle of vodka in the other. He took a long draught, tossed the pint in the sea, then aimed at the towering fin and fired, blasting two bloody holes into the albino hide.

"How do you like that, shark? You want more? I've got two full clips; come and get it!" Holding the handgun steady with two hands, he fired round after round into the beast's submerged back.

It took a few passes for the Megalodon's senses to recognize the familiar pattern of electrical impulses discharged by the yacht. Associating the strange creature with the excruciating pain that had cost it its eyesight, the predator went deep, heading back to the fishing trawler.

Believing the monster was preparing to ram his yacht, Bud Harris panicked.

Drunk, depressed, and suddenly quite terrified of meeting the same horrible fate as his lover, the millionaire shoved the gun into his mouth and pulled the trigger, blasting the back of his head open like a ripe watermelon.

* * *

Mac saw the returning wake and knew he was a dead man. "Okay, God, you win. How about this—no more sleeping with married women."

He jumped as the harness fell on top of him. Looking up, he was amazed to see the rescue chopper's silhouette hovering eighty feet overhead. Slipping his right arm in the harness, he frantically signaled to the crew to pull him out of the water.

He rose from the sea as the wake passed beneath him, his presence disappearing from the Megalodon's senses.

A minute later he was helped inside the open bay doors into the helicopter.

A cute brunette in her mid-thirties stood by with a medical kit. "Lieutenant Phyllis Jelley, I'm a medic. It looks like you've been shot."

"Feels like it too."

"Lie down, please. Joe, I'll need some towels and an antibiotic."

"Is this a test?"

"Excuse me?"

"You're married, right?"

"Please sit down; you're bleeding all over the cabin."

"Maybe you'd better just leave the bullet in me."

* * *

Down to his last seconds of air, with the beam of his flashlight fading fast, Jonas struggled to complete the last side of the triangular incision. Bearing down on the fossil, he sawed through the tough muscle and pushed his hand through the opening, releasing a current of seawater.

Slogging through waist-deep refuse, he fought his way back to the tail section of the Abyss Glider and forcibly shoved the mini-sub's nose into the hole, his effort aided by the slime coating the exterior of the craft. He managed to push the vessel halfway inside the severed muscle when everything started spinning.

You're out of air. Get inside the pod before you black out.

He dropped to his knees and yanked open the hatch, crawling inside the glider as the Megalodon suddenly descended.

The Abyss Glider rolled into the shark's esophagus clear up to its tail fin before jamming in place.

Jonas tore the mask from his face, sucking in deep breaths of air as he sealed the hatch. His bio-suit reeked of whale oil, the rubber shredding in his gloved hands from the prolonged exposure with the acidic stomach bile. Quickly, he climbed into the glider's harness, then looked out the nosecone, shocked by the new view.

The Megalodon's gullet was dark, save for a pair of fluttering deep blue gill slits and the beckoning sliver of daylight outside of the shark's open mouth.

Jonas felt the min-sub sliding backwards into the stomach as the Megalodon rose once more on a near-vertical ascent.

Reaching for the emergency lever, he ignited the hydrogen.

* * *

The fishing trawler's captain had just finished replacing the last of the engine's shattered spark plugs when his first mate yelled out from his post at the fish finder.

"Skipper, it's back! Four hundred and thirty feet and rising like a missile straight for our hull."

"Restart engines—all ahead full."

"What about the girl?"

* * *

Terry Tanaka was twenty feet from the fishing trawler when the boat's engines suddenly growled to life. Putting her head down in the water, she swam as hard as she could—her eyes widening underwater as a fireball ignited from the depths.

* * *

The igniter switch sparked the remaining fuel in the Abyss Glider's hydrogen tank, the flame in turn igniting the flammable whale oil within the Megalodon's stomach.

Jonas held on as the mini-sub shot through the darkness like a bullet before coming to a sudden halt between the creature's partially-opened jaws, the points of its upper and lower rows of teeth raking deep tracks in the escape pod's thick Lexan glass.

A split-second later the female regurgitated the charred remains of its stomach, expelling the scorched organ and the Abyss Glider into the sea. The ballooning black mass burst into a bright crimson lake of blood.

"Thank you, God, thank you…" His body trembled with relief as the pod continued to rise away from the dead beast, the numbers on his depth gauge dropping steadily.

Cold sweat dripped down his skull and the back of his neck. Jonas rolled over to look at the sun-drenched aqua-blue surface three hundred and twenty feet above him.

Then he noticed the deep grooves in the Lexan—the incisions created by the monster's teeth were leaking seawater into the escape pod.

* * *

The fishing trawler circled Terry, its captain forced by the crew of the *Kiku* to return. Alphonse DeMarco tossed her a life ring. She reached for it as gouts of blood began pooling around her body.

"Terry—"

"Al, it's okay, it's the Meg's blood. I saw a fireball. Jonas must have ignited the rest of his hydrogen tank."

"He's still alive?"

"Get me a mask and snorkel."

"Terry—"

"Just do it!"

DeMarco located a snorkel and mask and tossed them to her. She pulled the mask over her head, positioned the mouthpiece, and peered below.

* * *

The escape pod's ascent slowed as it took on water.

Below, the Megalodon continued sinking into the depths, trailing a river of blood. Jonas watched until the albino creature disappeared from view. He had escaped certain death twice, but to survive this day he still needed one more miracle.

Physically and mentally drained, lying in three inches of water, Jonas held his palms to as many leaks as he could. He stared helplessly at the depth gauge as it dropped below 270-feet, his mind calculating.

You're rising about forty feet per minute with three inches of water, adding another inch every minute or so. Got to at least make it within a hundred feet of the surface before you abandon ship ... a hundred and twenty feet at the most. If you lose ten feet of rise with every inch of water...

"I'm not going to make it."

Twisting around to face the escape hatch, Jonas began breathing slowly and deeply, attempting to expand his lungs as much as he could. He removed his rubber boots, then, locating the face mask, he detached the empty pony bottle.

He glanced over his shoulder as the water rose past his chest.

One-ninety ... one-eighty ... one seventy...

The pod slowed, barely rising.

Don't let it start to sink. Anticipate and get out quickly.

* * *

"Terry, get out of the damn water now," DeMarco demanded.

Terry ignored him, keeping her face down in the water,

360

breathing through the snorkel. The Megalodon was dead, that she knew. But her heart told her that Jonas had survived.

Andre Dupont felt dazed and depressed. All his efforts to save the creature—the lobbying, the expense—all for naught. The greatest predator of all time ... lost.

"I could have died today," he whispered to himself. "For what? To save my killer? What would the Cousteau Society tell my wife and children? 'Ah, Marie, you should be a proud widow. Andre died in the most noble of fashions, giving his life to feed an endangered species.'"

Dupont stood, stretching his sore back. The morning sun reflected sparks on the water.

That was when he sighted the fin.

"Hey ... get the girl out of the water!"

* * *

The bone-chilling Pacific reached Jonas's chest, the additional weight slowing the mini-sub's ascent to a crawl. He shivered in his bio-suit, afraid to move, then glanced at the depth gauge as the pod stopped rising.

One hundred and forty-two feet.

Inhaling a deep breath, he fixed the mask to his face and twisted open the rear hatch.

* * *

The two-foot-tall dorsal fin circled the fishing trawler. Eleven men as one screamed for Terry to get out of the water.

"That's a Great White," yelled Philip Prousnitzer. "Terry, it's homing in on the Meg's blood, you need to come aboard!"

The trawler's captain went below and returned with a shotgun. The dorsal fin circled the girl. The captain took aim.

Terry surface dived, disappearing below the waves.

The shark followed.

* * *

It had taken precious seconds to pull himself free of the

sinking pod. Starting toward the surface, he took long, easy strokes and kicks, counting backwards by three from a hundred and fifty. The pressure in his ears and sinus cavity was overwhelming, and he realized he could not pinch his nose to equalize while wearing the face mask.

Pulling it off, he squeezed his nostrils together and blew air into his cheeks, the pressure easing his pain.

By the time he reached a hundred and twenty feet, Jonas's muscles felt like lead.

Just a walk in the park...

Eighty feet—he could no longer feel his legs.

Don't ... stop.

At fifty-eight feet, the periphery of his vision became clouded by darkness.

At thirty-three feet, Jonas Taylor lost consciousness.

* * *

Terry grabbed her man by his right wrist as his body began slipping back into the depths. She kicked hard, pulling water with her left hand, using her right hand to pinch Jonas's nose and keep his mouth clamped shut. She felt the shark circling closer and swam harder.

As her face broke the surface, Terry pulled Jonas's head free of the ocean. His lips were blue and he wasn't breathing. She attempted to level him out to blow a few precious mouthfuls of air into his mouth as the dorsal fin surfaced eight feet away, the juvenile predator over-stimulated by all the blood in the water.

The fishing boat shot past Terry, its trawl net scooping up the shark as it launched its attack on Jonas.

Terry waited anxiously for the boat to circle back. Ninety long seconds passed before it returned; Jonas's pulse dangerously weak.

I'm losing him...

A minute later they were sprawled out on deck, Terry giving

him more effective breaths without any results.

She pulled away as Jonas vomited a lungful of seawater. His blue complexion faded to white, then red.

Terry was teary-eyed and all smiles as he opened his eyes. "Are you all right?"

He nodded. "Just … a bad case of indigestion."

He winced as invisible pins and needles stabbed his blood vessels.

"Jonas?"

"Nitrogen bubbles …"

"Try not to move. We're en route to the lagoon. We have a recompression chamber on site."

* * *

The young shark thrashed back and forth within the trawl net. Andre Dupont followed the captain into the pilothouse, attempting to reason with him. "Captain, you can't kill it," the Frenchman pleaded. "Great Whites are a protected species."

"Look at my boat. She's busted up. I'll kill this fish, stuff it, and sell it to some tourist from New York for twenty thousand. You gonna give me that much, Frenchy?"

Dupont rolled his eyes. "Good luck in prison."

Ten minutes later they arrived in the deep canyon waters located just outside the Tanaka Lagoon's canal entry. The giant steel doors had been left open for the *Kiku*.

The trawler entered the canal.

* * *

Jonas moaned, his head in Terry's lap. Every joint in his body was on fire, his muscles consumed with stabbing pains. "How much farther?"

"We're entering the canal. Medical personnel are waiting for us. We'll have you in a hyperbaric chamber in three minutes."

He looked up at her. "I love you."

"And I love you."

The pain increased; he was dizzy, nauseous. His felt as if the Megalodon's teeth were biting down on his back.

"Let me sit up."

Masao Tanaka was waiting by the north bleachers, his head heavily bandaged. Mac was there, too, leaning on crutches.

Terry saw her father and waved.

Tears of joy flowed down Masao's cheeks as he waved back, grateful his daughter was safe.

Doubled over in pain, Jonas focused on what appeared to be a juvenile Great White being towed in a trowel net along the port side of the stern. The shark was small, seven feet long, weighing between three and four hundred pounds. It was struggling fiercely, twisting within the confines of the fishing net, the action serving to wash the dead Meg's blood from the female pup's hide.

Jesus ... it's an albino.

For a brief moment, man and beast regarded one another, the creature staring at Jonas with its soulless gray-blue eyes, Jonas marveling at the presence of the Megalodon offspring. He closed his eyes at the irony and smiled.

And then the pain became overwhelming and the submersible pilot lost consciousness as two paramedics loaded him onto a gurney.

THE END of part one.

The MEG series continues in:
THE TRENCH (part 2)
MEG: PRIMAL WATERS (part 3)
MEG: HELL'S AQUARIUM (part 4)
MEG: NIGHT STALKERS
(part 5 … coming in Summer 2015)

To contact the author, receive free monthly updates, or to enter contests to become characters in his novels, go to www.SteveAlten.com

ATTENTION: SECONDARY SCHOOL TEACHERS

The MEG series is part of Adopt-An-Author, an innovative nationwide non-profit program gaining attention among educators for its success in motivating tens of thousands of reluctant secondary school students to read. The program combines fast-paced thrillers with an interactive website AND direct contact with the author. All teachers receive curriculum materials and posters for their classrooms. The program is FREE to all secondary school teachers and librarians.

For more information and to register for Adopt-An-Author, go to

www.AdoptAnAuthor.com